Laws and Prophecies

L.S. King

This is a work of fiction. Names, characters, events, and incidents are the products of the author's imagination. Any resemblance to actual persons, living or dead, or actual events is purely coincidental.

Cover designed by MiblArt

Loriendil Publishing
loriendil.com

DEDICATION

Johne Cook - thanks "Bro" for everything!

CONTENTS

Acknowledgements

Thanks to:

Shannon and Corrie McNear, Nichelle Belton, Rick Copple, Linda Paterson, Susan Szymanski, Jane Lebak, Bokerah Brumley, and Eric Myres.

Dr. Jonathan Crofts - My Very Own Physicist™ who has patiently waded through my questions and tried valiantly to keep me from breaking the laws of physics. Without him, the technology of this world would be much diminished, although to be honest, his brain would probably be in a much better state if he didn't have my stories twisting his mind into knots.

And as always:

Johnston McCulley and Guy Williams—for my love of capes, swords, and brave deeds.

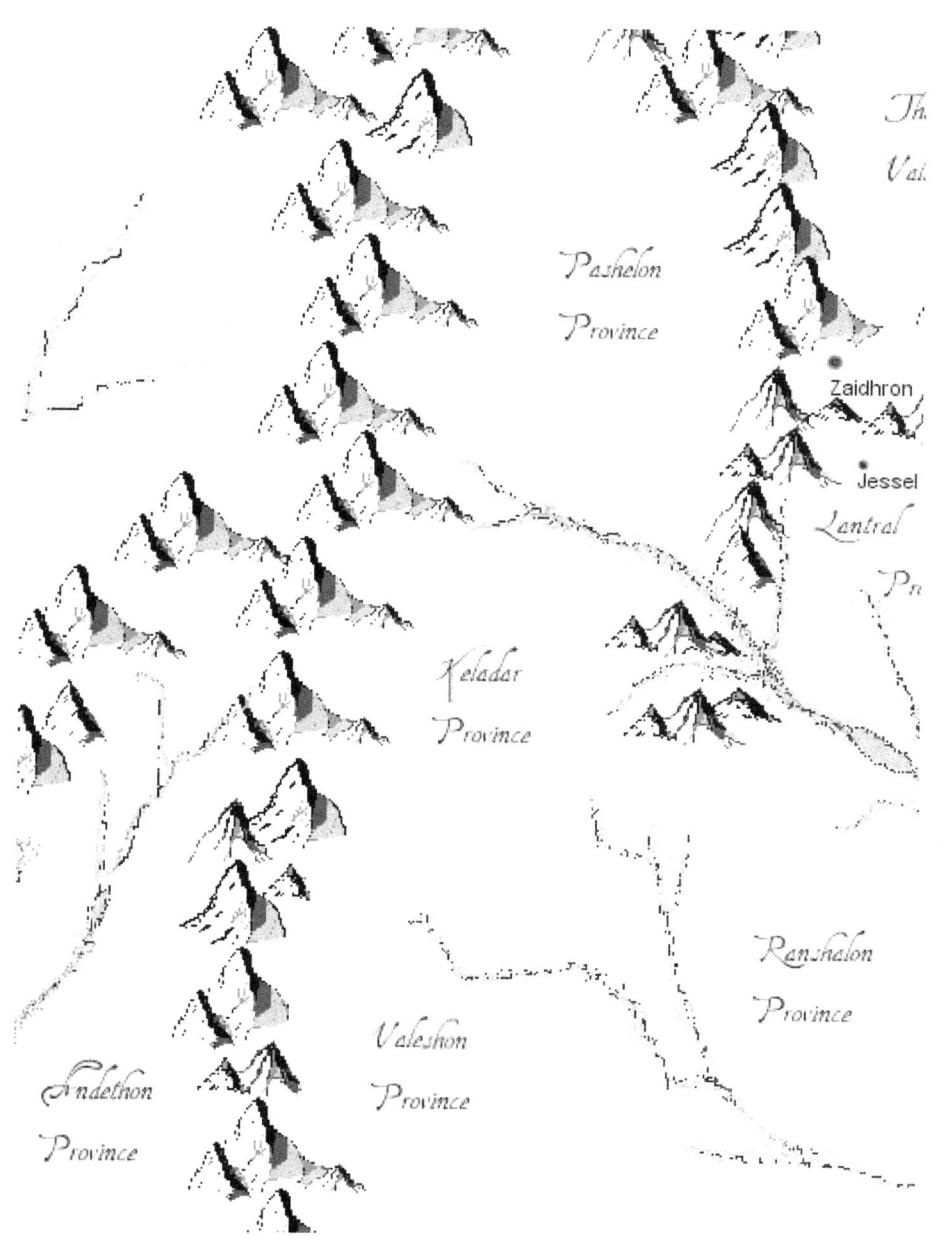

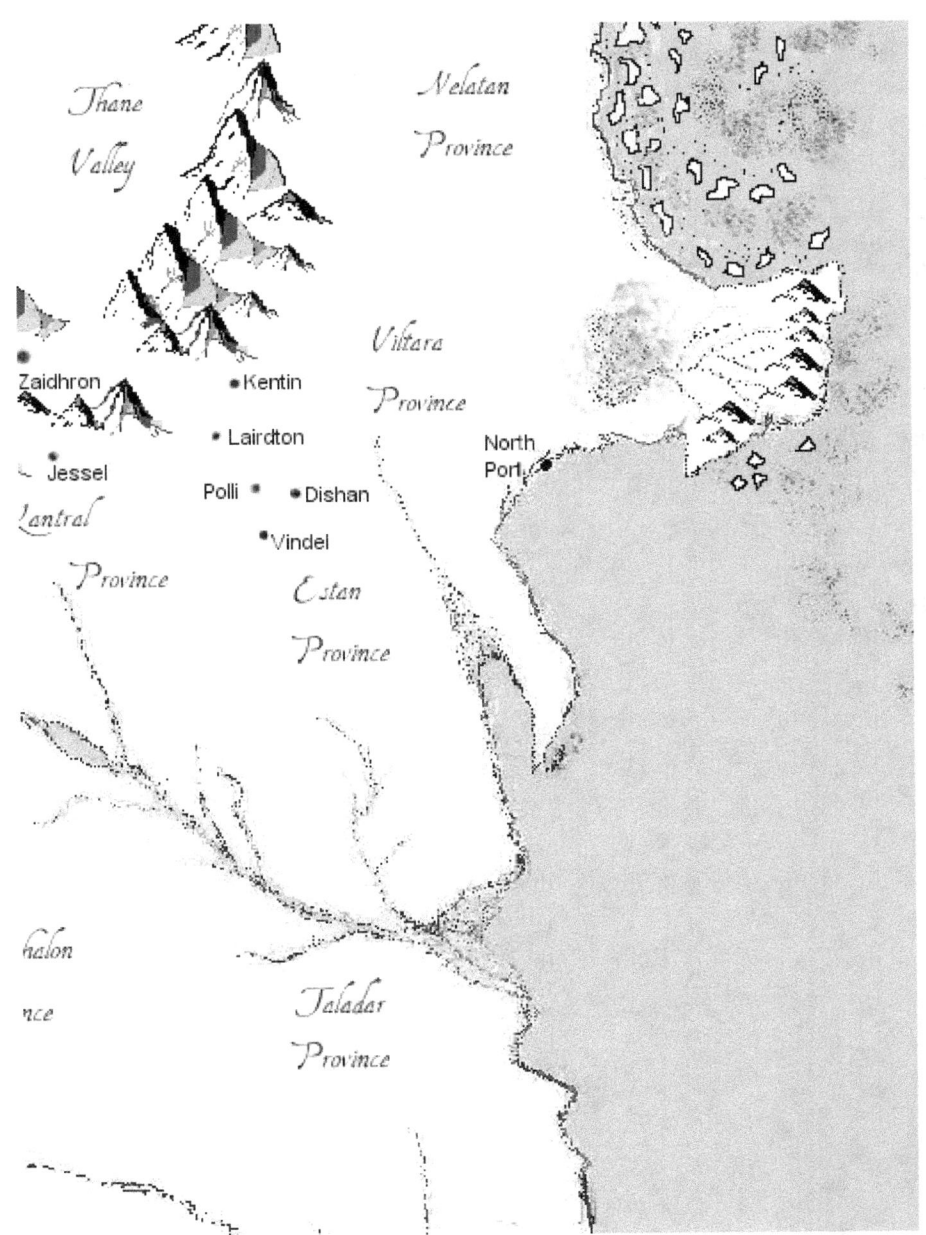

Thane Valley

Nelatan Province

Viltara Province

Zaidhron

Kentin

Lairdton

Jessel

Polli

Dishan

Vindel

Lantral Province

Estan Province

North Port

halon
nce

Taladar Province

PRONUNCIATION OF NAMES

Teldheri:

- ' indicates a glottal stop except when used after ch, in which case it indicates the ch is a hard sound (as in Scottish lo**ch**)
- dh indicates a fricative **d** (as in mo**th**er or **th**en)
- a is **ä** (as in f**a**ther), except in an accented syllable, in which case it is short
- e is short as in **e**gg
- i is short as in p**i**t, except as final vowel, then it is long **e**, as in Teldheri (or when followed by double consonants, such as is common in female names)
- ai is a diphthong, with the separate vowels pronounced as given above: **ä** and long **e**
- ei is a diphthong, with the separate vowels pronounced as given above: short **e** and long **e**
- o is long **o**
- u is long as in r**u**le
- gh indicates a soft g (as in **g**eneral)
- jh indicates a sibilant s (as in mea**s**ure)

Male names:

- accent is on the first syllable except when it is a three syllable name beginning with a vowel with a closed second syllable, in which case the accent is on the second syllable, therefore *El'adhrel* but *Alcan'dhor*

Female names:

- in names such as *Sarinna*, or *Colinn*, the i is pronounced as a long **e** and carries the accent, as indicated by the double consonant after the vowel
- in names such as Amara or Aleta, the accent is on the second syllable
- in names such as Sherel, accent is on the first syllable

"enh?" used at the end of a sentence to indicate a question does not carry a long **a** sound, but rather the nasal enh sound similar to "hein" used by the French.

LAWS AND PROPHECIES

Prologue

Year 1027 . Lunation Five . Day Ten
Thirty-one days past summer solstice

(sixteen years before current events)

Alcandhor's father stopped a moment on the steep path. "Look, son."

To their right the mountain fell away, and only a few trees stood between them and the cliff. Stars, they had climbed to a dizzying height above Thane Valley! Alcandhor stepped closer to the edge to view the landscape. The dark greens of the woods, the lighter greens of the farms, and little blue ribbons of the streams and rivers stretched out to a blurred distance.

They started on this journey with no explanation. He had asked, repeatedly, where his father was taking him, but Saldhor would only say, "Wait, and you shall see."

Now, with a touch on his shoulder, Father said, "Thane Valley shall be yours one day."

With Alcandhor having only fourteen years, Thaneship and its

1

burdensome responsibilities, as well as the resultant ownership of this beautiful land, seemed safely far away. Surely, surely, his father would live many more years, especially since he had the blood of the Enaisi in him, and those aliens were so very long lived.

"Come," Saldhor murmured.

Alcandhor turned and followed his father. They crested a rise and before them, in a secluded hollow, nestled a small cottage, surrounded by several pastures of animals and a large, tidy garden to one side.

Unable to contain his curiosity, Alcandhor blurted, "Who lives here?"

His father merely lifted an arm for them to continue on.

They drew near, and the door opened. A stooped man with long, silvery hair smiled at him. Shock rooted Alcandhor's feet to the ground, and he found his breath stolen away as the man's large, deep-brown eyes bored into his. His bronze skin, darker than any Alcandhor had ever seen—except in the gallery portraits of the Enaisi themselves—seemed tinged with grey, as if old age leeched the color from it. This man could not be an Enaisi; those aliens withdrew through the portal to their world centuries ago, shutting it down and locking it against use. But then, who was he?

"Aye, this is the one, Saldhor. This is the one. Bring him to me." The ancient man retreated into his cottage.

His father bowed full, eyes lowered, then with a hand on Alcandhor's back, urged him forward.

Apprehension warred with curiosity. The latter won out, and Alcandhor did not resist. He blinked to adjust to the dark of the interior. 'Twas sparsely furnished with only the hearth, a table and two chairs, a cot to one side, herbs and vegetables hanging from the ceiling; a typical poor farmer's cottage.

The old man lowered himself into the one chair, well padded with cushions, and gestured for Alcandhor to come to him.

Swallowing, and reciting to himself *Rangers do not fear,* he lifted his chin and stepped closer.

A dark hand, not gnarled but with the thin boniness of age, touched his temple. "Aye, you are the one." He took Alcandhor's hand and bowed over it. "You are also the last I shall see."

"Say it is not so!" Saldhor exclaimed.

"It is not long now. Even she has said so. But she is not alone anymore. Everything is as I have foreseen, my son. And I am not sad. For so many years, all who remembered have been gone. Do not grieve."

The old man stared into Alcandhor's eyes, and he met them steadily, not afraid, truly, but not understanding. The wizened hands rested on his head for a moment and then rose, turning palm up.

"Who are you, sir?" Alcandhor whispered.

With a grin, white teeth in a dark face, he leaned forward until his forehead touched Alcandhor's. "I think you know."

There was only one possible answer, but by all the Bells of the nebula, it could not be! *He* could not be! "But–but you are dead!"

"Obviously not, young Son."

"But then, you...*you* are the true Thare!" Alcandhor wheeled to his father, eyes wide, searching for...for denial or assurance or something that would stop his heart from pounding thus.

"Ha, nay. I passed that mantle on many generations ago. I am just an old man now, ready to die."

Alcandhor's eyes stung, and he blinked, taking a deep breath.

Straightening with a smile, the ancient one asked, "Shall we have afternooning? I prepared a stew that I find quite delectable."

~*~

Alcandhor sat on the floor near the hearth, his father on a chair behind him. His ancestor asked questions about the city, various provinces and their lords, about Saldhor himself, and Alcandhor's elder brother, Valdhor. Many times he seemed to already know the answers, although that could not be. Not up here on top of a mountain, alone. Shrewd guesses, aye, that must be what it was.

The wide, dark eyes now settled on Alcandhor, and he fidgeted despite all his efforts.

"You will see great things in your lifetime, young son. Great changes. Never doubt that."

"Will they...will they be good changes?"

"That will be for you, and your world, to decide." He sat up straighter in his chair, his eyes narrowed. "But you...you will know great sorrow and grief, and great joy."

"Do not all people experience those things?"

The ancient man laughed. "You are wise for one so young. Aye, you are correct. But take care, young son, as events will occur that will attempt to crush you. You have strength that you do not realize yet. Stand firm." Those large, disconcerting, too-knowing eyes bored into Alcandhor's. "One decision will come that will seem impossible to contemplate. You shall want to draw back from it, abhor even thinking it, but it is a decision that is yours to make. Thus it has been seen, and thus it shall be."

"If the decision is so difficult, how shall I choose? How shall I know what to do? Can you not tell me?"

"If I tell you, is the decision then yours?"

Alcandhor had no answer for that. Nay, he had, he just did not like it.

"You fear being strong enough, wise enough, but I tell you, young son, you are just what this world needs, just when it needs it. Hold fast to that."

With a single nod, Alcandhor dropped his gaze to his hands clasped in his lap. He was but a boy, a younger son, scorned by so many in the clan who saw what he was. Not strong like his older brother, not built like a fighter. How could he lead his clan one day? What could his world need that he could some day provide?

The old man stood slowly, steadying himself with a hand on the mantel of the fireplace. "Young son, at the right time, you will have answers to your questions and doubts. And to many other things besides." His hand, resting on the mantelpiece, tapped a steady tattoo, his smile sly, as if sharing a secret, but Alcandhor could not decipher what it might be.

With a sigh, the ancient man lowered himself to his chair once again. "Will you pour me some tea, young son?"

Alcandhor complied, honored at serving his revered ancestor.

~*~

The next morning, his father opened the door, and Alcandhor stepped outside, pulling his cloak tightly around himself. 'Twas not truly cold, but this high up, the strong wind had some bite. He stopped to say goodbye, and found the ancient man smiling at him. He set his thin hands on Alcandhor's head, as if blessing him, although he said nothing.

A muzzy warmth settled on Alcandhor. He smiled at his ancestor and turned to follow his father down the path.

Chapter One

Year 1043 . Lunation Nine . Day Twenty
Thirty-four days past autumnal equinox

(current year)

Irdhith, new lord of Lantral Province, paced in the sumptuous study that once belonged to Zantith, his uncle. He could not pretend sorrow that his uncle had been found guilty of treason and murder and exiled to a remote island, but he did regret that the man's plans to usurp control from the Rangers had not succeeded. So much had depended on that, not only for the independence of their province from outside interference but for his own purposes.

And on top of everything else, the Ranger Nandhal, complicit in Zantith's plans, had been declared outlaw and captured. Irdhith could not escape acquaintance with the man, but he must distance himself from him.

Now Irdhith was left to pick through the remains of the schemes and try to gain something. The sister of Thane Alcandhor—what was her name? Sarinna? A lonely widow. Aye, now there was a prize to be won and for many reasons.

He swept to the gilt-edged table and sat, staring at the polished wood, his eyes narrowed. Finally, he picked up the quill. This letter to the Thane must be carefully written.

~*~

Sarinna found herself barely able to breathe for the pounding of her heart as she pushed into the throng gathering at the gates of Zaidhron, their city. She awaited the safe return of her younger brother Alcandhor, Thane of their clan, Ch'shalna, who were the Rangers and peacekeepers of their world.

If only she could run ahead, across the plain and past the out-wall to find her brother. But that was not their way. So along with all the others, she waited for him, and the men accompanying him, to arrive at the main gate. Hopefully all alive and well.

"How close are they?" someone asked.

5

"I know not," another replied. "Have they passed the out-wall?"

"What did the drums say? Can anyone tell what the drums said?" called a woman, her voice querulous. "Did they capture the Rogues?"

Other than Trained Rangers, not many knew drum code. However Sarinna did. The message from the drum tower in Pashelon Pass, a half-day's march southwest, had alerted the city to the soon return of their kin.

"The drums merely sent word of their approach," she offered. "Nothing more."

"They near the gatehouse!" a woman shouted.

People milled, and Sarinna braced her feet to keep from being shoved off-balance. She pressed through toward the front, raising on tiptoe in search of her brother and cousins.

For too long Rangers who had forsaken their vows and gone Rogue had plagued their world. A recent hunt had rid them of all but two. The first, Monadhal, clever and vicious, had lived in the wild, managing to elude his former kin for years. Her first cousin Haladhon had claimed Capture Rights on the outlaw for not only once trying to kill him but more so for murdering his father. That meant Haladhon would fight the man alone, to capture or to death.

The other Rogue, Nandhal, had only recently fled, having plotted to murder the Thane and the chiefs of their clan, and had also well-nigh succeeded in killing the Ranger Marcalan, Sarinna's second cousin. Even though he was barely healed from the near-deadly attack, Marcalan claimed Right on Nandhal.

The Rangers surely would not be returning if they had not been successful in capturing the two Rogues, but had they paid in too dear blood for it?

A cheer rose and rippled through the crowd. They surged back, almost knocking Sarinna off her feet. Making way? For whom? Stars, was someone badly injured? But nay, everyone would not be cheering.

A wild yell and shrieking feminine laugh answered her worries before she even saw the cause. Marcalan had Tam, his new, young bride, slung over his shoulder like a sack of meal and pelted north straight toward where their family chamber awaited.

Sarinna found herself laughing with everyone else. Marcalan obviously had recovered enough from his near-fatal beating to consummate their marriage. Today would start their three days of nestling.

She turned her attention back to the gate, lifting again on tiptoe, searching for her close kin. The Rangers came through the entrance with less speed and more decorum than the newly married couple.

Alcandhor walked at the front with Haladhon at his side—both appearing hale, thank the Maker! And on her brother's other side, the incredibly long-lived alien, Mattan, their very own ancestor who had, only days ago, reactivated the portal, and come through from his planet to join them on this world.

From nearby, Sarinna's young niece squealed. The child and both her brothers rushed to their father. Alcandhor knelt down to embrace his children, his careworn face brightening.

Sarinna shared a smile with her mother, Taniss, as the older woman murmured, "They bring him to life."

His little daughter in his arms, Alcandhor drew near.

"All is well?" Sarinna asked while he embraced their mother.

"All is well. Monadhal and Nandhal have been captured without injury to anyone. They are already being taken to the cells."

Sarinna gave her brother a quick kiss on the cheek, but noticed his smile seemed forced. Using the limited empathic abilities inherited from her Enaisi ancestors, she sensed him as they strolled on the path between gardens of the sward and felt his fatigue. Was that all it was? Exhaustion, not worry?

"Truly? All is well?"

"As well as can be. Nandhal will be branded tonight, and cut off."

"Is it necessary with his execution only days away?"

"The branding must happen regardless, but in his case, I will not abrogate the law, not after he raped a woman and her daughter and killed the whole family. He will be cut off."

That explained her brother's brooding.

"But he is captured, and now there are no more Rogues. Surely that is a reason for joy."

"Aye."

"Come." She made her smile bright. "Let us feast tonight without reservation."

"I take it the preparations are already well under way?"

Sarinna nodded. She had not needed to tell Ganill, the head cook of the Great Hall, to begin readying for the banquet after the drums had finished echoing. The woman knew her business. "Aye, and with Tam and Marcalan nestling, we shall have yet another celebration in three days. With all these festivities, the city's schedule has been tossed into the midden."

"I am certain our city steward will manage to keep us from falling into chaos." He inclined his head to her.

"I will. As always." On the far side of the dark-skinned Mattan, a familiar face smiled at her, a few more laugh lines around his deep-set

7

blue eyes and his blond hair more silvery than when she last saw the sept chief from Pashelon Province. "Ordhral!"

"And how are you, Sarinna?"

"I am well. How is your wife? The last time she wrote she was glowing over a great-grandchild."

"Boy or girl?"

Sarinna thought for a moment. "Girl."

"Ah, then expect another missive soon. There is also a boy."

"Wonderful!"

Alcandhor squeezed her arm. "Do you keep track of all clan births, sister? That is the task of our head law-keeper."

"Or, since he is not here at present, his son." She glanced over at their cousin Andhrel, pacing them nearby, who grinned and inclined his head. "But nay, I keep correspondence with their sept, mostly through their chiefs' wives, and the other septs as well, not to mention with many of the provincial Ranger hold stewards. I receive better tidings that way."

"Does that fall within the purview of the city steward?"

"It falls within the purview of the clan matriarch, and our mother tasked me with that responsibility when she moved to the valley after Father died."

"But she is back now, living here." He frowned over at Taniss.

"And I have not wished to take full brunt of those duties again," his mother returned with a stern glare. "However, Sarinna does keep me informed."

Alcandhor inclined his head and said nothing more. Wise man, her brother.

"I do have other news." Sarinna raised her chin and met Mattan's gaze. "Several Worshippers arrived."

"Say not!" Alcandhor growled.

Anger kindled in the faces of both Ordhral and Mattan.

"The guards refused them entrance at the out-wall, and they left. But with an Enaisi here, they will likely return in greater numbers, insisting we allow them in."

"I refuse to permit those heretics access to the city," her brother hissed.

"Perhaps if Mattan talked to them, explained to them he was not a deity?" Alcandhor's son Teldhor suggested.

"They would fall down and worship, ignoring his words," Ordhral spat. "They have no sense, and one cannot reason with them."

"I agree, from what you have told me," Mattan said. "They would merely find an excuse to dismiss anything I say to them."

"What if you sent them emotions to show your anger, like cousin

Tam has done to several people?" Teldhor asked.

"Proof of my godlike powers, I daresay."

"I may not have the fabled foresight of the Children of the Enaisi"—Haladhon bowed toward Mattan—"but I foresee trouble ahead with the Worshippers."

"We may indeed," Sarinna said. "But never mind for now. You, brother, have an urgent duty. Hindhal wishes you to call upon him to see how fares the healing to your shoulder."

"I will do so tomorrow."

She met his eyes evenly. "You can stave off trouble by attending the healer promptly."

"Trouble from him or trouble from you?"

"Both."

Alcandhor sighed. "Thane of the Rangers, and I answer to my sister."

"That you do!" Sarinna smiled. "We shall go ahead to your family suite and await you."

"My thanks." Alcandhor kissed his daughter and set her down, then hugged both sons. "I shall join you shortly."

~*~

Tam slowly woke from some pleasant, muzzy dream and became aware of a weight across her waist. And legs twined with hers—and light snores muffled by her hair. A smile spread, and she stifled a giggle. Her new husband seemed to love to cuddle behind her and sleep with his face in her hair. She knew not why. Would not one feel smothered or tickled by it?

She stretched very carefully, hoping not wake him. He had managed to keep everyone convinced he was fine while journeying back from capturing the Rogues, but being empathic, she felt his fatigue, and shared the pain from his leg wound, still not fully healed. Now, he was leaden in sleep. Stars, if he was drooling in her hair—! Tempting as it was to feel to see if he had, she did not wish to disturb him; he needed the rest to heal completely.

She lifted her eyelids enough to tell their chamber was dark. She wriggled a bit to get comfortable and closed her eyes; she had no reason to stay awake, they did not have any duties for three whole days. Her eyes flew open—what would they do for three whole days? She felt her face warm, aye, *that* of course.

She had thought being loved by her uncle, aunt, and cousins was the most wonderful thing ever. And then she thought having *in love* was the most wonderful thing ever. But making love, that went beyond anything she could have ever imagined!

But surely they could not do *that* for three whole days!

Marcalan snuffled in his sleep and snugged her tighter, and Tam could not help but smile again. Their bond had increased much more after they had made love, and she could sense, even deep in slumber, the contentedness and completion of her husband.

Mattan had warned them how strong their bond could be. He had pulled them aside that last morning before they broke camp and sat on a fallen log, facing them.

"Now, you must both be careful, since you are both empathic," he had said, his dark brown eyes earnest. "You can sense each other, but do not send *to* each other while intimate. You particularly, Tam. You are strong and could cause a bond-lock."

Marcalan had looked as bewildered as Tam felt. "What is a bond-lock?"

Mattan leaned forward, elbows on his knees. "You grow so...involved with each other that you become lost in the bond. You become unaware of anything beyond each other."

"Bells!" her husband had exclaimed. "Does this happen among your people?"

"Aye, and it often does not end well if others are not there to try to break them out of it. So heed me, please."

Tam had nodded most gravely.

Glad she was of the warning too, because *that* had been so intense, she could not imagine what it would be like with them actively sending their sensations to each other.

A shock came afterwards too, when they discovered that they could actually read each other's thoughts. She knew not which of them had been more surprised the first time it happened. She did hope they would become accustomed to it, or perhaps learn to control it. 'Twas not always good to know what another person was thinking, especially if it was not meant to be heard.

Marcalan stirred, and a low, happy *Mmmm* erupted from him and a thought: *Stars, what a way to awaken!*

As he kissed her shoulder, she giggled and rolled toward him, her arms wrapping around his neck as his lips found hers in the dark.

A knock at the door startled her, and she broke the kiss.

"Evening meal," a woman's voice called through the door. "'Tis hot, do not let it sit out here for too long."

Marcalan groaned. "What timing!" He leaned forward to kiss her again, but Tam put a hand on his chest.

"Our meal will get cold," she said.

"I care not!"

"I do! I am hungry. And I am not going anywhere. We have all night. We have three whole days. Let us enjoy a hot meal. Go. Bring it in." Tam threw back the covers. "I will make tea."

With a moan, Marcalan sat up. Tam stood and felt her way around the bed hearing rather than seeing her husband pull on his trous.

"I can barely see by the embers in the fireplace," he grumbled.

"Wait and let me light a candle first. You do not want to stub a toe. Forget not the chair near the—"

A *thump* interrupted her, and a grunt, and she winced at the flash of heat throbbing in his right foot. His resultant curse, although only mental, seared into her mind.

Stars, you need not use such language!

I did not intend you to hear it. Shall we never have private thoughts again?

It seems only directed thoughts, and very strong thoughts, are sent.

Marcalan snorted as he opened the door.

Tam lit several candles from the embers, then swung the kettle over the fire. She tossed a few small logs made from salnais in the fireplace for both heat and light, then returned to the bed to get dressed.

You need not dress, you know. Marcalan's voice even seemed to lilt when it was only a thought-voice. *Such a view while eating would be glorious.*

The air is chill.

Aye. He chuckled, and her face grew warm as she realized the implication.

"Stars, Marcalan!"

"I cannot help it, Love-ling. You are beautiful. I want to appreciate your beauty."

"Let us eat first and appreciate later."

Marcalan's grin belied his serious bow.

~*~

Arms crossed, Sarinna observed her kin in the Great Hall, wearing a false smile. Inside, she worried about her brother. He had been subdued during the evening meal and left soon after with his children.

Granted, he rarely stayed in the Great Hall in the evenings. Sarinna could not say if it was more because he enjoyed playing kingsmen, backhand, or various other games until his children's time for bed, or to avoid his wife, Aleta. The latter no longer applied though, since he had

11

put her out, ending the marriage. As soon as she knew she lost her authority and privileges as wife of the Thane, the viper left the city, not even saying good-bye to her children.

But tonight, he seemed distracted and aloof, much more than usual. Sarinna had asked if it was anything the healer said, but Alcandhor claimed Hindhal had merely stated he was still on the mend. Perhaps that was all it was; he chafed due to the time it was taking to heal.

Mattan strolled over, drink in hand, concern on his fine, dark features.

"What troubles you?"

She did not ask how he knew. This was an Enaisi, after all, he could sense emotions—and even read minds, although he claimed he did not do so unless invited.

She hesitated, then replied, "My brother."

"His shoulder?"

"Nay. Well, aye, but he seemed more distant than usual this evening."

Mattan leaned close, smiling. "I think some of that is the attention he is garnering from the ladies, now that he no longer wears a necklet."

Sarinna bit her lip. "I had not thought of that. So you think that is all it is?"

"Stars, nay. His real problem is something much deeper."

"Oh?"

Mattan smiled. "Aye. He has deep wounds. He knows not how to begin healing."

"And it is affecting them." Sarinna nodded toward the center of the Great Hall, where Rangers and kin gathered. Tonight's celebration quieted when the Thane left, and everyone moved about in a ritual of feigned jubilation. Laughter gusted here and there, mostly from younger folk. The music reflected the subdued mood: soft, slow tunes, not the merry, lilting ones usually expected for such an evening.

"Aye, it is."

Sarinna turned to him and implored, "Speak to him, Mattan. He respects you and will listen to you."

The Enaisi vented a soft huff. "Not likely. He thinks me interfering when I try to discuss personal matters."

"But why?"

He shrugged. "Perhaps because he does not know me well enough yet. He has told me things I am certain he has shared with very few, but it was hard won to get it out of him."

"Believe me, it is no easier for any of us who have known him all our lives. Please talk to him."

"Nay, Sarinna, it is your place."

"He will not listen to me."

"Oh, I think he will. He wants help, but knows not how to ask for it. He is trapped, and needs to see there is way out. Ponder that as you go to him. He is in his Thane's chamber."

She met Mattan's eyes, searching for understanding. A veil lifted, and she gasped as she saw her brother as never before. "Thank you." She hurried away.

~*~

Upon hearing his sister's voice call his name, Alcandhor dragged his attention from his studies, blinking to clear his thoughts. Sarinna stood in the doorway, cloak wrapped around her.

She walked toward the table. "If you put a cot in here, you would never leave but for meals, would you?"

"Is it not the Thane's chamber?" he asked.

"My dear brother, I understood your long hours here to avoid Aleta, but why now?"

"You know I prefer books." He lifted the tome in his hands as proof.

"I know you well enough to know that is but an excuse. Stars, 'Candhor, if you wish to learn of our history, our laws, and the Enaisi, or more of the Enaisi's science you love to study, you have someone who can sit and teach you from firsthand knowledge. You sit here, shut up until all hours of the night and your people worry about you."

"You mean you worry about me."

"I mean your people worry about you." Sarinna leaned on the table. "And wonder if you are displeased with them. They are in the Great Hall celebrating so many things, the capture of the Rogues, Tam and Marcalan's marriage, the arrival of an Enaisi, the end of the treason, and also, forthrightly, your freedom from *her*. But here you sit as if the weight of the world were still on your shoulders."

"Is it not? I rejoice with them, but I have the burdens of my office. There are still traitors and those causing dissent, especially in Estan, and we know not if the new provincial lords are true or corrupt. It is a relief knowing we have no more Rogues now, but I grieve over the two awaiting their sentence. And although I understand why everyone is delighted that Aleta is gone, yet I know that I was a fool. I married her and brought her here, and I endured her for years, not realizing how the whole city suffered as well." He looked down at the text. "Nay, it is better that I stay here."

"You, dear brother, are more stubborn than a kinchou."

"My thanks," he replied dryly, returning his gaze to the page he had been reading.

"I mean it! You climb up to the heights and cling there on a spit's worth of ledge with astounding tenacity for what good reason?" Sarinna splayed a hand over the book. "You will not stay here, Alcandhor."

He leaned back with a sigh. "Why can I not be left alone?"

"Because you are Thane."

"It is because I am Thane that I am alone."

Sarinna pulled a chair close and sat across from him. "Talk to me."

He sighed, closing the tome. "Those Rangers need a man they can esteem. One who is—"

"Oh, spare me! I know the litany. You do not realize there is something more your people need: a Thane to whom they feel akin."

"What do you mean?"

"Remember how Father was? He would be in the Great Hall right now, tipping a few back, singing songs, laughing, dancing, being with his people. You used to be that way. You did withdraw somewhat over the years, mainly because of her, I think, but when you became Thane, you withdrew from us completely."

"Sarinna, how do I make you understand—"

"You cannot." Her grey eyes shone almost as steel in the candlelight. In even a more scolding tone, she repeated, "You cannot. You are wrong, Alcandhor."

Leaning forward, her eyes gazed intently into his. "You—are—wrong. You think if they see one spot of weakness from you they will no longer follow you. You give them no credit, brother. They demand not perfection from you—that is your own expectation." She grasped his hands, her face earnest. "I sense, I know what they feel. They understood why you withdrew to avoid her, but she is gone. They worry about you, and they wonder if they have done something to alienate you. They want their Thane with them. They need you, *Thane* Alcandhor."

He stared at her, shocked, then averted his eyes. Her fingers squeezed his hands, tacitly urging.

Finally, he replied, "You are right. I have been selfish." He rose, sighing. "Let us go to the Great Hall."

Sarinna stood as well, fists on her hips. "Oh, what a festive face you have, Thane."

Holding out a hand, she sent feelings of affection, and he returned them. How would he survive without being able to sense this? Her staunch love and belief in him had held him through so much.

Hand in hand, they left his chamber.

Chapter Two

The celebration in the Great Hall did indeed lack vivacity. 'Twas forced. Sarinna had hit the mark. Alcandhor met his sister's expectant gaze with a smile, determined to be happy this evening, and strode through the hall toward the kegs of ale.

"Thane!" Cordhan ambled over. "We thought you had retired for the night."

He filled a tankard and then turned to the Ranger. "Not at all. I had to sneak away to finish a few details for the morning meeting. Now, I am free from duty for a little while."

Cordhan visibly relaxed. "Thane, I have wanted the chance to ask you something personal."

"What is that?"

"I was wondering when your shoulder will be completely healed."

Alcandhor drank deeply from his tankard, delaying his answer. "Hindhal examined me today. Not for some time yet."

"Ah, I understand. It was a most serious wound. We were afraid we were going to lose you. But let me know, as I wish to regain one of my favorite match partners."

Before he could reply, several young Rangers swooped down on the keg table, laughing and jesting.

"Stars, is it our Thane?" asked Loch'alan with mocking amazement, jostling with another Ranger to fill his tankard next.

"You seem to be enjoying the evening," Alcandhor said, grinning.

"What is not to enjoy? Things will go better now, aye, Thane? And my brother is married. Perhaps he will find it more arduous to plan pranks with a wife in tow."

The Rangers hooted, and Alcandhor grinned. "I do not see anything slowing down Marcalan. Is there a wager on it yet?"

Loch'alan gave an innocent blink, much like his brother. "Stars, Thane, we would never wager—"

Cordhan laughed, shoving Loch'alan, who squawked as his ale slopped over the side of his tankard. "Think you the Thane knows not the wagering that goes on in the back halls? Stars, he has wagered enough himself in the past."

They stared at Alcandhor, mouths agape. How separated he truly was from his men. These younger ones did not know him at all. He hid his disquiet and let his eyes smile with wicked delight over the rim of the tankard as he took a drink.

"It is hard to imagine the Thane wagering," Loch'alan replied in a cautious tone.

"It is difficult for me to make a wager," Alcandhor said, straight-faced. "Everyone knows I have sight."

Amid the Rangers' laughter, he found himself relaxing, just a little. Stars, he needed this as much as they did. How long had it been since he had let them see he was one of them? Why had he felt it so necessary to—nay, he would not think on such things tonight. He vowed to be cheerful as he concentrated on watching his men enjoying themselves.

"It is so strange with Marcalan missing." Baidhrol glanced around. "I keep expecting him to either walk up with that too-innocent expression of his, or see him laughing as he runs off."

"Aye, so do I," said another young Ranger, "and it is unnerving."

"It is a relief to me," Loch'alan retorted.

"You really should not display such open affection for your brother," Baidhrol shot back.

Loch'alan snorted. "I love my brother best from a distance. I am happiest when he is roaming."

Alcandhor chuckled silently, knowing the young Ranger's heart too well. He had prowled worriedly around Zaidhron while his older brother was recovering from being beaten almost to death by the Rogues. And he begged to be allowed to join the chiefs when the word came that those outlaws were caught in the net, but Alcandhor had denied him—as he did their father and many others. Had he permitted every Ranger to go that wanted to be there, the city would have been emptied.

"And what think you of your new sister?" asked Cordhan, refilling his own tankard.

"My head runs in circles around her." Loch'alan grimaced. "First I see a slip of a lass, until she knocks me topside down. Then I see her as a Ranger. Now she has married my brother. So do I view her as a Ranger or a lass?"

"As a lass who is a Ranger. She is both." Alcandhor pointed at the youth with his tankard. "And you had best inure yourself to it, as she will be your Thane one day."

"Stars," Loch'alan muttered, wagging his head.

"Just think, Loch'y," Baidhrol said, his twinkling eyes belying his impassive expression. "One day you will be brother-in-law to the Thane."

"Stars!" Loch'alan repeated emphatically, staring at Alcandhor.

The young Rangers all asked questions at once.

"What is Marcalan's rank now?"

"What about their children?"

"When does she become Thane? When she comes of Age?"

"What about you, Thane?"

Silence fell after that last question.

The doubt and concern on the faces of all these Rangers filled his heart. Bells, if only all his men had this much love for their Thane! He took a long pull of his ale to give himself a moment to regain composure, then shrugged. "I will become her Second at Table."

"But...how can you just...stop being Thane?" Baidhrol whispered.

Alcandhor smiled and dropped a hand on the young Ranger's shoulder. "It would have been easier if we had known of her all along. It would have been understood that I was Thane in interim until she came of Age. You are accustomed to me as Thane, aye? This is sudden for you. For all of you." He grinned at them. "But you have five years to prepare for her ascension."

"You seem so accepting of it already, sir. How is that?" another asked.

"It is the law."

"Why did he not follow the law and have her birth registered?" asked Loch'alan with a frown. "He was strict to follow the law from what I have heard."

Alcandhor fingered his tankard. He did not want to make excuses for Valdhor, especially as none existed, but would not condemn him when the man was no longer alive to answer for himself. "We will never know, Loch'alan." He took a deep breath, hoping the conversation would not delve too deeply into what could bring him under condemnation himself, and continued: "That is my fault. I needed him too badly as I prepared for the traitors' attack and did not call Question on his actions, intending to do so after the treason had been dealt with."

"'Tis not your fault, Thane," Cordhan said in a firm voice. "You saw things, and knew you must have men placed strategically, especially Valdhor. Without him, you would not have had knowledge of where the traitors held the young Laird hostage. How could we blame you?"

"That is all past, is it not?" asked Lantalan, walking up with several other Rangers.

"Aye," Cordhan replied, exchanging quick glances with the older Ranger. "So, what think you of your oldest son finally marrying?"

Alcandhor did not miss the two older Rangers unspoken communication and abrupt change of topic. Did they both understand the danger to their Thane with questions about Valdhor and Tam's birth?

Lantalan snorted. "About time, although it took me by surprise. I am still adjusting to the idea of that incredible young lass with such abilities

17

will be Thane—and now she is my daughter."

"Perhaps she has ability enough to tame Marcalan," Loch'alan said, which drew snorts, guffaws, and hoots.

"Never happen." Baidhrol waved his hand.

"It would be nice to see him tethered, would it not, Father?" Loch'alan asked.

Lantalan draped an arm around his son's shoulders, while glancing at Alcandhor with a grin. "Aye, but somehow I have a feeling that Marcalan will continue to be Marcalan. What say you, Thane?"

"Aye. And you spoke almost word for word what Mattan said about him." Alcandhor smiled past Lantalan and his son. The alien approached, brows raised, obviously close enough to hear his name mentioned.

"What did Mattan say?" asked Loch'alan.

"He said that Marcalan is meant to be Marcalan."

Loch'alan blinked. "What did he mean by that?"

The alien stood silently behind the young Rangers, his lips quirking up.

"Ask him," Baidhrol said with a grin.

"Not bloody likely!" exclaimed Loch'alan.

"Afraid of him?" Baidhrol poked him in the ribs.

"If you have no fear of him, you ask him."

"I am not the one who wants to know what the Enaisi meant," Baidhrol shot back.

"What I meant by what?" Mattan asked.

The two jumped, and several Rangers snickered at Loch'alan's and Baidhrol's now red faces. The alien quietly filled his tankard, then turned toward them with eyebrows raised. "You wished to ask me something?"

Alcandhor fought the urge to burst out laughing. He took a sip of ale as he tried to compose himself. A rush of mirthful warmth flowed over him, the Enaisi empathically sharing his amusement in the situation as the two young men fidgeted.

Baidhrol nudged Loch'alan, who swallowed.

"Uh, the Thane...he said that you told him that Marcalan was meant to be Marcalan."

Mattan waited, his demeanor calm and open.

Loch'alan cleared his throat, his face still flushed. "I just wondered what you meant by that, sir."

"Simply what I said." Mattan shrugged. "Marcalan is meant to be Marcalan. Not what anyone else wishes him to be."

"It is not easy to live with that sometimes," Lantalan replied dryly.

The alien chuckled. "Nay, but be assured, you have done your duty well by him. And he did not cause you to turn grey after all, did he?"

18

Alcandhor and the older Rangers, as well as Loch'alan, all burst into laughter as that had been one of Lantalan's complaints since his eldest was a wee lad.

"Nay, sir, he did not," Lantalan replied with a grin when he caught his breath.

"You had better all learn to call me Mattan, just as you call your other chiefs by name. I despise formality perhaps more than your Thane." He winked at Alcandhor.

Lantalan gave a slight bow in acknowledgment. "I understand it is a deep cost and dangerous to you, so I wish to thank you—most heartily—for risking your own life to heal my son."

The Enaisi grinned. "I will remind you of that the next time he has vexed you."

"At least I have two more days respite before I need worry about it again."

"Now that is a indisputable reason to celebrate." Loch'alan raised his tankard.

Alcandhor chuckled, stepping away from the Rangers and their continued jesting, and retreated to a nearby table.

"Good to see you here tonight, Thane." The fair-haired Zandhral smiled, sliding onto the bench next to him.

"And how are you, cousin?"

Zandhral had a few more years than Alcandhor, and although not close friends, they had a bond because of their ability to sense. Also, his cousin used to keep watch on Alcandhor when they were young, as would an older brother, which had caused a few conflicts with Valdhor.

"Better now," Zandhral replied, his eyes twinkling.

Alcandhor's lips twisted in a wry smile, taking his meaning. The mood in the Great Hall had shifted, becoming more cheerful, as people realized their Thane was present.

"How is the shoulder?"

Alcandhor looked sharply at Zandhral, who just grinned smugly. "That is one thing you cannot hide, especially from me."

"'Tis true." Alcandhor sighed. "It heals very slowly."

"And you are worried."

"I cannot be Thane, or even a rostered Ranger, if I am permanently impaired."

"Has Hindhal said anything?"

"Nay, but I have sensed his worry. He is not pleased with how it is healing, or rather, not healing."

Zandhral leaned forward with an eager whisper. "What about Mattan?"

"What about him?"

"You could ask him to heal you."

"Could I?"

"Why not?"

Alcandhor drank some ale to give himself a moment to think of a way to explain it to his cousin, but Zandhral placed a hand on Alcandhor's arm, his chastisement apparent. "What think you your men will feel if they know their Thane has a way to be healed yet refuses? As long as you are not back to full fighting ability, we will worry. You insist going out on missions, as this one where the Rogues were captured. How can we allow you if you are not hale?"

"He speaks the truth and you know it," Mattan said from behind him.

Alcandhor twisted to look up at the Enaisi. "You have been listening?"

"I just walked up, but I heard enough."

"I am healing fine," Alcandhor said, "it will take time."

Zandhral looked from one to the other, his gaze finally resting on Alcandhor, rebuke in his eyes as he stood. "You are stubborn and prideful. Think hard about that choice, Thane, before some Ranger calls Question on your actions."

Alcandhor stared at Zandhral as he walked away. Hang the man, he always knew more than he should. He glanced up at the alien and scowled. "Are you going to say on about it?"

"He is right. You are proud. Too proud to let me heal you."

Alcandhor glowered at him as the Enaisi sat down next to him.

"One favor," Mattan said.

"And that is?"

"Allow me to sense the wound. I can discern if it would mend by itself. If it is a permanent injury, as you suspect, then permit me to heal it."

He sighed. "I begin to wonder why I ever wanted to meet you."

Mattan laughed. "Do not try to fool me."

Alcandhor lifted a hand.

"Do you agree, Thane?"

"Is that not dangerous for you, even fatal?"

"Aye, but for something as this, I can do it in stages and take time to recover."

He hesitated a moment, then sighed. "I will permit you sense the wound."

"And heal it?"

"First tell me what you find, then I shall decide."

Mattan glared, lips thinned, and laid a hand on his shoulder. Alcandhor kept his gaze on his tankard, holding his breath, as he waited for the Enaisi's pronouncement.

Silence dragged on, but he dared not look up.

Finally Mattan murmured, "There is much damage from that arrow. Damage to the brachial plexus and muscles, scar tissue that has already—" He stopped, his expression grave. "This will not completely heal on its own."

Alcandhor swallowed, his stomach tightening.

"Thane?" he asked softly.

An urgency, an insistence swept over him, and he searched surreptitiously for the source. Zandhral watched intently from across the hall, arms crossed. Their eyes locked in a silent battle, and finally, Alcandhor averted his gaze. "You are not fully recovered from healing Marcalan. Will it not make you weak?"

"Aye, but not dangerously so. Nothing strenuous has taxed me, nor will it. Being here is restful and healing."

Alcandhor did not reply.

"My son?" Mattan whispered.

He licked his lips, frowning. Why was it so difficult to just accept this offer. After two false starts, he muttered, "Do it."

"Let us go to my chamber."

~*~

The Ranger Sedhral crossed his arms, eyeing Alcandhor and Mattan ascending the staircase. What was that simpering by-blow of a thane scheming with that stranger? Enaisi—feh! Some trickery, that. Alcandhor had found some dark-skinned hill folk of their clan, likely related to that lass he claimed as niece, and brought one of them back for some inexplicable reason, probably to bolster his claim of Thaneship.

Sedhral would not be fooled as all of Zaidhron was! And it would not stop Pendhras, himself, and all who aligned themselves against Alcandhor from calling Question. As soon as the petition arrived with the signatures of all their allies, they would finally, finally be able to rid their clan of that weak excuse of a thane.

~*~

Upstairs, Alcandhor reclined on the bed, the Enaisi sat next to him, placing one hand slightly to the front of the shoulder. After a time, a slight warmth spread, and the constant ache gradually ebbed away.

21

Mattan remained still, head bowed, long after the pain had gone. He could not bring himself to look up at the alien—'twas true, he had too much pride. How could he resent such a gift?

Finally, the Enaisi leaned back with a sigh. "I have healed it somewhat. I need to recuperate. Later I will do more. But you must be easy with it. Keep up the strengthening exercises but gently. Before long you should be able to wield a sword."

Alcandhor made himself meet Mattan's gaze. "I thank you."

"It is a privilege to serve my Thane," he replied with a quiet smile, inclining his head. "But I tell you again, I am serious about you not pushing these next few days while exercising."

He nodded. For a man who claimed he would not read thoughts unless invited, the alien always knew quite a bit.

"May I ask a question, Thane?"

"I think you will whether I say aye or nay."

Mattan chuckled, but said nothing, his dark eyes probing. After an interminable silence, Alcandhor finally relented. "Say on."

"Why do you resent Thaneship so much? Certainly as you grew up you knew the chance of becoming Thane was there."

"If Valdhor had died and left this mantle, I think I would not have such resentment. But he simply walked away from his responsibilities, dumping them on me."

"So is it truly being Thane that you detest, or your brother?"

"Both."

"And you both detested and loved your brother, did you not?"

Alcandhor huffed. "Aye."

"And do you feel that way about Thaneship as well?"

"I know not what you mean."

Mattan chewed his lip for a moment. "You do enjoy control, and despise when it slips from your fingers."

"Aye, I admit that. But to have the lives of my clan in my hands, to know every decision I make could cause men's deaths, that I cannot abide."

"Think you that burden will be lighter on Tam?"

"But it is rightfully hers."

"I do not argue that point."

"Then what? Do you see or sense something?"

"I just wish you to honestly look at your reasons. Do not hide behind that conclave decision given to Valdhor. If you pass on Thaneship, make sure your heart is clear."

Alcandhor frowned with uncertainty at the Enaisi. How could this man unerringly find the mark and make him have to search his heart?

"Let us return to the Great Hall."

Mattan inclined his head.

Once back at the kegs, he filled a tankard and walked to a table, the alien following. He took a deep pull, trying to keep his mind from his meddling ancestor's advice. Females congregated nearby, distracting his thoughts. He groaned quietly.

His dark eyes glinting, Mattan leaned close. "Do you think you can escape them?"

"I only need not notice," Alcandhor hissed.

"Ha! That will not last long. They will merely become more bold."

"And I do not care for bold women."

"Do you not? What sort of woman do you like?"

Alcandhor spat, "One who is quiet and unassuming."

"Submissive?"

"Nay, just not domineering and overly willful." He ground his teeth. *Or childish and selfish and given to shrieking temper displays. Or unfaithful.*

"Too much of that the first time around?"

He stared at his tankard.

"Come, man, you need to discuss it with someone. I know her not, so I can listen without prejudice. Tell me."

"'Tis still too raw and hard to put into words. The years I tried, yet failed, to keep our marriage alive. My love for her alive. I lied to myself for years that there was hope, putting my children and all my kin here at Zaidhron through torment because I did not put her out long ago."

"Do you think you will marry again?"

"Stars, nay! I have no desire for another necklet to be about my throat. Who would wish for such torment?"

"Marriage is not always torment."

"I will not take the chance. I do not intend to marry again. Ever."

"That proclamation shall cause great sorrow among the women here."

"They have no heartache because of me, they are all only interested in marrying the Thane. There is not one woman in this city whose heart dies inside wishing my arms were around her. A plague on them all!" He drained his tankard, then stood, and gestured toward Mattan's. "Shall I fill it for you?"

"Nay, thank you."

Alcandhor strode to the kegs, hoping his brisk pace would deter the gaggle of women that eyed him. He determined to do one thing—avoid the dancing area of the Great Hall. Staying near half tipped back, jesting Rangers at the kegs would prove much safer.

He smiled as he filled his tankard, listening to the young Rangers nearby. He remembered times spent with Haladhon at that age, and the fun they had. He turned with a wistful sigh to watch them as they laughed, told stories on each other, and bragged on themselves. He found himself grinning at them.

"Were we ever that young, Thane?" Eladhrel asked, walking up beside him.

Loch'alan and Baidhrol doubled over laughing and gave each other playful shoves. The two chiefs chuckled and stepped away from the kegs.

"So, cousin, what think you of their opinion"—Alcandhor gestured over at the young cockerels—"that things shall begin to quiet now?"

Eladhrel pursed his lips. The man was a contradiction in some ways. He embarrassed more easily than even Alcandhor, and quick, witty comments would pass by him unnoticed. Yet despite his unassuming manner, he was a wicked fighter, always the first to rush into a fray, and had an instinct for assessing situations and people that was uncanny.

"Nay. I see it not. Even if we had not a woman who is Ranger and heir to Thane, and had not an Enaisi now in our midst, we have much to deal with. Rebellion roils. Most strongly in Estan, but in other provinces, too, and with inexperienced lords whose loyalties remain in question. And we have a young, untried Laird which will cause doubt and mistrust among the nobles, especially as he is an advocate of Ch'shalna clan. I suspect we still have much turmoil in our future."

Stifling a sigh, Alcandhor could only nod in agreement.

Chapter Three

Mists swirled about Alcandhor in the darkness. A nebulous shape slowly grew into a towering hulk. Dread overcame him, and despite himself, he took a step back. The looming structure glistened in cold welcome, and Alcandhor recognized it. Estan Hall. He shuddered, knowing, somehow, his steps must bring him hence.

Sitting up abruptly, Alcandhor gasped, sweat dripping down his face. He threw back the covers and swung his legs over the side of the bed, then dropped his head into his hands. Not another dream! Not again!

~*~

Alcandhor pulled his cloak close against the bitter wind, his long, dark hair whipping about his face as he marched across the grounds the next morning. He slammed into the Thane's chamber startling the two clan chiefs already seated at the table.

A pained grimace crossed Mattan's features. "Was that necessary?"

Alcandhor bit back a reply that a man who had lived for over a thousand years should have better sense and avoid a morning-after, but it was a celebration last night, and many suffered the same fate today.

Haladhon straightened from his indolent posture. "Is there a problem, Thane?"

"I apologize for being late." He strode to his study table. "This whole place has gone mad."

"Why say you that?" asked his cousin, a glint in his green-grey eyes.

"The women in this city are suddenly interested in greeting me, asking about my health, and wanting to discuss various aspects of the weather."

Haladhon threw back his head and roared with laughter, while Mattan winced, placing a hand on Haladhon's arm in a tacit plea.

Alcandhor planted his fists on his hips, teeth clenched. "What is so amusing?"

"You, my dear cousin. You have supplanted me, sir, in being the most sought-after male in our clan. I thank you." The tall Ranger inclined his head in mock gratitude.

Before he could retort, a knock came at the door, and Eladhrel and

25

his brother Andhrel entered, accompanied by the Pashelon Sept Chief Ordhral.

"Is something amiss?"

"Nay, Thane," Eladhrel said, holding out a missive. "But a messenger arrived from Viltara. Lord Krendhal has called a lords' conclave to confirm Randhal as the new Laird."

"I expected that would be soon. Ordhral, wish you to join us for the morning reports?"

"I would be honored, Thane."

Alcandhor waved Andhrel and Eladhrel to seats, wishing them to stay for the meeting. Mattan leaned back, eyes closed. His tall cousin nodded toward their dark-skinned ancestor and winked.

"I am not asleep," the Enaisi muttered. He rubbed his temples with a soft moan.

Ordhral asked, "You are in pain, Mattan?"

"The truth is," the alien said in a quiet voice, "that I am not well this morning."

"Aye, too much spiced wine," Haladhon replied with an insufferable smirk.

The Enaisi shot him a dirty look.

Alcandhor suppressed a chuckle as his tall cousin continued, "At his age, you would think he would know better than—"

"At my age?" spluttered Mattan, sitting upright and glaring at Haladhon. "What in the names of both moons does age have to do with it?"

"All the centuries you have lived and you know not the results of drinking too much?"

"Regardless of age, when one is enjoying himself during a celebration, one does not always think of how much one is drinking," he retorted, then sat back grimacing.

Alcandhor rubbed his lips, fighting a smile. The Enaisi glared at him. "What has you amused?"

"A grumpy clan chief suffering too much morning-after-the-night-before."

"I do not see how that is amusing."

"Stars, man, why do you put up with the headache? Can you not heal yourself of it?"

"It is taxing to heal, whether oneself or another person, and I would rather save my energies for something more worthwhile."

"In other words, the headache eases his guilt for overindulging," Haladhon put in, snickering.

Mattan glowered in Haladhon's direction, which did not subdue the tall Ranger in the least.

With a grin, Alcandhor pulled the pile of papers toward himself. Fortunately, today, the morning reports were routine save missives from the lords of the three provinces previously plagued by Rogues.

Haladhon snorted as he read the first, from the new lord of Keladar. "Gilendhar is not best pleased Rangers descended on his province, and has not said word one about the fact the Rogues have all been captured as a result."

"No surprise there. I fear he is as his cousin Paltor was."

"Aye." Haladhon frowned. "I think we should look into his activities."

"Let us wait for more reports from Keladar Rangers. Besides I will have a chance to meet and assess Lord Gilendhar at Laird Hall."

His cousin lifted a shoulder and picked up the next letter. "This is a little better. Lorwith of Pashelon sends greetings and thanks us for ending the Rogues' menace."

Now Alcandhor snorted. "I am certain he is grateful. He does not like competition in his thieving from his people."

Haladhon's eyes widened. "Cousin, how can you say on against such a loyal lord?"

"I take it," Mattan drawled, still leaning back with his eyes closed, "that Lord Lorwith is not as upright as he should be?"

"He is a traitor, but we have no proof," Alcandhor spat.

"He squeezes as much as he can out of his people," Ordhral added through gritted teeth. "Not to mention his border taxes make it difficult for his people to trade out of the province. We Pashelon Rangers feel the bite of the difficulties but are hindered in doing much. 'Tis beyond frustrating."

Mattan *hmmed* but said nothing more.

Haladhon cleared his throat and fluttered a missive in the air. "Irdhith, our new lord of Lantral Province, makes a bare mention of the dead or captured Rogues, despite the fact the murdered family's farm is in his province."

Alcandhor nodded. "I have only met him once or twice, but he appeared to be concerned only with his own comfort, not that of the province. I do wonder if his uncle gave him any instruction as to how to govern."

"How much did Zantith govern anyway?" Haladhon's lip curled. "He was only interested in gambling and gathering finery for himself."

"True. It is interesting, though, that Irdhith does express dismay and disbelief that the Ranger Nandhal, whom I had sent on assignment to his uncle some lunations before, had gone Rogue."

Haladhon nodded at Irdhith's letter. "I also find it noteworthy that he states a desire to visit Zaidhron, specifically mentioning meeting Sarinna. How did he word it? Known for her beauty and wisdom? He must be scheming something."

"You do not think he might be honestly interested in her beauty and wisdom?" Ordhral asked, grinning.

Before Haladhon could reply, Alcandhor said, "I am perhaps a bit biased, but I think my sister is beautiful and wise. However, I believe she is more widely known for her acerbic turn of phrase and the ability to cut men off at their knees. So nay, I agree with Haladhon. I do not think he is truly interested in her. Which makes me wonder what he is truly interested in." He straightened, trying to crack his back. "I think the lords' conclave at Laird Hall will be very informative. But now, shall we turn our minds to the morning reports?"

In Tam's absence, Haladhon recorded the summaries of all the daily tidings, then tapped the message from Lord Krendhal. "The conclave is in eighteen days. When are you leaving?"

"I mean for us to leave in three days' time for the Laird's conclave." With a meaningful stare at Andhrel and Eladhrel, he added, "And I am going to follow the precedent of the other noble clans. We are not going alone. Your wives will accompany you, if they wish it."

They all gaped at him.

"In the midst of what might be dangerous circumstances, Alcandhor?" Andhrel asked in a rough whisper.

"Once at Laird Hall, they will be safe. Remember 'tis our men who guard that hall since the siege. We will travel with a large detail of Rangers as well. However, this time of year is cold and not easy journeying for those not inured to it. It will not be an easy task for the women." He paused, glancing around the table. "Sarinna is going."

"Sarinna?" Haladhon stiffened. "Why?"

"I have no wife to attend. Taniss, as matriarch of our clan, is not willing to make the journey, so it falls next to Sarinna."

"And she has agreed to this?"

"Aye. She looks forward to it." Alcandhor frowned in surprise at Haladhon's disapproval.

"She knows of the dangers you expect?"

"Cousin, this is Sarinna we are discussing. Think you she would allow me to keep anything from her, even if I attempted it?"

The brothers snickered, and his Third at Table relaxed into his chair, looking abashed.

"Stars, man, you would think she is your sister," Eladhrel said.

"She is the closest I have, cousin," Haladhon said, his jaw set. "I alone of you am an only child. Sarinna is as sister to me."

"Think you I would put my own sister in danger?"

Haladhon met Alcandhor's eyes and let his breath out slowly. "Nay, Thane. Nay, you would not. I apologize. I overstepped myself."

"It delights me to know your feelings for Sarinna are as deep as they are for me." Alcandhor's humor rose, and he pointed a finger at the tall Ranger. "Take care, or you may reveal the depths of your heart and ruin your carefully constructed reputation."

Haladhon scowled and then sighed, leaning back again and stretching his legs under the table. In his usual mocking manner, he summarized, "So, we leave in three days, with our women, for Laird Hall. You have Rangers guarding nobles and Rangers guarding Laird Hall. And you have Tam and Mattan as 'secret weapons.' Marcalan too, if you consider his wit."

Andhrel huffed at that, and the others grinned.

Alcandhor sobered. "One more bit of business must be attended this morning. When do we hang the Rogues?"

Their countenances all grew solemn.

"Now, while they are nestling. Tam needs not see it again," Haladhon spat.

"She will know it," Mattan murmured. "She has a strong awareness of Nandhal. She will sense his death when he is hung. Give them their nestling time."

"Carry out sentence on the two Rogues the day after their marriage celebration. We can leave that morning after the hanging," Andhrel suggested.

"How can she sense Nandhal so strongly?" Haladhon asked with a frown. "Is that natural?"

"As strongly as she has inherited the abilities of my people, aye. She has met him, felt his presence, and he has sent to her and she to him, even though it was only negative feelings of hate, anger, and pain. I will need to be there for her, I think, in this instance. It might be a good idea to alert all those of Enaisi blood to be aware they might sense his death personally, especially if they knew him well."

"Marcalan," Haladhon murmured.

"Aye, he Trained with him for years."

In a low voice, Alcandhor said, "Empathic or not, it affects us all." He inhaled deeply, pulling strength from inside himself. "Any other business?"

"Aye. When do we announce Marcalan has been given chief status because of his marriage?" Haladhon asked.

"At their marriage celebration," Alcandhor said. "I have already ordered a chief's jerkin to be readied for him."

"And the announcement that he is a Child of the Enaisi?"

"Mattan," Alcandhor asked, "you are ready to explain to our clan the impossibility of Marcalan's genetics?"

"Stars, no one has been able to explain the impossibility of Marcalan himself," Haladhon said dryly.

Alcandhor glared at him.

"Aye, Thane. I can make an explanation that I believe would be simple enough for most people to understand."

"And do we leave our people to make their own assumptions as to whether Marcalan is the fulfillment of Zadhras' prophecy?" Andhrel asked.

"Until Mattan and I can discover where those prophecies are hidden so we have the exact wording, I will make no statement. Nor will any of the chiefs. Is that understood?" Alcandhor gazed around the table.

The chiefs all inclined their heads.

Ordhral nodded, indicating he knew he was included even though not a chief—save of his own sept within the clan. However, his eyes gleamed. Did he know something?

Alcandhor studied the man, but only received raised eyebrows. Stars, another who could playact innocence. "Any other business?" he asked again.

Eladhrel straightened, frowning. "Aye, Thane. I think planning to leave the same day as the executions is not a wise move."

"Why is that? Because of the emotions involved? I thought journeying would keep our minds off it."

"But it is not just us—it is the whole city. And forget you if we wait until afterwards, we will need to journey quicker to arrive at the journey station before dark, especially as we are nearing winter solstice and the days are shorter. That will be difficult on the women."

Alcandhor met Eladhrel's gaze. "Perhaps you are right. We had best wait a day. Are we agreed?"

The chiefs all nodded.

"Then this meeting is concluded."

Everyone rose. The brothers bowed and left, leaving Haladhon standing by the door. "Thane, I would like to go to the valley. I will return before Tam and Marcalan's celebration."

Alcandhor sighed, then belatedly smiled. "Aye. Visit while you can."

Haladhon returned the smile, tightly, then whisked out the door.

"What was that about?" Mattan asked.

Alcandhor shook his head. "I do not fain discuss it. Ask Haladhon."

The alien's brows rose, and he opened his mouth, but Alcandhor stopped him before he could begin. "Now, about those prophecies. Have you made any headway?"

Mattan glared but replied, "Nay, but I did want to know if you wished to accompany Delgan and me to the Portal Complex."

With frown at the mention of his friend and history-keeper, Alcandhor asked, "Why are you and Delgan going to the Portal Complex?"

"To work on breaking the encryptions on those files. Three might speed up the process."

"Encryptions?" Ordhral asked.

Mattan waved a hand. "I discovered files that were uploaded and encrypted—you might call locked—after the time that the portal had been shut down and complex closed off. Which means only Ismari or Ashani could have been responsible. We think perhaps those files contain the lost prophecies of Zadhras the Seer. The Thane and I—" Mattan stopped and frowned, fists on hips. "What is so amusing, Ordhral?"

"I do not say the prophecies were not stored in the Portal Complex as a safeguard, but I know for certain that is not where Zadhras kept them."

"And where are they then, Sept Chief?" Alcandhor asked.

Brows raised, Ordhral replied, "You know, Thane. Think about it. You have been there."

Alcandhor frowned, shaking his head. "I know not what you—oh!" *Stars!* "You know of that, do you? Of him?"

"Of Zadhras, aye. I met him, long ago. As did you, not so long ago."

"Now, wait." Mattan lifted a hand. "Ashani's son, Zadhras—he cannot be alive. I would know."

"Nay," Ordhral said. "He died when our Thane was but a stripling."

Alcandhor hesitated, then nodded. "'Tis strange. It was to be a secret. I was not aware anyone else knew of him."

"To my knowledge, you and I are the only ones now alive who ever met him, or knew he still lived."

"Stars, Ordhral, you continue to astonish me!"

"I have been most blessed to know many things, through knowing Ismari, and Zadhras as well."

"Any other secrets you must keep from your Thane?"

Ordhral smiled. "Not for much longer, I deem. 'Twill be an ease to be unburdened soon enough. I apologize, but I only follow the instructions set down by my first mother."

Alcandhor forbore pulling out his hair. He took a deep breath and focused on the prophecies. He would fain know the literal wording of the one that might concern Marcalan, but also, what others existed that they knew not about? "So, then, if the prophecies were stored at his cottage, they might still be there, safe and undamaged."

"You would know more of that than I would, my Thane."

"Rangers guard what was once his home, keeping it intact and free from squatters. They do their duty without even knowing why." Alcandhor closed his eyes. "Can you imagine if Worshippers found out..." He stopped, sighing. "Aye, we need to visit and find those prophecies. But I would wait until after the hangings. By both moons, this might mean a delay in leaving for Laird Hall."

"All will be well, and done orderly, Thane," Mattan said.

"Sight, Enaisi?"

"A lifetime of experience," the alien replied with a grin.

"I wish I shared your optimism." Alcandhor stood. "So, if we are not going to the Portal Complex just now, I need to find Amadhor, Monadhal's father."

"'Tis a hard task, Thane," Ordhral murmured.

"Aye."

Chapter Four

Mattan stood in the sward, pulling his cloak about him. It had been so long since he experienced weather. War-ravaged Anatai had none; the planet was but a barren desert, a hollow victory. The underground world to which most of his people had retreated and hid while he and others fought off the invaders, had been almost like a prison. Yet at the moment, he was not appreciative of the biting wind.

He frowned, sensing for Haladhon. The man was at the barracks, or leaving them anyway. Aye, he was moving, and his emotions roiled with both bitterness and happy expectation. Mattan plotted an intersect course, and soon came across his tall son.

"May I walk with you?"

"Has the Thane set you on me?"

"Set me?"

"You asked, did you not, and he told you to ask me directly."

"He said he did not fain discuss it."

Haladhon snorted. "He would not discuss my *shame*, as he deems it."

Mattan stepped fast to keep up with Haladhon's long strides. "What is this grievance that hangs between you unspoken?"

The tall Ranger's lips thinned, the veneer of lightheartedness stripped away. "I have two children who live in Thane Valley. Their mother is listed as my legal mistress."

"Why do you not marry the mother?"

"Panill does not wish to leave her home. And by *law*, a chief and his family must reside in Zaidhron." Haladhon's lip curled. "Except Valdhor. He married, had a child, and lived in Pashelon with a bounds."

"What was the reason for that?"

"I know not, save it seems the law is more fair to some than others."

"There must be some explanation."

"Oh, aye, so 'tis said, but sealed by Thane Saldhor and Lamadhel and my father. Only Lamadhel now remains alive to tell the reasons, but he claims he is bound to secrecy."

So this explained the resentment simmering under his laughter. Rubbing his aching head, he asked, "You would readily give up that jerkin, would you not?"

Haladhon stopped, blinking. "Nay."

"Stars, you would lie, knowing I can sense the truth?" Mattan flung his arms out, indicating the lack of people nearby in the sward. "There is no one else here, my son."

The Ranger's lips peeled back. "Aye, I would."

"But a Ranger chief cannot relinquish his jerkin, can he?"

"Nay. Even for those not a chief, 'tis not easy, but I would likely be able to come to some arrangement or compromise, living in the valley near my girls, roaming a bounds, perhaps even smithing a little. But I am not allowed to live outside the city, much less give up this jerkin once earned—unless it is snatched from me for a breach of the law."

"And so twice the law prevented you from what your heart's desires. No wonder you are so bitter. What has stopped you from doing something to get that jerkin taken from you?" A revelation shot through Mattan. Was that why Haladhon flouted the law with his dalliances? Did he secretly—or perhaps unconsciously—hope Question would be called?

"And take the chance of being stripped of more than just this jerkin?"

Mattan bit back asking why, if he truly feared that outcome, he would philander at all, instead merely replying, "Aye. I am certain some Rangers would try stretch the law as far as possible. I have sensed there are those who despise you as they do Alcandhor. You dare not give them reason, enh? You are torn. You wish to forego the jerkin, but you also fear what might happen."

He did not answer, but resumed his march, staring ahead, jaw set. There was much more that he was not saying. Something deeper. But now was not the time to pry further. Mattan lifted a hand. "Forgive me for being so intrusive. I do tend to meddle."

Haladhon said nothing, but the tension in his shoulders eased slightly.

"I would ask a question, though, if you do not mind me meddling in Alcandhor's business."

With a snort, he shrugged. "Ask."

"What is the story of Alcandhor and his wife—ex-wife?"

He sneered, and Mattan need not sense to know how much execration this topic held for the man. He kept himself from prying into Haladhon's thoughts, instead asking for the information he sought. "What is the source of the anger and hatred I feel from you?"

"It is her. Aleta. His former wife. She never loved him. She ate away at him like a festering sore, destroying him. I—" Haladhon stopped walking and glowered, a fury rising in him startling in its intensity.

"If it is too personal and painful, you need not tell me."

"It is too personal and painful for *him*! He still cannot bring himself to discuss it. And all I could do all these years was watch helplessly as the man I love dearer than brother slowly destroyed by her venomous mouth. She loved him not. She married him for the power she thought he could wield when he became Thane. She considers mercy and compassion weaknesses and scorned him for them. She whispered her poison that he was weak and unworthy for years. What you see is the result."

So many things were explained. So very many things. He leaned closer to the tall Ranger, meeting his eyes earnestly. "Then we have to work to undo that, Haladhon. You and I. At least now I know the cause of his doubts."

"Some but not all."

"What do you mean?"

Haladhon's forehead creased as he sighed. "He wanted to be a history-keeper and science law-keeper as well. He despised his elder brother Valdhor for giving up heirship and dreaded that the mantle fell on him. It affected him. Not too noticeably when he was younger, but when his father, Saldhor, died, he withdrew. Between living with her, dealing with Saldhor's untimely death, and coming to terms with being Thane, he changed. I have never really seen him happy since he took on Thaneship."

This was not news, but the man need not know it, not when he had shared something obviously held tightly in his heart. He put a hand on the Ranger's shoulder. "We will have to work very hard then, will we not, to bring out that cheerful, mischievous rascal that is hidden away deep inside him?"

Haladhon stared at him. "How can you know so much?"

Mattan managed a smile. "Do not think it a gift."

~*~

Alcandhor found Amadhor matching his son Albardhal in a secluded, walled section of the training grounds. They stopped as they saw him, lowering their staves.

"You need say nothing, Thane," Albardhal said. "He has been dead to us for years."

"He was your brother," Alcandhor replied. "Laws or not, Monadhal—"

"Say not that name, Thane!" Amadhor's hand chopped downward in the air. "My son died years ago. That, that man in the cells is a soulless creature in my eyes." He lifted his chin, one fist clenched to his chest. "*My son* was a Ranger. That man has no regard for life or the law. He chose to disregard all that was ever taught him. He chose his punishment, hardening himself to any chance of redemption by his clan or family. He chose his fate, and when he did, my son died."

Both men's pain crushed Alcandhor's heart. "I come not as Thane, but as a fellow Ranger, and a friend. I hear your words, but I hold grief over this, so then, how much deeper is yours? How deep has it been all these years?"

The silent cold stares defeated him.

"We can finally put an end to our shame when he is dead," Amadhor said.

"What shame?" Alcandhor threw out his arms. "Did you do less than your best with him? You have two fine sons who are upstanding Rangers, and grandsons who are promising striplings and Trainees. Because one son strayed you feel shame? You cannot fault that. Personality will out, at times, no matter what effort we put forth. I have never faulted you, nor did my father. I would dare any Ranger to speak against you. Has it been so?"

The older Ranger licked his lips, his pride and reluctance more telling than words.

"I ask again, has anyone spoken against you?"

"Not directly," Amadhor muttered.

Alcandhor gritted his teeth. "Who?"

"I wish not to say, Thane."

"By the Bells and both moons, I will not have any Ranger speak against another unless they are willing to call Question on actions or deeds! I will know who, man!"

"It is never openly said, sir." Albardhal spoke up upon his father's silence. "It is implied, or it is a look, or a moving away from us."

Alcandhor stepped forward, and both men backed up. "You should have come to me," he hissed. "I will have your family stand next to me when the time comes. I will show by actions that I count you worthy as Rangers and friends. I cannot control individuals, but I will do what is in my power to see that my clan understands that blame is laid at a person's feet, not on his family."

He took a deep breath and willed his anger away. Dropping a hand on each man's shoulder, he sent compassion and peace to them as he gazed into Amadhor's eyes then into his son's. "I sense your grief, and I am sorry. Sorry for his choices and for the pain it has inflicted on you. Sorry it has to end this way."

Both men turned from him, just as they had done every time in the past when he had approached them. He dropped his hands in despair and failure and walked away.

~*~

Lessons with his children cheered Alcandhor, but now, following afternooning, his heart again weighed heavy. He ignored the scattered splatter of cold rain as he trudged alone across Avadhron's Sward.

"Thane!" Gardhal jogged toward him. He stopped and waited. The Elite bowed, not seeming to care about being soaked. He blinked as random drops hit his face, but charged ahead with his report. "An event has unfolded. Casinn visited Nandhal in the cells."

Alcandhor stared at him, lost. "Casinn?"

"A servant who formerly worked in the Great Hall, but now in the family ranges."

"Why would she visit Nandhal?" Before Gardhal could reply, a thought occurred to him. "Think you she is enamored of him?"

"Aye, and it explains much. I have made inquiries, and found the last few lunations she had been prone to sullen moods, about the time Nandhal left for his post at Lairdton's Ranger Hold."

Alcandhor groaned. "Has she spoken to anyone? Asked for counsel or comfort?"

"Not that I could discover, but then, she keeps to herself, and her attitude has not won her friends."

He nodded, not remarking that the same could be said of the dour Gardhal. "Was their conversation monitored?"

"Aye." The Elite crossed his arms. "She cried and declared she loved him, and wished they had been married already. He mocked and cursed her, and she ran out."

"Stars, he has no compassion even for a woman who loves him."

"Nay. Cold to the marrow."

Alcandhor gazed up at the thick, low clouds. "Perhaps...we should apprise the range mistress. She might help the lass with her grief. Nay, best tell Sarinna, and let her handle it."

"Aye, sir."

"Any other news? Has anyone else visited either Rogue?"

"Only Edhron. And they both scorned him."

"Aye, that I knew." Alcandhor stared ahead at nothing. "Has either wished to talk to anyone?"

"Nay. Nandhal cursed and kicked at the healer who came to check him, and he had to sedate him." The Elite grimaced, as if in pain. "If he thrashes about, the wound may open."

Alcandhor flinched.

Gardhal lowered his voice. "The cell guards also report Nandhal weeps from time to time." After licking his lips, he continued, "'Tis sorrowful, Thane. It does affect us all. But..." He stopped, then blurted, "you cannot hold it to your heart."

Such a statement from the taciturn Ranger? Did he see his Thane's grief so clearly? "How can I not? I am their Thane."

"Nay, sir, you are not. They rejected you. They rejected our clan. And our laws. They chose this, knowing the outcome."

He could not meet the Elite's eyes. "Thank you for the report, Ranger Gardhal."

After the man bowed and walked away, and Alcandhor stood for a long while in the rain, trying to bring his emotions under control.

~*~

Alcandhor looked around the Great Hall that evening. If only he could leave. He joined the Rangers in some jesting, but his heart was not in it; his thoughts returned too often to the Rogues' hanging. And also, the fear of having Question called on Tam's birth record loomed darker than ever before.

Mattan walked up, smiling, and tossed an arm casually around his shoulder. How much had the alien imbibed already?

"My dear Alcandhor, you need a diversion. Excuse me, Rangers, but I am going to steal your Thane away for a little while."

The men bowed, grinning.

"You look as if you need to steal away to your bed, not try to divert or amuse me."

"I have only had one ale. Know you not the difference between a man relaxed and one sotted? Come, son, you will enjoy this."

Alcandhor sighed in resignation as he followed Mattan to the back hallway and to lift to the Portal Complex, only recently made accessible, thanks to Tam. "And where are we going?"

"Ah, that I must show you. Get in. This is someplace special." Once inside, the alien touched a letter on the panel. "You will see in a few moments."

Alcandhor did not say it aloud, but the entirety of the Portal Complex was special to him.

The door opened. As always, this place awed him, although all he saw was a corridor, now fully lit. He reached out to touch the Enaisi's grey-white oldstone walls, built ages before Alcandhor's people even came to this planet. Older than the white shimmerstone of the city. He turned, smiling, but Mattan's gaze sobered him. "What is it?"

Mattan paused a moment before answering. "You have sight. Strongly, from what I have been told. How much do you share of what you see?"

Alcandhor shrugged. "Little, especially where it concerns a person. I am loath to tell what I have seen, as I am often unsure if I see correctly."

"Then you will understand that I see things about you, and yet am hesitant to discuss them."

"Not even a hint? Is it good or bad?"

"You jest, but I feel your trepidation, Thane. Come. Let me show you the main library housed here."

Walking down the dim hallway, Mattan said, "Even before knowing what was happening when I came here, I realized this is a time of instability and changes. There are those of your people that are important to the future of your world, and particularly in times such as these they are needed."

"Aye. Chosen ones."

"If that is the term your people now use. You are one, you know."

Alcandhor avoided Mattan's gaze. "I have been told so."

"Do you know the others?"

"Perhaps not all. But a few."

"You worry if you have done well by them—by one of them especially. You have. By all that I can sense."

"My father tried to instruct me concerning him..." Uncertainty threatened to choke him, and he fought it down.

"You learn well. Things are almost beyond what you can shape now, but your duty is not done. There is a nebulous darkness before you, my son, and I cannot see past it. But tasks face you. Hard ones. You are stronger than you give yourself credit for. You will prevail."

Alcandhor met his eyes, searching for meaning, for guidance. "Will these tasks come while I am Thane, or after?"

"I cannot say. I see little. It is more a feeling."

Did Mattan's vague wording mean he could not tell him because he did not know or because something that he saw or felt warned him not to? That cursed shadow rose up, threatening to grip his heart again. Would someone call Question? 'Twas foolish to think it would not happen; 'twas more a when than an if. Could he evade the worst penalties? Would the clan stand by him?

Mattan turned and tapped in a code on a small panel next to a door, which then slid open. "This is the library." He touched a spot on the inside causing lights to flood the room.

Alcandhor's mouth gaped at the enormous chamber—perhaps the size of the Great Hall. Books filled shelves built into the oldstone walls and more were on freestanding shelves set in sections on the floor. On the tables scattered throughout sat computer consoles. He stepped cautiously inside as if the books would disappear if he were not reverent enough. He swallowed to clear the constriction in his throat and to try to control his breathing.

"You are a cruel man," he whispered.

"Why say you that?"

"You introduce me to this library, knowing in a few days we will be away, and I have no time to begin reading."

Mattan threw back his head, laughing. "But you have me to ask questions of. Why need you a library?"

"You do not always answer questions."

"Questions that I will not answer, I doubt you will find answers to in these books."

"You can be infuriating."

"So I have been told," Mattan said with a grin.

Alcandhor smiled, then grew serious, chewing the inside of his cheek. "What knowledge is here? Anything dangerous to my people? To our way of life?"

"I cannot say. Some perhaps. I would have to check the indices, and that would take time."

He let out a long, slow exhale. "Then we shall lock this for now. No one shall know of it."

"But—"

"I have spoken, Chief Mattan."

The Enaisi hesitated, then bowed. "Shall we then return to the Great Hall?"

Alcandhor nodded. "First let us stop in the wine cellars. I feel a need to have a drink."

~*~

Sarinna turned at the sound of her brother and the alien guffawing to see them stagger into the Great Hall. Stars, 'twas late; she thought Alcandhor had left for Family North long ago. Those still present watched them with amusement as they sang an old tavern song. Mattan stumbled over words and melody, obviously attempting to learn the tune from his Thane, who could not sing well.

She smiled with tolerant affection, one hand over an ear. They reeled toward her and attempted to bow—unsuccessfully, and ended up on the floor, laughing.

"I cannot believe how sotted you both are. This is very unlike you Alcandhor. And this is the second night in a row for you, Mattan."

"I think she likes you," Alcandhor said in a feigned whisper, pulling on the Elder in an effort to get him to his feet.

"Indeed? How can you tell?" Mattan wobbled, holding on to the Thane for support.

"She is treating you as an errant child That is proof she likes you. If she did not, she would pay no attention to the fact you are a wretched sot."

"Ah, I see. I am grateful to know—" the alien stopped and drew himself up in indignation. "I am not a sot!" Mattan shoved Alcandhor, and they both fell over again.

"Oh, stop. You two cannot truly be that tipped back."

Her brother peered up, melting Sarinna with his loving gaze. He had become so withdrawn these last years—she rarely saw that look anymore.

"Do you know, my dear sister, that you are beautiful when you are angry?"

"I am not angry," she said evenly, trying not to smile.

"True," Alcandhor said. "Aggravated?"

"Irritated?" Mattan suggested.

"Annoyed?"

"Exasperated?"

Sarinna threw up her hands, rolling her eyes, which caused both men to laugh once more.

"A fine pair you two make. Is that the best thing you men can find to do to relax—drink?"

Her brother snickered. "It worked. I must say, I am very relaxed."

"I agree." Mattan poked Alcandhor's arm. "I think you have no bones in your body, Thane."

Sarinna groaned.

"Like the drunkard in the song." Alcandhor sang, out of tune, the last line of the verse again: "And rolled himself right out the door."

She shook her head and gazed at nearby Rangers. "Will you help these two hopeless rascals to bed?"

Grinning, the Rangers came over and helped both boneless men to their feet.

To the ones holding up their Thane, she said, "Give me a moment to grab my cloak, and I will join you."

"I can walk," Alcandhor muttered as Sarinna and the Rangers headed for the door. "I need not my men to escort me."

"You can barely find the floor with your face," Sarinna said. "And I cannot carry you if you pass out, so these Rangers are going with us, whether you like it or not."

"See what injustice there is in the clans, men?" asked Alcandhor.

41

"Even the Thane is able to be bullied by a sister."

"We all endure such, Thane," answered Mardhral, grinning at Sarinna.

"Aye, and you have three sisters, so you understand," Alcandhor replied.

"Indeed."

It was quiet as they walked across the grounds, her brother leaning on her. His guard lowered from the drink, his emotions could be easily discerned. Although pleased to feel his affection, she was relieved none of the accompanying Rangers was a Child of the Enaisi; Alcandhor despised letting his feelings be revealed in front of his men. He would unhappy enough that they had seen him tipped back.

She was also thankful his suite was only on the first level of Family North; they only had the challenge of getting him up just that one flight of stairs.

"Thank you. I will see to him," she told the Rangers, once they were at his door. She helped him inside. He made his way to his bed and sat on it heavily as she lit a candle from the fireplace.

"Oh Sarinna, 'tis marvelous," he mumbled.

"What is?" she asked, kneeling to help him unlace his boots.

"Mattan showed me the Enaisi's library. It is magnificent! You should see it—it is as large as the Great Hall, and filled with books. Not just computers with files one can access, but real books!"

"No wonder you wished to celebrate."

"Ah, nay, I worry. Is there knowledge in that library that could entice our people, make them dissatisfied with our way of life, or wish to try new inventions or enact new ideas which could destroy our world? Our forefathers warned us of this. We will not disclose the library until I can reach a decision. Such riches, but as all other kinds, it leads to temptation. And if I have the slightest concern for our world and our future, I will not sanction it."

Sarinna shivered as his anguish pressed on her like a weight. Despite his love of learning and of books, he would readily give it up. No wonder he drank so much tonight with Mattan. She need not answer; they could sense each other.

"I will build the fire for you as you undress." She knelt at the fireplace. "It has burned low."

She tended the blaze, still discerning the aching sense of loss in him. At times, her brother was too noble. He had given up so much for duty's sake. As a child, he would come to her for comfort, and she would rock him, cradling his head as he cried. If only she could hold him now and let him cry. But he would not weep; he was Thane, and would do what he felt was best for his people, and say his loss was negligible. She could hear the words as if he had spoken them aloud. For a moment, she despised Valdhor. If only she could have 'Candhor back; the little brother that had so openly loved and laughed—the one that withered when he gained heirship, and died when he became Thane.

She rose after hearing the bed creak and crossed to him. He was already asleep—or passed out. She sat next to him, brushing the hair away from his face. The worry lines were gone for the moment, and he seemed at peace. She stood, adjusting the coverlet over him, and kissed his forehead, murmuring, "Sleep well, little brother." She blew out the candle and left.

Chapter Five

Andhrel and Eladhrel greeted Alcandhor and followed him into the Thane's chamber, discussing inane details of their plans in leaving for Laird Hall. He gritted his teeth against his pounding head. Why this morning of all mornings did they wish to chat?

Slowly, he lowered himself into his chair, nodding at Ordhral and Mattan. The former he had asked to join him since neither his Second and Third at Table were there. The Enaisi looked as afflicted as Alcandhor felt.

"So," he took a breath. "Any news I should be aware of—inside the city or without?"

"Only what is in the reports, Thane." Ordhral gestured to the pile of papers. "No changes of importance. Tensions are building, of course."

Mattan cleared his throat, rubbing his temples. "Regarding Eladhrel's point of leaving too soon after the hangings. I think perhaps we should delay an extra day."

Andhrel frowned. "Why say you that?"

"I know not how often Rogues are hung, but I would wager there may be families here who are distressed. It would be more comforting to them if their leaders were here not only that day but also the next."

Their eyes all locked on Alcandhor. He sighed. Even without that dream, an urgency to get to Laird Hall and to Estan Province grew in him, but he could not deny Mattan made sense. He leaned back in his chair, nodding, then winced as the motion increased his headache. "Two days."

"I look forward to tomorrow night," Andhrel said. "I only hope Haladhon has not made any special preparations of his own for the evening."

"He would not," Eladhrel said, wide-eyed. "Not at their marriage celebration."

"Stars, know you not what he has done to them during nestling?" asked Alcandhor, grinning despite his headache. "He arranged for the legs of their bedstead to be cut almost all the way through."

Andhrel and Ordhral burst into laughter. Alcandhor grimaced, and Mattan winced.

Eladhrel gaped. "That goes too far!" He frowned at them all. "You think it amusing?"

"Brother," Andhrel said, his eyes twinkling, "you need to remember this is Marcalan and Haladhon."

"But it is Tam, also."

"If she is not amused, I will wager she can bring payment to Haladhon that he will not soon forget," Alcandhor said.

The men chuckled, and he gazed about, hoping his expression was pointed not peaked. "If there is no more business, Ordhral, Mattan, and I are going to read and order the morning reports so they may be archived."

~*~

Irdhith ground his teeth upon reading the missive from Lord Krendhal. A conclave to confirm Randhal as Laird in eighteen days, nay—this arrived yesterday. Seventeen days. That gave him little time to plan his journey to Zaidhron to meet and woo this Sarinna.

If even half of what Nandhal said was true about empaths and their abilities to share not only emotions but physical feelings were true, then he must have this woman!

Perhaps a short visit to become acquainted, then after the conclave, a longer visit to Zaidhron. Protocol dictated that he dare not write to the woman directly. A letter to her brother would have to suffice. He licked his lips in anticipation of such a conquest as he dipped the nib in the ink and began to write.

~*~

The reports finished, Ordhral blew on the ink of one document, and Mattan sorted the rest. And Alcandhor's headache had eased off somewhat, thankfully. Small mercies.

The door opened with a soft knock, and Feladhrel stuck his head around timidly. "Thane? Someone is here who wishes to speak to you. I am not certain of protocol—"

"Who is it?"

"A farmer from the valley."

By both moons, not Sonvil or Lanwin. "His name?"

"Halcom, sir."

"Halcom..." Alcandhor frowned in thought. The broad plain of the valley took four days to cross at minimum by a Ranger's pace, if one did not consider having to detour around the little lakes and rivers, and eight for its length. That did not include the hanging valley at the northwest end, nor the high shoulders. He could not know all the tenants who lived there. "Show him in."

A fit, lean man with a weathered face shuffled in. He fingered a hat, his slicked-back hair and neat shoes bespoke of a wash and cleaning up after his journey. His clothes were likely his best, although the cloak had subtle mending by a skilled hand. He stopped as if gut-punched at seeing the dark-skinned alien. His mouth moved for a moment, then he blinked and turned to Alcandhor with a plaintive expression.

Alcandhor rose. "News has probably not reached all of the valley yet, good man. This is Mattan, an Enaisi who has returned to us through the portal."

The farmer kneaded his hat, threatening to crush it. He bobbed bows to Mattan, Ordhral, and a third time to Alcandhor. "Thane," he murmured.

"You are a farmer in my valley, Halcom?"

"Yes, sir. From my great-grandfa's time. Forwin his name was, and..." He dropped his gaze. "Clanless. But he was taken in by the Thane and given a home in Dandrin Shire."

Alcandhor smiled in recognition at the ancestor's name. "Aye. Then you have clan-tenant rights."

Halcom's head snapped up, his eyes wide. "Clan? But we are of no clan, sir."

"Your family has proved the land for four generations. That has earned you clan status, so you are not clanless, my good Halcom. You are adopted kin."

The farmer's back straightened a little, the corners of his lips twitching up.

Alcandhor made a mental note to have Rangers go through the records and make certain those who had adopted-clan status knew of it, and the benefits. But for now: "So, how may I help you?"

"It's my neighbors, see? Lanwin lives the farm next over. He says he was given eviction, and I say good. For him an' Sonvil. They don't do right by the land, sir. But they won't leave."

"You do know they are allocated time to find a new home before being evicted?"

"Yes, but they say you won't make good on it. I told the Ranger about it, and he laughed."

"What Ranger?"

"Fandhrel his name is. He said you wouldn't make them leave. An empty threat, he said it was."

"Why would a Ranger think I was not serious about evicting them when I ordered the writs scribed and delivered?"

Halcom stared at the floor. "They say...they say you are weak." He bobbed his head in a bow. "Your pardon, m'Thane."

Alcandhor's back stiffened, and his teeth clenched. "They say?"

"The Rangers, Fandhrel and Inradhor. Rangers for Dandrin shire, they are, for 'most the last year or abouts. They always say things like that. It's not right, sir."

Ordhral uncrossed his arms. Alcandhor's nostrils flared, but he took three measured breaths while he let himself sense the farmer. Timidity and awe—*stars! of him?*—and fear, but no guile. The man appeared genuine. He glanced at Mattan, who nodded, giving tacit confirmation that Halcom spoke the truth.

"Have you discussed this with the Ranger Rendhol?"

"Yes, sir. He did not want to believe me, back when I first told him they didn't do right. The two Rangers, they threatened me if I talked again. But Rendhol, he's a good'un, and I had to tell him what Fandhrel and Inradhor said. He sent me here, sir. Said to tell you what I heard. Said you'd know what to do."

"I thank you for coming to me, Halcom. You must have started your journey before dawn to arrive so early." Alcandhor pulled the cord. "I will see you are given some refreshment. And consider this matter resolved. You have my word."

The farmer's brow furrowed. "I...I wouldn't like those Rangers to know I was here, m'Thane."

"Worry not. I shall have a Ranger accompany you back to your farm and be certain they do not make good on their threats." Alcandhor lifted his chin. "Despite what you seem to have been told, I am Thane, and my word is law."

Feladhrel arrived, and he instructed the stripling to show the farmer to the early room of the Great Hall and see the man was given a meal.

As the door shut behind the two, Alcandhor clenched his fists. "Fandhrel has ever despised me as Thane, and I knew Inradhor leaned in that direction as well, but I would not expect their dislike of me to affect their duties. This speaks of dereliction."

"Do you think their feud was fed by these Rangers' disaffection?" Mattan asked.

"That is what we shall discover, among other things. An Elite is to leave today to find out what in the name of both moons is going on in that shire. Gardhal is a good choice. He will brook no foolishness. Inradhor and Fandhrel are recalled immediately to Thane Hall while we investigate. I shall find two Rangers to replace them, they can depart with Gardhal and Halcom."

Ordhral rose with a frown. "Rangers are not normally recalled during an investigation, Thane. At least, not based on the word of one witness."

"If they have intimidated the locals, we may get better answers if they are absent."

"Shall I call Gardhal in for you, Thane?" Ordhral asked.

"Aye."

The Pashelon chief bowed and left. Alcandhor sat back down, sighing. "Good man, Ordhral. I wish I could have him to hand more often."

"I have a feeling he will stay to hand for quite some time."

"Sight?"

Mattan shrugged. "More an intuition. He was close to my sister, saw her as a mother perhaps. I detect a longing from him. Besides, he has more to do here, I can sense the duty of...something weighing on him. With your permission, I would like to have him assist Delgan and a few other historians. I am giving them limited access to the Portal Complex to gather history and look for the prophecies."

"Allowing him further excuse to stay here? He needs none, but if he wishes a task to hand besides assisting me at times, that should keep him occupied."

Mattan inclined his head. "When you have done with Gardhal, let me sense your shoulder and give it more healing. You may then resume matching, albeit lightly at first. Would that not allow you an outlet for your frustrations?"

Huffing a laugh, Alcandhor nodded. "Aye. That it would."

~*~

Jholinn sat with Amara, as usual, and Sarinna eyed the quiet woman. What a shame that she had become widow before having any children of her own—any living children. The news of her husband's death had brought on her birth pains, and the baby had not lived. Caring for the newborn Amara and being her wetnurse had at least given her something to live for. But soon the child would be old enough to not need the constant companionship. What then?

Sarinna's eyes narrowed with a thought, and she allowed herself to sense the widow. She felt...what? A coldness? Nay, more a chill apprehension. And loneliness. If only Tam—Sarinna blinked. Stars, she had Mattan to hand. Should she ask him—not to read the woman's thoughts, nay, but to sense deeper? Was it right to do so? Would he think her meddling?

She turned to her mother and whispered, "Does Jholinn have many friends?"

Taniss shook her head, her lips thinned. "I tried to befriend her early on, and had some success. But then I left the city after your father died, and cannot say. I have not seen her with anyone but Amara since I have returned."

"That is not good. Why have I never realized it before?"

"As busy as you are? And how many friends do you have?"

Sarinna shrugged. She had cordial relations with her cousins' wives, certainly. And daily interactions with masters of ranges, warders, and their assistants with which she worked, most of them amiable. Had she filled her own life with so much work that she had no time for friends? How could she not realize how lonely her life was? Her gaze slid to Jholinn again. Perhaps she could remedy that emptiness for her niece's nursemaid as well as for herself.

Her brother stood, indicating the meal was at an end. Sarinna turned to the Enaisi, sitting next to her. "I would ask a favor."

"What is it, daughter?"

Daughter. Stars. Is that how he saw them all, as his children? Aye, surely. Better than thinking them all *pets*! She dismissed the not-so-amusing notion and lifted her chin. "Jholinn seems so isolated. I sense that, and also that she is...fearful. Can you detect anything more?"

"And why do you wish to know more?"

"Just tell me."

Mattan's brown eyes searched hers. Was he reading her mind? Bedamn him to the fires of Teledhar if he was! His lips quirked, and Sarinna's fists clenched.

"She is lonely. And yes, she has a fear of something. She has learned to keep her emotions closed tightly, as if afraid of having them sensed."

"But why? Oh, how would you know unless you read *her* mind?"

"I can sense more deeply, and more easily. It does not mean I have read *your* mind. But I will say, her ability to suppress her emotions thus is quite a formidable achievement. You would not know it to look at her"—he nodded toward the widow, who knelt in front of Amara to wipe crumbs from the child's frock—"but she is very strong of spirit."

Sarinna raised an eyebrow. "Thank you."

Alcandhor lifted his daughter into his arms. He strode away, his sons trailing, and after a few moments, Jholinn seemed to take a deep breath, and her shoulders straightened. The fear in her released, revealing a sorrowful longing as her eyes followed the Thane. Stars! Indeed she was formidable to keep thus hidden!

Her skirts swayed as she wove over to the younger woman. "Jholinn. May I have a word?"

The widow's fists clenched in her skirt, her emotions again

knotting. "Aye?"

"I have been thinking. Since Amara will soon be of an age where you are needed less—indeed you do have more free time in the afternoons now—you may wish to look into other employment. Or, do you already have something in mind?"

"I do not, Lady Sarinna."

"Just Sarinna, please. And since you do not, will you come with me and let us discuss a possibility?"

"I...I certainly."

The two women threaded past those lingering and chatting as well as servants clearing tables. Once out the double doors, Sarinna pulled her shawl tighter.

"So," she began, as they strolled along the path toward Thane Hall, "what do you do with your free time, now that my brother has Amara with him in the early afternoon?"

"I...nothing really. I mend clothes, or sew, or take a book to read while waiting for her lessons with her father to be finished."

Hiding her dismay at this woman's want of a life, she lightly replied, "Stars, woman, then you might be just what I need!"

"What is it you need, La—Sarinna?"

"An assistant. I have a Second who helps with the city stewardship, but still we are often overwhelmed. Someone to aid us would be a boon. And also, I tire of obligations of hospitality which should have been Aleta's domain. Taniss does not wish to resume them, either."

"Could not one of the chiefs' wives take on those duties?"

"They help, but nay, they have other responsibilities which demand their attention. So, as city steward, it is on me to provide someone to assume the post. What say you to being trained for the task? You would work closely with me, as is wont, and right now, the obligations are not onerous as we have few visitors. That may change with the new provincial lords in place, and also with many history-keepers and science law-keepers undoubtedly already making plans to descend upon Zaidhron with an actual Enaisi present, and the Portal Complex now available."

"You truly think I could manage such a responsibility?"

"Your care of Amara, and of the boys when needed, has shown you are dedicated, hardworking, and anticipatory. Aye, you are perfect for this. Will you accept?"

"I am honored. I shall do my best."

"Good! And I can show you what is necessary for special occasions, such as the marriage celebration tomorrow night. A joyous first task as trainee to the position. When we get to Thane Hall, I will let that stripling—what is his name?"

"Feladhrel?"

"Aye. We will let him know if you are needed for Amara, you can be found in the steward's chamber. Not very far away from the Thane's chamber and my niece, is it?"

Jholinn shook her head with a timid smile.

~*~

Alcandhor strolled toward the Great Hall with his children, Amara holding his hand and skipping, while the boys chatted about the divergences between what Mattan told them was their history compared to their books. He had tried, mostly unsuccessfully, to steer them away from that topic during tutoring, and concentrate on their other studies.

"Why the differences, Father?" Teldhor asked.

"You keep asking, and I keep saying I know not. Some of the books we have now were written from oral tradition, and many books from centuries ago are missing. Even Mattan does not know why much of the old knowledge is lost. A mystery you can be certain he and the history-keepers will do their best to solve."

"But what shall we do about our books, which are inaccurate?"

Alcandhor laughed. "That is a question to take up with the scribes and history-keepers. I imagine there will be much rewriting."

"Thane!" Loch'alan ran toward him and skidded to a halt with a rough bow. "I am bid tell you, Worshippers have arrived at the out-wall. The guards are refusing to let them through, and they are becoming agitated, making claims they have the right to come to the city."

"Tell the guards to keep firm, as always. I will discuss what might be done with Mattan at the meal."

"Thane." Loch'alan bowed again, a proper one this time, and hied off in the direction of the main gates.

Teldhor shook his head. "How can people be so stupid? Mattan may look a little different, with his very dark skin, but he is just a man."

"The Enaisi have genetic differences, some of which seem amazing to us, such as their longevity and ability to read minds, but aye, they are just men." He recalled the night before when the two of them had gotten beyond tipped back, and the morning-after they both suffered today. "All too much 'just men.'" He smiled at his children. "Come, let us not allow this news to throw a shadow on afternooning."

~*~

After Alcandhor sat to begin the meal, he leaned toward Mattan, sitting on the far side of Sarinna. "Have you heard the news?"

"No." The Elder grimaced. "Nay. Stars, I must be getting old. Adjusting my speech to your new patterns is much more difficult than it was to learn your language to begin with." He held up a hand. "I apologize for the digression. Now, what news?"

"Worshippers are at the out-wall, demanding entrance."

All those within hearing responded with groans or sounds of dismay. Taniss *tsked* and shook her head.

Mattan sighed. "It did not take long."

"Nay. And we have not discussed how we should handle the situation."

"Rather, we both have avoided it."

"I still say you should send to them, like cousin Tam does," Teldhor said.

"It is tempting," Mattan replied. "But I fear it would only cause them to revere me more for having 'powers.'"

"But if they truly think you are some god, could you not order them to not worship you?"

"So I would use the claim of being a god to tell them not to treat me as one?"

Teldhor frowned at his plate.

"Have you had such problems on other worlds you have visited?" Alcandhor asked.

"We have not stayed long on many planets, just researching and leaving so rarely do they learn much of us."

"But surely a few have. Did you not say some of your people had been trapped on other worlds when you had to shut down the portal?"

"What has been discovered about us on those worlds I cannot say. My team are not the only adventurers of our people. We are the only ones who—" he stopped, dropping his gaze. "We are the only ones who cared about your people, and this planet."

This cut close to the shame Mattan hid. Alcandhor veered away. "So how do we scatter these Worshippers? I fear 'tis not an easy task."

"I wager if cousin Tam were not nestling, she would storm out and make them leave," Eladhor said, wide-eyed. "She can be scary."

Amid the chuckling that ensued, Sarinna said, "I think we should take counsel with each other after the meal to try to sort out this absurd difficulty."

"We? Should this not be a matter for the chiefs?" Alcandhor asked. "Or do you speak as a Child of the Enaisi?"

"As the steward of Zaidhron who does not want an uproar

disrupting the city."

"I would say that is a legitimate reason for inclusion," Mattan murmured, winking at Sarinna. "Shall we all convene at Thane Hall after meal to discuss this?"

Alcandhor glanced down the table to Andhrel and Eladhrel and then nodded to Ordhral, making certain the sept chief knew he was included. "Aye. Although I am doubtful we shall find any workable solutions."

"Before we go to Thane Hall, though," Mattan said, "we should see how many have arrived at the out-wall, and what they are actually doing."

"A sound idea."

~*~

Alcandhor ascended the stairs to the allure of the out-wall to find quite a few residents of Zaidhron already there. Gawking at the Worshippers appeared to be a new pastime. Hopefully a short-lived one. Mattan pulled the hood of his cloak close around his face, but at this distance, and with so many assembled at the embrasures, it was doubtful anyone would spot the dark-skinned alien.

'Twas not a few people, but a crowd gathered on the Settlers' Plain, smashing flat the tall salnais grasses, which had not yet been harvested. Granted, compared to what was grown through the valley and in other places, it was not a large loss, but 'twas still willful destruction of a crop, and an important one at that. Fashioned into paper and fiber for clothes, pressed for oil which could be used for torches and sconces, as well as other uses, salnais was essential.

Many of the Worshippers knelt in prayer, others gathered by the gatehouse, calling insults and yelling for the gates to be opened. Stars, some had erected tents!

"Enough," Alcandhor spat. He pelted down the stairs and ordered the Rangers to open the one gate and let him through.

The rabble quieted a moment.

A burly man with dark hair and a beard stepped forward. "You cannot deny us entrance! We demand to be allowed in to see the Enaisi."

"You come onto Ch'shalna land and dare give orders? You will all leave now."

"You cannot make us leave. We demand—"

Alcandhor jabbed a hand toward the man. "You are trespassing on Ch'shalna land, and you are destroying the salnais crop. If you do not decamp now, you will be fined to cover the cost of the loss."

"This is not your land! It's outside the out-wall!"

"Learn your geography, and history, man." Alcandhor's arm swept west to south to east. "From mountain to mountain including to the top of the switchback yonder"—he nodded to the south—"is *our* land, ceded to us by the Enaisi when we first settled on this planet. You have no business here."

A woman came forward, hands clasped to her chest. "You have met the Celestial, haven't you? Touched him?" She reached a hand out to Alcandhor.

He flinched away. "He is not some god!"

A chorus of voices rose, clamoring to see the Celestial.

"Why?" Alcandhor shouted. "So you can worship as a god, a mere man?" He waved an arm behind him, toward the city. "If he wanted anything to do with your worship, he would be out here now, instead of remaining in Zaidhron. I say again, leave."

The crowd hushed, staring up toward the crowds at the crenellations of the out-wall.

The spokesman however, raised his chin. "And if we do not?"

"What is the penalty for trespassing?"

The man blinked. "What?"

"If you trespassed on a provincial lord's property, what would they have the right to do?"

Some of the Worshippers exchanged glances. The spokesman scuffed a foot on the trampled grass. "Lay hold."

"Then you have your answer. And believe me, I have enough guards and cells to accommodate all of you. I see children here. Wish you to have them thrown into dank cells?"

"You wouldn't dare!"

Alcandhor took a step closer, teeth clenched. "*You* dare to come onto *my* land and make demands of me and then challenge me?" He lifted his head. "You have until sundown. If you have not cleared this plain by then, you will be all put in cells."

"But it's almost sundown now," a nearby woman wailed.

Indeed. The clouds glowed with smudged, pale pinks and oranges in the west, and the eastern sky deepened into dark purple. The guards should be lighting torches soon. Alcandhor nearly faltered, but nay, he would not give one breath's space to these unreasonable people. "Then you had all best leave quickly."

Arms crossed, he waited for their reaction. Would they back down? Stars, he would hate to follow through, but he would if necessary. Slowly, the Worshippers gathered their things, some weeping. A few protested but were silenced. Alcandhor nodded to the gate guard, who widened the entrance, allowing him to pass through.

"Bells, but that was well done, Thane," the Ranger murmured.

"They will return, or others will come. This nonsense is far from over."

"Aye. Glad I am not to be a chief and need worry about finding an answer to this *nonsense*."

Alcandhor clapped a hand on the man's shoulder with a smile.

Mattan and the others clambered down the steps. "Well done," the Elder said. "Forceful, yet not overly so." He leaned close, smiling, and whispered, "Zaidhron would have likely given them until morning. He would have liked you, no doubt. And even Avadhron, I think, would have found no fault with your handling of the situation."

"He would have had more to say, from what I have read about him."

"Oh aye, much more. And much more loudly too."

From what Alcandhor had seen of Avadhron in that holographic viewing years ago, he tended to agree.

Walking back toward the city gatehouse, Eladhrel asked, "Other than not letting the Worshippers into the city, what can we do?"

Andhrel shook his head. "Even if they do not arrive in great numbers, they will come. As merchants, for example. We cannot deny every person entrance to Zaidhron."

"We have had Worshippers here before. It is inevitable with all the trade we do," Sarinna said. "But they have never caused any problems, to my knowledge."

"Nay," Alcandhor said. "Once or twice a Worshipper has come to 'pray' at the Statue of the Elders, but they were chased off. I worry not as much for one or two arriving. It is the large numbers, such as we saw today. It shall happen again, be assured." He grimaced, detesting the notion of those deluded people gathering on the plain. What if they decided to harry merchants or other travelers?

"The crowds can be kept out," Mattan said. "The out-wall serves a good purpose there. It was built to stop a large attack force, after all."

"After the war, you mean?" Alcandhor asked.

"You know the history?"

"I know *a* history, Enaisi, but as we have been discovering, our history is not always accurate."

Mattan raised a hand. "And I will not attempt any lessons at this time."

Ordhral scratched his cheek. "I perceive some may try to scale that wall, probably at night, but with patrols on the allures, I doubt that will be successful. Despite its original intention"—he inclined his head to Mattan—"the out-wall does us a great service."

"Now wait," Mattan said. "Do not give me any credit for that wall.

That was Zaidhron, Dandhral, and others of the First Table."

"I thought you were not going to give us a history lesson," Ordhral said, smiling.

"Do not get saucy, nephew!"

"Can we return to the problem?" Alcandhor grumbled.

"Dealing with a few at a time should not be a worry," Sarinna said. "What if they begin...infiltrating though? A few merchants, a few travelers wandering in, all seemingly at random, then they gather and demand to see Mattan?"

"I will do the same as I did today," Alcandhor said, "order they leave or throw them into cells." He gazed upward. "If only there was a way to...to make them stop believing you—and the other Enaisi—are gods."

"I see no way," Mattan said. "People will believe what they will, regardless of facts."

"'Tis not right," Eladhrel muttered. "To foist themselves upon Mattan. To treat him in a way he despises."

"I agree," the alien said. "The notion disgusts me." He turned to Ordhral. "How did my sister handle it?"

"I think it is one of the reasons she lived high in the mountains, away from people."

"Your sister? Ismari?" Andhrel asked, looking from the Elder to the sept chief.

"She was here," Mattan murmured. "She stayed behind with Ashani."

"But then, where—?"

"She was Tam's mother," Alcandhor said softly. "And Tam remembers her not, so say nothing for now."

"By the Bells and both moons," Andhrel muttered. "No wonder Tam's abilities are so strong!"

The wind gusted, and Sarinna pulled her shawl tighter. "Are we continuing on to Thane Hall? It appears we are nowhere nearer to an answer about the Worshippers. Further discussion is fruitless, I would think."

"Probably not," Eladhrel replied. "What say you, Thane?"

"I see no point in a meeting. We have said all. We cannot stop them from journeying here, and can only refuse admittance."

"But today's incident may help spread word among them that we do not tolerate them here. That may be helpful."

"For now." Alcandhor grimaced. "I cannot see them giving up easily, though."

"Neither shall we," Sarinna said, chin set.

"I think your son might have the right of it, Thane," Ordhral said, his eyes crinkling. "Send out Tamissa—and Sarinna. They would properly affright the Worshippers."

The men chuckled, but Sarinna just smiled grimly. Alcandhor knew that look, and thought, just perhaps, there was more truth there than Ordhral intended.

Chapter Six

After breakfast, Alcandhor made his way to the gatehouse of the out-wall. He nodded at the Rangers standing guard. "They have all decamped?"

"Aye," one said, "although some left rubbish—and worse. Probably as a statement of their disdain for you making them leave."

The second scowled. "We have already called for assistance in cleaning up their messes. What do we do if more show up thus?"

"Immediately send them away. Do not permit them to camp or even rest. If they do, lay hold of them as trespassers. I will not knowingly admit Worshippers to Zaidhron."

The first Ranger sighed. "Except that now, instead of mostly avoiding the city, knowing the decree that has been set down for years, they will flock here anyway, because of the Elder."

"Aye. They have never been more than the buzz of an irritating insect, but I fear they shall become worse than a patch of deep-rooted stingweed or star-flower thorns." Alcandhor nodded and clapped a hand on each of their shoulders. "Yours is the first defense against these plaguing nuisances. I do not envy you the task, but I do have trust that you will do it well. And I am going to station two extra men at this gate, expecting repeats of yesterday's attempted incursion. That will allow you more flexibility in guarding as well as repelling the insistent."

The Rangers bowed, murmuring thanks.

Alcandhor nodded, and headed back to the city. Now to do some matching and regain the strength in that shoulder and arm. Perhaps today would be peaceful, save the frenzied activity in the kitchens of the Great Hall preparing for tonight's celebration. 'Twould be good to see Tam; he missed her these few days. And Marcalan too, although he would never admit it to the rascal.

~*~

A knock at his door interrupted Alcandhor helping Eladhor straighten his new tunic. Sarinna, at Jholinn's suggestion, had both boys measured for new dress clothes, and Amara for a new frock. Stars, what would he do without those two women? Aleta had never bothered, and he must admit he did not pay attention to such things as his children outgrowing their clothing.

He gestured to Teldhor to finish helping with the tunic.

Eladhor flung his arms up. "I need not my brother. I can do it."

Alcandhor waved in resignation as he strode to answer the knock. Haladhon leaned on the frame, his face haggard. "I not know what to do."

Opening the door wider, he nodded at his cousin to enter. Glancing at his sons, he walked through the alcove into the bedchamber and pointed at the chair by the wall, then sat on the bed. "Tell me."

Haladhon thudded into the seat, his voice low but urgent. "I talked of Tam and Marcalan and their marriage celebration tonight. My girls wanted to come with me. They have asked before to visit the city, and Panill always becomes unreasonable, as if she fears that if they leave, they will not return. But this time they pleaded and cried, and she became hysterical. She threw things, and it took both her father and me to settle her." He rubbed the back of this neck. "She has become increasingly unstable since her mother died. Her father confided he worries greatly for her and his granddaughters. His health is failing fast. My girls see it: their grandfather's approaching death, her increasing irrationality. I worry for them."

Alcandhor chewed the inside of his cheek, thinking. "What are their ages now—Lonill is eleven, aye, and Haliss nine?"

"Aye."

"I know not what I can do, but we shall discuss possibilities later. I will send a healer for her father. And perhaps if I personally give her a guarantee of my cousins' safety and return at a given time it will relieve her concerns and allow a visit."

"I...doubt it. But I will not dissuade you from trying. I am at my wits' end. My girls—" Haladhon scrubbed his face with his hands. "This is not easy for them. They feel trapped and cry whenever I leave."

How did one ease the pain of a parent worrying over children? Alcandhor whispered hoarsely, "I will do all I can, cousin."

"I thank you." Haladhon peered through the alcove at the boys, bickering quietly over the proper way to lace their new tunics. "'Tis almost time for the celebration. I had best wash up." He stood. "Tonight is a great cause for joy."

"Shall you be able to rise to the occasion for it, with these worries?"

"Aye. As always. And as you always do."

Haladhon stopped long enough to offer advice on the lacings and give each boy a playful clout on the shoulder before leaving.

~*~

59

The boys and Amara laughed, skipping as they crossed the sward.

A voice called, twice, and Alcandhor slowed, turning. Rendhol ran toward him, fist over his heart. "Thane!" he gasped.

"Why are you here? Wait." He gestured for the children to continue to the Great Hall without him. "Amara, you will let one of your brothers hold your hand. Hear you me?"

After his children were far enough away to not overhear, he nodded to the Ranger. "Say on."

"With Inradhor and Fandhrel gone, the locals all too gladly are telling their stories to Gardhal. Not only farmers but some townspeople as well. He has sent some of the reports ahead with me, but will come in a day or two with more. I left them with Elites in Thane Hall, as he instructed."

"That does not answer my question. Why are you here?"

"I wished to speak to you personally. Gardhal gave me leave. He said you would understand."

Alcandhor stifled a sigh. So close to evening meal and the marriage celebration. He must be there to start the proceedings. "To my chamber."

Rendhol almost ran to keep up with his long strides.

As they entered, the Ranger said without preamble, "I should be relieved of duty, Thane. I have been—"

"I will make that decision. You give me the facts." Alcandhor leaned against the front of his table, arms crossed.

"Sir. I...I noticed that unrest in our shire rose after Fandhrel and Inradhor were assigned. Not that unrest did not always seem to simmer under the surface, but—"

"Tell me of your assignment to Dandrin Shire. From the beginning. How did you find it?"

"The residents were wary and untrusting, and at first I thought it was because I was new, but it persisted. I took my concerns to Pendhras, and..." Rendhol rubbed his temple, shaking his head. "Every time I tried to discuss the matter with him, I ended up feeling a fool. My worries faded, and I would leave relieved, as if all were well. But it would not last."

Lips pressed together, Alcandhor fought to keep his voice and expression from displaying his ire. "Tell me, Ranger Rendhol, how you feel at this exact moment."

"I..." He dropped his gaze. "Shame. I have failed in my duty."

Alcandhor took a breath and released it as he strove to will away his anger and summon emotions of peace and serene reassurance. Once in control, he sent them to Rendhol. "And now?"

The young Ranger's shoulders straightened a bit, and he blinked, frowning. "I...I feel more at ease. I..."

"As when you would talk to Pendhras?"

Rendhol hesitated, then slowly nodded. "Aye, as you mention it."

Through clenched teeth, Alcandhor said, "Continue. When Inradhor and Fandhrel came, what occurred?"

"I had gained some trust with the residents over time, but after they were assigned, it...lessened. They grew distant as when I first arrived. I have been there for over three years, and thought I had a rapport with them. I asked my fellow Rangers, and they dismissed my concerns. They claimed such ignorant folk, many from clanless families, just could not understand what we did, nor why. I did not like their replies, but again, when I took my thoughts on the situation to Pendhras—"

"He eased them."

"Aye. And..." Again the Rendhol paused. "And I begin to suspect the feud between Sonvil and Lanwin might have been, not started, nay, but...fueled by the other Rangers. I do not have proof, but—"

"I will gain proof, if it exists, Ranger. You remain here, as I may have need of you as witness." Alcandhor pulled the cord.

"Your pardon, sir, but what of my bounds?"

"I have sent two already. I will send more. And am recalling Pendhras as well. Speak to no one about this."

"Aye, Thane."

~*~

Despite Rendhol's interruption, Alcandhor managed to get to the Great Hall before his niece and her new husband arrived. Many claps on the back or shoulder greeted him as he wended his way to the head of the main table, his stiff, highly polished black boots clicking on the shimmerstone floor. Taking his place near his chair, he tugged on the suede, azure formal jerkin, not comfortable with the slimmer cut or the added length, past mid-thigh.

Marcalan's parents waited next to him, Lantalan grinning, and Kalinna looking resigned.

Alcandhor left off adjusting his jerkin as cheers thundered through the Great Hall. Hand in hand, the couple stood in the doorway, Tam blushing and Marcalan laughing. Unsurprisingly, she wore a formal jerkin, as did her husband. Sarinna had made certain long before that her niece had proper Ranger garb, winning an argument with the seamstress over a lass not wearing gowns to official functions. What would he do without his sister's ability to anticipate?

Children lined the area between the door and the start of the tables, carrying brightly colored ribbons tied to the end of long sticks to wave over the heads of the newly married pair.

The tables themselves had been placed farther apart in the center, offering a wider walking space. Along each side, family and friends gathered, grasping hands across the aisle. To denote the strength of their union, the couple, never breaking their handhold, would force their way through the impediment of all those standing between them and their parents at the front of the hall.

Usually those in line offered token resistance, but near the end, Loch'alan and Baidhrol, wearing fierce grins, braced in a lunge, hands grasping each other's wrists.

"This is going to be interesting," Lantalan murmured.

The pair stopped before the two cockerels, and Tam tipped her head. A smile spread on her face, and she tickled her brother-in-law in his armpit. He yelled and jumped back, and they rushed past.

"Not fair!" Loch'alan shouted, but he was drowned out by laughter.

As the couple approached and bowed, all of Alcandhor's burdens sloughed off, and he felt pride would rend his jerkin. Tam's large, golden eyes shone, and Marcalan—he smirked as if he had just surpassed his best prank. *Rascal*!

He knew he grinned like a fool as he embraced one then the other. Lantalan and Kalinna in turn hugged each of them.

The couple turned to face the assemblage holding hands. Alcandhor stood beside them, arms raised. "Marcalan and Tamissa have pledged their lives to the Maker and to each other privately, as is our custom. Tamissa has made a necklet for her husband, braiding her hair in with the string, to show her heart is twined with his in love. She has set into it beads of various colors representing their commitment of devotion, faithfulness, gentleness, and hearts guided by peace and generosity toward each other. Marcalan has accepted this necklet, and the binding vows that go with it. They present themselves publicly as a declaration to you of their union, and to ask the blessing of their clan." He lowered his arms, now speaking as her uncle, not Thane. "As Tamissa's nearest kin I grant my blessing, and wish them every joy."

Lantalan stepped forward, with his wife at his side, but she did not join in as her husband spoke the traditional words. "As Marcalan's parents, we grant our blessing, and wish our son and new daughter a full and happy life."

Alcandhor lifted his arms again. "I present Marcalan and Tamissa. May their marriage be peaceful and fruitful, blessed in full measure by the Maker, and may they live to love each other in their elder years."

The hall thundered with cheers as Marcalan threw his head back laughing, then lifted Tam by the waist, and swung her in a circle.

Another duty waited to be performed. Alcandhor raised a hand in a tacit command for everyone to sit. Clasping Marcalan's shoulder, he nodded at a nearby servant, waiting with a garment folded over his arm.

Alcandhor ordered, "Take off that jerkin, Marcalan, son of Lantalan."

With a smug expression, the newly married Ranger obeyed, taking his time undoing the laces, his eyes twinkling.

"Scoundrel," Alcandhor said softly.

"I am enjoying this, Thane. Should I not?" Marcalan murmured.

"I thought you despised the notion of being made a chief."

"'Twas done whether I wished it or not, so shall I be glum or make the most of it?"

A sigh escaped Alcandhor, but he could not help a twitch of a smile. He lifted the new formal jerkin for all to see the chief's crest. Susurrations rippled and echoed throughout the immense chamber as Marcalan donned the garment over his silver shirt.

Alcandhor then announced, "Based on precedents of the past, and by conclave decision, you are now elevated to status as chief. Your rank, however, remains Eighth at Table."

He saluted, his fist over his heart, while all the Rangers in the hall stood, following suit. Marcalan bowed. Then naturally, having to destroy a solemn moment, he exclaimed, "Stars! And I had hoped to rank my father."

Laughter erupted, and more than a few groans. Alcandhor raised his arms for silence. "A most singular circumstance has also arisen." He stepped aside and gestured to Mattan.

The alien came forward, gazing about before speaking. "It has been discovered that Marcalan is a Child of the Enaisi."

Gasps and chatter burst forth. Mattan lifted a hand. "Now, I know this is astonishing, and seems impossible, and before any prurient speculation begins, I have done genetic tests in the Portal Complex, and there is no doubt of Marcalan's parentage. This is unprecedented, and I am researching to try to determine how this happened. Anything I discover, I will make known. For now, if anyone has questions, they should approach me directly. But be it acknowledged that Marcalan is not only a chief, but also openly recognized as a Child of the Enaisi."

The rascal again bowed deeply, but his amused expression belied the seriousness of the moment. Alcandhor muttered, "Get to your seat, vagabond."

With a wink and grin, the prankster obeyed.

The Thane sat, and the gong sounded, starting the meal.

~*~

"What think you of married life?" asked Haladhon, breaking a piece of bread off a hand loaf.

Marcalan smirked. "I finally found someone to scrub my back."

Everyone sitting near chuckled, while Tam nudged him with her elbow.

"By the way, I thank you for a most interesting wedding present," Marcalan said. "I have to admit, it was brilliant."

"Coming from you, that is a great compliment." He looked over at Tam. "Did you enjoy the present, as well, cousin?"

Tipping her head and with wide eyes, she asked, "What present?"

He gaped at her, then slowly grinned. "You are learning, enh?" He leaned close, leering at the both of them, but before he could say anything, Tam replied, blushing, "Aye, he is, Haladhon."

Marcalan chuckled, and he stared at them both, open-mouthed. "How knew you what I was going to ask?"

Tam smiled. "We are fully bonded and can share thoughts now. Marcalan anticipated you, so I just answered before you asked."

Haladhon closed his mouth, absorbing the implications of her proclamation, and said to Marcalan, "You will have to tell me details later of this thought-sharing."

His cousin shot him a wicked grin. "Perhaps. Who was your conspirator?"

"Ah, I think I shall protect him."

"It is a man, then. A Ranger?"

"I shall divulge no more."

"Want you details?"

Haladhon barely hesitated. "It was Tandhral."

Marcalan nodded. "I thank you."

Andhrel called over, "How does it compare living in a suite after so many years in a barracks?"

"'Tis very different. Stars, to not hear dozens of Rangers snoring each night was worth marrying. Someone should have told me that years ago. Now I just have to listen to one Ranger snore, and she does it so prettily."

The table burst into laughter as Tam slugged him in the arm. "I do not snore!"

"Now, how would you know that if you are asleep, hmm?" her husband asked, his voice lilting.

"Be warned, Marcalan, you are on dangerous ground," Sarinna said, with a raised eyebrow and hint of a smile.

"Stars, aye." Eladhrel leaned forward. "You have three sisters, so you should know the danger. Yet you would risk her wrath?"

Marcalan chuckled. "I have heard that making up after a fight is very pleasant."

"If one survives the fight," Haladhon said. "You do remember she is Trained, do you not? And by Valdhor?"

"Stars, is she?" Marcalan exclaimed, in astonished innocence. "I wondered why she wears a jerkin and trous!"

Tam swatted him, and he yelped. "You are right. She is merciless!"

Amara giggled. "Cousin Marcalan is funny."

They all burst out laughing.

Haladhon lifted his tankard. "Here is to our funny cousin and his dangerous, merciless wife."

"Hear, hear!" called several voices as they all raised their glasses and tankards to the toast.

Chapter Seven

As soon as they had risen from the table, Kalinna rushed over to hug her son. "Oh, my baby, it is so good to see you married."

Tam frowned, confused, as the woman's emotions did not match the display of affection. She was rather vexed.

Marcalan winked to Tam over her shoulder. His mother then turned, putting her hands to Tam's cheeks. "I have to allow, you are a pretty girl. But you really should have some dresses. Those trous are just not fit—"

"Mum," her husband interrupted, "My wife is very fit. I should know." His leer made Tam blush.

"Such bawdy talk." Kalinna wagged a finger. "You know what I mean. It is not fit for women to dress thus."

"She is a Ranger."

"But she need not wear those trous all the time."

"Oh, stars, Mum," he said, laughing, "I can see her wielding a sword in a skirt!"

Marcalan's ire rose, though he covered it with banter. His desire to protect Tam was a new, beautiful feeling—someone loved her and wanted to keep her safe, even from domineering mothers. However, as her father taught, 'twas not right for another to stand up for her. But how did one deal with such a person? Should she speak up? And would she— could she find the appropriate thing to say?

"Rangers do not usually wear their swords in the city—"

"I know that, Mum—"

"Do not interrupt! The girl must learn certain proprieties—"

Tam took a deep breath. "Any proprieties I must learn, I am confident that my husband can teach me, Kalinna, but I thank you for your concern."

"A man does not know some things, child, things that should be discussed woman to woman."

"Taniss and Sarinna have already offered me advice about matters my father did overlook."

"Well..." Kalinna drew herself up. "Taniss is level-headed. I am sure she will properly instruct you on lady-like dress and comportment. I certainly hope she does offer to help you learn to style your hair. It is very unbecoming to wear it down and loose. It makes you look like a man. You should braid it and—"

Tam stiffened. "Rangers never braid their hair." Braiding was for ladies and the vain nobles. She had tried once, several years ago, to do braids after seeing women in a village with their hair pulled back thus. It seemed to make more sense; it would out of the way and easier to do tasks. Her father had been incensed. Rangers did not braid their hair, he raged. If they want it out of their way they pull it back with a thong, but they never, never braid their hair!

"But you are a lass."

Tam's eyes narrowed. "I am a Ranger first. I was raised thus by my father, and I will not braid my hair."

Kalinna glared. "It seems you are much like Valdhor."

"I thank you."

"It was not a compliment."

Lantalan approached. "You have stepped out of turn, Kalinna. We should already be in the marriage queue." He smiled at Tam and Marcalan, then took his wife's elbow. As they walked away, he spoke softly to her, but his tone was as a steel blade. Kalinna's voice protested in response, although Tam could not hear the words.

"Oh, stars, this will take all bloody night," Marcalan murmured, his hand sliding around Tam's waist. "The bane of every wedding celebration—the marriage queue." He led her to the front of the Great Hall, by the stairs. Everyone drifted toward the circumference of the chamber to form a seemingly endless line. What was supposed to happen now?

"Just keep smiling," Marcalan said.

Alcandhor stood at the head of the queue, grinning. "I see Kalinna got some words in beforehand." He reached out to embrace Tam, which she gladly accepted. Sometimes she wished time could stop so she could just let him hold her. She did not pretend he was her father, but he loved her as one, and it was a soothing balm. She closed her eyes and let herself cling to him for a long moment.

"Aye, and now she and Father are far down the line. He has had words for her." Marcalan chortled. "For what she said and for not following custom by queuing right away."

Alcandhor brushed the hair back from Tam's face, and gently kissed her on the forehead, then grinned at Marcalan. "I think your mother will find that her new daughter is not easily managed."

The two men chuckled and embraced, pounding each other on the back. Her uncle moved past, letting the next person step up.

Tam quickly discovered what her husband meant. She kept smiling, as person after person passed, hugging, kissing, crying, wishing them well, offering advice, teasing—on it went. The never-ending press still wrapped around the Great Hall, even after greeting so many people that their faces all blended into each other. If only they could escape back to their chamber.

Finally the line ended, and Tam sighed, feeling more exhausted than if she had matched all day.

Eladhrel walked up, grinning at them. "I wanted not to talk in the queue and hold it up, but I saw Kalinna caught you beforehand. What was she going on about?"

Marcalan chuckled. "Tam's attire and comportment. She is of the opinion that female Rangers should wear skirts, and braid their hair."

"Oh great Bells!" Eladhrel dropped a hand on Tam's shoulder, concern on his face. "Do not let her compel you, she can be—"

Bursting into laughter, Marcalan playfully punched his cousin. "Stars, to whom are you talking? This is Valdhor's daughter! Think you she cannot handle my mother?"

Eladhrel blinked. "You are correct." He inclined his head. "My apologies, Tam."

She giggled. "Accepted, cousin."

"Excuse us, Eladhrel," Marcalan said, "but we have not danced yet."

The chief bowed, grinning, and the couple walked toward the dancing area. She shook her head, comparing Marcalan's irrepressible personality to his mother's domineering ways, and looked up into her husband's twinkling blue eyes. "How did such a woman have a son like you?"

He chuckled. "That question has been asked before."

"How does your father deal with her?"

Marcalan leered at her. "When we get back to our suite, I will show you."

Tam blushed, but realized he had deflected the answer. She followed his lead and changed the subject. "I know not how to dance."

"I can teach you."

She nodded toward the couples, the ladies swaying and spinning in their long, flowing skirts. "I would feel foolish dancing in trous. I–I think for dancing your mother might be right. I should have a skirt."

"I think you are beautiful in trous, Love-ling. But if you decide to wear skirts, do it because it is what you wish, not to please my mother. Believe me, there is no pleasing her. If you yield to her wishes, she will feel she controls you, but will still find fault."

"I wore a skirt once," Tam said slowly, watching the women curtsey and men bow as the dance ended. "While posing as a servant in Laird Hall. I did not like it."

"Then do not wear skirts. Love-ling, I care not that you wear trous, and you do not wish to wear skirts, so then why should it worry you?"

Tam sighed. Marcalan's love wrapped about her like a warm blanket, and she leaned into him, closing her eyes. They just stood still, and the intensity of their entwined feelings made her blink, fighting back tears. She had never known one could be loved thus.

You will never be without this, Love-ling. We will always be together.

With a smile, she snuggled even tighter against him, listening to his heart beating and feeling the rhythm of his breathing. A new melody started, and he released her, taking her hand, his eyes gentle but insistent. "Dance, Love-ling. I will teach you."

He led her onto the floor, and she found that it was indeed easy to dance, at least with a husband who, through a bond, could help anticipate what to do.

After two dances, they walked across the Great Hall to get something to drink, fingers laced together. So many changes had occurred in her life in just a couple of lunations. How could ever believe such grand things could happen? Yet...the empty place where her father's presence should be caused an ache deep inside. She missed him so much, but if he had lived, what would he have thought of this, of their marriage?

Marcalan's thoughts broke into hers. *Stars, he would have wanted to thrash me—and you as well, I would wager.*

She turned to look at him. "You did not fear him at all?"

He shrugged. "I remember him mostly from a small child. I saw him the...the day of the ambush. He was not delighted to see me, and I confess I did not try to appease him." His eyes searched hers. "Perhaps I should have. He died bravely, and I did not give him the respect he deserved as a chief."

"I think you acted as Marcalan. As you always do," Tam said, touching his face. "Would trying to appease him have made him act any differently?"

"Nay." Marcalan smiled. His voice lilted as he continued, "I did see him once when I was a stripling. It was over ten years ago, by my memory. He had come to Zaidhron for some assignment, I suppose, and was at luncheon. When we all got up from the table, he saw me and glared at me as if he wanted to rip my limbs off and beat me with them. I just grinned and walked away."

Tam shook her head in disbelief. How could Marcalan not fear her father? How could he so casually smile and walk away from him? Was he brave or a fool?

"I have been told I am both," he said, his eyes twinkling. "I know not if you will ever have more answer than that." He dipped a cup of something for Tam. "Try this."

She peered at it, wrinkling her nose. "Is that wine?"

"Nay. You will like it. It is called cider, have you not had it before?"

Tam sipped it and smiled. "It is delicious! Nay, I have not had it before. I only had water and the teas I would make until I came here." She closed her eyes and took another drink. It was sweet and so good!

"Enjoying yourselves?"

Her eyes flew open to see her tall cousin towering over them with a mischievous smirk and peered at him in suspicion. "What are you scheming, Haladhon?"

"Me? Nothing."

She groaned at his innocent expression. "Oh, stars, what have you planned?"

He grinned, shrugging, and repeated, "Nothing, cousin."

"I believe you not." She stood on tiptoe and reached up to tug on the strand of hair that always curled onto his forehead. Since she had first seen him, she wondered why he had that one short lock when the rest was all so long. "And how did your hair get cut here anyway?"

The two men exchanged conspiratorial glances, and Tam backed up a step. "Never mind! I have a feeling I would be better off not knowing. Stars, what men are in my clan!"

Haladhon backhanded Marcalan in the chest. "And you married the worst of the lot."

"Think you I know it not?" Tam asked wryly.

Her husband chortled and bowed. "My thanks."

"I cannot wait to see you two having your first argument."

"Too late." Marcalan smiled, eyebrows raised. "We had it the first day of nestling."

"Oh ho, what is this? And what was it about?" Haladhon's eager glance flitted from one to the other.

Tam frowned. *What argument?*

The one we are going to let him think we had, yet tell him nothing about.

She bit her lip, ducking her head a moment to hide her smile, and then lifted her gaze to her cousin. "That is our business."

"You are too cruel." Haladhon turned to Marcalan. "Come, cousin."

Pointing a finger at her husband, she said, "And you will not say on, either!"

"Not word one!" He pulled her close and kissed her forehead. *And now to further tease him, I will change the topic.* "I am told we leave in two days rather than tomorrow morning for Laird Hall."

Haladhon hesitated before nodding. "Aye, and glad I am too. I am going back to Thane Valley just for a day."

"Your girls will be happy about that, I wager," she said.

Haladhon smiled broadly. "Aye. I am, too. I do not see them enough."

"I would like to meet them." Tam gazed up at her tall cousin. "Do they look much like you?"

Marcalan grinned. "Lonill favors Haladhon more than Haliss, I think."

"They must both be pretty."

"Stars, how can Lonill favor her father and be pretty? I mean, look at that face."

Tam pursed her lips to keep from smiling, shaking her head. "Haladhon is much handsomer than you, Marcalan."

Her husband slapped a hand on his chest, rolled his eyes melodramatically, and fell to the floor. "Oh, she has broken my heart! Oh, wretched girl!"

Before Marcalan could continue moaning in grief, hands grabbed Tam and spun her around. She found herself in an embrace.

"Ah, my new sister," Loch'alan exclaimed. "Have you tamed my brother yet?"

How much had her new brother been drinking? She glanced at her grinning husband as he scrambled to his feet. "Stars, I think that is not possible."

"Oh, sister, surely you will try." Loch'alan went down on one knee.

Tam looked into his sparkling blue eyes, so like his brother's, and smiled. "You can be a rascal too, can you not?"

The Rangers with him laughed. Baidhrol shoved him. "Shall we tell her stories, Loch'y?"

Marcalan handed his brother a tankard of ale just then; Loch'alan took it, murmuring thanks. Stars, he was handing ale to all the nearby young Rangers. *What are you scheming now?*

Keep them busy.

"Tell me some stories," Tam said, gazing at Baidhrol intently, trying not to burst into giggles. "Is Loch'alan truly like his brother?" From behind the men, she noticed Ganill, the head cook, approaching the keg table. Oh stars!

Loch'alan groaned. "Oh please. Do not compare me to my brother!"

Her husband handed his brother another tankard, and before the younger Ranger could ask, Marcalan said, "Just hold it for me for a moment."

He quickly gave all the other Rangers a second ale as well, then said, "Excuse us, Tam and I need to talk to Mattan." Taking her elbow, they hurried away as Ganill neared, her voice carrying as she exclaimed, "What ails you boys to be so bold and gluttonous as to have two tankards of ale for each of you? Is one at a time not good enough? Shame on you!"

Tam just shook her head as Marcalan snickered, and behind them, they heard Haladhon laughing.

~*~

Alcandhor looked around but did not see Tam and Marcalan anywhere. He walked over to Haladhon. "Where are they?"

"They have left."

His eyebrows rose, but he was not really surprised; tradition spoke that couples should try to sneak out early and back to their chamber, but few managed it. Considering Marcalan's many years of planning pranks, and Tam's abilities, he had wagered they would disappear before the night grew old. What did surprise him was that it appeared Haladhon had not planned anything for the celebration. But what was the tall Ranger scheming? He knew him too well to think he would forego the chance of springing something on the new couple.

"So tell me what you have contrived, cousin."

Haladhon grinned. "Nothing."

Alcandhor scowled at him. "My thanks for trusting me."

"Honestly." He leaned close, a conspiratorial smile on his face. "But it will drive them both mad waiting for something to happen, will it not?"

~*~

Tam and Marcalan ran, giggling, to their chamber. It amazed her that they had been able to steal away, but day by day she realized just how devious he could be. As they got to the door, he caught her around the waist and kissed her. She eagerly kissed him back, reaching for the latch, but he grabbed at her hand. "Nay," he hissed. "Hold here."

Marcalan inspected the door with great care and cautiously opened it. He held up a finger indicating she should wait and disappeared inside. Although she understood the necessity of vigilance, she soon grew tired and peeked inside. *Is it safe?*

I know not. Come in and close the door.

Tam did, noting he had lit candles. Marcalan peered into the bathing room, candle in hand. Fascinated, she watched as her husband scrupulously examined their chamber. She would not have thought to check so thoroughly. He was methodical and detailed. No wonder he had been made an Elite.

Finally, he nodded. "Everything seems safe."

"But then, what is Haladhon planning?"

"I know not. Perhaps we left before he could spring it on us."

"Let us hope so. I still fear he is scheming something."

"I am suspicious, too, Love-ling." He pulled her close. "All we can do is be careful." He kissed her, and she wrapped her arms around him.

"I love you," she whispered after he broke the kiss.

Marcalan smirked. "I know. You cannot help yourself."

Tam swatted him, and he laughed.

Chapter Eight

Alcandhor rose before dawn, unable to sleep knowing that the two Rogues would be hung at sun-up. He crossed the sward to the Great Hall to find Mattan waiting in the early room, a pot of morning tea and several cups on the table.

"You were expecting me?"

"I expect quite a few. I found no sleep, and I barely know them. And I can sense the anguish many feel."

Alcandhor fell into a chair, not knowing how to respond. He poured a cup of tea. "I would like to go see them. I cannot reverse their sentence—that was set when each of them became a murderer. But I wish..." he broke off, grieving too deeply to even continue.

"To find a heart hidden in either one?" Mattan asked softly.

"It is so impossible for me to believe anyone can die without conscience. Without recognizing that the Maker calls our hearts, and waits for us to come home to His Halls."

"I know. But it does happen. These two are beyond hope. I am sorry, I wish I could tell you differently, but I have sensed them, and they are completely hardened."

Alcandhor bowed his head and silently drank his tea.

Before long, Tam and Marcalan came in, and his niece sat next to him, rubbing his arm, her golden eyes fixed on his face. He embraced her, and she snugged into him. Her love helped a little—nay, not only her love but Marcalan's too, mingled together in their bond. Bells, how amazing!

A low, mournful blast on the horns pierced the air and Alcandhor's heart. Dawn had arrived. He rose, and took a step toward the door, but Tam put her hands on his chest, staring up at him, tears in her eyes. "Do not block us this time, Uncle."

Stifling a moan, he pulled her close and held her tightly. After a few moments, he kissed the top of her head and pushed her back a little, trying to smile. "I will be fine. I worry for you and Marcalan. And others."

He did not hurry to cross the grounds toward Thane Hall, where the gallows awaited, prepared for the somber event. Many had arrived already.

"I never realized what that was," Tam murmured, her gaze on the huge, overhanging beam even with the ceiling height of the ground level

74

on the west-most building of the chiefs' range.

"This is where all arbitration, laws, and sentences are given. So this is where the law is carried out." Alcandhor glanced about. He touched Marcalan's arm. "Can you find Amadhor and his family? I wish them at my shoulder."

Marcalan bowed and strode away as Tam, Alcandhor, and Mattan continued toward the platform built underneath the beam.

"Who is Amadhor, Uncle?"

"Monadhal's father."

Tam did not reply right away, but finally asked, "Has Nandhal any kin?"

"Nay. His parents and grandparents are dead. He has no siblings. His only close kin is Amadhor, his father's brother."

"Monadhal and Nandhal are first cousins?"

Alcandhor nodded. "It is a double-blow to Amadhor and his family. They carry it as shame. That is why I wish them at my shoulder. I will have the whole clan know it is not counted to them."

"It must be a heavy burden," Tam whispered.

Where was Haladhon? Ah, his cousin stood alone by the wall of the chiefs' range, arms crossed, a forbidding expression on his face.

Rangers brought the two Rogues across the grounds in a dray, and murmuring grew into loud, angry talk as they passed toward the platform. Alcandhor ordered, "I will have a respectful quiet here."

Word spread, and the crowd subsided. Marcalan approached with Amadhor, his family following, their faces wan.

"I meant it when I said I wanted you standing with me, Amadhor. You are a Ranger, as are your sons, and you have nothing to be ashamed of. I am proud to count you as close kin."

"I thank you, Thane."

"Have you met our new Second at Table?"

"Nay, sir, we have not."

"Tam, this is Amadhor, your first cousin, twice removed. These are his sons, and eldest grandson."

Amadhor bowed to her, then said, "My wife did not wish to come, Thane. And the younger ones we left with her. I apologize."

"Why? Tam has fifteen years and that is too tender in my estimation, but she is Second at Table and cannot be excused. I would fain give her permission to leave. I would not insist your grandson be here. They have the same age."

"I will be fine, Uncle." His niece looked over at Amadhor. "I hope you will be, too, cousin. And your family."

"This simply ends a nightmare, cousin Tam." He gave a firm nod, his lips thin.

She tipped her head, arching one eyebrow, reminding Alcandhor of Sarinna.

"I am a Child of the Enaisi, cousin. You may say what you will, but I sense strongly. I wish I could take away your pain. I am sorry."

Amadhor swallowed heavily and turned to face the gallows. Alcandhor glanced at him and at Mattan, who seemed preoccupied. Marcalan put an arm around his young wife as the two men were led into place upon the platform, hands still tied behind their backs. Both gazed about arrogantly; their pale faces the only sign of their impending execution.

Now it was time. Alcandhor took a deep breath and stepped forward to address the two condemned Rogues. "Nandhal, in the short time you ran Rogue, you have committed heinous crimes. The rape of two women and the murder of their entire family, including a small boy and a babe, all for mere plundered goods. You conspired with the traitors who murdered the Laird and Rangers, including Chief Valdhor, and attempted to murder your Thane. And you attacked and did attempt to murder the Ranger Marcalan. The punishment for all these crimes is death.

"Monadhal, you are guilty of many crimes over many years, but I will list only your most recent. By your own confession, you murdered three Rangers, one of which was Chief Bardhor, Haladhon's father and my uncle. As well, we know of your complicity in the capture and attempt to murder the Ranger Marcalan. The punishment for which is death. Your sentences will be carried out immediately. So be it."

Rangers placed nooses around the Rogues' necks with careful adjustment.

Nandhal's face contorted with rage. He screamed, "Curse you! Curse you! I will have my last revenge, you incestuous by-blow! May you rot without a grave, you—"

Mattan held up a hand, and Nandhal seemed to choke. "Have it done now, Thane, while I stop him."

Alcandhor nodded at the executioner. The doors dropped, and the bodies fell. Mattan slumped and fell back against Marcalan, who grabbed the alien.

Alcandhor took his arm to help keep him upright. "Let us take him to the solar, it is closest." He glanced up at the gruesome sight of the two bodies, then over at Monadhal's father, whose face was white. By both moons, he needed to see that Mattan was cared for, but he also worried about Amadhor.

"Come with us," Alcandhor said to the stricken man.

The Enaisi straightened, pushing away their attempts to assist him.

"I am fine."

"You will obey your Thane. To the solar. Tam, see that hot tea is brought up."

"I will tend to that," Sarinna said from behind him.

"My thanks," Alcandhor said, as they walked toward the main door of the chiefs' range, but he doubted she heard him; she already outpaced them, skirts flapping in her wake.

"I need no assistance, Thane," Mattan said. "I can walk."

"We will still accompany you. I am certain you know the way to the solar, my dear Enaisi?"

Mattan huffed as Alcandhor held the door open for him.

"Thane, wish you truly that I accompany you?" Amadhor asked from behind him.

He turned, eyeing the Ranger with worried frown. "Aye, you and your family. Please, join us."

They continued up the stairs, Alcandhor never taking his hand from Mattan's shoulder. In the solar, servants already knelt on the hearths, lighting the fireplaces; Sarinna worked fast.

Alcandhor gestured to a divan, and Mattan obediently sat.

"What happened?" the Thane asked.

Mattan sighed. "I probed their thoughts, Thane, for just a moment, and discovered Nandhal had planned an emotional assault on you, so I set a block over his mind. That is why he began cursing."

"So he was cursing you," Alcandhor said. "I wondered about that."

"I continued to block, to protect all of you, but as he died, I did not pull away quickly enough."

The chamber fell silent.

"But what could he have done, Elder?" Amadhor asked in a hushed voice.

A servant entered with a tray. After she set it on the low table by the divan and left, they continued the conversation. Tam poured tea.

"He wished to connect with the Thane's mind, sending his emotions to him as he died."

"By the names of both moons," Amadhor hissed. "What would that do to the Thane?"

"He would feel the sensations as Nandhal died. It is not pleasant."

"But how could blocking cause you to be affected?" Marcalan asked, as Tam handed the cup to Mattan.

"Ah, thank you, Tam—you see, I was not blocking, not as you understand it. Nandhal was trying to send his emotions. If he could not get to the Thane, he might try Tam, you, his uncle Amadhor, or anyone else he thought he could cause more anguish. Those of you who are

77

empathic have the ability to block and protect your own mind, if given warning, but those who have not Enaisi blood have no protection at all. What I did was go into his mind, and create the block from inside, preventing him from sending to anyone."

Alcandhor blinked, leaning forward. "So you were connected to his mind as he died?" Just what were the Enaisi capable of?

"Essentially, aye. I had to pull back at the last moment, when it was too late for him to send. I almost waited too long, and he tried to hold the connection."

He sipped the tea, and Tam knelt by him, searching his face.

"What is it, Tam?" he asked.

"I...I am trying to sense if you are truly well."

Mattan placed the backs of his fingers to her cheek for a moment. "Be assured, Tam. I took no real hurt from it. Just momentary weakness." He sipped the tea quietly, seemingly unaffected by their stares. Finally, he set the cup down and regarded Amadhor. "May I have a word with you, alone?"

As Amadhor sat next to Mattan, the other Rangers all moved to the far side of the solar. Alcandhor watched the fire to keep from staring at the two of them. He hoped Mattan would not inadvertently say something to cause the man more grief—he had lived with enough.

Albardhal crossed his arms as he glared across the chamber. "What is he saying to my father?"

Amadhor burst into sobs, and Mattan held him as he wept. Albardhal strode over, snatching his arm free as Alcandhor tried to stop him. Before he got to his father, he halted as if physically restrained, and he stared at Mattan in astonishment. Tears started in his eyes, and he fell to his knees next to his father. The rest of their family joined them, putting their arms around their kin.

What should Alcandhor do? He slowly backed to the fireplace, giving as much privacy as possible to the family.

"What is happening, Thane?" Marcalan asked.

"I know not for certain. I would say probably that Mattan is sharing whatever he found in Monadhal's mind. I hope it brings healing and not more grief."

Tam lifted her chin. "Mattan would not hurt them."

"Not intentionally, nay. But sometimes one can judge incorrectly. What might bring peace to one heart, may not to another." He peered at his niece and her husband. "So how do you both feel after this morning's event?"

"Saddened," Marcalan answered.

Alcandhor scrutinized him. "You seem unlike yourself this

morning, cousin. I remember not you jesting once."

"It is the emotions of those around me, Thane. I feel...heavyhearted."

"He can sense what I do now, Uncle. The bond is stronger now that we are..." she paused, blushing, then murmured, "intimate."

Marcalan slipped an arm around her waist as she leaned into him. They seemed meet for one another; why had he not seen it?

"Why are you smiling, Uncle?"

"It makes my heart light knowing you love each other so much."

Marcalan's head cocked to the side, and his eyes twinkled. "You know, you never did tell me what I should call you now. As Tam's foster-father you are as my father, too. Should I call you 'Father' or 'Uncle?'"

Alcandhor glared at him. "You are going to enjoy making sport of me about this, are you not, you vagabond?"

"Have I ever missed an opportunity yet?"

Alcandhor rolled his eyes, but the jovial moment passed, and Marcalan's eyes faded. "Should we leave, Thane? This is so difficult for them."

Alcandhor was not used to a serious Marcalan, but he pushed the one concern out of his mind for that of the grieving family. "Aye, I think we should."

Amadhor got to his feet, his face flushed and wet from tears. "Thane, I thank you."

"Thank me, Amadhor? For what?"

"For–for caring about me and my family. You tried many times to talk to me, and I always walked away. Today would have been much worse without you and this Elder you brought back. I am deeply indebted to you."

Alcandhor did not know what to say. He took his cousin by the shoulders, and whispered, "I hope you find some measure of peace."

"I thank you, Thane."

"Would you honor me by walking with us as we go to the Great Hall for breakfast? The mealtime horns will sound soon."

"Thank you, but nay, Thane. I will stay a little longer with my sons and grandson, if you will allow us to continue to use your solar."

"Use it as long as you need, cousin. Have your morning meal here in private. I will have it sent up."

"I thank you again."

Alcandhor gripped the man's shoulders tightly, then left with his niece and new nephew. Mattan joined them, and Alcandhor looked at him questioningly.

"They wished to be alone," he explained, still looking drawn.

Tam gazed up at the Enaisi with a worried frown. "You should have tea made with taihala."

Mattan stopped, gaping at her. "How do you know about *tai'ala*?"

Alcandhor blinked at the different pronunciation the Enaisi used for the word, an almost hissing sound, one that hailed back not just to Enai, but to the more ancient Amhan'ai—which contained that same sound. So from which language did this word originate? Would the vast amount of things he desired to learn from this man ever be plumbed?

"I just remembered it." She tipped her head. "Am I not correct? It is not an herb used to help you gain strength from such an ordeal as you have had?"

Mattan stared at Tam, mouth open. "Where did you learn this?"

"From my book. I have a book of herbs and garden lore. I used to wonder about certain entries such as the one about taihala. I knew not what it meant that it was a restorative for empathic distress, but now I do."

"I would like to see this book."

"I will fain show it to you. After breakfast?"

Mattan nodded.

Alcandhor eyed the Enaisi as they all walked across to the Great Hall. Tam and Marcalan walked ahead of them, and Mattan watched the lass with a frown.

"Is something wrong?"

"Ah, nay, Thane. I just...she is so much like my sister. In some ways, the loss is more keen, and yet in others, it is lessened to see my niece. I miss Ashani too. She was a good friend."

"What was she like, Ashani?"

"Wise, intelligent, quiet—unless you roused her ire." Mattan's white teeth flashed in a quick grin. "She had a sweet face, and I..." He inhaled sharply. "It is silly, but I remember her long, slender fingers. So expressive. To know she was murdered by her own great-grandson, that is vile."

"It is a shameful part of our family history."

Mattan nodded, and they continued along the walkway in silence.

~*~

Sedhral waited in a secluded alcove in Avadhron's Sward, sheltered from the chill wind. His fellows soon joined him, including Pendhras and Fandhrel from the valley. Good.

"Have you the petitions?" Sedhral asked.

Ch'oralan held up two scrolls with a smug smile.

"Then we are ready." And just in time too, before Alcandhor could call conclave on Pendhras and Fandhrel. Once that happened, their standing would be affected, and they would be culled from participation in calling Question. Fools! To cause such mischief with so much at stake!

Bandhral's lip curled. "I cannot wait until we rid our clan of that by-blow of a thane."

"That shall be accomplished by the end of the day," Pendhras vowed. "And we shall be acclaimed for restoring our clan and its traditions!"

Chapter Nine

As soon as the morning reports were finished, his niece left to get her book. The Enaisi took the opportunity, as he waited, to visit Andhrel in the law library and answer questions.

After a brief knock, the door opened and the stripling Feladhrel peeked in. "Thane? A messenger arrived from Lantral with this letter."

Alcandhor took the missive and broke the wax seal. Lord Irdhith requested a visit, now, before the Laird's conclave. What was that man scheming that he wanted to rush to Zaidhron? Again, he mentioned Sarinna specifically.

He would have Maradhor compose a reply stating they were leaving in mere days for Laird Hall and there he could meet them all, including Sarinna.

He pushed aside the letter just as Tam arrived, hugging the book to her chest. "Where is Mattan?"

"Upstairs, with the law-keepers." Alcandhor held a hand out for her treasure. He glanced through it, stopping occasionally to read a page. Years of study went into the writing of this! "You say you think this was your mother's?"

"Aye. I was not to ask my father about my mother, so I know not for certain. But it is in a fine script unlike my father's and is all about plants and herbs and their healing abilities."

Alcandhor continued to leaf through the pages. He stopped when he came to the last section—this one was not about herbs, but was a private journal written in Enai. In a low voice, he asked, "Tam, what is this?"

"I know not. Writing of some sort, but I have never been able to figure it out. But it seems to be the same hand that wrote the book."

"Call Mattan."

She nodded. "He is coming, Uncle." Leaning forward, she asked, "What is it?"

"It is..." How could he tell her what he had read? "I need to discuss this with Mattan. Please, go into the forechamber and wait. I wish you close to hand. Or take Marcalan with you up to the library and study. And I mean the history texts, not your husband."

A hearty laugh echoed across the forechamber from the Elite's chamber. Alcandhor grimaced. Would he ever again be able to have a private conversation with his niece? "Stop eavesdropping, scoundrel," he said to the air.

Tam smiled, all dimples, as she left.

Mattan came in. "What is it?"

"Close the door and sit down."

The alien frowned but obeyed.

"Tam told me she suspects this is her mother's," Alcandhor said, handing him the book.

"Aye." He flipped through the pages. "It is Ismari's handwriting."

"Turn to the back."

The Enaisi did and looked up, with a shocked expression. "Have you read this?"

"Only the first few lines. When I realized it was a private journal, I had Tam call you. Do you wish me to leave?"

He hesitated then shook his head. "I...I may need a friend when I am through reading all this."

Alcandhor sat quietly, avoiding looking at Mattan, whose emotions roiled—was it intruding on his privacy? Surely not or he would have blocked this grief and sorrow. Tears coursed down his ancestor's cheeks and, after a time, he carefully closed the book and set it on the table.

"I thank you, my son," he said, his voice breaking. He stared downward, fists on his knees.

A knock at the door broke the silence

"Come in, Tam," the Enaisi called.

"I felt your sorrow, Mattan, I could not just..."

"I know. I will be fine."

"What about my book has made you so sad?"

He sighed, his dark eyes searching Alcandhor's, his expression pleading. He did not pose the question aloud or mentally, but the Thane knew what he asked. "I know not. You read minds and hearts. I will leave it to you."

Tam bit her lip. "I can feel your grief. It...it is so deep."

Marcalan entered the chamber and shut it, face implacable. Gaping a moment at the audacity, both amusement and annoyance welled in Alcandhor. "Getting bold since your marriage, are you, cousin?"

"As you explained," he said, walking to his wife and putting an arm around her waist, "I am bonded and have no choice. I feel her anxiety and will not be kept away from her."

Not wishing to take the Ranger to task in the midst of Mattan's turmoil and Tam's response to it, Alcandhor merely replied, "So be it." He returned his attention to the alien. "Tam has had much impact on her life in a very short period of time, and I wish her not to be overwhelmed. I will leave it to you, Mattan, to tell her more. You can tell her mind—"

"Leave it to me, not Mattan," Marcalan spat. "She is my wife, and I know her mind."

"Marcalan..." Tam chided softly, but her gaze did not waver from the alien.

Alcandhor stared, shocked, at his cousin. Stars! He was no easy-going prankster now!

Mattan smiled through his tears. "It has taken you by surprise, has it, Thane?"

His lips twisted. "You are right. I may have known about this intellectually, but seeing it happen is very different."

"What are you talking about?" asked Marcalan.

"You. The bonding has changed you," Alcandhor said. "You realize not what you have done? You have entered the Thane's chamber without being bidden or being granted permission, and you have given command to the Thane."

Marcalan's face paled, and he swallowed. After a moment he managed, "My apologies, Thane. I did not—" He stopped and frowned down at his wife. "Tam? Are you all right?"

~*~

Tam took ragged breaths. Something significant and compelling was about to happen; she felt the weight of it, the fear of it. Barely conscious of the conversation around her, she asked, "Why were you crying?"

Mattan shook his head, his face still wet. "I know not if you are ready to know about this. There is a block in your mind, suppressing memories. One set there when you were very young. And it is weakening."

Tam frowned. "Who would put a block in my mind? Certainly not my father."

"You did. To protect yourself."

"How did I do such a thing? And as a child?"

"Once you remember all, I think you can answer that question yourself." Mattan's dark eyes met hers. "I can remove the block, or we can wait for it to crumble on its own one day. For it will. When it will happen, I know not, nor how you will react when it does. You have a husband who can help you through the pain of it, and your uncle, and myself, if we are there."

"But you know not when?"

"I think it will not be long. I felt it beginning to weaken in camp as we returned with the Rogues. I can remove the block and allow your mind to remember as it will. But it is your choice."

Marcalan's arm tightened around her, his love warming her through. She was not alone. "I...I do wish to know..."

Are you certain? her husband asked.

She nodded. "I am sure."

Mattan sighed, his smile sad, and then—something *snapped* in her mind. Almost as when her back felt out of adjustment and suddenly cracked into place, but this was mental not physical. With a sense of a *tugging* in her thoughts, she frowned at the Elder; he knew what she could not remember.

"Shall we let the remembrance come on its own? Or shall I tell you?" Mattan asked softly.

Indecision tore at her. What did she hide from herself? Marcalan's protectiveness desired for her to wait, but she wanted to know. Had to know. "Tell me."

"Let me try to nudge your memory on its own first," the alien said. "Let us go to the clan hall above."

Whatever this was, she was certain not only that Mattan knew, but her uncle as well; the same worry radiated from them both as they ascended to the large hall where clan gatherings were held, and where portraits of all the Thanes and their families hung.

Tam glanced over at the family portrait that included her father, and the men waited as she walked over to it, staring up. The scornful face, the narrowed, grey eyes—they intimidated her even in a painting, yet she missed him. She tore her gaze away, her heart aching, blinking tears, and followed them to the other end of the hall.

She paused, smiling at Mattan's likeness, then he took her a little further along the wall and stopped. Tam gazed up to see a family portrait and gasped at the woman in it. It was like looking in a mirror save the woman's skin was so very dark, much darker than hers. Like Mattan's.

Tam had looked into those eyes before! Pretty, delicate, brown hands had held her tiny ones. A sweet voice sang words she did not understand while embracing her and dancing or rocking her. She had run across the floor to waiting arms, to that face. A tumbling of memory flooded her mind, then...then she remembered a cold body, a void inside her—emptiness, such emptiness, crawling onto the bed to her father for comfort, a slap that tumbled her from bed to floor, then all went dark.

~*~

Mattan caught Tam as she fainted.

"Stars!" Marcalan gasped, staggering, almost collapsing, and Alcandhor grabbed him, surprised that the expected pain did not pierce his shoulder. "Are you all right?"

"I will be." His cousin put a hand to his head. "She remembered. Oh, Bells, if her father were alive, I would kill him myself, right now!"

Alcandhor's mouth dropped open at Marcalan's black eyes. "Stars, I believe you would!"

"Why?" Holding Tam in his arms, the alien glanced from one to the other.

"It is the first time I have ever seen him angry. Look at his eyes, Mattan."

"Aye, that is normal."

"Not for Marcalan. The rascal is never angry. Never. He is the most easy-going scoundrel I have ever met."

"You saw not what I did, Thane. What that man did to my wife is unforgivable, and if he were alive, I would kill him."

"I saw it too." Mattan cradled Tam like a child, his cheek resting against the top of her head.

His new nephew scowled and stepped forward, arms outreached to take his wife.

"Marcalan, be not angry that I was in her mind. I needed to safeguard her in case the memories were too strong. And please, let me hold her a moment longer."

"Why?" Marcalan spat, his eyes still dark.

"Can you not figure it out? Look at that portrait."

"I see a woman who looks like Tam, save her skin is much darker, like yours. From seeing Tam's memories, I know it is her mother."

"It is my sister, Ismari. She was trapped on this world for over five hundred years when she closed the portal to safeguard your people."

Marcalan groaned. "By the moons, I am a fool."

"Now understand you why I wish to hold her? She is all I have left of my sister. My twin sister."

Marcalan's eyes faded to blue as they filled with tears. "Facing all these memories is going to be hard for her. She had not had one easy moment in her life. How much more must she go through?"

Alcandhor exchanged glances with Mattan as he placed a hand on young man's shoulder, sending him understanding and comfort. Marcalan flinched, as if to pull away, but then relaxed, a slight smile on his face. "Thank you." He gazed over at Tam. "This is overwhelming to me. I was starting to get used to what we called our 'connection' but after...after nestling, it has been so strong. I feel I am getting lost..."

"You will adjust." The Enaisi still held Tam close. "The beginning of a bond is like a melding of personalities and thoughts. After awhile you will both find you are stronger in who each of you are separately, and although it seems a contradiction, the bond actually reinforces that."

"Mattan, is the solar available, or are Amadhor and his family still there?"

"They have gone, Thane."

Alcandhor gestured toward the door. "Then let us take her to the solar. She can rest until she awakens."

The chamber had no chill—the fireplaces had not yet burned out. With great care, Mattan lowered Tam onto a settee. Marcalan knelt on the floor next to her and held her hand. Alcandhor pulled the bell rope, then came to stand beside the alien, watching her.

"How long before she wakes?" her husband whispered.

"That will depend on her. I know not whether she will attempt to shield her own mind from what she has remembered and rebuild that wall."

"Is that possible?" Marcalan turned to look at Mattan in astonishment.

"For her, aye. But I think she will not hide from this. I believe it is the real reason she feared me. She knew, subconsciously, that I could be a threat to her hidden memories. The mind is a fantastic thing, and has incredible mechanisms in place to safeguard itself." Mattan lifted a hand. "You need to know that you will experience her pain and grief when she awakens."

A servant appeared in the silence that followed, and Alcandhor murmured a request for hot tea and a tray of food.

A slight frown passed over Tam's face.

Softly send her comfort, Mattan said mentally. *Let her feel the bond you have with her. She will need your strength.*

Alcandhor did as he was bidden, his niece's heartache gnawing at him as she awakened. She lay still, staring at them, tears brimming in her eyes. Marcalan leaned closer, and she held out her arms to him, clinging to him tightly as he pulled her into an embrace. She closed her eyes, resting her head on his shoulder.

"I know," Marcalan murmured several times, rocking her slightly.

Before long, the servant reappeared with a tray. Alcandhor poured a cup of tea for Tam and brought it over.

With a shuddering sigh she sat up, and Marcalan slid in beside her, his arm still around her waist. She took the cup with a sent feeling of gratitude and sipped it.

She nodded, glancing at Mattan. The Enaisi must have mentally asked her something.

After a few sips, she gave the tea to Mattan, then held her arms out to Alcandhor. He sat and let her cuddle into him, as she liked to do, her

87

legs drawn up and face buried in his chest. Leaning back, he lightly stroked her hair, softly sending his love. A woman grown, yet still a child in so many ways.

She looks to you as a father. Your love can help her against the pain of her childhood.

Alcandhor met Mattan's eyes in acknowledgement.

Marcalan rubbed his wife's back gently, his face wet. "I am glad she has you, else the pain would be worse."

Alcandhor kissed the top of her head, hugging her tighter. Wishing every moment he held her could erase a painful memory. He gritted his teeth—oh, how he wished Valdhor were alive! Tam slowly relaxed into him and the strength of her emotions faded. Had she fallen asleep? Mattan nodded. *Let her rest.*

"Can we have luncheon here?" Marcalan whispered.

Alcandhor nodded. "Ring the bell," he mouthed.

"What things did Ismari write in there?" Marcalan asked.

The four remained in the Thane's solar, Tam curled next to her husband, his arms around her, and Alcandhor across from them, beside the Enaisi.

Mattan brushed a hand over a page of his sister's journal. The depth of his sorrow cut Alcandhor, and he took a breath to keep tears from welling his own eyes at the Elder's pain.

"She loved Valdhor. He irritated her beyond belief, but she loved him. She writes of her two children by him in here."

"Sandhor," Tam said abruptly, staring ahead as if at nothing. "He was so tiny. I helped birth him. But the fever killed him. It almost killed all of us."

"Ismari used her abilities to heal you and Valdhor, but it was too taxing on her, as she was ill herself." Mattan swallowed several times to clear his throat so he could continue. "Her last entry was that she knew she had not long, and that she hoped Valdhor would keep his promises to her."

"Promises?" Tam tipped her head.

"To Train you, from what I understand of her entries. And to love you."

Marcalan's face hardened. "He certainly kept the first promise, but as for the second—"

"He is dead, love, do not let such feelings control you," Tam murmured, touching his cheek.

"I saw and felt what he did to you! How can I not—"

"You must! I lived it and hold him no ill will. It was the most he could give of himself. I have to accept that."

He turned away, clenching his jaw. Never had Marcalan held onto a anger or a grudge until today. What did he see in his wife's mind to cause thus? Alcandhor dragged his thoughts back to the book. "Does she say why it was so important for Valdhor to Train her?"

"She foresaw it. She saw that Tam would become a Ranger. Valdhor's heir. He did not want to accept it. He despised that she was a girl."

Tam choked back a sob. Mattan rose, but she shook her head with a sad smile. "I am all right. I just...I remember him always being ashamed of me."

"This is accomplishing nothing except bringing more grief to my wife!"

Tam arched an eyebrow. "I need not be coddled."

Marcalan met her gaze, his expression one of love and worry. After a few moments, he let his breath out. "I will try to not be so protective, Love-ling."

More mental discussion. "Stars, this is infuriating," Alcandhor mumbled.

The Enaisi chuckled. "For me as well." He raised a hand. "Just because I can read thoughts, does not mean I will allow myself to pry into a private conversation."

"Life is getting more complicated and interesting every day," Alcandhor said dryly.

Tam gazed at Mattan with a pleading expression. "Can you tell me more of my mother?"

"I would fain talk of her with you."

Alcandhor stood. He knew they would not mind him staying, but this was going to be a very emotional time for his niece and her other uncle, and they should have privacy. "My children are doubtless waiting for me."

He kissed her on the forehead and strode out.

Before he was halfway down the stairs, a Ranger raced up, two and three steps at a time. "Thane!" he gasped, eyes wide and face white.

"What is it, man?"

"We could not stop her! We tried! I swear we tried!"

"What? Who? Who could you not stop? What happened?"

"A lass jumped from the allure!"

"What? Who?"

"Some servant. Haladhon says her name was Casinn."

"Haladhon? Stop. Tell me all, in order."

"She came up to the allure and climbed onto the embrasure. We ran toward her, yelling for her to get down. She was crying. She said—this was strange—she said it was not supposed to be this way. She said Nandhal was to be Thane, and she, his wife. Then she jumped before we could grab her."

Alcandhor closed his eyes with a groan. "Who is tending to the body?"

"Haladhon has arranged that, Thane. We came to him as we knew not where to find you."

With a nod, he continued down the stairs. He found both Sarinna and Haladhon waiting for him at the bottom, faces grim.

He inclined his head toward the door of his chamber, and they followed him inside. He leaned on the front of his table, shoulders sagging. "How did this happen?"

"I talked to her," Sarinna replied. "Twice. I could sense her grief, and resentment and anger, but she kept insisting she was fine. I asked if she wished to visit her family in Jessel, but her only response over and over was that she was fine. All was well."

Arms crossed, Haladhon said, "I knew she had been enamored of Nandhal, and that he flirted with her, but nothing more. The guards claim she said Nandhal was to be Thane, that means she knew of the plot between him and the lords to kill all the chiefs." He stopped, scowling, fists clenched. "I am Chief of the Elites! How could this happen under my nose and I not discover it?"

"We never even knew Nandhal was involved, and he was at Lairdton for several lunations before the ambush and siege. How could you have known? You may be Chief of the Elites, but you are not all-knowing, cousin."

"I try."

Alcandhor managed a wry smile, then clenched his jaw. "How do we tell her family?"

"They despise us," Haladhon said, "as did she, so it will not be easy."

"Why did she then wish to work here?" Sarinna asked.

"She wished to find a powerful husband," Haladhon said.

"And how know you this?"

With a wry smile at Sarinna, his Third at Table replied, "Because she tried to catch my eye, until she found out I was not a catch. Not married, yet not available, because of Panill."

Sarinna raised one eyebrow, her lips thinned, and Haladhon's shoulders hunched slightly. What in both moons was that about? No matter, Alcandhor needed to think of this lass and her family.

"So she latched onto the highest ranking Ranger of the first table that she could, is that it?" Sarinna asked, peering up at Haladhon.

"Likely. And I would wager Nandhal secured her affections with empathy."

"That seems to fit," she murmured. "Granted, a lass in love can be so overcome by the death of her lover that she might kill herself, but if he had used empathy, she would be as if enthralled."

Alcandhor found his sympathy for the lass tempered by the knowledge she had been on the hunt for a high-born Ranger. She was no better than Aleta, by that reasoning. Nay—she grieved when Nandhal died. Granted, empathy may have been involved in luring her into a relationship, but she had a heart; Aleta had none. He let out a slow breath, and finally said, "And so I must tell her family."

"Let me compose the letter, brother," Sarinna said. "You can sign it."

"Aye, you are better with words in such occasions."

"It will not assuage them," Haladhon said. "They do not like us, and did not want her to come here."

Alcandhor threw out his arms. "What more can we do?"

"Nothing," his Third at Table muttered, then rubbed his neck. "If she had not jumped, and if she had told anyone her knowledge of Nandhal's–and his conspirators'—plans, she would be tried for treason."

"I do not know if it is too late to stop those guards from telling the full tale, but let us try to halt such talk. Gossip may have wings in this city, but I would not bring further shame to her family or her memory."

"I will do what I can."

"As will I," Sarinna said. "We can state she talked nonsense due to grief."

"And if we pursue nothing as far as inquiries, then perhaps it will die down," Haladhon added.

With a nod, Alcandhor closed his eyes. "Bells, what a day. Not only the hangings but another death besides. What else might this day bring?"

~*~

A shadow indeed settled heavily over the city; Eladhrel and Mattan had been wise in their suggestion to delay leaving.

His children stayed with Jholinn in Family North and did not see the hangings, but they heard talk. He decided he would not have studies with them this afternoon. Perhaps they would spend time in their family suite together. Aye, that would suit.

When he arrived, the widow curtsied and hurried away.

Trying to explain Rogues and the law to them was not easy. The boys were learning the laws, and had some intellectual understanding, but they both had known Nandhal; he was a close cousin. They could not comprehend he had gone Rogue, done very bad things, been caught, and hanged.

"It is so strange to think I will never see him again," Teldhor muttered.

"He was mean," Amara said matter-of-factly from her blanket in the corner. She was setting out a play set of wooden dishes to have an outing.

"Why say you that, Sweetling? Did he ever do anything to hurt you?"

She shook her head, pouring imaginary tea into little cups. "Nay. He talked mean to me, and to Jholinn. He scared her, and she almost cried."

Alcandhor frowned. "When was this?"

"Mmm, I remember not. But we were happy when he left the city."

"Aye, we were all relieved when he was assigned to Lairdton," Teldhor said. "He was never pleasant to be around."

Alcandhor silently agreed, chastising himself. How could he show such leniency to those who did not deserve it, and in turn cause pain to those who deserved better? He had done so with Aleta, and with Nandhal. Did he have misplaced compassion? Or was he just a fool? He sighed. "I think we have had enough gloomy talk for one day. Let us have an outing with Amara."

Teldhor snorted, rolling his eyes. "An outing? That is for little girls."

Alcandhor chuckled. "You two can be roaming Rangers who happen upon us, and we ask if you would like to share our food."

The boys agreed to that with stipulations that they were chasing roadway bandits and only stopped to see that the family was unharmed.

Later, they set up the board to play backhand. It was a strategy game, and Amara far too young for it, but Alcandhor let her help him plan his moves as she sat on his lap. They played several games, then they gathered together by the fireplace while he read them a story.

Afterwards, Teldhor asked, "Is there truly going to be a lords' conclave?"

Eladhor looked up, frowning. "I thought you said you would be here from now on."

Alcandhor tousled his son's hair. "I said I should not have to be gone as often or for as long. But when the Laird calls a conclave, I must go. Do you understand?"

The boy sighed.

"I am sorry, son. We leave the morning after tomorrow, but I will try to be back for winter solstice."

"That is less than two lunations away," Teldhor whined. "And every time you go to Laird Hall, you stay there longer than you say you will."

"I know. It seems other things always happen while I am there. But I shall make every effort to be home by then."

"Promise?" Amara asked.

Alcandhor sighed. "I cannot, Sweetling. But I will try."

Chapter Ten

The enjoyable afternoon drove away the gloom of the hangings and the fact that Alcandhor must soon leave for Laird Hall. After a walk on the grounds, he had their evening meal brought to the family suite, then they played the journey game, marking their routes through the provinces on the map board with colored tokens.

Eladhor had just passed the border of the final province when a knock on the door interrupted them. Haladhon appeared, his face carefully neutral, his tone formal. "Thane? Rangers have arrived to see the chiefs. They are calling conclave."

Alcandhor caught his cousin's manner and expression and sat up straight. This was it. The nightmare he had dreaded since becoming Thane, that had recently been even more of a shadow over him had grown to fruition, a black blossom. He stood. "Find Jholinn or Taniss to stay with my children. Have the chiefs all meet in the conclave chamber. I will be there as soon as I can."

Jholinn soon arrived, and after giving each child a long embrace, Alcandhor strode out. The cold night air seemed to chill his heart more, and the fog rising gave the sward a funereal atmosphere. He did not look at the Rangers waiting in the forechamber, but climbed the stairs to the conclave chamber and sat at the head of the table, knowing in all likelihood he would not sit there ever again.

Once the chiefs seated themselves down the sides of the long table, Andhrel summoned the Rangers calling Question.

The men entered, their expressions smug yet grim. Although Alcandhor knew most of them, by protocol, they each gave their name, rank, and status. Pendhras' presence was not unexpected. Nor was Ch'oralan's; he was the one who had contested Tam at Lairdton's Ranger Hold. Raised in Zaidhron, his bounds now were in the southern province of Ranshalon.

Bandhral and Sedhral, who both resided here in the city, had always been vocal of their dissatisfaction of their current Thane. Again, no surprise. Galedhel from Lantral Province Alcandhor did not personally know, but he had seen the man talking with Bandhral several times.

Fandhrel stood next to Pendhras. The recall of those Rangers from Dandrin Shire seemed to have worked in their favor. Or did their recall cause this petition to be hurried before they were called to conclave over their misdeeds in the valley?

Nay, these were Rangers from different provinces and bounds, who came united to conclave. This was a well-planned maneuver.

They bowed toward the table, then Pendhras frowned at Mattan and Marcalan. "Who is this? We have called conclave and will have only chiefs here."

Alcandhor sat back in his chair, trying to ease the tension he felt in his shoulders. "This is Ranger Chief Mattan. Surely you have heard the news that an Enaisi has returned and dwells among us again. He is our oldest chief—and forefather."

"Now, why make remarks about age, Thane," Mattan muttered. "'Tis not comely."

"I have seen him. I do not accept his claim, or that the portal works. It is some trickery."

"Ah, Pendhras," the alien said, leaning back, "you bring back memories. It is good to know that willful ignorance is still in abundant supply in our world."

The older Ranger glowered, fists clenched.

Alcandhor rubbed a hand over his mouth. "That was not nice," he murmured.

"I am not nice," Mattan replied flatly.

"I see a stranger," Pendhras spat. "I would have proof."

Meeting the man's glare, Alcandhor said, "You are a Child of the Enaisi. You know their abilities, such as telepathy?"

"Aye."

"So be it. Mattan, if you please."

Moments later Pendhras stiffened, his face going ashen, then he whispered to the alien, "You–you are indeed an Enaisi."

"Oh, come, you cannot believe—" Galedhel stopped. All the other Rangers' eyes widened, and they grew pale, their mouths dropping open. Finally, they all nodded.

The older Ranger straightened and took several deep breaths. Finally, he cleared his throat and jabbed a finger toward Marcalan. "He is not a chief."

"Since his marriage to Tam, he is," Haladhon said. "Based on precedents from the past. Marcalan retains his family lineage and rank, but is counted as a chief."

"We will see about that. It is part of the reason we are here." Pendhras drew himself up. "We have requested a conclave convened to call Question on two items. We have a list of Rangers that we speak for on each one." He took a scroll from the pouch at his side and held it up. "Here is the first. We call Question on Tamissa being Confirmed, Presented, and accepted as heir to Thane."

"On what grounds?" Haladhon asked, passing the document down the table.

"On the grounds that Valdhor never entered record of having any children, and there is no proof she is his daughter."

"Then who would you think she is, man?" Eladhrel asked.

Alcandhor unrolled and scanned the paper, then gave it to Mattan to read, glancing down at Tam's impassive face as he did so. The Question petition passed from one chief to the next as the conversation continued.

Pendhras shot a scornful look at Tam. "She could be a foundling for all anyone knows."

"Valdhor claimed her as daughter," Andhrel said.

"He never recorded her birth. She should have no clan standing without a proper birth record. We only have his word she is his daughter. Now he is dead, and we cannot get answers from him. We know not who her mother is—"

"That we do know," Haladhon spat.

The Questioning Rangers stared, open-mouthed.

"Then tell us," Pendhras demanded.

"My sister, Ismari, was her mother," Mattan said.

"Impossible. There have not been Enaisi here in centuries."

"My sister stayed, as did Ashani. She chose to seclude herself for reasons we do not know. But she did marry Valdhor, and she is Tam's mother."

"And you have proof of this?" Ch'oralan asked, his eyes flashing.

"Other than the fact that she is the likeness of my sister, has abilities that indicate she is at least half-Enaisi, and that she now remembers her mother? Not to mention my sister kept a journal naming Valdhor as husband and Tamissa as daughter?" Mattan spat, half-rising from his chair. He exhaled and sat back down. "I have ways to test her and show genetically who her parents are. I can provide proof of Tam's ancestry, maternal and paternal."

"That does not resolve the lack of a birth record," Pendhras replied. "Such a testing would require a clan vote."

"Would it?" Mattan asked softly.

Pendhras glared him and lifted his chin. "We have a second grievance on which we call Question." He pulled out another scroll, this time his expression openly triumphant.

After reading it, as before Alcandhor passed it to Mattan. As each chief read it, he simply sat, regarding the Rangers calmly, although his heart pounded in maddening fury. They had a valid point, and it just might be that by day's end he would at the least, no longer be Thane, and, at the most, be clanless.

What he had to do was keep the focus on him and off the chiefs. Although never spoken among them, he knew they were aware of the rumor that Valdhor had a child, and did not act on it due to Saldhor's orders. If that became known, all the chiefs could be found guilty of breaking Clan Law. That could not be allowed to happen. He must force them to concentrate on him as their target.

Ire radiated off Haladhon in hot waves, but his cousin kept quiet as everyone at the table read the document. When the paper returned to Alcandhor, his best friend finally burst out, "You use this as an excuse! You know the Thane had a valid reason—"

"Haladhon," Alcandhor chided in a gentle voice. "Before this goes on. I want to go back to this first Question. Would you accept Mattan's proof for Tam's parentage?"

Pendhras chin jutted out. "I would not, as she would still have no legitimate birth record in our archives from her parents, and besides, does not the use of such testing go against our laws? Our ancestors came here shunning advanced ways, giving us laws that keep our lives simple, so we would not destroy ourselves again. However, I cannot speak for all who signed with us in calling Question. It would have to go to a clan vote. But think you we Rangers will accept her if we say nay?"

Marcalan shot to his feet, but Eladhrel pulled on his arm, and slowly he sat back down. Alcandhor wondered how much mental discussion flew around the chamber. Despite his appearance of sitting idly, Mattan was probably very busy.

With open scorn, Haladhon said, "I think you presuppose too much, Pendhras."

"The burden falls on you to show proof that Tam is not Valdhor's daughter, birth record or not," Alcandhor said. "Valdhor claimed her as daughter, and the word of a Ranger is accepted as fact."

"The word of one who would not obey the law by sending a birth record, and who would not accept the responsibility he was born to?" Pendhras sneered.

"You would not speak so if Valdhor were present," Haladhon retorted.

"But he is not here, and there is no proof she is truly his daughter. His claim alone is not enough."

"It is enough," Tam said, tears in her eyes. "He wanted a son and despised me for being a lass. If he could have passed off claim of me, he would have."

"Then why did he not?" Pendhras asked.

Tam's eyes narrowed, and her chin set. "Because he promised my mother he would Train me. My father would never break a vow."

Pendhras sniffed. "I still accept it not. If those who signed with us do not accept it, it will go to a clan vote."

Alcandhor sighed, staring at the first document, wondering how to help Tam before Thaneship was stripped from him. How would the clan vote if it came to that, and what would become of her? Mattan's voice spoke in his mind: *I will see to her. You need not worry about Tam— these men know not the law as well as they should and cannot force their claim. I can guarantee she keeps rank and status in our clan.* Alcandhor swallowed, relieved, knowing he could trust Mattan. *But you, my friend, I worry for. I cannot help you.* Alcandhor knew this. For all his abilities, the Enaisi had not the power to change or abrogate the law.

"Since the fate of Tam is not something that can be judged today, I will have to forego that, and continue to the second Question," Alcandhor said, "which is the fact that I never pursued calling Question on Valdhor when I discovered he had a daughter."

Andhrel leaned forward earnestly, gazing at the Rangers. "Do you understand not why the Thane acted as he did?"

"Clan Law is our highest law," Ch'oralan blurted, "and he violated it. We call Question on him."

Pendhras put a hand up to silence the blustering Ranger. "Any time Clan Law is broken, an accounting must take place. No open proclamation has been made that this has been done, so we call Question on the Thane."

With a weariness that ached to his bones, Alcandhor sighed and folded his hands in front of him. "I had intended on calling Question on Valdhor's actions after he completed his mission. I know that is not proper procedure and breaks—"

"Ha! You did nothing!" Ch'oralan shouted, his face red. "You broke Clan Law."

Pendhras turned to the younger man, jaw set and his eyes dark. "You will keep your place and let me be spokesman, as was decided."

Ch'oralan glowered, but subsided, inclining his head. Pendhras again faced the table, his bow overly dramatic. "My apologies. Please, continue."

Alcandhor nodded. "Let me start at the beginning. I went on a search for Valdhor, having had foresight through a dream that I needed him for a mission. I knew that the traitors' plans were ripe, and that time was short. I did, of course, discover he had a child, and I brought him and Tam both back here as quickly as I could. The chiefs did confront me that I had not called Question about Tam's birth record when I called them for conclave, but the sense of urgency, of foresight, that had sent me to find him, I used as a reason to wait. I needed him too badly."

He stared at his hands, remembering Valdhor's face as he lay dying, and in a softer voice continued, "I intended to call Question on his actions when that mission was over. I did not foresee his death."

"That is your claim, but there is no proof—"

Pendhras whirled to Ch'oralan, as Haladhon shot to his feet. "Enough," both men ordered simultaneously.

"You will follow protocol for the meeting, Ch'oralan, or you will be removed," Haladhon stated, his eyes narrowed.

Ch'oralan inclined his head once again. His tall cousin seated himself. "There is proof. The Thane discussed with us calling Question on Valdhor the same day Tam was Presented. He told us that he wished to delay it because of the imminence of the traitors' plans being put into action. We all bore witness of his intentions, and the chiefs all—"

"Nay," Alcandhor said, slamming his hand on the table and glaring at Haladhon. He had to stop the chiefs from chancing coming under condemnation themselves by admitting they acquiesced to his wishes instead of demanding he follow the law. The ensuing chaos would provide too many opportunities for nobles who wished to be rid of Ch'shalna clan and the Enaisi's laws. "You will not attempt to turn the focus away from my crime. The chiefs confronted me about it, and I resolved to postpone calling Question. It was my decision, Haladhon. Mine alone. I did not pursue calling Question on Valdhor. Regardless of the dire circumstances at the time, by doing so I put his worth above the law, and set myself above the law as well. I take full responsibility for it. The chiefs asked me to call Question, and I refused. It is my crime alone. I freely admit guilt in this, and accept the punishment."

He stood and stared at the stunned chiefs. By confessing guilt to a high crime, he was automatically stripped of rank and status. With Tam's birth record disputed, Haladhon was now interim Thane. "So be it." Haladhon should have made that last statement, but Alcandhor knew his cousin would never utter those three words and condemn his dearest friend.

A horrified silence settled on the chamber, then in a rough whisper, Haladhon began, "Alcandhor—"

"No more discussion is necessary," Alcandhor stated. "I would suggest, Thane Haladhon, since Ranger Chief Lamadhel is not here that you drum him the details, and get his acknowledgement so sentence can be carried out." He slid his dagger from its sheath, placed it on the table, and strode to the door, striving to keep his composure.

"Where are you going?" Haladhon's voice cracked.

He turned to face the man who was closer than brother, his voice low, their eyes locking. "You know where I will be."

His cousin's face turned white. He strode out and down the back hallways listening to the echo from his boots on the white stone, then out into the sward, trying not to think of what was happening. What had happened. Best not to think.

He finally reached the western tower for the gate.

One of the guards, Baidhrol, good friends with Loch'alan, bowed. "Thane."

"Ranger, show me the cells."

"The cells, Thane?"

"Aye. Bring the keys."

The young Ranger stared in puzzlement for a moment, then took a torch and led the way down the stairs. He stopped at the lower landing and peering expectantly at Alcandhor.

"The bottom cells."

"Aye, sir."

Down another flight of stairs. Baidhrol stopped, frowning in the flickering light of the torch.

"Unlock a cell," Alcandhor said, his voice a rough whisper.

"Thane?"

"Do as you are told, Ranger."

Baidhrol opened a cell. Once inside, he turned and swallowed, hoping his voice was steady as he gave what would be his last order as Thane. "Shut and lock it."

"I...I cannot leave you in here, Thane."

"Do it, Ranger Baidhrol. Just...do it."

The young Ranger seemed ready to weep as he pulled the door to, his face full of confusion. Left in the dark, Alcandhor felt his way to the stone shelf that doubled as a bed, and sat down. His stomach knotted, but he refused to give in to the horror and loss.

Not caring about the icy feel of the stone beneath him, he laid down, putting one arm across his eyes and wondering how he could have avoided this. From the time he became Thane he had feared this would happen. But what could he have done differently?

His father had refused to discuss Valdhor or any alleged children with anyone, and had left a letter to be opened by Alcandhor upon becoming Thane, instructing him to leave matters be regarding Valdhor and to quash any inquiries into whether he had any offspring. He knew his father had keen sight, and so obeyed, although it left a dread on his heart because if his brother had children and had not recorded their births it meant breaking Clan Law. Their highest and oldest law.

But he saw now the wisdom of his father's orders. If he had pursued the rumor that Valdhor had a child and had brought Tam to be raised by the clan, where would they all be? He reviewed all that happened since he found her. She saved the life of Lord Krendhal, and the young Laird, and Alcandhor's life, too, for that matter—twice. She helped find the truth concerning the traitor Tanadhon. She put them in contact with Mattan, and with her help, ended the threat of the Rogues.

What would their world be like now without Tam as a Ranger? The Laird's clan, Viltara, would be no more, and all would be in upheaval with greedy, power-hungry nobles vying for control. Without Tam to stop the traitors and the Rogues, all the chiefs would likely be dead. Which would have left Nandhal in the position to bid to become Thane, fruitless, aye, but causing turmoil and confusion in Ch'shalna Clan. There she left a mark too—it was after being thrashed by Tam and upbraided by Alcandhor and Haladhon that Nandhal became apprehensive and ran.

Nay, he would not change anything if he could go back. He had to do what he did. It was worth it all to know he had done much to preserve his world. Even if it cost him everything. And it had. As Thane, for him to be guilty of breaking a High Law brought the maximum sentence save death, thus he would be branded and cut off—his gut twisted and his legs twitched together involuntarily at the thought. He would be disowned. Clanless. He was glad he had spent a wonderful afternoon with his children—he would never see them again. The reserve he had fought to maintain broke, and he sobbed in the dark.

Chapter Eleven

Before the drums' echoes faded, Sarinna rushed from the steward's chamber down the back hallways of the chiefs' range, her throat clamped shut. She took the stairs two at a time, skirts high, and flung the conclave chamber door open. The sight in front of her froze her in place. Tam, white-faced, cradled in Marcalan's arms. Haladhon paced like a caged beast. Andhrel and Eladhrel both sat, silent and pale, as did Mattan, his hands folded and head bowed.

"Tell me this is a jest," she said, trembling with both anger and fear.

"It is not," Marcalan whispered.

She stared at them, terror gripping her heart. She strode to the Enaisi. "Can you not do something?"

"I cannot abrogate the law," he murmured, his voice breaking. "He admitted guilt."

"Guilt? To what?"

"Not calling Question on Valdhor about Tam's birth record," Andhrel said.

Sarinna's nails dug into her palms. "But he intended to, he stated thus to me."

"We all know this, and we could have argued it in his favor, but he admitted guilt."

"But are there not provisions in the law for those who admit guilt but are not truly guilty? Those who confess under duress or where—"

"Those do not apply when guilt is known beyond a doubt, and acknowledged," Andhrel said.

Haladhon slammed a chair into the table. Andhrel jumped, glancing at his enraged cousin. "If Alcandhor had pleaded extenuating circumstances, we could have called for a clan vote, but he simply stated he was guilty of the crime, and accepted punishment. He took any choices we had out of our hands."

"But why?" Sarinna asked, trying to choke back sobs.

A voice behind her made her turn to the open door. A teary-eyed Jholinn stood at the top of the stairs with Alcandhor's three children, all sobbing.

"Oh, my heart," she murmured. "Let us all go to the solar."

She twisted around to look at the chiefs, pinning each of them with her gaze. "You must do something," she ordered, then left to help with her niece and nephews.

Taniss entered the solar to see both her daughter and Jholinn attempting to comfort the children. Teldhor ran to her. "Gran, you can make them listen, can you not? They cannot stop Papa from being Thane."

She lifted her chin. "I will do what I am able as clan matriarch. But you must learn to be strong in trying times, so your father will be proud of you." She held her eldest grandson's gaze until he nodded, sniffling, then she turned to Eladhor. So softhearted, much more like Alcandhor than the older boy. She was glad they did not understand the full import of what was happening. Amara, of course, did not truly comprehend any of it, save that she knew her papa was in trouble, but her brothers' tears increased her own distress.

She put her hand on Eladhor's head and smiled at him. "Your father is strong, and you are like him. All of you. Be strong. For him."

The boys nodded, and Eladhor wiped his face. Taniss straightened. "Now, I am going to see the chiefs."

The children's hopeful faces made her heart ache as she left. What could she do against a conclave?

She met Lantalan coming up the stairs and inclined her head to her late husband's best friend. He gravely bowed.

Haladhon's ranting could be heard through the door. "This is ridiculous! Tam has proven herself! She is loyal to our clan!"

"The law is the law," Andhrel yelled, "and we cannot abrogate it, regardless of our feelings, or else Alcandhor would be here, not locked in a dank cell!"

Taniss gazed up to see Lantalan's jaw clenched and his nostrils flared.

A loud slam brought silence, then Mattan said, "Do not worry about Tam. Her standing is secure. Think you, man. Despite Pendhras' claims, the burden is on him to disprove her parentage. She was Presented to the clan as Valdhor's daughter, in his presence, and he did not dispute it. His word as a Ranger, whatever Pendhras may say, is taken as oath. And he is mistaken about being allowed to use advanced technology according to your laws. I know those laws—I sat at table when Zaidhron, Cosdhral, and the others drafted them. Trust me, Tam is safe. It is Alcandhor that I am helpless to assist."

Opening the door with a bow, Lantalan waited for Taniss to enter.

"I cannot believe this is happening." Haladhon raged, pacing. "Curse the law if it punishes a good man like Alcandhor!"

"Calm yourself, cousin," Eladhrel said, grasping the tall Ranger's shoulder.

With a snarl, Haladhon slapped the arm away.

"Enough," Taniss said.

The men stood in deference to her, all with anguished expressions. Marcalan's arms encircled Tam, her face blotchy and tear-streaked. Taniss forbore her instinct to go to her granddaughter; this was not a time for emotion. A broken chair lay against the wall, no doubt the result of Haladhon's temper.

"Can you tell me what this nonsense is about?" Lantalan demanded.

The chiefs frowned at him, and Taniss bristled. "Do not dare to say it is not his business."

"It is not. It is a conclave matter," Andhrel said.

"As closest to chief of the First Table, I have been asked to represent all our kin," Lantalan said. "It is not merely a conclave matter, it affects our whole clan. We want answers. Why is our Thane in a cell, charged with a high crime?"

"He is no longer Thane," Andhrel said, his voice dull and thick. "He admitted guilt. Haladhon is now our Thane."

That statement brought a growl and slam on the table from their new Thane. "Mattan, there must be something. You were here when our laws were written. You must have an answer."

The Enaisi stood, his eyes black, although tears welled in them. "I have told you, Haladhon, as Andhrel has, there is nothing we can do. When Alcandhor—"

"I want not to hear it!" Haladhon shouted, his face red.

"I want to hear it!" Lantalan shot back. "Why is Alcandhor in a cell?"

"Rangers called Question on his decision to *not* call Question on Valdhor over neglecting to record Tam's birth," Mattan said.

"So the crime of the elder brother falls to the younger because of a delay in calling Question?" Lantalan asked. "We all knew of that situation. A clan vote would clear Alcandhor of wrong doing."

"He admitted guilt," Eladhrel said.

Taniss stood as stone, hope dissolved, seeped out of her body and down through the floor. How could she possibly assimilate the knowledge her son was now dead to her? Nay. It could not be true.

"What?" Lantalan took a step backward. "But why?"

"To save the chiefs," Mattan answered. "He knew there was a chance these Rangers would accuse all the chiefs as they did not force Alcandhor to call Question on Valdhor at the time. He was also afraid that they might bring up the fact that there were rumors that Valdhor had a child, and that could cause Question to be called on the chiefs if it could be ascertained they were aware of that, and the lack of her birth record."

"But a clan vote would surely clear the chiefs," Lantalan said.

"A clan vote on the chiefs in the middle of all this uprising? What would happen?" Haladhon demanded. "What would those who are of the mind to overthrow the Rangers and the Laird's rule do knowing our clan has such upheaval in it? Despite the siege and trial, we cannot trust at least half the provincial lords. Alcandhor knew what he was doing. He sacrificed himself."

Lantalan closed his eyes. "Oh, Bells!"

Taniss tightened her throat, striving to keep control. Haladhon resumed pacing, cursing under his breath.

"Stop it, Haladhon," she ordered. "It helps nothing."

"What can help? What can be done?" he spat, striding over.

Upon his mother's death shortly after his birth, Taniss had become her nephew's wet nurse and foster-mother, often suckling both Alcandhor and Haladhon at the same time, as they were just under a year apart. She loved him, and would censure him as she would her own children. The pain in his eyes tore her heart, but a man could be not hugged and comforted as a child. Instead, she gave him a stern glare. "Put your energies to thought, to solutions, not cursings."

He turned away. She fastened her attention on the Enaisi, knowing the answer before she asked the question; she had been wife of the Thane and knew their laws well. "There is nothing that may be done?"

"I am sorry, Lady Taniss, nay. The law is clear. He purposefully stepped into this, we cannot stop sentence."

"So my son will be sacrificed for the sake of this miserable world?" Her gaze swept them, then came to rest again on the alien. "Think you he was right to do what he did?"

"My opinion will not sway anyone, nor change the law."

Taniss closed her eyes in an attempt to keep her composure. Lantalan cleared his throat. "I will relay all this to our kin."

As he left, she wilted, unable to deny the hopelessness to herself any longer. "I will be in the solar with the grandchildren."

Oh, Maker, her son was as dead! And his children—how did she prepare them for losing their father? They would be orphans. Sarinna and she would foster them, but would Haladhon stand in as father, or would that go to the more restrained Lamadhel or his sons? Perhaps Lantalan...

She could hear loud voices as she approached the solar. She opened the door as Teldhor yelled, "I hate her!"

"You do not mean it, Teldhor. Do not say thus," Sarinna said, her arm going around his shoulders.

He shrugged her off. "I do mean it! If she had not been brought here, no one would have known about her, and Father would not be under judgment!"

"That is enough!"

They all turned to Taniss. She shut the door, locking eyes with her grandson. "To blame Tam when she is not responsible is folly, and beneath a Ranger. You are facing a grave loss, but that is no excuse for lashing out at kin."

Teldhor fell onto a divan, arms folded, face forbidding. Never did he look so much like his mother. She sat down next to him. Amara ran over and climbed into her lap.

"You have the right to be angry, son, but do not aim it amiss. Can you understand?" Stars, if only Haladhon could learn that lesson. But Haladhon was Haladhon, and not likely to change at this time of his life. Teldhor on the other hand...

"I suppose," the boy replied, then his brown eyes lifted to hers, filled with tears. "But what of Father?"

Taniss swallowed. She could not bring herself to tell them of his sentence. "He...he is in a cell."

Amara burst into a scream, her shrill voice echoing through the chamber. The boys clapped hands over their ears, while Jholinn scooped her up and held her close, cooing to her. Her arms wrapped tightly around the woman's neck, and her screams slowly reduced to mere tears. With jerky sobs, she said, "I do not want my Papa hanged!"

Taniss and Sarinna both rose to soothe her. "Why think you he will hang, child?" Taniss asked, smoothing her granddaughter's hair.

"Nandhal was in a cell, and he was hanged." Her face scrunched up, and she wailed, "I want my Papa!"

Eladhor openly cried, and Teldhor dropped his head to his arms on the side of the divan. Tears streamed down all three women's faces as they tried to comfort the children. How did she dare tell them their father's fate, and that they could never see him again?

~*~

Ch'oralan's apprehension grew upon hearing the angry susurrations and seeing the baleful glares as he crossed the Great Hall to the First Table for the evening meal. He did not need empathy to know their calling Question infuriated the entirety of Zaidhron. His father and brothers would not speak to him, and his cousins muttered imprecations of what should be done to those who acted as traitors against the Thane. Even having his second cousin Galedhel several places down from him brought no comfort as he received the same treatment.

The seats where the chiefs should be at table remained vacant; no one moved up to fill those spots as was custom. Sitting at the upper left across from those empty places somehow boded ominously.

He tried to speak to his father, but Terdhrel turned his back to him. When he tried a second time, his father swung around, hissing, "Speak not to me, you rogue! You have all but killed our Thane!"

"I only followed the law."

"Do you deceive yourself so thoroughly? You bear ill will against Tam and Alcandhor for what happened at Ranger hold when you contested her and she bested you. You have no sense of loyalty to our Thane or our clan. You know not what love is."

"Love and loyalty cannot excuse breaking the law," Ch'oralan said.

"There are times when love may forgive many things," Terdhrel spat, "but I wager you remember that not from reading the Laws of the Maker. If you have not learned that yet, I wonder if you ever will."

"So you would allow the Thane of our clan to break the law with impunity?"

"I, and all here, granted him leniency because of the extraordinary circumstances that existed at the time. Necessity effected a postponement in executing the law. How can you not understand that? If Valdhor had lived, he would have stood in front of conclave. Those of you who have called Question do so from sullied motives." He jabbed a finger into Ch'oralan's chest. "You mostly because of your objection to Tam."

"So you would have had a lass as Thane one day?"

"It does not sit well with me to think of a woman as Thane, but she has been proving to be a worthy Ranger. I would have given her a chance to see if she had the qualities of leadership and the strength necessary. Now, that is all past and done. We have lost our Thane and at least one chief. More if you and your accomplices have your way."

"Accomplices? You make us sound as criminals."

"Are you not? You have stolen from Ch'shalna clan that which many, nay most, of us find most precious—our Thane." His father's voice broke with emotion, and he turned away.

Ch'oralan frowned.

After the meal, Galedhel and Pendhras joined him in a corner.

"I think we misjudged terribly," Galedhel hissed. "There is too much loyalty to the Thane."

"It will not save him," Pendhras said, fists on his hips. "And the trull will be gone, too. Haladhon has been guilty of breaking Clan Law, and proof will be easy to find, even without bringing up that bawd he calls his mistress. So that is three gone. Lamadhel will be Thane in a matter of days at the most."

"Why are you so adamant that Lamadhel become Thane?" Ch'oralan asked.

"He is older and understands the past traditions. He will not discard them as Alcandhor has done. Things will be as they ought to be. I do not regret what is going to happen to Alcandhor—he was lax and left himself open to attack."

"What about that Enaisi?" Galedhel asked.

"The clan may fawn over him, but he is nothing. He must obey the same laws we do."

"The whole city is in an uproar." Ch'oralan cut his eyes to those about them. "It makes me fearful."

"Stand firm," Pendhras said. "We wait for one drum message to get rid of Alcandhor. Tamissa is gone as well since there is no birth record. That is the law. Then we attack Haladhon. That licentious by-blow should have been branded, cut off, and disowned years ago."

Galedhel shook his head.

Pendhras leaned close and snarled, "We are following the law. We will lead our clan back where it belongs. You remember that."

Chapter Twelve

The door opened, and Alcandhor's stomach fell. Was it now time for sentence to be carried out? He fought the urge to hunch in on himself; a man who had been Thane and a Ranger should face his nightmares without flinching.

"Thane?" Baidhrol stood with a torch in one hand and a tray in the other.

"Call me not that."

"A-aye, sir," the Ranger replied, his voice hoarse. "I brought a meal for you."

Alcandhor let out a silent breath as the young man set the tray on the shelf next to him.

"Take it. I cannot eat."

"I will not, sir. It is your choice to eat or not, but I will leave the food."

As loudly as the drums echoed throughout the city of Zaidhron, could they be heard in the subterranean levels? "Lamadhel has not drummed back then?"

"Nay, sir."

The young man shifted from foot to foot. The last thing Alcandhor wanted was to speak to anyone, or listen to emotions expressed, but he could not just tell this lad to leave.

"I am sorry this duty fell to you, Baidhrol. I hope no one holds it against you. You are a good Ranger."

"Thane—sir, I..."

"I can sense. You need say nothing for me to know what you feel. I thank you. But I wish to be alone."

"Aye, sir."

After the door shut, Alcandhor set the tray on the floor and stretched out on the stone shelf. He had lied to Baidhrol; he had not sensed him. He dared not stop blocking or who knew what he might feel—Tam might send to him, or Mattan. He could not cope with that. His rough response after the alien mindspoke with him had stopped the man from repeated attempts.

He stared into the dark. How much longer must he wait for the inevitable?

~*~

Ordhral burst into the conclave chamber. "What in the name of both moons has occurred?"

Tam jumped. This enigmatic Pashelon cousin had always been reserved and gentle. Now, his black eyes and thunderous expression confounded, nay even frightened, her.

"Where have you been that you know not what has happened?" Andhrel asked.

"Mattan gave Delgan, me, and a few others access to the Portal Complex to archive information of our history. But we came back to have a late meal, and all is in uproar."

Ordhral frowned as all the chiefs talked at once, but slowly his expression grew from comprehension to shock. His lips drew back in a snarl. "I knew I was to come. I knew it!" He pulled a sealed letter from inside his jerkin. "Now is the time. Finally." He went down on one knee. "Take it, Tamissa. It is your right."

Tam took the missive and broke the seal, the wax cracking into bits. Her eyes widened. "Stars! 'Tis my birth record! Recorded and witnessed by"—she gazed up in astonishment at the Pashelon Ranger—"you!"

Ordhral's smile reminded her of Uncle's, and oh, what love flowed from him! She would need to talk to this cousin later!

"But then why it is not in the family genealogy?" Eladhrel asked. "'Tis a break from—"

A drum message interrupted her cousin: "Unseal the records."

The chiefs all exchanged glances, frowning. Andhrel's mouth gaped, but then understanding lit his eyes, and he smiled. "Ah. We should go to the clan archives."

Tam rushed up the stairs behind Andhrel to a vaulted chamber, and crowded close, peering over his arm, as he lifted the tome that bespoke their lineage. The book fell open, and a thick, folded sheaf of documents, sealed by wax, fell to the floor. Marcalan picked it up. "'Tis the Thane's seal."

"I would wager at least one of those papers bears the same message as mine," Ordhral said.

After breaking the seal, Marcalan riffled through the contents. "It is."

"Two copies of her birth record," Andhrel murmured, turning to peer at Ordhral. "Someone took no chance. Ismari, I would guess?"

"Aye. She foresaw much, but only shared what she felt she must."

Tears sprang to Tam's eyes. "Does this mean Uncle is no longer in trouble?"

"He cannot be charged with breaking Clan Law by not calling

Question on Valdhor over having your birth recorded when it is in the archives." Andhrel said. "But what I do not understand is why it was kept secret."

"The answers probably lie in those other papers," Haladhon said.

"Then let us read them." Tam snatched them from Marcalan's hands. They all stared at her, and she lifted her chin. "Whatever this all is, it seems to be connected to me. Have I not the right?"

"Since your birth cannot be contested now, Second at Table," Haladhon said with a formal bow, the twinkle returning to his eyes, "I would say you have the right to do as you please."

Tam smirked and spread the papers on a nearby table. "Some I can read, but this is another sealed paper with writing I cannot decipher, similar to what is in my book."

"It is a message for me," Mattan said. "My name is written on it."

She handed it to him, then scanned the first of the missives. "It is a letter to Thane Saldhor from my mother. She gives all my birth information to him, and tells him to seal it as I must stay with my father. I must be Trained and will not be if I am brought back to the clan—" her voice choked and she could not continue.

Marcalan pulled the paper from her fingers. "'I cannot see the future, Thane, and the only conclusion I can reach is that I will die. You must guarantee Tamissa stays with Valdhor. Seal the records so that certain knowledge of her will not be known until she has Confirmation age, in the year 1044.'" He paused and read on silently, then said, "There is more, but it is of a private matter. Some directed to Saldhor, some to Tam, and some to Alcandhor."

"And your paper, Mattan?" asked Haladhon.

"A letter from Ismari," the alien said in a hushed voice, "to be delivered to me, or to any of our people, if the portal ever opened again."

Haladhon crossed his arms, frowning. "So Thane Saldhor, between his own foreknowledge and that of an Enaisi, abrogated the law because of the advice of an Enaisi—"

"He did not abrogate the law," Andhrel said. "Tam's birth was dutifully recorded as it should have been. But the record was sealed, and not disclosed until now, which is a completely different—"

"What does all this do to Uncle?" Tam interrupted.

"Both Questions called are null and void," Andhrel said. "Your birth was recorded. Alcandhor acted in good faith, obeying his father's advice to not inquire into Valdhor's family record, trusting to Saldhor's sagacity. Tradition has always been that when the foresight of an Enaisi is offered, it is given weight as if law. I can name many precedents. He cannot be faulted. And your standing in the clan is solid."

Tam shot to her feet. "Then let us get Uncle out of that cell!"

"We must first reconvene and explain exoneration to the ones who called Question," Andhrel said.

"And if they still try to argue or do not agree to drop their dispute?" Tam asked.

"They must have legal grounds to continue. They have none. Is this not correct, Mattan?"

"Aye. You need not worry, Tam."

"But can we hurry? Uncle is in a dark cell and knows not what we have discovered! And he must be very cold and hungry and scared."

"Worry not, Tam," Eladhrel said, grasping her shoulder with a smile. "Put your anxiety to rest."

"Anxiety?" Haladhon exclaimed. "Is that what you call it?"

"Leave off, cousin," Andhrel murmured, then more loudly, "Shall we summon those Rangers and explain all to them?"

"By all means," Haladhon growled.

~*~

Alcandhor stared at the stone walls, listening to the gurgle of water in the basin at the corner of the cell. Earlier he heard a dull booming, likely drums, but he could not ascertain enough to know what they said. It mattered not. Lamadhel could only confirm what must be done according to the law. He waited for the inevitable now. Would they deliver sentence tonight or wait until morning?

A rattle at the door sent a sharp, painful shiver through his body, and he clenched his fists in his lap. Light flooded in from Baidhrol's torch as in a hushed voice he said, "The chiefs bid me tell you they require your presence."

How did his hammering heart not break his ribs? He followed the young Ranger up the stairs, feeling the cold deepen as they left the depths of the cells. As he exited the door of the tower, the hair on his arms rose, but not from the chill night air.

The stubborn fog rendered the many torches hazy, amid a darker cloud filling the grounds. Stars, 'twas people! Every Ranger, and all other kin in the city as well, seemed to be present. Were they all wishing to see their former Thane stripped of rank, status, and clan? Did so many despise him?

His morbid thoughts halted as all the men went down on one knee, inclining their heads, and the women responded similarly, either curtsying or bowing. His fists clenched. One did not behave so to a man disowned, even if he had been Thane! He stepped toward the nearest men to jerk them to their feet, but before he could take more than one pace, several Rangers at the front rose—the ones who had called Question. They bowed again and walked forward.

"Thane, we apologize for our actions," Pendhras said with stiff formality. "We called Question without understanding the situation and do know now that you have been faultless in your duties. We beg your forgiveness."

Words failed Alcandhor. He was guilty—he had admitted it. He stared at the man in total bewilderment, then heard Haladhon laughing nearby. "He is lost! More so than in a complete fog in Hillsdown. Look at his face! Stars, 'Candhor, I wish I could have it painted!"

Haladhon could laugh? Now? What in the names of both moons was happening? He peered into the mist for his cousin.

"You are cruel, Haladhon," Tam's voice called. She strode out of the dark haze, her arms out. "It is all right. Your father entered my birth record years ago. But it was sealed by order of an Enaisi, my mother."

She embraced him, but stepped back as his children ran up, tears on their faces. The news washed over Alcandhor as he knelt, hugging them tightly, relief flooding through him, his own face wet. Hands caressed his hair in a familiar manner. Taniss. He stood and embraced his mother, then Sarinna threw her arms around his neck, almost pulling him off balance. His shoulders were grasped, his back clouted, then Haladhon grabbed him and shook him, still laughing.

His Second at Table knelt and held out his dagger. "Take back all that is due you, our Thane."

Smiling, he accepted the weapon and sheathed it. Someone must have coached her on the words. Tam rose and bowed.

"Come, eat, *Thane*," Sarinna said.

"Aye, you must be starved, Thane," said someone from nearby, then a general clamor arose, and he was pulled in the direction of the Great Hall. He picked up Amara and managed to walk with both sons trying to hug him. Haladhon's hand still rested on his shoulder as his friend and cousin strode besides him. "How fared you as Thane?" Even as he asked, he amazed himself that he could speak lightly of what had almost cost him all.

"Oh, he was magnificent," Marcalan said. "He waged war on all the furniture in the conclave chamber on your behalf."

They all laughed—Haladhon as well, despite his embarrassed grin.

The good mood prevailed as they entered the Great Hall, and Ganill herself brought out a platter filled with juicy slices of herdbeast, then patted Alcandhor's shoulder before going back to the kitchen. He exchanged grins with Haladhon; who would have thought their head cook would ever show him affection? She had named them both a bane to her kitchens when they were lads. Scullery work was frequently given to naughty boys at Zaidhron, but the two of them often found as much mischief to get into while working in her kitchens as anywhere else.

Amara sat on his lap, burying her face in his hair and chest, and his boys hung on his arms with a desperation borne of the horror they must have lived through for those few hours thinking they had lost their father.

With a soulful pout, his daughter placed one hand on each side of his face. "Papa, you must never worry me again!"

Alcandhor kept the smile off his face, barely, wanting to laugh and cry at the same time. Instead, he met her expression and tone. "I will remember, Littlest."

"Jholinn and I cried and cried worrying about you."

"I am sorry, Sweetest. But it is over."

His baby girl snuggled against him with a happy sigh.

Alcandhor did not mind trying to eat with three children clinging to him; he had them and would not lose them. His nightmare was over. The realization of that still sank in, no more dread. How long would it take before he felt free of that shroud that enveloped him for years?

When he finished eating, Rangers and close kin descended on him again, and the ale flowed freely. The city seemed ready to celebrate all night.

Jholinn came over to take Amara to bed, her eyes red and puffy.

He picked up his daughter. "I will go with you and settle her in. Today was difficult for her, I think it will be more comforting with me there."

"Then do you wish me there, too?" Jholinn asked.

"Aye, if you mind it not. Amara likes you there as she falls asleep."

"I don't mind, sir."

Why must she always look away when he tried to talk to her? He smiled at his sons. "Wish you to go with us to Family North? It is almost your time to ready for bed anyway."

Both lads eagerly accepted, and as they crossed the sward in the deepening fog, he asked how their Training was, and listened as Eladhor told a story of how two Trainees found out the hard way that they should not try to practice falls until they have been taught how.

Alcandhor chuckled. "And how bruised are they?"

"All black and purple, Papa. But Cordhan said that would teach them."

"Indeed."

The walk seemed too short, even holding Amara most of the time. The boys readied for bed, while Jholinn helped his daughter into her nightclothes. He then sat on the sofa, hugging them and telling them he was proud of them, and that he wished he could take them with him to the conclave. "But you boys will both go to Laird Hall with me when you are striplings. And will be there often when you are chiefs one day."

They asked questions about Laird Hall and the Laird himself. Alcandhor answered them, and they spent a little time playing and tickling. Finally he said, "Time to sleep."

"You are not staying with us?" Eladhor asked.

"I should go back to the Great Hall for a little while. Wish you Jholinn to stay here until I return?"

Teldhor rolled his eyes. "I am almost a stripling. I need not be watched over."

"Then you will be responsible for your little sister, and not tease or frighten her?"

Lifting his chin, Teldhor said, "I would not do such a thing!"

"With that response, I think I need Jholinn to stay to watch over Amara until I return," he said dryly.

"Truly, Father. I will care for her."

At Alcandhor's skeptical gaze, Teldhor shook his head, his eyes wide. "Upon my vow as a Ranger!"

"You are not yet a Ranger, son," he said, laughing.

"I am almost a stripling."

Still smiling, he nodded. "With your vow, and knowing Eladhor will likely tell on you, I think I will trust you to watch over Amara."

He hugged both boys and after they had gotten into bed, he picked up his daughter. "Wish you me to rock you to sleep, or to put you straight to bed?"

"Rock me, Papa."

She wrapped her legs and arms around him as he walked to the chair and sat down. How long he cuddled her he knew not, but finally she fell asleep. He rose, hoping not to wake her, and Jholinn pulled the blankets back for him. Gently, he placed his daughter in her bed and covered her. He brushed her dark blond curls back from her face and softly kissed her forehead. Such a feisty little bundle she was.

Alcandhor and the widow silently left the suite. As the door closed, he said, "I am at peace knowing she has you, Jholinn. I thank you again for taking on the burden of a child that is not yours."

"It is my delight to care for her, sir."

"I am deeply in your debt, nonetheless."

She averted her eyes, curtsied, and headed toward the stairs.

"Jholinn? You are not returning to the Great Hall?"

"N–no, sir."

"Then I wish you night's rest." He bowed.

"Sir?" She met his eyes as she murmured, "I am so glad..." Her gaze dropped, and she finished in a softer voice, "I am glad you are free."

"I thank you, Jholinn."

She nodded, then dipped in second curtsey, whirled, and hurried down the staircase.

Alcandhor stood for a moment, frowning, before heading down the corridor. Ah well, he had more important things to concern himself with than a young Ranger widow who disliked him.

The chill of the walk across Avadhron's Sward did not touch him; relief warmed him through. Entering the Great Hall, he searched for his close kin. They gathered around Pendhras, who, by his gesticulating, made excuses for his actions.

Alcandhor drew close in time to hear the man say, "We were only obeying the law—"

Taniss interrupted with a slap across his face that echoed a sharp crack. The older Ranger's head slung back at the assault, then he gaped. Alcandhor winced in remembered pain—his mother had a strong arm. Pendhras straightened up, the whole side of his face blotchy red.

"Liar!"

"Dare you call me a liar, woman?"

"You will address me as Lady Taniss, Ranger. I am your clan matriarch. And aye, I call you a liar. Do you tell me that if Tam came to Zaidhron wearing a skirt instead of Ranger garb you would have called Question on my son about her birth record? Ah, you probably would, enh? You had your own agenda, ever wishing to strip my son of his legal claim to Thaneship, defying the authority of the chiefs. Even knowing the wishes of an Enaisi were involved, still you would wish to press your suit against my son if you could."

"Nay, I—"

Her fingers jabbed his chest. "Your hatred blinds you. So do not point to the law as an excuse. Take responsibility for your own actions. That is what my son did, even though he thought it would cost him all he had."

Under her steady gaze, Pendhras hesitantly bowed and walked away.

Alcandhor crept silently behind her, grinning at Haladhon, whose eyes twinkled, then quick as a viper, he slid his hands around his mother's waist, kissing her cheek. She stiffened a moment, then leaned back into him, her hands caressing his arms. He murmured into her ear, "You are a wicked woman, Taniss."

"So your father used to say."

He chuckled. "I am glad I have not received such a slap in years. I remember the sting full well."

"You deserved them, as I recall. You could be a handful."

"Me? I was always the good son."

She turned around, an eyebrow rising. "Good at getting into mischief, you mean." She seized hair from his chin beard in her fingers and tugged hard enough to make his head jerk down—his eyes widened at the sudden assault. "You ever frighten me like that again, and I will thrash you until you are blistered!"

"Aye, Mum," he whispered, then realized how ridiculous for the Thane to be upbraided by his mother in public. He chortled, wrapping his arms around her more tightly.

"Stars, what ails you, son?"

He could not reply for laughing. As his mirth subsided, he kissed her on the forehead. "Will you dance with me?"

The light in her eyes was answer enough, and Alcandhor proudly led his mother to the dance floor.

~*~

Before heading to his family suite, Alcandhor stopped in the chiefs' range to make sure the conclave chamber was set in order. Secretly, he wanted to see if Marcalan had been exaggerating about the furniture.

What was once a chair indeed lay against the wall, reduced to kindling. A smile tugged at Alcandhor's lips. Fortunately, nothing else seemed to have been a victim of Haladhor's temper.

At the sound of a boot scuffing, he looked up. Mattan stood in the doorway, arms crossed, a frown on his face.

"What is it?"

"You were almost mutilated and disowned by your own people over a birth record," the alien said with disgust.

Alcandhor stared at him, confused. "Do you have a question about the law?"

"Nay, a comment."

"And that is?"

"Your laws stink."

"Pardon me?"

"You heard me. They reek like a dung heap."

He drew himself up, fists clenching, meeting his ancestor's gaze. "You vowed to live by our laws when you became part of our clan."

"To abide by them, aye, to agree with them, nay." Mattan pointed a finger at Alcandhor. "You explain how the punishment fits the crime."

"Clan Law—"

"Spare the speeches, Thane. You don't know the debates Zaidhron and I had over your laws. I will never understand the importance your people place on clans and family. But to do what they would have done to you over something as simple as a birth record, I cannot fathom it."

"It does not matter which Clan Law was broken, it was the fact that Clan Law is High Law. If I were a parent who had neglected duty, the discipline set would be very different. But when I became Thane, I took a vow to uphold our laws. I am considered the embod—"

"'The embodiment of the law,' yes, I know," Mattan said in a derisive tone, "I have heard it all many times. And as the embodiment of the law, if you are found guilty of breaking High Law, the highest penalty is automatically passed."

"Exactly." Why was the Enaisi so disturbed over something so easy to understand?

"*Tohni teg'ha.*"

Alcandhor stepped forward at that vile expletive in Amhan'ai. "That is not a comment I would expect to hear from a Ranger chief."

"You have not heard such sentiments from a chief before, Thane? Haladhon feels much as I do."

"Haladhon—" He stopped, grinding his teeth for a moment in an effort to control himself. This was a sore spot for him; he had fought desperately more than once to keep his cousin from coming under condemnation for his indiscretions. He took a deep breath and in a calmer tone answered, "Haladhon is a bitter man."

"Do you think I don't know that?"

Alcandhor was not going to discuss his best friend. At least, not now. He went back to their original topic of contention. "Our laws are sometimes harsh, I deny that not. But they are not debatable. The lesser laws may be amended, but not the High Laws, not by other than a king's decree. And we have no king. You know this, so why do you contend with me? I cannot change them."

"Because I am furious!" Mattan waved his arms, his eyes flashing black. "Your law condemned you, and you were willing to sacrifice yourself, and aye, I know you would do so again, which further infuriates me."

"Do not make me sound like some noble martyr."

"I hope to make you sound like a fool!"

"I will not argue with you. It is done."

"Is it? What if Question is called again? What will you do?"

"How can I answer that? I know not what I might do unless given exact circumstances. Why does this bother you so?"

Mattan stepped forward, grasping Alcandhor's shoulders, mingled chastisement and affection flowing from him. "I thought I had lost a son today."

He swallowed heavily as he stared into the dark, intense eyes. *Do not block me, my son.*

Not wanting any more exhausting emotions to break his control, he turned away from the alien. "Whether you agree with them or not, you have vowed to live by our laws. Discussions such as this are fruitless, High Laws cannot be changed."

"You had alternatives today. You did not have to accept guilt and punishment."

"I did what I felt I had to do!"

"Just promise me if a similar situation occurs you will not dismiss your options!"

"Leave off! It has been a long and exhausting day, I need this not." Alcandhor's voice broke, and he inwardly winced.

The alien slowly let out his breath. "I apologize. You are right, this is not the time."

Jaw clenched, he could not answer if he were to keep his emotions in check. The silence stretched out and became awkward, but he would not move. He dared not.

Mattan cleared his throat. "I bid you night's rest, my son."

After the Enaisi left, Alcandhor took a shuddering breath and ran his hands through his long hair.

Chapter Thirteen

The next day, Alcandhor gathered the chiefs to him for the morning meeting. Tam ordered the reports, after all the routine matters had been taken care of, and Alcandhor apprised them all of what Casinn said before jumping from the allure, with strict instruction they were to dismiss any questions brought up concerning it.

"She was not nice," Tam said, staring absently ahead. "The first day I was here, she acted very superior to me." Tipping her head, she continued, "But I am sorry she is dead."

Marcalan rubbed her back, and she returned a slight smile. Would that his niece always maintained such a tender heart. Alcandhor took a deep breath and asked, "Any other business?"

Haladhon sneered, "Other than the Rangers who had called Question scattering like crid bugs? Nay."

"Not those from Dandrin Shire, though, surely?"

"Nay. Most in the city are not pleased with them, so they creep about or stay in quarters, since they have no duty."

"As soon as Gardhal arrives, we shall see if they return to duty." Alcandhor rubbed his hands on the table. "Now, a message has arrived from Lord Krendhal, I hear?"

"Aye." Andhrel held up a paper. "He suggests we bring scribes with us to Laird Hall."

"Does he say why?"

The law-keeper shook his head. "Perhaps there is doubt about the veracity of some of Laird Hall's scribes, and he does not wish to say so."

"That is a possibility." Marcalan arched his back in a stretch. "So who shall we take?"

"How many does he suggest?" Alcandhor asked.

"Three."

"Maradhor is my first choice, of course." Alcandhor looked at Andhrel. "Who else?"

"Jonadhan was sent on from Pashelon to Laird Hall. Is Lord Krendhal aware he is a scribe?"

"I know not. Possibly, but I will not assume. We shall bring three as requested. I would recommend Riladhral." Alcandhor frowned. "He is teaching, though. Have we anyone who can replace him?"

"Aye, leave that to me," Andhrel said. "With Delgan in judicious charge of recovering documents from the Portal Complex, there is much to do. I will set our journeymen those tasks to keep them busy, and we have enough master scribes to oversee their work." His cousin grinned. "The apprentices already are moaning at all the extra nibs they must cut with this new industry, as well as all the fetching of more paper, the making of more ink, and message running."

Alcandhor smiled, but kept on topic. "Think you Mordhal is ready?"

Andhrel nodded. "He has been to some arbitrations, and his copy work is exemplary."

"Then we have our three."

"Thane, why are you taking only scribes who are also Rangers?" asked Marcalan.

"'Tis generally a safe profession, but since we know not why Lord Krendhal has requested Ch'shalna scribes, and not knowing if there might be traitors still lurking in Laird Hall, I would rather take those who can easily defend themselves."

Marcalan nodded. "It is good for the guards at Laird Hall who are still in training, as Maradhor is a most excellent teacher of swordsmanship as well."

"A point." Andhrel smiled, leaning back and running a hand through his light red hair. "We have not many dual masters."

Eladhrel chuckled. "What else does he have to do with his time? He has no wife."

Tam frowned, her expression puzzled. "But Maradhor is old. He has as many years as you, Uncle, does he not? Why has he never married?"

Alcandhor tapped the table with his finger, pursing his lips. Stars. He supposed he did seem old to a lass having but fifteen years. What must she then think of her great-uncle Lamadhel, or of Edhron? "He has a few years on me, he is your father's age. But your question has never been answered satisfactorily, and this meeting is not the place to conjecture about it." He smiled to let Tam know he was not seriously chastising her. "I would caution you though, my dear niece, to not ask Maradhor. He seems as smitten with you as the rest of us, but you might find you have crossed a line."

She looked ready to pursue the subject, but her large, golden eyes slid to Marcalan, and she gave a brief nod and subsided. Stars, would he even become accustomed to those two having mental discussions?

A knock at the door interrupted Alcandhor before he could dismiss the meeting.

Gardhal entered, carrying a thick packet, his face red from the chill and probably from journeying at a fast pace much of the way from the valley. Indeed, he must have been up before dawn to arrive so early.

"The results of my investigation, my Thane. Wish you me to stay?"

"Nay, go warm yourself and eat while we review them. And I thank you."

Alcandhor read the first report, then handed it to Tam, and from her, they made their way around to each chief.

Alcandhor's ire rose, and by the time he finished the last paper, he slammed a hand on the table. "We are calling conclave."

"Bells, Thane!" Haladhon gestured about the room. "We each need to read these."

"Do you not all agree from what you have seen so far?"

"Aye," Andhrel murmured. "But let us all finish, Thane."

"Besides, Lamadhel is not here," Haladhon said.

"This is not High Law. We have a quorum. And Mattan."

"Now wait, I have never voted as a chief!"

"Aye, but you can listen. And offer your opinion. And more so than even Tam, you can sense the accused."

"Is that considered legal? Or proper?"

"'Tis not illegal. Those of us with Enaisi blood have always used our abilities in arbitration as we deemed necessary. How much more an actual Enaisi?"

"But a conclave is not arbitration."

"I have spoken, Chief Mattan."

The dark alien lifted his hands and let them fall into his lap.

Alcandhor leaned back. "Haladhon—nay, Tam, as my Second, after this meeting see to it a Ranger is posted at my door when we leave. I want no one in here but chiefs until after the conclave. Also, apprise Rendhol and Gardhal they may be needed as witnesses."

Tam nodded, then gazed down at the document in her hands. Fuming, Alcandhor rose and paced until Haladhon pleaded with him to be still and not distract his reading. He returned to his chair and thudded into it, grinding his teeth, waiting for all the chiefs to finish. Mattan placed each report into a pile. When, finally, the last one had been added, Alcandhor asked again, "Do you agree we should call conclave?"

Faces grim, they all nodded.

"Then since the Rangers in question are to hand, we shall call conclave later today. Directly following luncheon. Tam, another duty. Advise Maradhor of the conclave, we will need him as scribe." Alcandhor stood. "We are adjourned."

Hopefully, some hard matches would knock the edge off the anger those reports caused.

~*~

Washed and refreshed, although a bit sore, Alcandhor strode to his chair. Families scurried to their places in anticipation of the gong. Amara stood next to her grandmother and reached her arms up to her father with a smile.

"Where is Jholinn?" Alcandhor asked his mother as he picked up his daughter.

"With Sarinna, probably dining privately in Thane Hall."

"Sarinna?"

"Aye. She has become her new assistant. And I am instructing her as well."

"You—? But why?"

"Amara will soon be of an age to not need her. During her free time, she is learning new duties. She must have something besides her widow's allotment to live on. And she is not the type to be idle."

Alcandhor could see that, but he always imagined her with children. Granted, that was likely because he only ever saw her with his own, but... "And what are you teaching her?"

"Hospitality. I do not wish to take on all those duties as when I was the wife of the Thane, and Sarinna cannot constantly be shouldering the double load when we have visitors. And I think we shall have many more now that, hopefully, the nearer provincial lords are not traitors. Indeed, we already do, mostly history-keepers, due to the attraction of this handsome alien." Taniss nodded to Mattan, standing next to her, and he inclined his head with a smile.

"But that position has never been apart from the Thane's family."

"And who in the Thane's family do you suggest assume that duty, enh? Jholinn is more than capable, and has been almost as family in her love and attention to the children. Besides her care of Amara, you know well she has washed scrapes and bruises, settled fights, and tended your boys through sicknesses."

"I do not deny that. She has my undying gratitude. I could not have asked for a better carer than she has proven to be."

His mother's inscrutable expression confounded him, especially since the main emotion he sensed from her was exasperation. Over what? Did she think he did not appreciate all that young woman had done for his family?

"Ah, my son," she murmured, shaking her head. "You had best sit before Ganill comes out to see why the gong has not rung."

Alcandhor obeyed his mother. His perplexity over this change concerning Jholinn and his turbulent thoughts of the conclave lessened with the task of urging his daughter to eat her greens.

~*~

The chiefs and Maradhor all gathered outside Thane Hall, cloaks pulled tight against the bitter wind.

Alcandhor nodded, sending his children inside ahead of them. They had not been happy about going to the tutoring class today instead of staying with their father for lessons.

Mattan inclined his head toward the door. "Shall we then start this conclave?"

"You are in such a hurry to proceed?"

"The sooner this mess is started, the sooner it is finished."

Alcandhor could not disagree. "Then let us go up."

Gardhal and Rendhol gave testimony first, with the chiefs asking questions and taking personal notes of the various reports. Maradhor studiously scribed all from his side table.

Afterwards, the Rangers were called in one at a time. Fandhrel clumped in to stand at the end of the table, his expression one of mingled disgust and martyrdom. Alcandhor took in his appearance as he pondered what little he knew of the man, other than his constant harping that Alcandhor was too weak to be Thane. His glowering brows dominated his round face, and despite his Training, he tended to slouch. The Ranger had been shuffled between several bounds over the years, appealing for reassignment for various reasons, some seemingly tenuous. This last posting had been at Pendhras' request.

Tam rose and read the charges. Fandhrel cut her off, spluttering denials.

"You will cease," she commanded. "You do not interrupt, Ranger."

Alcandhor resisted raising his eyebrows at her imperious tone but was secretly pleased that she took charge. It was her responsibility after all, as Second at Table. And future Thane. And she did have experience, having done this same duty with the traitors on trial at Laird Hall after the siege.

Fandhrel's lip curled, but he obeyed, staring at the chiefs with an angry, puzzled expression and growing increasingly indignant.

Finished with the charges, Tam asked, "Have you anything to say, Ranger Fandhrel? Any circumstances which might mitigate the weight of the evidence we have presented?"

"Words of farmers? Of clanless nothings? This is not evidence, but empty mouthings. I have done nothing wrong!"

Andhrel jabbed a finger on the table. "You are accused of intimidating townspeople and farmers for no more purpose than to preen at your power over them, and you have done nothing wrong? You broke

124

one tradesman's window when he dared speak up, and threatened harm to not only him but his family if he reported it, and you have done nothing wrong? You incited two families to continue their feud, openly stating the Thane would do nothing to them, and giving each of them misinformation or outright lies concerning the other family to fuel their contention, to name only a few incidents. And you have done nothing wrong?"

"They are all lies. That window was broken by accident. The two families—"

"These are all corroborated statements of witnesses of the various events," Andhrel replied. "They are not lies, Ranger! If you have nothing else you can add, you are dismissed."

"I stand by what I have said. The truth has been twisted. I am the one besmirched."

Fandhrel was led out, and Inradhor replaced him at the end of the table. This Ranger waited silently while the charges were read, his lean face flushed and gaze downcast. Alcandhor took in the lanky youth with fair hair and pale grey eyes, shoulders hunched as he was called to account on his first bounds. He knew little of the young man, being distant as kin, and not raised in Zaidhron. His family lived in Lantral and were thrilled to have a son recommended to a bounds in Thane Valley. What would they feel now?

When Tam finished and asked for a response, he said, "You do not understand what we Rangers face. These clanless have no understanding. Perhaps we went beyond what we should at times, but—"

"I can sense, Ranger," Tam spat. "Your guilt attaints you, yet you make excuses. Did you enjoy the sensation of power over the people you are supposed to protect?"

Inradhor's eyes widened, his face blanching. "Nay, I—"

"So you merely incited trouble for what reason?" Haladhon asked. "You feel the Thane is weak, so you cause disturbance instead of keeping peace? How does that show weakness in the Thane? Does it not rather show weakness of character of Rangers?"

Eladhrel clenched a fist on the table. "You speak of these farmers and townspeople as if all were clanless, which is not the case. This bespeaks of mere mouthings you have heard from Fandhrel, Pendhras, and others perhaps. Have you no mind of your own? Do you truly find those in your bounds are—without course—ignorant, unlearned, and incapable of reason?" He half rose out of his chair. "And even if true, what of that matters in keeping order and dispensing justice? Do Rangers weigh out our laws with variable scales by clan or rank or education?"

Inradhor's head dropped, and Alcandhor did not need to sense to know his shame.

"I asked you a question, Ranger Inradhor."

Alcandhor leaned back at Eladhrel's vehemence.

"Nay, sir, we do not."

"Then what reason—not excuse, but proper reason, do you give for your actions and behavior?"

"I...I have none, sir," Inradhor murmured.

"Do you admit to the charges, then?" Eladhrel asked.

"Aye. I do," he muttered.

After a short silence, Tam said, "You are dismissed."

Inradhor shuffled out, and Pendhras sailed in, head high, openly sneering. Being a Child of the Enaisi, he did not look the seventy-three years he had. Grey barely started in his dark hair, just above his ears, and a streak downward from his mouth on each side of his chin beard. His skin had only a slight weather-beaten appearance, despite his having roamed a bounds for many years. His brown eyes narrowed, glaring into Alcandhor's.

Tam rose to read the charges to Pendhras, but he spat, "I do not recognize the authority of a trous-donning trull in Ranger clothes!"

The chiefs all shot to their feet, their chairs either scudding back or falling over. Eladhrel grabbed Marcalan's arm as he surged forward. Amid all their denunciations of Pendhras' statement, Mattan's rose above them all: "You will not speak in that manner to the daughter of my sister!"

"She is a female, she ought not be a Ranger!"

"Why not? Women were Trained as Security in Ch'shalna clan back on Teledhar. Many were Elites, several on Chief Avadhron's own team. They only reason they put a moratorium on females as Security, later just called Rangers, was because your population was so diminished they did not wish to chance losing even one woman to more dangers than was necessary. It was never meant to be permanent. And you read my sister's letter to Thane Saldhor last night, where she claimed sight that Tam needed to stay with her father be Trained. Do you deny this?"

"I do not deny it, but I know not that was truly your sister's writing."

"Bells and stars, think you I know not my sister's hand?" Mattan stopped and drew himself up, fists on hips. "You deny anything which does not fit reality as you wish it to be. Very well. Tam, read the indictments."

All the chiefs sat, save Tam. She glanced at Alcandhor, one eyebrow lifted, then at Mattan.

"I do not recog—" Pendhras' protest ended in a groan, and he doubled over.

Tam lifted her chin, lips thinned. "You will be silent while the charges are read."

Pendhras straightened slowly, fists clenched. "You are no Ranger, much less a chief. I have no need to obey you."

Eladhrel slammed a fist on the table. "What gives you the right to choose which chiefs have authority over you?"

"To sharpen the blade," Alcandhor added in a low voice, "what law gives you the right to *choose* who are the chiefs?"

"She is no—"

"I asked you a question, Ranger. What law allows *you* to choose who is a chief?"

Pendhras met Alcandhor's gaze with open hatred, but said nothing.

"Answer the question. What law?"

"Females are not—"

"What law?" Alcandhor repeated.

Pendhras glanced from one to another, his lips compressed. "I can state no law."

"Because there is no law. You do not choose who are the chiefs. That is by birth and Training."

"If Lamadhel were here, he would back me! A woman as a Ranger, much less a chief?"

Andhrel burst into laughter. "My father backs Tam as a Confirmed Ranger, chief, and future Thane. If he were here, he would likely knock you topside-down for this insolence."

"'Tis not possible."

"The transcripts of the conclave Confirming Tam as a Ranger, and of the second stating she is heir to Thane are both available to read. Maradhor was the scribe at both conclaves, and sits there. Wish you to ask him of the content?" Andhrel lifted a hand. "You may speak, Ranger Maradhor."

Pendhras turned, lips thinned, to the side table.

The Ranger scribe's wide-set brown eyes sparkled. "I can attest that Lamadhel backed Tamissa, daughter of Valdhor, as a Confirmed Ranger, as Second at Table, and as heir to Thane."

"But she is a *lass*! Women are not—"

"By all the stars in the sky, man," Eladhrel said, "can you not accept that your prejudices have no foundation? Does the tradition of the past carry more weight than the law?"

"If the law is what we follow blindly, then why does Haladhon still wear a jerkin when he has flouted it continuously?"

"Ah, nay," Andhrel said. "He is not on trial. You are. And you splutter and stall in even allowing the accusations to be heard. Do you then fear your own guilt is that apparent?"

"He should be on trial! He has—"

"Enough," Alcandhor said. "*You* are on trial. The charges will be read, with your consent or without it."

"I will not be silent while a bawd—" Pendhras stopped, gasping, his eyes wide, one hand clutching his throat.

Mattan nodded at Tam, and she recited the list of charges and then looked up. "What have you to say in your defense, Ranger?"

Pendhras exhaled loudly and leaned over, hands on his knees, panting. He slowly straightened. "What did you do to me, Enaisi?"

Alcandhor wanted to know the same thing. It was as if he were able to choke the man with his mind. And, thinking on it, was that what he did to silence Nandhal as well? He would have to ask the Elder afterwards—he had never heard of the Enaisi causing physical reactions. Although... Tam, they had discovered, could send pain to another. Perhaps this was similar. He kept his peace for the moment; now was not the time.

"What do you think I did, my son?"

"I am not your son!"

"Oh, you are. Unfortunately. I have looked into the genealogy of every Child of the Enaisi. You are a descendent both of me and my friend Ashani. And I can assure you she would be not only ashamed but furious at your willful pride and disdain for the law, ah"—he held up a hand—"unless it suits your purpose, of course. So tell me, what explanation can you give for your actions in the valley? And if you cannot back up your reason by stating a law, we none wish to hear it. Do not speak of lies or being besmirched, we have too many witnesses as to your guilt."

"It appears you will accept nothing from me but full confession and penitence. So I will give you the former. But I am not sorry for any of my actions. They were done to further my clan, which has sunk to disgrace."

"How will inciting a feud raise the clan?" Eladhrel asked. "Or causing unrest?"

"Enough, Eladhrel," Mattan said. "He will not listen."

"Aye, I agree," Alcandhor said. "You are dismissed, Pendhras."

The Ranger shot a disdainful glare at Alcandhor and marched out smirking as if he had beaten the indictments and emerged victor.

"By all the stars and both moons," Eladhrel murmured.

"He is so deluded, I think no reality can touch him," Mattan said.

"Being denounced, made clanless, branded, and cut off might touch him," Haladhon growled.

"I want to avoid creating any more Rogues," Alcandhor said softly, tracing a whorl in the table's wood grain.

"And that was exactly what Pendhras was thinking, Thane," Mattan replied. "You are too soft and will do nothing to him."

"I allowed you could sense, not read minds, Enaisi. I expect you to adhere to your moral code."

"My apologies, Thane. I admit my guilt, but felt in his case, a slight brushing of his surface thoughts might be telling. Although one needed only see his attitude as he left to know what he thought and felt."

"Then you should not have brushed his thoughts." Alcandhor stared at Mattan a moment, until the alien inclined his head. "Let us confer about judgment."

~*~

Seemingly endless discussion took place, but finally, Alcandhor ordered each man be brought in to hear judgment.

Firstly, Inradhor, who held himself rigidly as he listened to Tam read the chiefs' decision that he be stripped of rank, standing, and status. His shoulders sagged, but when told he might regain what he lost, a sense of hopeful disbelief radiated from him.

As was custom, his Thane stood before him as he unlaced his jerkin, the sign and pride of every Ranger. His face contorted, and he swallowed repeatedly. He squeezed the soft leather of the jerkin in his fists, clutched to his chest for a long moment before he handed it to Alcandhor. With unshed tears in his eyes, he whispered, "I will earn it back, Thane. I vow this!"

"I will hold you to that vow, Inradhor."

The ex-Ranger bowed and fled out the door.

Fandhrel sauntered in, head high albeit frowning. Was he shaken by seeing Inradhor rush out without his jerkin?

Without preamble, Tam read his judgment, stripped of all save clan affiliation, but he cut her off before she could finish.

"This is a mistake! This is wrong!"

"You will be silent while I read, man," Tam ordered.

Alcandhor pursed his lips to keep from smiling at her usage of *man* instead of *Ranger*.

"But I broke no laws. I upheld them! The ignorance of those in the valley is—"

"You will be silent." Tam's voice came out commanding, sounding much like her father.

Fandhrel blinked as she finished reading aloud.

"If there is no avocation you have studied, as some Rangers are wont to do, we shall appoint you to a work position which requires no training," Eladhrel said. "Do you have anything that you may use to earn a living, man?"

"Nay. I have ever only been a Ranger."

"Then we shall consider positions and offer you a choice. I would vote for farm hand in the valley. Or perhaps you would prefer to stay in the city? You could be drudge for the Training halls, enh, or haul the midden?"

Alcandhor put his fist over his mouth, feigning a cough to keep control. Eladhrel usually was the most mellow of his chiefs. What had brought about this vehemence?

Andhrel added, "Also, considering your penchant for mouthings against the Thane and the chiefs, you will likely be monitored to see that you do not try to incite discontent."

His upper lip curling, Fandhrel seemed about to reply, but Mattan spoke first. "You will only make your situation worse with any outburst. You have lost almost everything. You are still Ch'shalna clan. Hold fast to that, or you will truly lose all."

Hand held out, Alcandhor stepped forward. Fandhrel's fists clenched and unclenched before he reluctantly unlaced his jerkin. Unlike Inradhor, there was no sorrow, no sense of tragic loss, just a banked-down fury, much like a tantrum held in check. The man whipped off the jerkin and threw it down.

Through gritted teeth, Alcandhor ordered, "You will pick up that jerkin and hand it to the Thane of your clan as is protocol, man."

"Or what?"

"We can always choose a harsher course for you. Do you wish to be branded, cut off, and disowned?"

"You would never dare."

Alcandhor hissed, "Try me."

Confusion flitted across Fandhrel's features. Finally, he blinked and then bent to pick up the jerkin. He looked away, hatred emanating from him, as he held it out. Alcandhor accepted it, and Fandhrel stormed out.

Turning to Eladhrel, Alcandhor said, "Stars, man, you have become decidedly severe and outspoken of a sudden!"

His cousin's face flushed. "I may be a second son, but I am a chief."

Alcandhor frowned. "Have I—or anyone else—ever suggested otherwise?"

"Nay, but..." Eladhrel licked his lips. "I have felt it in myself."

"And now you do not?"

With a sheepish smile, his cousin shook his head.

Alcandhor lifted his brows, but did not inquire further given his cousin's silence. After a pause, he gestured toward the door. "Let us finish this."

Pendhras openly seethed as he stood before them. He did keep silent at first while Tam read, but when she said that he would be stripped of rank, standing, and status he cursed. Mattan shot to his feet, and Pendhras, his neck cords straining, fell to his knees, clawing at his throat.

Alcandhor rose, lifting a hand. Tam stopped reading. Mattan slowly sat while Pendhras struggled to his feet, gasping for air.

Holding out a hand to stop his niece from continuing, Alcandhor said, "As my Second at Table has pronounced, you are stripped of rank, status, and standing. For *now*, you remain in Ch'shalna clan, but that may change." He stepped around the table to face Pendhras. The man's fists clenched and unclenched.

"You have manipulated others—both Rangers under your command and the residents of the shire in which you are supposed to *serve*—in order to further your own ends, and for what purpose, man? What did you wish to accomplish? Creating strife and causing chaos in one shire of the many in that valley? You claim I am weak, but how does any of this prove that? Is your mind so small and your hatred of me so complete you cannot see beyond the reach of your hand?"

Pendhras' lips peeled back from his teeth, his brown eyes now black with rage.

"We have discussed whether to cast you out, cut off and branded, but that takes more than a quorum. To be disowned requires the vote of every chief. We are sending the full transcript of this conclave to Lamadhel. He shall need time to peruse it, and when we arrive at Laird Hall, we shall convene there to render our decision—"

"It is not right it is done away from Zaidhron—"

"Do not interrupt your Thane!" Alcandhor kept his voice low and even. "If Lamadhel has questions, or doubts, then we shall wait until we all return here. Until a decision is made, you are remanded to the cells."

"What! How dare you!"

"I have spoken."

Pendhras launched at Alcandhor with a snarl, but doubled over and fell to the floor. Alcandhor twisted to see all the chiefs on their feet, faces grim. He sought Mattan's gaze, however 'twas not the alien this time, but Tam.

Her eyes gleamed black, her countenance fierce. "You dare attack the Thane?"

Moaning, Pendhras fought to an upright position on his knees. "If only you had died at Lairdton. If only Tanadhon had succeeded!"

131

"Do you say you were in league with him?" Andhrel asked.

"Nay. I am no traitor. I only wish this weak excuse for a Thane dead."

Stunned, Alcandhor found no words would form. Could this man not see such a statement itself was treason?

"You have brought sentence upon yourself," Eladhrel said softly. "We have no need now to send for Lamadhel, only to inform him of the outcome."

In the silence, Alcandhor could feel their eyes on him. Staring at the floor, he murmured, "You ever said your loyalty was to Valdhor. Yet you did not see that my brother called me Thane, accepted me. Backed me as Thane."

"Aye," Tam whispered. "In the Great Hall, in front of everyone, he censured Loch'alan for how he addressed the Thane."

"Even more, he protected me in the ambush, not because I was his brother, but because I was his Thane. He died for his Thane. Yet *you*—" Alcandhor stopped, his emotions threatening to overtake him on remembering his brother's death. He cleared his throat and glared into Pendhras' eyes. "Your words and actions have brought disgrace to my brother's sacrifice. You are—" he stopped as the former Ranger interrupted with cursings and then grabbed the man by the jerkin, hauling him to his feet. Through gritted teeth, he declared, "You are disowned and guilty of treason. Sentence will be carried out when we return from Laird Hall with Lamadhel. You are to be kept in the cells until then."

He paused and ended the conclave: "So be it."

After the dazed former Ranger had been escorted out, Alcandhor skimmed the faces of his chiefs. "I wish to visit Dandrin Shire to personally apprise the people of our judgments, and reassure them, and also to visit the two families of the feud. Tam and Mattan, you two shall go with me."

"I would go as well, if I may, Thane," Marcalan said.

"And I," Haladhon chimed.

Alcandhor hesitated. He had a second reason to visit the valley. Did that need to remain a secret now? He caught Mattan's eyes and raised his eyebrows.

It is your decision. You are Thane.

Alcandhor glared at the Elder. "You are not helpful."

Mattan smiled. The chiefs glanced between the two of them.

Alcandhor sighed. "I think...all the chiefs should go, and Ordhral as well."

"But Thane," Andhrel said. "I would like to help with some of the work in the Portal Complex before we leave for Laird Hall."

Eladhrel nodded. "And I have tasks I wish to finish before we leave as well. Some of the law-keepers who will be tutoring my students for me while I am gone need—"

"Nay." Alcandhor splayed both hands on the table. "I have need of all of you. After we visit Dandrin, we shall journey on to another place. I will say no more of it now, but it is to be kept secret. Understand you all, you will tell no one of this second purpose. Gardhal shall accompany us to Dandrin since he did the initial inquiry, but then he shall return to the city."

He slowly met the eyes of each chief. Their expressions all changed from surprised or curious to grave. Aye, they may not know the secret, save Mattan, but they all caught that something of serious import awaited in the valley. He nodded. "'Tis settled then. We shall leave in the morning."

Chapter Fourteen

"Do many who are not clanless live in the valley, Uncle?" Tam asked, her breath misting. She pulled her heavy cloak tighter against the wind as they plodded up the road from Zaidhron toward the mouth of the valley. At least the sky was clear with few clouds. Rangers were supposed to endure without complaint, so her father said, but that did not mean Tam enjoyed journeying in the rain.

"Very few, save those who have clan-tenant rights as adopted kin. All those in a clan pay levy to their clan to provide for those who cannot care for themselves. Allotments for the elderly, widows, and so on. And those in the valley pay tribute to Ch'shalna, which is how Zaidhron is supplied with much of its need. So a person who is not clanless is paying two-fold. Not many would choose that."

Tam nodded. Her gaze swept the landscape as they topped the rise. Although she knew from viewing the maps in Uncle's chamber that Thane Valley was ever so wide, she had expected to see a valley similar to the ones in the high mountains where she grew up in northwest Pashelon: steep, rough slopes, tall, always-green trees, and falls splashing over tumbled stone with little farms snugged in narrow bits of land between tors and hills, eking out what they could from herding hillbeasts and farming the rocky soil.

This valley, however, was broad and spread far beyond what she could see. Stone fences and hedges separated large tracts of farmland and pastures, most not green at this time of year, but varying between shades of golden yellow to dull brown. Patches of fog clung to certain low spots, but when the sun grew high enough, they would likely burn away.

"'Tis beautiful," she murmured.

"Aye. And it is peaceful and prosperous, which causes some dismay to those who would claim we should not take in the clanless."

"Do we take in anyone who is clanless?"

"Nay. We scrutinize those who appeal to live here. Those with a history of lawlessness, especially violence, are denied. Mostly we give a second chance to those who have had misfortune, or who were tossed out of their clans but do not exhibit a lifestyle that continues to be contrary to the law. And families or widows more so than single men. Many if not most of the Rangers in the valley are older who have much experience and wish a quiet life. They brook no nonsense, but have the wisdom to handle disputes and dispense justice evenhandedly.

"Pendhras had been given his position for such reason. He requested Fandhrel. I should have suspected something, but took it as mere friendship."

"I still do not understand how he thought disrupting one shire of the whole valley would reflect badly on you, Thane," Marcalan said.

"Perhaps he had plans to spread the bad feeling to surrounding shires," Andhrel said, shrugging.

"He might have, given more time," Alcandhor said.

"But he did not know that our Thane kept close scrutiny on that feud."

Eladhrel nodded at Haladhon. "True. And did not predict Rendhol would come to us rather than either join him or keep quiet." He smiled over at the shire Ranger, who remained subdued.

Tam needed not sense to know guilt filled the man. Part of her wanted him to just accept the blame, but Pendhras had used empathy to create a feeling of ease or surely Rendhol would have reported the problems long ago. So he claimed, and Tam felt no guile in him, only sorrow and remorse. Uncle had brought no charge against him and made no final decision on his situation. Perhaps he would do so when they arrived.

"For a Ranger to underestimate his fellows and his Thane is rank idiocy," Gardhal grumbled.

"Even so," Marcalan said, "his mind must be utterly twisted to conceive of such a scheme."

"I think he did not conceive of a scheme, not at first," Mattan said. "Most likely he sought a way to erode confidence in Alcandhor by whisperings, such as he did with the feuding families, telling them the Thane would not make good on his threats. And over time, it escalated."

"And in the end, all it did was erode faith in the local Rangers," Ordhral said. "Perhaps in all Rangers."

"Aye," Alcandhor murmured. "Who knows what we shall find when we arrive in Dandrin."

~*~

Despite the cold, onlookers filled the main street of the tiny town. All activity ceased as the ten Rangers walked through. What appearance did Tam and her kin present? Did they know what the Thane looked like? Even if not, they should know by the crest on the jerkins most of them were chiefs. And Mattan, with his so-very dark skin, always caused people to stop and stare. She supposed she did as well.

A few of the locals called to Rendhol, who raised a hand or nodded in acknowledgement.

"Glad to see you back," one said, grinning, then stepped back, head down, as if afraid the Rangers would take affront.

Stars, how had Pendhras treated those under his domain for them to have such a response? Tam had wondered about the advanced age of the replacements at first, but now could see why her uncle had set the men he did. Bardhon, Zandhral's grandfather, replaced Pendhras. He was one with Enaisi blood, but unlike his predecessor, would not abuse such a gift. If he were half as wise as Zandhral, the shire was blessed to have him as new steward.

The others also were old men: Valdalon—Gardhal's father, who seemed not quite as grumpy as his son, and Doralan, the father of one of her regular match partners, Cordhan.

At first Tam had been confused about the leadership in the valley. In the provinces, the provincial lord and his appointed representatives ruled in the various wards and administrative districts, and the Rangers provided the constabulary role as well as their other duties such as roaming bounds and arbitration. But the valley belonged to Ch'shalna clan, so rule was directly the task of Rangers. The steward of a shire's Ranger hold was also the steward of the shire. 'Twas simpler, to be sure.

Bardhon stood on the slate porch of the building marked with Ranger banners, and he bowed as they drew close. "Thane."

Tam followed her uncle as Alcandhor walked up the few steps and clasped the new shire steward's shoulder. Bardhon returned it with a smile.

"How go matters here?"

"Well. There is suspicion and mistrust, but that is to be expected. Tensions have eased though." He leaned close. "I am honored you charged me with this task, Thane. We all are."

"You three have my unreserved trust."

Bardhon bowed.

"Have you a place for us to meet with the people?"

"Aye, we had planned to use the arbitration hall, but many more have shown up than we expected." He nodded toward the curious, gathering crowd. "I fear we may have to stay outdoors to accommodate everyone."

"Ah, nay. 'Tis cold. Have you no hall here, such as used for celebrations or dances?"

"Aye, but it is unheated at the moment."

"Then lead us to it. We can help make it warm and ready for a shire meeting."

Bardhon hesitated, then a smile slowly spread. "Aye, Thane. Just the thing."

~*~

After they had built the fires and lit the sconces Tam saw that her uncle had done a wise thing. Did he realize it, though? The shire folk had watched as the Rangers worked, including the Thane—carrying salnais logs to a hearth and kneeling down to do the work himself, then helping to carry benches for everyone to sit. Before long, quite a few surged forward to help. A lad shyly grabbed the far end of a bench to assist Alcandhor, who grinned and thanked him.

Uncle was not afraid to work, or do menial chores, but his duties precluded such things, having to spend his time worrying about all the problems and paperwork in his Thane's chamber. Although she liked the young Laird, Tam could not see *him* kneeling to start a fire or carrying furniture. So was this just Alcandhor being Alcandhor, or was he being artful in showing he was not above them by not denigrating or designating to others manual labor?

She set down her own bench. Marcalan grinned as he lowered the other end. *Perhaps both. He would do this regardless, but he knows the display of watching even the Thane himself doing simple chores is helpful in breaking down the wall between these people and Rangers.*

With a frown, Tam tipped her head. *Were my thoughts that loud? I was not sending.*

I know not. I think we should ask Mattan for guidance.

Tam nodded. For all his reputation of being a prankster, Marcalan had much sense.

My thanks.

She straightened with a glare. *Stop it!* But at his mischievous grin, she rolled her eyes, unable to keep from smiling.

Once all the benches had been set out, and the hearths had taken much of the chill out of the air, her uncle lifted his hands and gestured for everyone to enter. The people pushed through the double doors like gushing river water. The benched filled, and yet still more crowded in.

"Are we all inside now?" the Thane called. "Are there seats enough?"

"We can stand," rumbled a burly man at the back, arms crossed.

Tam joined her kin, standing next to her uncle on a small platform at the front. Alcandhor introduced them all, and of course, she and Mattan drew stares. At least with her other uncle present—stars 'twas difficult to remember the alien was also her uncle—not all eyes were on her.

137

At the Thane's nod, Tam pulled out the document with the decisions of the conclave, unrolled it, and read the contents. That the two Rangers were stripped of rank, standing, and status brought some mutters and susurrations, but Tam sensed not a feeling of anger but of approval.

Loud gasps and exclamations filled the hall upon the declaration that Pendhras was disowned. And that was all the information given. Eventually it would be known he had committed treason when his sentence was carried out, but the Thane wished to keep that quiet for now, to keep focus on his crimes in the valley. Was it dishonest to not give full disclosure? Part of her thought so, but mostly she agreed with her uncle that it was shameful, private clan business.

The Thane turned, lifting a hand, and Rendhol stepped forward, head down.

Alcandhor did not have Tam read the verdict for the young Ranger, but lifted his chin and addressed the crowd directly. "I return this Ranger to his post in this shire. His youth and inexperience caused him to hesitate in questioning what he saw happening. After all, we teach ourselves that Rangers are above reproach. How could they behave in such ways? But when it became more apparent and could not be denied, he repeatedly shared his concerns with his shire steward. Pendhras used his empathic ability to ease Rendhol's worries, yet he did not toss away his doubts or cave to the pressure to become like the other Rangers in his shire." He turned to the new steward. "I trust you, Bardhon, and the others with you, to mentor this Ranger. He has great potential."

Rendhol slowly raised his head, his lips pressed together. "I do not deserve this, Thane."

"You stood for what was right, for the people of your bounds, even though it meant standing against your own kin—elder Rangers, one of whom was your direct superior." Alcandhor turned back to the assembly before him. "What say you all? Do you find him fair and just?"

Despite a few mocking calls, the overall response was a cheer, accompanied by stamping of feet and clapping of hands.

He clasped a hand on Rendhol's shoulder. "I return you to duty in this shire. Continue to be honest and keep the trust of these people."

The young Ranger bowed.

The burly man at the back bellowed, "What about Lanwin and Sonvil, and them getting kicked off their land?"

Alcandhor stopped. He drew himself up, stared at the man, and around the hall. Everyone stilled. Her uncle said nothing. The quiet become more quiet—not a boot scuffed, no one even moved. Then, in a low voice, he asked, "*Their* land?"

The man shifted his weight from foot to foot and uncrossed his arms. "Your land."

Andhrel stepped forward. "Are they present?"

"No. Both families are on their—the Thane's land, saying they will not let you turn them out."

"Then we shall journey there," Andhrel said and nodded at Tam.

She lifted her chin. "This meeting is concluded."

~*~

The shire Rangers joined the chiefs in the trek to the two farms involved in the feud. 'Twas, Tam was told upon asking, but an hour's walk west of the town. A few people followed them, the burly man among them. Tam bit her lip, watching them, and finally asked her uncle, "Think you they will cause trouble?"

"I believe they wish to see how the situation is handled. I doubt they plan any violence. However, we have several with empathy, and Mattan as well, to warn us, if needed."

"I sense mostly curiosity," Tam said. "Some little resentment, but not much."

"I would wonder if the resentment is for us, or for those on those farms," Ordhral said.

"What do you mean?"

Her Pashelon cousin shot her a tight smile. "From what I have heard discussed, some of the neighbors have found both tenants lacking in properly caring for the land. So it is not just the feud which has caused so much tension in the shire."

"That is true," Alcandhor said. "I am glad they joined us. They can bear witness, and hopefully will see that the truth is given wings, not some rumor." He turned to the shire residents behind them. "Walk with us, if you will."

After surprised expressions and a moment's hesitation, the small group quickened their pace to join the Rangers. The Thane asked a few questions of them, about their occupations and families, and the other Rangers joined in. Well, some of them. Tam found herself feeling shy. Uncle, she realized, slowly quieted, allowing the more sociable among them to carry the conversation.

Marcalan and Haladhon, along with Mattan and Ordhral chatted amiably, and the locals relaxed and asked questions themselves. Even bold enough to ask about the Elder, and finally about the tenants of the two farms.

"You shall see for yourselves," was all Uncle would say. The other Rangers followed his lead, and the conversation shifted away from that topic.

A stone wall bordered the road and separated the various fields beyond, although at times hedges marked the boundaries instead. Some tracts of land obviously grew crops. Many had been reaped already and been sown with a winter grain, as evidenced by tiny dots of green peeking through the stubble of the previous harvest. Other parcels sported herdbeasts grazing.

Once, a herder taking his charges from one pasture to another blocked their path. The valley folk called out for him to hurry, but he replied with a rude gesture belied by a grin.

The Rangers chuckled along with the locals, and when at last the road was clear and the gate shut, they continued, albeit more carefully to avoid the gifts the beasts had deposited. Would anyone bother to scoop up such wonderful fertilizer?

A drastic change from one parcel to the next caught Tam's attention. Whoever had sown the salnais in the new field had done a poor job—sparse in some areas, and clumped too closely to grow well in others, and weeds spread throughout. Was this the land of one of the farmers being evicted?

"Sonvil's tenancy," Bardhon murmured.

"I can see what the farmer Halcom meant when he said they do not do right by the land," Ordhral muttered.

Alcandhor turned to their followers. "You may witness, but do not interrupt."

Amid nods, the burly man crossed his arms again, but Tam sensed keen interest, more than suspicion or mistrust.

She viewed the extensive garden as they walked up the dirt path to the house. Hers often would be a bit overgrown and need weeding upon return when she accompanied her father as he roamed his bounds, but nothing like the neglect here. Weeds entangled and strangled the plants. Redfruit rotted on vines that had toppled from lack of support. The parik, bata, and several other ground plants had leaves with some little green to them, and if properly mounded with mulch and straw, should still be sound. The corbita was ruined, however, decaying amid soil and weeds; they had never been tied to a trellis or cage.

The condition of the herbs nearly made her weep.

Had this family cared for or harvested nothing—for their own use at least, if not to send on to Zaidhron?

A heavyset man stepped onto the porch and crossed his arms. Behind him, in the doorway, stood a woman with an ill-fitting frock, her hands on the shoulders of a tall, thin boy with light, blond hair sticking out in all directions.

"You can't make us leave," the man bellowed.

"Sonvil, you still have twelve days until the eviction is carried out," Alcandhor said. "You had best pack your belongings and arrange to move to another home—outside the valley."

"It ain't right! The Rangers said we could stay!"

Rendhol shouldered forward. "Not all of us did. I warned you."

"Fandhrel, Pendhras, and Inradhor are gone," Eladhrel said. "Stripped of rank, standing, and status. Along with Rendhol, these are your new shire Rangers: Bardhon as steward and Valdalon and Doralan. You will find they obey the orders of the Thane, and his orders are that you are to be evicted in twelve days."

"But we haven't done anything wrong! It's all that by-blow Lanwin's fault!"

Fists clenched, Tam stepped ahead of her uncle. "Nothing wrong? I have seen your fields. They are a disgrace. Your garden is worse. How can you feed your family, much less send your tribute to the Thane from what you have done, or rather not done, with his land?"

"Who are you, girl, to speak up so? Are the rumors true of a Ranger-trull?"

By word or motion, every one of her kin reacted. Tam held out both arms, silencing and stopping them. She knew not why she felt she had to respond herself, perhaps to show she was truly a Ranger, and not some lass that needed her kin to speak for her. A memory of her father handling similar situations rose in her mind.

And that word. She had heard it once before, from Pendhras. She was not certain of the meaning, but had some notion. No matter, she knew it was not a nice word.

Once it was quiet, she met Sonvil's gaze. She did not even send to him, but just stared, as her father had been wont to do, as the Thane had done in the town hall. The man looked away almost immediately. Tam still did not move, her eyes resting on him. He shifted his weight, glancing up, then away again. The boy finally called, "Don't hurt him!"

Tam marched up the steps, glared for a moment at the boy, then the woman, and then edged close to the—stars, but he stank!—man. "In twelve days, if you are still on this property, you will be removed. Forcibly if necessary. Do you understand me?"

The man nodded.

"I said, do you understand me?"

"Yes, mim."

"'Yes, Ranger Chief Tamissa.'"

He shuffled his feet and mumbled, "Yes, Ranger Chief Tamissa."

Tam backed away and rejoined her kin.

141

Bardhon said, "We shall also oversee the grounds and house. Anything stolen or damaged will be assessed and charged to you. If you cannot pay, you will be remanded to a labor camp, as is custom."

Tam followed as the Thane turned away and retraced his steps to the road. The woman wept, and Sonvil cursed her. Stars, what a miserable family! She could not feel very sorry for them, though; they had obviously not kept the agreement they signed when allowed to move to the valley as tenants, even if not including the feud with their neighbors.

Her mood flagged as they journeyed on to the next farm. This part of being a Ranger she did not like at all. A rustle caught her attention as the wind whipped, and she looked up to see a great many birds, a bigger flock than she had ever before beheld, blotting out almost half the sky. They appeared to be flying—nay riding!—the currents of wind, swelling upward and rolling down, as if sporting in the invisible flow of air. She found herself smiling. A chuckle came from Marcalan, and they exchanged grins. His hand touched hers, and their fingers entwined.

At a certain point, Tam could tell they had passed to Lanwin's tenancy. The fields told of somewhat better care. The path to this house was a wide lane, rutted with cart tracks and overhung by several large trees. A man with straggly brown hair and clothes which looked well lived-in stood at the end of the lane, chest out, and jaw set. "She can't make me leave. You can't make me leave!"

"This is Lanwin, Thane," Rendhol whispered.

A woman stepped off the wide porch and marched toward them, holding a babe in her arms. "He isn't welcome here!" Another woman followed her, accompanied by a sun-bronzed man with broad shoulders who was very old—perhaps Uncle's age or more.

"She can't kick me off the land! The family's tenancy was made over to me!"

"He won't do anything!" The woman stopped, blinked, and dipped a short curtsey. "Thane. Please, you can give the tenancy back, can't you?"

"You are Lanwin's wife?" Alcandhor asked.

"I was. Akima I am called, sir. I've put him out! He's lazy and spends more time wagering and drinking and dallying with—" She choked back a sob. The other woman put an arm around her. She adjusted the baby onto her shoulder and said, "This is my sister and her husband. They are willing to stay and help with our Fa's land. I mean, *your* land, but that was our Fa's tenancy. He was right proud of what we built here. But I want *him* gone!"

"You do know you were all given eviction."

"Yes, sir, but please, give us a chance without *him*."

"You ungrateful wench! You wouldn't have anything without me. I work hard—"

"At what, you by-blow?" the sister asked. "She put you out over a lunation ago, and you skulk around here—"

"Enough."

Tam bit her lips to stop a smile at her uncle's ability to silence everyone with one word. And he thought she could be Thane one day and control people's actions thus?

"I think I comprehend the situation." Alcandhor nodded at the sister's husband. "You, sir, what is your name and from where to you hail?"

"I am Dannel, Thane. Elesa and I lived on my parents' farm in the next shire over, Calwillin, but we are willing to move here. My folks have more than enough help, we wouldn't be shorting them. It's a good farm, my parents'. We can get this one back where it should be."

Her uncle's face contorted as he chewed the inside of his cheek, a sign he was also chewing over the problem. He had empathy, but he might wish to know what she could sense, since she had a stronger ability. But, with Mattan here, should she bother? Nay, she should do her duty as if it were up to her.

No deception came from Dannel. He was as straightforward as he appeared, she would wager on it. Hatred radiated like heat from both women toward Lanwin, and his attitude reminded Tam of Nandhal and Fandhrel, and Pendhras too, with his arrogance and anger. Him she did not like or trust at all.

But Uncle did not ask anyone for an opinion, unless perhaps Mattan mind-spoke to him.

"I will give temporary reprieve on the eviction so that Dandrin's new shire steward, Bardhon, can confer with Calwillin's steward. If all is as you say, you will have two seasons to prove this farm."

Lanwin's fists clenched. "Hold on—"

"Nay. You will leave this land, and this valley. Now. Do you understand?"

The man riffled his untidy hair with a scowl. "It's not fair!" He stared from one to another, then whined. "At least make her give me some food and—"

"You have given up all right to anything on this land," the Thane said. "Leave. Now."

Lanwin still hesitated.

"Doralan and Rendhol, be certain he leaves my valley."

The two Rangers stepped forward, and the man backed up, his shoulders hunched. He plodded away, and Tam had an overwhelming feeling that his was an act, an affectation of being a victim and trying to create pity. The valley folk parted and let him pass without comment.

Weeping, Akima thanked the Thane, as did her sister and brother-in-law. Tam was glad when they retreated from the farm.

Alcandhor nodded to the two shire Rangers remaining. "Ascertain the status of that farm in Calwillin, and keep eye on Sonvil and his family. Gardhal, if it seems all is well, you can return to the city, but you may remain to help if these men have need."

The Rangers bowed and turned back toward town, the locals following. The burly man paused and nodded at the Thane before joining the group.

The chiefs and Ordhral continued on the road alone.

"And where is this other place we are to visit?" Andhrel asked.

"You shall see," was all Uncle said.

Chapter Fifteen

Alcandhor could not help but smile as his niece clambered up the rocky, tree-lined slope. She turned to look back at them, her eyes bright. Aye, she was raised in mountains, and this must seem like home.

"Bells, slow down, Tam," her husband called. "Have pity on us old people!"

She laughed and all but ran up the steep path as if a kinchou. With exaggerated wheezing, Marcalan climbed after her, begging for mercy.

Ordhral smiled. "It is good to see Tamissa happy."

"You care for her a great deal."

"She is my sister."

"Surely much less than that."

"By our culture and language, and direct genealogy, aye, but by the Enaisi, there is no other word. She is the daughter of my mother, generations removed."

"Truly," Alcandhor said. "Interesting they have no word beyond mother and father or son and daughter in Enai."

"Not so remarkable," Mattan said from just behind them. "My people grow offspring in laboratories. There is no sense of generational family. Many do not know or even care who their biological parents are or were. Ismari and I were different. An experiment. Twins allowed to gestate together. We developed a bond. And instead of being their ultimate triumph, we were a failure—and worse, 'contaminated' those around us."

"Your team?" Alcandhor asked.

"Yes. And some others." The Enaisi nodded ahead. "Look at her. So like my sister."

"Aye." Ordhral inhaled. "I know your loss is immeasurably greater than mine, Mattan, but your sister was as a mother and dear friend for the whole of my life. Tamissa I tried to watch over as much as Valdhor would permit. He was not best pleased with me most of the time, but I stood my ground when I was there to see he was not too severe."

"By both moons," Alcandhor murmured, "how did he ever allow that? He was a chief of the clan, and granted you are sept chief, but he still had rank."

"But I had the pledge I made to Ismari to watch over her young daughter. He would not abrogate a man's honest vow or the wishes of his late wife. He threatened to thrash me a few times. I told him to try."

Alcandhor laughed long and low. "You rise even more in my estimation, cousin. And I am glad someone was there for my niece."

"Ah, but I was not. He did not wish me to be close to her—so I am but a stranger. But she is dear to me as if my own full sister in truth."

"Stars, we should have had you to hand when she recalled her blocked memories."

"Nay, Thane. As I said, I am a stranger to her. She would not have wanted me there."

Alcandhor clasped Ordhral's shoulder, then looked ahead. They continued the ascent, and Eladhor commented, "Someone has kept this path clear."

"It has been a task assigned to Rangers to roam here as part of their bounds and be certain this place, and the way to it, are maintained."

"You ordered this, Thane?"

"My father, originally. But I have followed his instruction concerning it."

"I wonder why."

Alcandhor had pondered his father's orders too, many times, but perhaps today's excursion was the reason. The incline of the slope decreased, and, as he remembered, a small distance from the right of the path the mountain dropped off. Through the few trees one could see the valley far below. Memories, not forgotten but seemingly clouded—by time and a visit at a young age, likely, returned like a fog evaporating in the sun. "We are close now."

Tam stood high above, waiting, Marcalan with her. The rest climbed to join them, following the path as it curved to the left, away from the cliff.

"There are fields in this small valley, Uncle, and a cottage. It is strange, though. It is deserted, no crops planted, no herdbeasts, but everything is tidy and kept up."

"Aye. I hope we shall find many answers here."

Silence reigned as they passed both the pasture and the area that had obviously been a large garden. The cottage seemed even smaller than Alcandhor remembered. He hesitated before lifting the latch.

Once inside, an ache rose within him. No dried herbs and vegetables, no fire in the hearth, no *life*. Zadhras was gone. He had known it, but seeing the vacancy made the reality, and the grief, real and fresh.

"Truly, Thane, Zadhras lived here in seclusion?" Andhrel whispered. "What was he like?"

Alcandhor took a deep breath while trying to find the right words. "He was...at peace. Content at the least, if not happy. I remember he smiled almost all the time. And his eyes..." How could he describe those eyes? They had haunted him for years.

"He gave the impression of knowing much and telling little, and of enjoying holding those secrets," Ordhral murmured.

"Aye. That exactly."

"And I know his prophecies are here. Written in his own hand. But...where?" The sept chief turned in a circle. "I think, Thane, you are the one with the key to unlock this mystery."

Alcandhor shook his head. "He told me nothing. I remember him telling my father I was the last one he would see, that I would face hard times and hard decisions, and observe many changes in the world. That is all."

Haladhon rubbed his neck. "I do not enjoy the idea of pulling this place apart stone by stone to uncover hidden prophecies."

"That would seem sacrilege," Eladhrel muttered, peering into a dark corner.

"Do not say that. My people are not gods. And Ashani's son was not some demigod anymore than Tam is."

The Rangers all halted and stared at Mattan and then at Tam. She glanced up with a shocked expression.

"Say then, irreverent," Eladhrel murmured.

Mattan's lips thinned, but he did not reply.

"What was the reason given, if any, for preserving this place?" Andhrel asked.

"Zadhras' request."

"I am in Hillsdown." Ordhral scratched his cheek. "You remember nothing more, Thane?"

"Nay. But then, I was a stripling having but thirteen, nay fourteen, years. I have a good memory, but 'twas long ago and a short visit."

"All the more reason you should remember." Mattan frowned. "I would venture he would not have wasted time on useless chatter. Every word would have purpose. Can you try to recreate the visit in your mind?"

"I suppose, but as I said, it was years ago, and my memory is as hazy as the fog in Hillsdown."

"Let us light a fire and have a repast, Thane. Perhaps a little time will nudge your recollection."

Knowing they might be in the valley for more than a day, they each had each brought provisions. Tam took charge. She demanded that water be drawn while she lit a fire, found pots and ordered them scrubbed, commandeered the small table and both chairs to use for her cooking needs, prepared tea, and a soup for later. Alcandhor hid a smile at her peremptory attitude, and how quickly the Rangers scattered to do her bidding, including himself and Mattan.

Before long, they all sat on the floor or leaned against the stone walls chewing strips of smoked meat and sipping tea, while appreciatively sniffing at the soup simmering over the fire.

"Does anything more spring to mind, Thane?" Andhrel asked.

"It will likely come more easily if you do not prod him," Haladhon said from where he stood near the hearth, arm propped on the mantelpiece.

With a glare at his tall cousin, Andhrel leaned back against a wall and drank his tea. Alcandhor did the same, staring up at the bare rafters while his kin chattered among themselves, seemingly ignoring their Thane while surreptitiously watching him. Irritation swelled, and finally he could not stand it. He rose and banged out of the cottage.

The cool air soothed his agitation a bit. What was it he was supposed to remember? They had only stayed that evening and left the next morning, and most of what the ancient man discussed had been with his father. But what else had he said? That he was stronger and wiser than he thought, that grief, sorrow, and great joy would come into his life, that he was what this world needed just now. Zadhras had said naught more. Nay! With a slight smirk, he had said one day Alcandhor would have answers. Stars!

He burst into the cottage and shoved Haladhon away from where he lounged against the end of the hearth.

"Steady on, Thane!"

He ignored his tall cousin, his fingers scrabbling at the stone blocks of the mantel. It was here! The secrets he would one day find were here, he knew it! The last piece lifted slightly as he pushed on it. Haladhon grabbed and lifted it for him. Alcandhor reached in and pulled out a roll of leather. He cradled it for a moment, unable to breathe. With great care he knelt and unwrapped it to reveal sheets of parchment.

All his kin silently came close, squatting or kneeling, save Mattan. Did he have no curiosity? Aye, but Alcandhor sensed irony besides. What a different view the Enaisi must have of these events. Ah, well, Alcandhor returned his attention to his find. The top sheet read:

One will be born in defiance of the law, and in his day that which is lost shall be found and many things will be revealed.

"What does it mean, Thane?" Eladhrel whispered.

Andhrel sighed. "And why are prophecies always riddles?"

"I know not the answer to either question." Alcandhor lifted the page and read another:

When that which is closed opens, then shall all be restored.

"Could that one be more vague?" Andhrel muttered.

The world shall rage and strive to slip its moorings,
But the Storm shall sweep through bringing amity in its wake.

"And now he turns nautical?" Andhrel shook his head. "What will follow, poetry?"
"Hush," Alcandhor murmured, continuing to the next sheet.

Hail to the lesser one,
May his hair ne'er be shorn.
From the fire he shall rise,
And shall reclaim his bourn.

Andhrel rocked back on his heels, and Haladhon and Ordhral both laughed aloud. Alcandhor stared at the words, his heart thudding. This could not mean what it seemed—
"Bells, it is as if he knew!"
"Perhaps he did," Ordhral said. "And he had a wicked sense of humor."
"Have you read these prophecies then?" Eladhrel asked.
"Nay, but I talked to Zadhras more than once. He said the hardest part was not seeing the prophecy, but how to communicate it, and that he tried various methods over the years. He also wondered what his children would think of his attempts."
"Why not just tell us what he saw?" Tam asked. "Why the riddles and the poetry?"
"I believe..." Alcandhor cleared his throat. "I believe he wanted to convey the message, but not take the chance of telling someone what they should do."
"What do you mean, Uncle?"
"When I met him, he told me I had, in particular, one hard decision to make, and it would seem impossible. I asked him to tell me what it was, and he said if he did that, it would not be my decision."
"A true puzzle, this one," Andhrel muttered.
"'May his hair never be shorn.' That is an ancient blessing indeed!" Eladhrel commented.
"Aye. One rarely used today, but perhaps in his time 'twas more

common."

"But what is his bourn?" Tam asked.

"Bourn is also seldom used," replied Eladhrel. "It means a small rill."

"But that makes no sense," Tam said.

Haladhon said, "It can also mean a bounds."

"One who shall reclaim his bounds?" Marcalan asked. "That seems a dull prophecy."

"Bourn can also mean goal," Andhrel murmured. "Or—"

"It matters not for now." Alcandhor rolled up the sheets. He must cut off this conversation. Andhrel of all of them should know what else *bourn* could signify. And he would not allow that subject to be brought up. "We should return these to Zaidhron and study them." He tied the leather cover back around them, his gaze on his task, meeting no one's eyes.

"We are not going to read them all here?" Andhrel asked, his voice plaintive.

"We have glanced at some of them, but I want them safely in the city. I wish scribes to copy them so they cannot be lost."

"But what if there are more?"

"I think not. I remember now the look and the hint Zadhras gave me when I was but a stripling. These are what he wanted me to come back and find." Alcandhor tucked the leather roll into his pack. "If any of you wish to tear stone from stone, you have my permission. But I think this place has served its purpose. I am not certain I need to have Rangers continue to oversee its maintenance."

Most of his kin gaped at him. Ordhral gave him a tight smile, and Mattan a sardonic one.

Tam tipped her head. "In that first prophecy, what does he mean, *in defiance of the law*?"

Andhrel snorted. "That is a very good question."

"One such as Monadhal, or another of the Rogues," Eladhrel said. "They surely defied the law."

"Aye," Tam said, "but it says *one shall be born in defiance of the law*. Defiance of what law? And how shall one's birth *be* in defiance of the law?"

"One born outside the law? A by-blow perhaps?" Eladhrel asked.

Andhrel shook his head. "But there are many types of law. We have the Clan Law, the Laws of the Maker, Ranger Laws, and civil laws to guard morality and the treatment of our fellows, which also includes laws of arbitration, and the Laws of the Enaisi, which is our guide to guard our planet against abuse, and also we have the laws of all the sciences."

"I would suggest, by the wording," Ordhral said slowly, "that the law being defied is one surrounding his birth."

"But what does it mean?" Tam asked. "I mean, defied. How does a birth defy the law?"

"The obvious meaning would be a by-blow," Eladhrel suggested again.

"Not necessarily," Haladhon waved an arm. "Look at Tam. We thought her birth had not been recorded. That could be considered a defiance of the law."

"Aye, but it was recorded, just kept sealed," Andhrel said.

"I do not argue that, just that the circumstances of not recording a birth might be considered a defiance of the law."

Andhrel shrugged.

"And look at Marcalan, he certainly defies the laws of science. He is a Child of the Enaisi and yet his parents—" Haladhon stopped, his mouth dropping open.

The Rangers' responses all tumbled over each other, and Alcandhor held up a hand. They all fell silent and stared at the rascal. The object of their scrutiny sat, arms crossed and eyebrows raised. "I am pondering the pose I should use for my statue."

"Be you serious," Tam said, slapping his arm.

"Have we not said I am the likely answer to Zadhras' prophecy? This—"

"Stars, cousin, give way," Andhrel groaned.

"We know nothing for certain," Alcandhor said. "That is one possibility. A strong one, I grant you."

"Bells," Haladhon said. "You ever switch sides of the stream on Marcalan and the prophecy."

"Because I am not certain. And I am not afraid to state my confusion on the subject."

"If this is the same prophecy we have been wishing to find, then I would say Marcalan—"

"We can talk in circles," Alcandhor said, "but I would rather wait until we are gathered at Zaidhron with others who are our best history-keepers and law-keepers."

"But—"

Voices outside the cottage caused them all to hush. The door banged open, and two Rangers entered, swords drawn. Their mouths gaped, their weapons drooped, and they bowed.

"By both moons!"

"Thane!"

Alcandhor smiled up at both men's shocked faces. "Well met."

The first Ranger gazed about, swallowing, his gaze flitting between Alcandhor, Tam, and Mattan as the second said, "We did not know you had all journeyed here. We saw the smoke and thought some intruders found this cottage."

"'Tis good to know you are diligent in your duty to guard and maintain this place."

The two bowed again, and Alcandhor bit back a smile at the confusion and curiosity he could discern. "Come men, sit you down and join us. We have tea, and soon the soup should be ready as well. You must have questions. Perhaps we can answer them for you."

The Rangers exchanged glances and hesitantly sat down.

~*~

The valley Rangers stood outside the cottage the next morning as Tam and the others descended. Her uncle turned and lifted his fist, opening it palm out in salute to the two Rangers who bowed in return.

The men had been shocked to find their inexplicable duty had actually been safeguarding the erstwhile home of the legendary Zadhras the Seer. Everyone knew a hermit had once lived there, but that it had been Zadhras shook them deeply, and they vowed to continue the task as long as their Thane ordered it.

They had also been quite unnerved by both Mattan and Tam, but the former set them somewhat at ease by serving them the soup and chatting with them. Tam wished she knew how to talk so openly with strangers. Shyness always seemed to overcome her.

"Where to now, Thane? Back to the city?" Eladhrel asked, pulling his cloak close against the chill morning air.

"I will leave the choice to each of you, but Haladhon and I shall journey to Tarillan Shire."

"Tarillan?" Andhrel asked. "You mean to visit Haladhon's family then?"

"Aye. I have not seen my young cousins in some time, and their grandfather does poorly."

"Oh, I wish to go!" Tam exclaimed. "I would love to meet them. Shall we join them, Marcalan?"

Her husband grinned. "I would be glad to see them again myself."

"I think you and Marcalan may safely join us, but too many may cause Panill panic," Haladhon said. "She does not favor much company."

"Then the rest of us will return to the city," Mattan said. "Although one day soon I would like to meet her and your daughters."

"Aye. Give her and our young cousins our greetings," Andhrel said.

They stopped at a small tavern in Dandrin to have an early luncheon before continuing on. Marcalan eased the nervousness of the stripling serving them by sharing the hard-won knowledge that one should not pick one's nose if one has the hot spice pimin on one's fingers. The lad and her kin all laughed, but Tam just rolled her eyes.

As they came to the crossroads near the mouth of the valley, Andhrel asked, "Wish you me to take the prophecies to the city, Thane?"

Alcandhor grinned. "Nay, they shall stay with me. You shall not have a chance to give them an early peek, cousin."

Marcalan chuckled, and Andhrel's mouth twisted in a wry smile.

The chiefs—Tam found she thought of Ordhral as a chief, even though he was only a sept chief—split off to go back to the city, while the four of them continued on to Tarillan.

"How far is it, Haladhon?" Tam asked.

"About another hour's walk. The road narrows after we pass a small pond and follows next to a stream for a bit to their far pasture."

Haladhon's reply and his mood were noticeably subdued, even without using her ability to sense. "Do you not want Marcalan and me to go with you and Uncle?"

Haladhon frowned. "Nay, why do you ask?"

"You are not happy. Are we too much company?"

"I am merely...worried about Panill's father, their farm, and my girls. I hear they hired a herder to help, which gives my concerns a little ease."

Haladhon did not tell all, Tam could sense that. But before she could even frame another question, Marcalan shot her a mental warning. A glance over at her husband brought a subtle head shake and a frown.

What is wrong?

This is an unhealed wound for him. Do not pick at the scab. Once we arrive, I think you will understand. Marcalan lifted his arm, Tam snugged into his embrace, and they walked silently in step. At first. He seemed to start limping, or hesitating, every few paces, throwing off her balance slightly, but she felt nothing wrong—not even the sense he had a stone in his boot or a blistered foot. Amusement burbled in him, and she pushed him away. *Behave!*

I always behave. I do not say how, but—

"Stars, Marcalan!"

Haladhon and the Thane both turned to look at them and grinned.

"Does he ever stop, Haladhon?" she asked, her voice more plaintive than she intended.

"Nay. Become inured, cousin."

They all laughed, and Marcalan quieted. Tam was not certain if that was good or not, probably an indication he was scheming. She took advantage, however, enjoying the beauty of her surroundings.

The stream and path next to it, indeed, led them to a pasture with many herdbeasts grazing. When the rill wound off to their left, they continued straight on the narrow track. Soon a thin ribbon of rising smoke became visible, and not long after, the cottage—and chimney—from which it rose. The buildings and grounds appeared, from this distance anyway, to be well-tended. The garden certainly was, which made Tam more approving of this Panill and her family.

A girl lifted a bucket from the well. She stopped for a moment, then dropped the bucket and ran toward them, arms flung out. "Papa!"

Haladhon fell to his knees, arms outstretched, and the girl threw herself at him, crying, "Papa!" over and over.

The door opened, and a second girl hesitated in the doorway, then with a shout, pelted to Haladhon.

Tam scarcely breathed, watching the girls cling to their father, crying and laughing. Their desperate love and joy, and Haladhon's, almost made her weep. Marcalan pulled her close.

Now I understand, she thought to him.

Her husband squeezed her tighter.

Picking up his daughters, one in each arm—despite their size, Haladhon walked toward the cottage. Stars, but her cousin had strength! The older girl had almost Tam's height and she knew the girl to have eleven years. She likely would be tall as her father.

They entered the girls' home behind Haladhon. A shapely woman stood at the hearth, swinging the kettle over the fire. Her wide smile faded as she saw others crowding in the door. Her large, brown eyes narrowed, and her full lips pouted.

Tam stared at the ample-breasted woman, assessing her body and comparing it, and finding herself lacking. She averted her gaze, her face growing warm.

Marcalan's arm slid around her waist. *You are more beautiful to me than any other woman. I am not displeased with your figure, Love-ling. Why should you be?* He tightened his embrace. *Perhaps tonight I can show you how pleased I am.*

Tam stifled a giggle and set her attention on Haladhon's mistress and his children.

Now that the two had loosened the hold on their father, Tam could more clearly see them. The older one, Lonill, had the full lips of her mother, but her eyes were blue and shaped more like Haladhon's. Her hair was lighter than either of her parents. Haliss was darker and looked more like her mother. Both chattered to their father, interrupting each other, but her cousin seemed to be able to understand and track their conversations.

Panill bobbed a hesitant curtsey to Alcandhor, her gaze darting between the intruders—as Tam easily sensed the woman felt them to be.

"Greetings, Panill. This is my niece, Tam, and I believe you know Marcalan."

The woman did not even nod in salutation. "Thane. Are we—is there trouble?"

"Ah, nay, Panill. We had need to be in the valley and wished to visit. I do not often get the chance to see you and my young cousins. Are you well?"

"Yes. My fa isn't though. The healer came out two days ago. He's doing poorly and..." She blinked, tears welling in her eyes, clutching her apron in her fists. "I don't know what to do."

Haladhon held out an arm. She burst into sobs and rushed to him.

Her cousin's emotions confused Tam. Sympathy was strongest, and some affection was there as well, although it seemed...impatient and worn thin.

"Someone there, Panni?" a weak voice called from the next room.

"Haladhon is here, Fa. With...with the Thane and some others."

"Thane? Ah, ah, need to see you, Thane! If you please."

Alcandhor smiled tightly, slipping past Tam to go into the darkened chamber. From her place near the door, Tam could hear the conversation between her uncle and Panill's father.

"And how are you, sir?"

"Poorly, poorly." He gasped between every few words. "I haven't long. Know that. The girls. I'm worried for them."

"Haladhon has vowed to care for them, sir, and I back him."

The old man's voice dropped even lower. "Haladhon is a good man."

"We will see they are cared for, sir. You have my word as Thane."

"Thankee. Thankee." He gasped then called, his voice querulous. "Panni? My tea, Panni?"

Alcandhor backed out as Panill rushed in with a cup, breathlessly murmuring an apology.

Uncle smiled at Haladhon's girls. "And how are you both, other than worrying about your grandfather?"

"We are well, thank you, Thane," Lonill said. She did not have the commoner accent of her mother or grandfather, although something was off to Tam's ear. Did Haladhon tutor them, or did they try to mimic his accent?

"You are my cousins, and I am not here as Thane, but as kin. You should call me Alcandhor."

Lonill dipped a curtsey. Haliss blurted, "Kostan does not really believe that we are daughters of a Ranger chief."

"Who is Kostan? Is he the neighbor's son who comes to help with chores and does herding for you?"

"No—nay," Lonill said, catching her slip. "He is a man who comes around and offers to help. He helped with harvest and has returned several times. I think he is trying to catch Mum's affection. We have told him she is..." The girl hesitated, her eyes pleading. "We say married, sir. I know it is not right, but people think the wrong thing if we say legal mistress."

"I understand, and it is of no consequence. I am sorry. If I could change the law, I would. It is no harm to say she is married, the legal differences in this case are slight."

"Not so slight. I cannot live here—"

"Stars, Haladhon, I know! But in every other legal way, we have made provision that it is as a marriage. You know this." Alcandhor turned back to Lonill. "Is this Kostan in any way improper in his words or actions to any of you?"

"Not directly," the girl said. "But he scoffs at Rangers. And he says we are lying about Mum being married."

Tam stiffened, and her uncle frowned. "Where does this Kostan live?"

"I don't—do not know." The girl turned pink.

Alcandhor's lips thinned. Haladhon's narrowed eyes and jaw set.

"Haladhon, stay here until we must leave for Laird Hall and spend as much time as you can with your family."

Tam need not know her uncle's thoughts; they were easy to perceive. He hoped this Kostan would make an appearance. The girls jumped up and down, tugging at their father's arms.

Eyes bright, Lonill asked, "Will you stay for afternooning?"

"I thank you for asking, cousin, but I have need to be back at Zaidhron by night. Perhaps after the conclave at Laird Hall we may return for a longer visit. I know your cousin Tam wishes to become acquainted."

The girls peered at Tam. She smiled, not sure what to say to her two new cousins. Before she could say word one, Marcalan put his hands on her shoulders, grinning. "Aye, upon our return we shall have to visit."

"Shall you tell us more stories, cousin?" Haliss asked.

"What stories?" Haladhon stared hard at Marcalan.

"Stories about you and cousin Marcalan, Papa. And the funny things you have done."

Tam could not help but smile at Haladhon's aghast expression.

"Aye, and Tam has not heard all the stories either, so we will have a jolly time, will we not?"

Haladhon cleared his throat, but Marcalan blithely continued, "And we need to have a grand outing near the stream with lots of food and games. But come spring, mind. I think I would not wish to sit upon blankets and eat with snow on the ground."

The girls giggled.

The Thane gave each girl a hug, and promised to bring his children as well for an outing in the spring. Panill came out of her father's room just as they left. Had she been hiding from them or tending her father? She said nothing as they left.

Tam reflected on the woman and the girls as they walked back toward the mouth of the valley. Uncle and Marcalan said little. If only Panill would come live in the city, they could be properly married. Why was she so fearful? She said little, so 'twas hard to know how simple she truly was. Perhaps Mattan would be able to tell more. Not that it would make a difference; she would not leave the farm, so Haladhon and the girls would continue to be unhappy.

Chiefs must abide at Zaidhron, yet Tam's father was allowed a bounds while Haladhon was denied one in the valley. No wonder he was bitter.

"How many days until we leave for Laird Hall, Thane?" Marcalan asked, startling Tam from her brooding thoughts.

Her uncle did not answer right away. Finally, he sighed. "Five days. I would give more time to journey since we have our women with us. The roads will likely be muddy or frozen with winter approaching."

Stars, if it took them five days to journey to Laird Hall, and they left in five days... "But Uncle, that means we will arrive just as the conclave will start."

"Aye. However, I have never known a conclave to begin on time at Laird Hall. One or another of the lords is always late in journeying. I had wanted to arrive early enough to go to Estan beforehand, and I still have a strong compulsion to do so, but seeing Haladhon with his children... I feel I must give him some days with them." Her uncle inhaled swiftly. "By both moons, I would fain change that bloody law!"

"Without a special circumstance," Marcalan said, "such as Tam's mother having sight, 'tis not possible. It was made High Law."

"Aye."

"Why was it made High Law?" Tam asked.

"We do not know. Mattan might. He was there. But the fact remains, the High Laws cannot be changed."

"Except by foresight of an Enaisi," Marcalan said.

"Or a king's decree."

"And we have no king," Tam said.

"Nay," Alcandhor murmured. "We do not."

Chapter Sixteen

The Valley Gate had a different feel than the Main Gate. There was as much travel and vendors and bartering, but it had a comfortableness to it as folk from the valley traded and bought and sold all the time, not like those who might come from afar to try to sell goods.

The Rangers relaxed a bit more at their posts. It was not apparent in their posture, but Tam could sense it. They did not have the alertness of the guards at the Main Gate and out-wall gate. Of course, it would be difficult if not impossible for anyone other than someone from the valley to show up here. They would have to come through—or over—the out-wall and around the city to this gate. With all the men guarding the walls and towers, how easily could that be done? And all the gates were shut at night, only opened if the guards saw fit.

As they drew close, the Rangers brought their hands over their hearts in salute, and one called, "Thane, Chief Andhrel has requested your presence in the law library."

Her uncle inclined his head in thanks, muttering, "What now?"

"Most likely the prophecies," Marcalan said. "You know the history-keepers are all waiting, wanting to drool over them."

"'Tis almost dusk. I would like a meal."

"Stars, it is too bad you are not Thane. You could then order that food be brought to the law library."

Alcandhor shot a disgusted look at her husband, and Tam stifled a giggle. "I will see that a tray is sent to you, Uncle."

"Let Marcalan do that. Keep him busy. I wish you with me, Second at Table."

"Aye, sir." With a quick fist over his heart and mocking laugh, the rascal trotted off. Alcandhor shook his head and quickened his pace across the city.

The law library was brightly lit and filled with people. Scribes' quills fluttered and twirled as they waited in obvious impatience, and men and women gathered about tables conversing in quiet tones.

As Alcandhor entered, everyone stopped and bowed to him. With a studied expression, he pulled out the leather roll from his pack and offered it to Delgan with a smile. The stout, older man bent over the Thane's hands, tears in his eyes. Despite the history-keeper being a commoner, the two were close friends, both with a love of the past. What did it mean though, that Delgan received the roll? Was he senior even to

159

Andhrel as a history-keeper, or was it friendship that made her uncle give the prophecies over to him?

Almost everyone rushed forward, and Alcandhor raised an arm. "Let the scribes copy them first."

They all crowded in as Delgan unrolled the leather. Slowly, with loving care—which also afforded him time to read every page, he gave each scribe a sheet of parchment.

People huddled behind the scribes, murmuring.

"You may read over their shoulders if it does not disturb them," Alcandhor called. "But do not speak. I wish them not distracted and perhaps copy amiss."

The susurrations dropped into silence with only an occasional mutter and resulting "Shu!" from others.

Marcalan arrived with two helpers, setting trays of food and urns of hot tea on a table near the door. Tam helped arrange the offerings. Frowning, she picked up a pastry, almost like the ones from the Great Hall, but this was not a sweeting. Unwilling to speak and disturb the scribes, she raised it, asking her husband, *What is this?*

'Tis a meat pastry. The history- and law-keepers often wish to continue their obsessive work while eating so this allows them to forge ahead without interruption.

Her eyes widened as she took a bite. A filling of chopped vegetables and meat oozed out from the crust. Stars, but this was good!

"Wait for the ink to dry."

Tam turned at Maradhor's voice. Several people hovered around him, hands clutched to their chests in an obvious effort to keep them off the still drying copy. Marcalan was right; they almost drooled.

Despite his stated desire for food, her uncle lurked at a table. Andhrel did too, but with his gaze locked on Alcandhor, not the scribe or the prophecy being copied, and he murmured something in his ear.

"Leave off, Andhrel!"

"I will not, Thane!"

All activity stopped. Tam took a step forward, but Marcalan touched her arm and shook his head.

"This is important. Maybe the most important prophecy of them all!"

"Why say you that? Have you read them all, and understood them?"

"I know what that one claims, and—"

"Regardless, this one prophecy I wish kept quiet for now." Alcandhor took the still drying paper by the edge and said to the scribe, "Make one more copy and then store it and the original away."

"But Thane—"

"I have spoken."

"This is not right—" Andhrel spluttered.

"Enough. I wish to eat. We can discuss this in private. Later." Alcandhor blew on the copy, then rolled it up and tucked it in his jerkin. With long strides, he crossed the chamber to the food-laden table.

"What about the one we think is about Marcalan?" Tam asked.

Andhrel inhaled and turned his glare from their Thane to her husband. "Stars, as if he is not insufferable enough," he grumbled, "now he is in a prophecy."

Marcalan chuckled, winking at her.

"I think," Delgan said slowly, "that there may be two that are about the same person, whether it's about Ranger Chief Marcalan or not, I can't say."

"Stars, history-keeper, just call me Marcalan."

"Makes it easier when one is bellowing at him," Andhrel muttered.

Her husband laughed aloud, and Tam shook her head. Stars, Andhrel was right. As much as Marcalan loved attention, being the subject of prophecies might not be good.

Why not?

Tam gazed up at her husband. *I wish you not to think yourself of some great importance, and become insufferable in truth.*

Bells, Love-ling. I find it all a jest, whether truth or not.

Do you not take it seriously?

I take it might be truth, but nay, not seriously. I am merely me, a Ranger, a prankster, and proudly, your husband. Despite my jestful boasting, I do not aspire to be more than that.

Tam leaned into Marcalan, closing her eyes as his arms wrapped around her.

"What is this other prophecy that may be related, Delgan?" Andhrel asked.

The history-keeper handed a paper to her cousin. Tam broke free of Marcalan's embrace and rushed to peek over Andhrel's arm:

Heralded one, born of two Teldheri, gifted by the Enaisi: a bane and boon shall your birth be, a portent of woe, joy, and great change.

She turned to find Marcalan behind her, and he had obviously also read the paper. For once, no humor lingered in his eyes. Before she could even mindspeak to him, he murmured in her ear, "I take the prophecy seriously, Love-ling, but not myself. Give over your worry."

After clearing his throat, Andhrel stated, "Zadhras certainly was correct about the 'bane' part."

L.S. King

"There you have it, cousin," her husband said, his voice lilting. "I cannot help the way I am, 'tis prophecy you should blame, not me."

Andhrel rolled his eyes as everyone burst into laughter.

"Tam," Alcandhor said, "why do you not take your *bane* from here, since neither of you are history-keepers. I fear he shall continue to disrupt the chamber."

"Aye, sir."

His eyes alight and without any indication of chastisement, Marcalan snagged several meat pastries and strode out with a grin. Tam followed with a worried backward glance at her uncle and his dark mood.

~*~

Soon after his niece and Marcalan had gone, Alcandhor left with a cup of tea and a meat pastry. Before he reached the bottom of the stairs, Andhrel called his name. Stifling a groan, he entered his Thane's chamber.

"That prophecy—"

"Leave off!"

"The others did not know. But I do. I know what bourn can also mean."

"Leave off! It cannot happen. Will not happen!"

"You think Delgan, or some of the others who are as steeped in not only history itself but the history of our language will not discern what it means?"

"That is why I want it safely tucked away. I want no speculation as to meaning."

"But—"

"It cannot happen! Leave it, Andhrel."

His cousin straightened, blue eyes piercing, fists on hips. Finally he blew out his breath in a strong puff, spun, and stormed out.

Alcandhor sat, staring at the wood whorls on the table, shaking. *It cannot happen!*

~*~

The next morning, after the reports were done, Alcandhor and Tam went to the Training halls. Finished with his first match, he rubbed his face with a sweat cloth while watching his niece spar with a staff. Her techniques displayed superior training and effort. 'Twas easy to see this was her favorite weapon.

162

Tossing the cloth down, he glanced about for another match partner, but the young Ranger Baidhrol ran up with a sketchy bow.

"Thane, I am bid tell you more Worshippers have arrived at the out-wall."

"Who bids you tell me? Are the gate guards not dispersing them?"

"Aye. Well, we have tried, but they state they will not leave. They are doing something strange, and stopping merchants trying to enter and—you are asked to come."

Tam walked up with a frown. "What is this?"

"Join me, and let us see what these mad layabouts are doing. Last time they trampled the grasses and left rubbish and ordure when finally they departed."

"When was this, Uncle?"

"You were nestling. Wash up, niece, and attend." Alcandhor nodded at Baidhrol. "We shall be there shortly."

The young Ranger bowed and hied away.

~*~

Tam climbed the out-wall stairs behind her uncle. The huge plain had been harvested of the grasses, and from what she could see of what these Worshippers did, she was glad of it. She hoped the new crop had not been planted yet.

A man in a dark robe walked in a circle with some people following suit. Others made a barricade, stopping merchants' wagons from continuing on to the city. The wagon masters gathered to yell at the Worshippers, and if not stopped, Tam had no doubt they would come to blows.

"How dare they!" She flew down the steps, ignoring her uncle's calls to wait, and ordered the guards to open the gate. She marched out, fists clenched, to the men blocking the road. "You will move, now!"

Behind her, she could hear her uncle groan. Why was he not happy with her? As Second at Table was she not supposed to take charge in such situations? The answer came to her as they all fell to their knees. Her stomach knotted, and bile rose to fill her throat. She was dark-skinned—not compared to Mattan, but much darker than the Teldheri.

Still, she must maintain order; she could not back away now. "Rise to your feet, you fools! I am no god. But I am Second at Table for Ch'shalna clan, and shall have you all in cells if you do not leave!"

"But you are Enaisi!" one of the men said in a hushed voice, still on his knees.

"I am not. I am Teldheri. My father was Valdhor, son of Thane

163

Saldhor. And I say again, you will leave."

"But your skin, your eyes darken..."

"Away with your madness! Move and allow the wagons into the city."

The kneeling man touched his head to the ground, then rose and spread his arms for the Worshippers to give way.

Rangers must have followed her or else Uncle ordered them out, as they forged a line on each side of the road, and the drivers ran to their wagons with happy shouts. The ugly dray beasts snorted, and a few bellowed as they heaved against their traces.

The Worshippers who chanted while walking in a circle stopped, the man in the black robe gaping at Tam. She strode toward him and could now see the vestment had blue circles all over it. "You also will leave."

The robed man lifted his hands making a circle with his fingers and thumbs, and he closed his eyes, murmuring under his breath.

"Did you not hear me?"

"I pray you would give blessings to us, Child of the Celestials!"

"I am no god or child of gods! And blessings are not what I will give you if you do not cease this foolishness and leave. Now!"

He did not move, nor stop his mutterings—prayers were they supposed to be?

Using a force-hold on his wrist, Tam took him to his knees and held him there, calling to the nearby Rangers, "Take this one to a cell."

"I am blessed!" He tried to kiss her hand. Tam's ire rose, and with it, the urge to pound this Worshipper's face. She raised a fist.

Do not, Love-ling! Do not give in to the temper that controlled your father!

With a gasp, Tam released her grip and stepped back. Rangers dragged the man away. Blinking back tears, she strode to the gate. Surely her uncle could manage those simpletons.

Inside the gate, Mattan and Marcalan stood shoulder to shoulder. She dove into her husband's arms. Her alien uncle rubbed her back, murmuring, "It is all right, niece. You did well."

"I wanted to hit him. I wanted to pummel him until he was bloody!"

"But you did not."

"Because Marcalan stopped me."

"You could have ignored your husband instead of heeding him. Come. It is almost luncheon."

Tam sniffled then asked, "Will they ever stop trying to get into the city to see you?"

"I do not know. I would hope so."

"At least when we leave for Laird Hall the guards can honestly say there are no Enaisi here," Marcalan quipped.

"Ah, but then they will probably turn up there," Mattan replied with a snort.

"Bells, imagine the welcome they will receive! I doubt the Laird's Master of the Guards will allow any of their nonsense any more than we do. That will be a sight, enh, Love-ling?"

Tam managed a smile, but still, her worry that she had almost lashed out in anger as her father often did alarmed her. Would she end up being like him?

~*~

Tam chewed, her mind on what the Worshipper had said, not on the food. *Child of the Celestials.*

Aye, she knew—now—that her mother was an Enaisi, and had some memory of her. More feelings and flashes of a face and dark hands than true remembrances, but she did recall being held and rocked and sung to, praised for little triumphs and cooed at for bruises and scrapes.

Alcandhor ate silently, still glowering. She looked up at Mattan, next to her. After that one time, she asked naught of him about his twin sister, knowing how deeply the pain and grief cut him, but now she took a long breath. "Could you...could you tell me more about my mother..." It seemed odd to say it, but she added, "Uncle?"

The alien smiled. "After luncheon, we could sit and talk at our leisure. Would that be all right?"

Tam nodded.

He leaned closer, his eyes so kind. "And I know it bothers you to call me 'Uncle.' That is your name for your other uncle, is it not? Uncle Mattan, perhaps, if you can accustom yourself to it, but I mind not if you just use my name. 'Tis your love I hope to gain, not a title for myself."

"But I do love you."

"Aye, as you love many of your new kin, but you are the daughter of my sister, and my only link left to her. Can you understand my wish to become more beloved by you as close kin?"

Tam hesitated and, with a tentative smile, whispered, "Aye."

~*~

Tam stared up at the portrait of her mother in the clan hall, listening to Mattan's descriptions and memories.

"I wish I could have known her," she murmured. "I wish I could see her."

"You can, you know. Images of her anyway, in the Portal Complex."

"How?"

"Let us go there. I will show you."

She followed her mother's brother down the stairs and over to the Great Hall and its lift entrance, still listening to stories of her. How she loved plants and studied them so much that she became something called a botanist. She had helped plan some of the gardens in Avadhron's Sward, not merely out of love of nature, but of her first husband.

"This may be intense for you," Mattan said as they entered the lift.

Tam stared up into his dark eyes. "I want to see my mother."

Just look into a mirror.

The thought intruded loudly, making her blink.

Mattan grimaced. "You heard that? I apologize. I forget you are not only strongly empathic but have telepathic abilities as well."

"That is why Marcalan and I can share thoughts?"

"Aye. You can mindspeak to any of us—to any Enaisi, and I can see that you hear any intense thoughts we have. I should have remembered that."

"Remembered?"

The lift shot downward. "Ismari and I both had children here, half-Teldheri, half-Enaisi. They had abilities as yours. Amazing I should have forgotten that." He frowned. "Perhaps I did not wish to remember..."

The doors opened, and Mattan smiled, gesturing with his hand. Tam said nothing as she followed him down the brightly lit corridor, but did he think she could not detect the pain behind that smile? He had lost so much here. His wife, his children, his friends, and even his sister. How did he bear it? Was such a long life indeed desirable then?

Laughter echoed from up ahead.

"The history-keepers appear to be enjoying themselves," Mattan murmured.

"I am surprised Uncle is not here."

"He does sneak over, but with all his duties he cannot stay long. It must chafe him raw." He opened a door. The circular chamber appeared almost empty except for one piece of...furniture? 'Twas a bit like the rostrums in the law library, save it had markings similar to the computers she saw the one time Uncle brought her here.

"This is a holographic chamber. We can view recorded meetings, gatherings, so many things. There are quite a few that include your mother. Let me see what I can find."

Tam stepped close to watch his fingers almost dance over the... "What is that called?"

"This?" Mattan stopped and turned to face her full, smiling. "So much you do not know, my dear niece. This is the console for the imager, and also a computer—do you know what that is?"

"Uncle said it is a machine with a way to..." she paused to remember his words precisely. "A way to store and retrieve information."

"Very good. Well, this computer can recall any recorded event saved anywhere in the complex."

A flash at the center of the chamber caused Tam to gasp. The light solidified into shapes, into people—as real if truly there, standing at a raised, round table, talking in some language she could not understand—mostly, save a word here and there. They all dressed strangely. Some with dark skin, like Mattan, and others pale, like her people.

Stars, one of them *was* Mattan! And her mother! Tam did indeed look like her, save her own skin was not so very dark. She stepped forward, walking through the moving images to stand near her.

"Mimma," she whispered. One hand reached out, but passed through her mother's face as if it were fog.

Ismari spoke seriously to one of the Enaisi, then her expression and voice softened, and dimples flashed in her cheeks. Tam found tears tracking down her own. "Mimma..."

The image stopped, froze, and she stared at her smiling mother. She seemed almost to be looking at Tam.

"She was beautiful," Mattan whispered. "And her heart as lovely as her face."

Are you well, Love-ling?

Tam mindspoke to her husband. *Aye. Mattan is showing me my mother. I am fine.*

Ismari stood before her, appearing as real as if there in truth, yet in essence only a mist, a fog, a trick of lights and Enaisi magic. "The pain seems worse, seeing her, yet it...eases it as well."

"Aye. The grief never leaves, but it becomes more bearable over time."

"Like a scar that still aches sometimes..."

"Aye."

"Take her away, Mattan. I...cannot do more. Not today."

The imaging disappeared, leaving the chamber even more empty. Tam turned. Tears filled Mattan's eyes. Some final reserve snapped, and she dove into his arms. "I am sorry, Uncle. I am sorry for the hurt!"

Love wrapped around her as thick as a cloak.

"It is all right, Tam. We go on. We must."

A scrape at the door made her loosen the embrace. Ordhral stood in the entrance. "I apologize. I heard voices. Pardon me." He turned away.

"Do not leave," Tam called. "You knew my mother. Please, do not leave. Mattan showed me a...an image of her. You can tell me of her too, can you not?"

"I will gladly stay and talk of Ismari, my little sister."

Tam frowned. "I am not your sister, but your cousin."

"Aye, but by the Enaisi language and their way of thinking, you are. They have no words for grandparents or other ancestors. She was my first mother, and you are her daughter. By their ways, we are siblings. Or half-siblings. And she treated me as if I were her son anyway."

"Then...perhaps we could have tea and talk of my mother more?" She looked up at Mattan for approval, and he nodded, smiling.

~*~

Alcandhor smiled as Tam chatted amiably with both Mattan and Ordhral at one of the tables after the evening meal. Whatever had caused the reticence in her appeared to have dissipated. Marcalan watched, listening more than participating; he seemed to understand this was healing for her and remained content to just stay near. Was the rascal actually showing some measure of maturity at last? Not too much though; he would miss it if the Ranger stopped all his pranks and jesting.

Marcalan twisted slightly to gaze at Alcandhor and winked. Stars! Did he somehow know what Alcandhor had been thinking, or was his ability to sense so acute he could tell? With a knowing grin, the rascal returned his attention to the discussion, one hand absently rubbing his wife's back.

"Thane!"

Haladhon stormed across the Great Hall. His furious intent and his use of Alcandhor's title bespoke of something dire and official.

As his cousin drew near, he asked, "Need we go to my Thane's chamber?"

"Nay." Haladhon inhaled sharply, and his voice lowered. "That by-blow Kostan is a troublemaker!"

"What has he done?"

"It is mouthings and attitude, but it is impacting my girls. And I do not trust him around them. I have taught them to defend themselves since they were young, and told them to keep guard. I think I put a fear in him, and stopped at the Ranger hold and instructed tight watch be kept until I return from Laird Hall."

"Good."

"I hope it is enough. Something about him is wrong. I cannot say on, but he is wrong."

"I will send a note to the Tarillan Rangers reinforcing your orders. When we return, we can look into him more thoroughly."

Haladhon rubbed his neck. "I thank you, Thane."

Chapter Seventeen

Irdhith came through the gatehouse and scanned the white stone of Laird Hall. Even with the overcast sky, the walls glittered like diamonds. His mouth dropped open, but envy quickly overshadowed any awe. His provincial hall was grand, but this was more ostentatious than anything his uncle could achieve. Why was his own hall not built of this alien stonework as well? His lip curled. Some lords obviously had preferential treatment centuries ago, just as they did now.

He inhaled the icy air and let it out slowly. He must keep himself in check, especially if the Thane or his sister were here since, from what Nandhal said, they could sense emotions. But just how much could they detect of another's feelings from across a chamber or across a table? He must exercise strong control, surely.

Was there some method more advantageous in gaining the affections of an empathic woman? Too bad Nandhal was dead; he could use the Ranger's advice, but wine spilled was not worth weeping over.

Lifting his chin, he smiled to himself. He had more than enough assets in his favor. Not only his looks, which turned every woman's head, but his wealth, position, and power. Aye, he would win this Sarinna.

~*~

Tam muttered under her breath as they walked down the muddy road. With an indulgent smile, Alcandhor asked, "Think you that you can repeat it?"

Amilla squealed just then, slipping in the mud and almost falling. Her husband and Haladhon steadied her.

"It could be worse," the tall Ranger said in a feigned whisper. "It could be snowing or sleeting."

"Some comfort," Eladhrel's wife replied with a wry smile.

Alcandhor chuckled, then turned back to his niece with an expectant expression.

Tam tipped her head. "I will try. My grandfather, and your father, was Saldhor. His father was Handhor, whose father was Nardhor, then Sardhel, Alcandhal, Pandhal, Tardhrel, Randhor, Zandhor, Taidhrol, Maidhrol, Maidhras, Sandhras, Pandhral, Zadhras, known as the Seer, Tidhrol, Taidhral, Canadhor, Paladhor, Valadhor, during whose time as

170

Thane the portal was closed."

"Correct."

"And that is still only half the years back to Mattan. I see not how I am to learn all this. I know some Rangers' names, and that is hard enough to remember sometimes, but to learn whose son each one is, and whose grandson, and which each cousin is to me, I think not that I can do it!"

"We will all help, Love-ling." Marcalan tugged her hair. "Fortunately, you married a Ranger who has a remarkable memory."

Tam rolled her eyes, then said to Alcandhor, "I know not how most cousins are related to me. That seems more important than learning my distant ancestors."

Mattan chuckled softly. "Careful. Some of your distant ancestors might resent that."

With a smile, she replied, "Most are dead and care not. Those that are living I will fain learn about."

"The young never appreciate the past," the Enaisi said, winking at Alcandhor.

"What is the next list of names I should learn?"

"Do you know all the names, and clan lineage, of those at First Table?"

Tam sighed, her gaze sliding to her husband, who lifted his eyebrows with an innocent expression. Another private conversation. "Nay, not all their names, Uncle." She glared at Marcalan. "Nor the lineage of most of them. I am sorry."

"Your first cousins are easy, of course," Alcandhor said.

Brightening, she exclaimed, "Oh, aye, I know all my first cousins. By sight and name."

"Then next, I would suggest learning your second cousins."

Her shoulder's sagging, Tam asked, "How many are there?"

"Oh, stars, shall we name them all?" Haladhon's eyes twinkled.

"And each one's lineage, so she can—" her husband stopped as she slapped his chest with the back of her hand, but he snickered.

"Since you are so eager, Ranger Chief Marcalan, you are her instructor. By day's end, see she knows all the Rangers of the First Table, their lineage, plus their wives, children, and grandchildren."

The rascal made a sweeping bow to his Thane, slid his arm around Tam's waist, and pulled her close. "I will fain teach this student at any time." The couple walked, embracing each other, Marcalan murmuring who her cousins were, between quick kisses to her temple.

"Now that is the way to have instruction." Haladhon nudged Alcandhor. "Too bad none of us can give such lessons."

Mattan peered over at him with a wry expression. "I am sure you have given plenty of lessons in your time."

"Do not get him on that subject, please," Alcandhor said, shaking his head.

The rake laughed but thankfully did not expound on the topic. Probably because of the women; they would all round on him if he became bawdy.

Alcandhor's thoughts turned to Nandhal's hanging and Pendhras' trial and the questions he had wanted to ask Mattan. With the flurry of preparing to leave and discussing "just one more" last-minute detail several times with Ordhral and Lantalan, and with Gardhal as well, and the frenzy over finding the prophecies, not to mention spending every moment he could with his children, the time had not presented itself for him to broach the topic. He called the alien over and pulled him a little away from the others.

"I have wanted to talk to you about what you did to Nandhal and Pendhras. It did not seem like the mere sending of pain but more as if...you could physically stop them from speaking. Choke them."

"Ah. I wondered if you would ask about that."

"So it is something beyond what Tam can do? And you would say nothing unless I first ask?"

Mattan stared ahead. Alcandhor waited, listening to the sound of all their boots sucking mud as they walked. Finally, the alien murmured, "There are things I do not fain discuss unless necessary, Thane. For the fear it can induce in others."

"Fear of what?"

"Fear of my people. Of...me."

"Think you I would come to fear you?"

"I know not. Your initial reverence evaporated rapidly, and you see the flawed man I am."

Alcandhor considered that for a moment. "So you have abilities about which we know nothing? And you wish to keep those secret?"

"Not secret. But only revealed prudently."

"Be prudently revealing then."

"You are single-minded, are you not?" Mattan asked with a fleeting smile. "Aye, I will say on. Or try anyway. It is difficult to explain. I can create a sensation so intense it seems as if they are physically affected."

"It appeared to be stronger than that."

"It is very effective."

"And that is all it is? It is not some ability to 'physically affect' others?"

Mattan flashed a real smile then. "Stars, would you make of me a god?"

"That is not an answer."

"It was meant to be. Do not try to credit me with some outlandish powers such the Worshippers might invent."

With a frown at Mattan's flippant attitude and lack of direct reply, Alcandhor sensed the alien, but found only amusement with a touch of derision. Was it only his fatigue that made him doubt his Enaisi Ranger Chief? Most likely. That bloody dream drained him of sleep, energy, and wit. He vented a long sigh.

"What is it?" Mattan whispered. "Do you distrust my answer?"

He shook his head. "Nay. I just..."

"What?"

"Our world, our people owe you so much. Our clan owes you so much. The abilities we have inherited from you are simply incredible. But there are times..."

"What? There are times—what?"

"There are times I almost curse those gifts."

"Have you seen something?"

"I have dreamed. Again. Several times, the latest last night. I know not what it means, but I feel exhausted as if I did not sleep."

"Those are the worst."

"What can I do?"

"About the dream, or the lack of sleep?"

Alcandhor snorted. "Either one."

"About the dream I can do nothing except commiserate. The lack of sleep can be remedied fairly easily."

"Oh?"

"Ask Tam. She knows more of herbs than I do."

"Aye, she has as much knowledge as a trained herbalist."

"Is that all that troubles you?"

Cutting his eyes to the Enaisi, he asked, "Shall I become irritated with you now, or wait until I find out what it is you wish to instruct me about this time?"

They shared a brief grin, then Mattan replied, "I simply wondered how you are feeling. After some of the morbid recent events."

"Nay, I am well," Alcandhor said after a moment. "I mourn the deaths, and the decisions that had to be made, but 'tis all over. As is that nightmare I have finally put to rest."

"But? What has you so filled with dread?"

"The dream. It...haunts me."

"Ah. So tell me."

"There is not much to tell. I see Estan Hall in my mind. I am compelled to go there. That is all."

"So it is more what you feel when you dream of Estan Hall, rather than dreaming of events?"

"Aye."

After a long silence, he looked over, curious that the alien had said nothing. "No guidance or opinion?"

The Enaisi lifted his eyebrows and shrugged. "Follow the dream."

Alcandhor grimaced. Was he more irritated when the man gave him advice or when he did not?

~*~

Tam understood why her uncle wished to stop at Lairdton's Ranger Hold. It was only proper respect to personally update the steward, Capalan, of events and allow him to meet Mattan. The poor, stunned man could only stutter, but the hold-keeper, Sherel, acted as if she met Elders every day and offered everyone tea.

Alcandhor refused for them all, disappointing the women, stating they must continue on after he received a brief report from Capalan about Estan.

"We could have stayed for tea while you Rangers discussed that province," Amilla said as they trudged down the path away from the hold.

"Aye, and turned it into another long discussion, delaying our arrival by that much more." Uncle nodded toward his chiefs. "I can apprise everyone on this last leg."

"Then do so," Haladhon grumbled.

Tam smiled up at her tall cousin. He must have wanted tea as well.

The Thane lifted a hand. "The accord between the governing council and the Esteni Rangers has broken down. The council seems to be playing favorites and disregarding advice and law references provided by Rangers. Factions are siding with and against the council. But each side blames us.

"The one faction, who call themselves simply the Rebels, claim the Rangers guidance caused the council to render wrongful decisions. Their goal is to rid their province of us and our influence as well as our appointed council. They reject the notion of a central government, desiring to set up regional councils, with locals appointing their own rulers, arbiters, and constabulary."

"That breaks every law we have, both our own, and those of the Enaisi!" exclaimed Andhrel, eyes wide.

"Aye, and the other faction is no better. They call themselves

Royalists and clamor for the council to be disbanded because of its bias and control returned to the nobles. They extol the idea of a province where the nobles would provide justice without Ranger interference, and that a constabulary established by Estan's lord would keep the peace. In essence, they wish their provincial lord to become their king."

"That is against all our laws too!" Tam said. "Do they not understand that?"

"I think they do not care. Some, of course, wish the traditional laws kept, but they are not vocal nor violent, so we have no concept of how large a percentage of the population they are."

"Not large enough a proportion, I would wager," Haladhon murmured.

"We shall discover more when I talk to the new lord of Estan Province, and when I visit myself."

"I do not like your talk of journeying to Estan," Haladhon said.

"It is my decision."

"But—"

"Do not say on!" Uncle's lips thinned, and he strode ahead.

Haladhon's worry weighed on Tam. Was her cousin unnecessarily fretting? Marcalan squeezed her around the shoulders, shaking his head and shrugging. So he did not know either?

Silence reigned while they passed through the town of Lairdton and along the tree-lined road. The women showed some sign of fatigue, and the Rangers seemed subdued. She could sense their concern, but was because they shared Haladhon's opinion or merely because the Thane was being stubborn?

When they finally came out from the trees lining the road, the women sighed with relief. So did Tam. One final climb up the road to Laird Hall, built atop the rise at the center of an enormous glade. The imposing edifice sparkled like ice in the late afternoon sun. At last, this journey was over. Traveling with women was not enjoyable. Oh, they did not complain; but they were not used to journeying, and the slow pace irritated her. The memories of how difficult it was urging the young Laird to continue on day after day when she rescued him helped her try to be patient.

So many changes happened in the short time since Tam had first been there less than three lunations ago. Then she felt she was not much more than the mountain lass she had pretended to be when she was sent in to spy at Laird Hall. Now, she knew who she was: a Child of the Enaisi, Ranger chief, and heir to Thane. Then she had been a child, now she was considered a woman grown.

She could not wait to see her friend the Laird again. What would he think when he found she had wed Marcalan?

Her husband's proud claim of her, and his love, washed over her. She would not have believed she could feel thus. Her childhood felt empty upon remembrance now that she knew what it was to be cherished.

They passed through the gatehouse and into the bailey. Tam half expected the Laird to come running out to greet them, but that would not be proper behavior for the high lord of all the noble clans. With Lord Krendhal here, the young man would be more reserved and tend to follow proprieties.

Lamadhel did meet them however, grabbing Alcandhor's shoulders in an unusually open display of affection. Perhaps because of how close they came to losing him when Question was called? The Thane pulled his uncle to the alien. "Lamadhel, I wish to introduce Mattan."

The older Ranger bowed. "It is an honor, sir."

The Enaisi clasped his shoulder in the traditional greeting. "Call me Mattan. I am a chief, as you are."

"I understand you are also my forebear." A smiled played on her great-uncle's lips. "It is disconcerting to know you have so many years as to make me a babe, yet look so much younger."

They all laughed, then Alcandhor asked, "How is our Laird?"

"Well. In fits over his cousin's determination to marry him to the likeliest young lady he can find, but other than that, fine."

"The poor boy," Uncle muttered.

Blinking with total innocence, Marcalan said, "Perhaps if you feel such sympathy for him, you will offer assistance by distracting some of the women, Thane."

"Stars," Alcandhor groaned. "If you all do not cease with your jesting my hair shall turn grey."

Marcalan chuckled. "Now he sounds like my father."

Lamadhel slapped a hand on her husband's shoulder. "Congratulations, Marcalan. And to you, Tam."

She reached on tiptoe to embrace him. "Thank you for sending the message to save Uncle."

The older Ranger held her for a few moments. As they parted, he looked over the contingent of Rangers that had traveled with them. "You all know where the barracks are. The Laird bids you all welcome." He turned to the chiefs. "The Laird will receive you in the Great Hall, then you will be shown to your suites."

Galran, Master of the Guards, stood at the entrance to the antechamber. Although still thin from his captivity during the siege, he looked more hale now. For a time they had not been certain he would live. Alcandhor clasped his shoulder with a grin. "Good to see you regaining your health, my friend."

"And good to see you, Thane."

"Visit when you can. I would fain play you a game of kingsmen."

"I would enjoy that. Thank you, Thane."

Journey-worn and muddy, the Rangers entered the Great Hall. The many nobles present, arrayed in sumptuous finery, turned to whisper among themselves. With Alcandhor leading, they walked through the enormous chamber to the estrade at the center of the wall on the northern side. Tam needed not sense to feel the stares and curiosity, especially toward her and Mattan.

The sun, streaming in through wide windows of colored glass, blazed a rainbow across the floor and walls. Ornate carvings decorated the columns, moldings, and buttresses made of the glittering, white stone, some overlaid with gold.

Brightly colored tapestries depicting stories hung on the walls. One was obviously a picture of their arrival on this planet, complete with the dark Enaisi, hands spread in bestowment, and the pale Teldheri staring about them in wonder. Tall mountains towered majestically behind them against a backdrop of blue sky. Another tapestry showed the aliens on bended knee before a man in a silver and blue surcoat with Teldheri crowded around as witness. Tam glanced at Mattan. Would he give her details of the events of those tapestries? Indeed, he must be one of the Enaisi pictured in them!

Lord Krendhal stood on the estrade next to an ornate chair, regal in his dark purple surcoat, edged with white. The Laird, in a similar surcoat, only white edged with purple, rose from his seat as they approached, his face solemn. "Welcome to Laird Hall, Thane Alcandhor, chiefs, and ladies of Ch'shalna clan. We are honored by your presence."

"We are your servants, Your Grace." Alcandhor and all the Rangers bowed, and the women curtsied. "I wish to present to you our newest chief, Marcalan, husband to Second at Table, Tamissa, daughter of Valdhor."

As he gave his congratulations to the couple, the Laird grinned—too wide and not as decorous as was wont from Lord Krendhal's frown. The young man glanced at his First Minister and cleared his throat, his expression becoming more serious.

At least Marcalan only smirked, resisting the urge to jest. She sensed his mental giggle and squeezed his hand, tacitly telling him to behave.

"Also, my Laird, I wish to introduce you to Ranger Chief Mattan, an Enaisi who has come back to us."

The young lord returned Mattan's bow with slow reverence, his light blue eyes round. "I am honored, sir, to meet you, and on behalf of all our people, I welcome you."

"I thank you, Your Grace. I am delighted to return to my adopted people and my descendants," Mattan replied, bowing once more. "I am honored to serve."

The Laird swallowed but found his voice after a few moments. "I know you have journeyed for days. You Rangers are hardy, and while I have no doubt your ladies are as well, they are not as inured to such travel. This servant will show you to the chambers prepared for you. Please refresh yourselves. I look forward to seeing you at evening meal."

"Many thanks, Your Grace." Alcandhor bowed again then they all continued to the east end of the Great Hall and the main staircase.

"Uncle," Tam said once they were in the upper hallway, "the Laird was so formal, much more so than I expected. Save for that smile to Marcalan and me, he treated us as if we were strangers."

"He is not yet of Age and the object of scrutiny, surrounded by nobles who would fain find reason to call Question on his ability to be Laird. He is bound to show all propriety in front of them."

"How sad. He must be very lonely."

"Aye." Alcandhor dropped an arm around Tam's shoulders in a quick squeeze.

~*~

Turning the corner at the southeast side of the keep on the second floor above ground, Alcandhor saw standards at each end of the hallway displaying Ranger colors. The servant bowed. "The chambers along the outside wall of this corridor are all appointed for your clan." He stood back by two small stands, as was custom, waiting to see which suite the Thane would choose so he could place the banners with his crest on each side of that door.

Marcalan raised his eyebrows, a mischievous glint in his eyes. "Think you that you both can remember which chambers are yours this time?"

"Vagabond," Alcandhor muttered as Haladhon laughed. Stars, the younger Ranger recalled that tidbit from the night he and Haladhon tricked Alcandhor into getting drunk, and then they all told stories from their youth? What else did the rascal remember? No matter. He nodded down the hall. "The chambers in this section of the keep are all suites, and along the southern side with wide windows. And he gives us choice as if this were our own home. The Laird will undoubtedly receive some complaints for thus favoring Ch'shalna clan."

Mattan walked down the corridor with a frown and pointed at two of the doors. "These suites, if memory serves me correctly, are doubles. Two bedchambers joined to one living chamber. It might be better for Sarinna, and Tam and Marcalan to choose from the single suites further down, which would give them more privacy."

"A most thoughtful notion," Marcalan said with a lilt, winking at Tam. She blushed as he took her hand and led her down the corridor.

"We brothers might share a double. What say you?" Andhrel asked his wife. She exchanged a glance with Amilla, who nodded.

"That would suit us," Cariss replied with a smile.

"You two are fortunate your wives are friends," Mattan said with a chuckle. He pointed to the next door down. "We single men can share a double suite."

Alcandhor grinned at Haladhon. "Aye, I think sharing a suite would be just the thing."

The rake straightened, eyes wide. "Alcandhor, you would not be so cruel!"

"Would I not? What better way to be sure you behave yourself."

From down the corridor, Marcalan's laugh floated back. "See what a difference marriage makes, cousin?" he called as Tam opened the door. "What is considered misbehaving for you, is considered proper behavior for me. Especially with a wife who—" he squawked as Tam swatted him, then pulled him into the suite. The door slammed.

They all chuckled, then Haladhon turned back to his cousin. "Thane, you are not truly serious."

Alcandhor lowered his voice, mindful of the waiting servant. "This is a lords' conclave, and nothing must happen that could bring censure to us or the Laird. One indiscretion could set tongues flapping all through this hall. Mattan can have the one bedchamber, and we can share the other." His lips twitched with a smile. "Worry not, cousin, I mind not your snoring."

Haladhon grimaced.

"It really does make sense," Lamadhel said. "There are so many lords and ladies coming, that to give a suite to a single man would be looked upon unfavorably. And there are no single bedchambers on this level."

"'Tis not fair. Sarinna is single yet has her own suite."

"It is assumed any lady will be sharing her suite with all her garments and the sundry items that women seem to require in order to appear at court." Lamadhel said with a wink at Sarinna.

A raised eyebrow and pursed lips were her only reply.

Haladhon gave Alcandhor a despondent look. "Lead the way to our chamber, Thane."

~*~

Alcandhor gestured for Mattan to answer the knock at their door before setting his pack in the bedchamber. He returned to the parlor to see the Laird and Lord Krendhal standing in the doorway. Both hesitated, eyes on the Enaisi. With an inviting sweep of his arm, the alien bowed.

The two lords entered, and the Laird said, "We wanted to explain the need for scribes, Thane."

"Ah."

"If you remember there were scribes among those here that were found to be traitors when the siege ended?"

"Aye, I do."

"We have discovered we only have one faithful scribe. And we have been inundated with petitions."

"So that explains the mystery." Alcandhor nodded toward Krendhal. "We brought three, as you requested, milord."

"I thank you," the First Minister said. "We shall set them to their duties tomorrow."

A sly grin spread on the Laird's face. "Now, that we have dispensed with the important business that forced us away from the Great Hall and our other guests, tell me how you all are doing." He turned to look at Mattan, wonder in his eyes. "And how we are so honored by a visit by an Enaisi after all these years."

"We are all fine—"

"Ha!" Haladhon interrupted with a grin. "'Fine,' he says. But he will tell you little of what has gone on lately. He no longer wears a necklet, if you notice, Your Grace."

Alcandhor shot his cousin a dirty look.

The Laird's wide-eyed stare fastened on Alcandhor's neck.

His Third at Table chuckled. "You will not be the only eligible male of high rank at court, my Laird."

With a glare, Alcandhor shot back, "Forget not that you are not married, cousin."

"Nor is Lord Krendhal, nor Mattan. I hold myself in good company." Haladhon inclined his head, grinning.

Alcandhor *tsked*. "Pay him no mind, Your Grace."

"Of course." The young lord's eyes twinkled. "But now, please, let me become more acquainted with Ranger Chief Mattan."

The alien smiled and bowed. "I am honored, Your Grace."

The Laird returned the bow, then shook his head. "I am the one who is honored, Enaisi. To think it is in my time that the portal is reopened, and your people walk among us again."

Mattan held up his hands. "Treat me not as a god, Your Grace. I am just a man, as you are."

"Save his life span is longer than our years on this planet," Haladhon said in a dry aside.

Alcandhor bit back a smile at the young man's astonished look.

"His life span is what?"

The Thane clapped a hand on the alien's shoulder. "Your Grace, this is the same Mattan that came to Teledhar from Elyria with our forefathers one thousand years ago."

Krendhal's low, firm voice rumbled, "Impossible."

"'Tis hard to believe, aye, but it is true."

The lord's eyebrows raised as his cynical expression gave his answer.

"I had wondered what you meant when you said you had returned to your descendants." The Laird shrugged with a smile. "But...it seems no more impossible than Rangers who can send emotions which drop people to the ground. For myself, I will try to get past my disbelief. Now, tell me how you came to be with us again."

Alcandhor grinned, walking over to the sideboard where refreshments had been laid in for them as Mattan explained all to the Laird and Krendhal.

Chapter Eighteen

Even at Laird Hall, Rangers usually only wore their daily garb, but being at court with other nobles present, it was necessary for the chiefs to dress accordingly. Twice in so short a time, Alcandhor was forced to don his formal attire. An onerous duty. Especially since here he could not avoid the silver-edged azure cape and worse, the gold sash, fastened at his right shoulder and resting at his left hip. Considering all the nobles wished to avoid any acknowledgement of his historical status and rank, one would think he could forego wearing that despised sash, but always they insisted that formalities be observed.

Soft music filled the Great Hall as the Rangers descended for that evening's banquet. Haladhon was correct; Alcandhor dreaded the courtly evening affair. But he was proud to have Sarinna's hand lightly on his. He swallowed the horrid thought had it been Aleta instead.

Marcalan never looked more smug than at this moment with Tam on his arm, slender and straight as a water reed in her formal Ranger garb. Alcandhor's chest swelled with pride and love for her, too. Soft billows of affection wafted over him, letting him know she felt and returned his sentiment.

Long tables filled the sides of the enormous chamber, draped in cloths of each provincial lord's colors, allowing those of their clan to sit together. Nay, upon a second look, not only each lord's clan, but also those noble clans within their borders. And mostly occupied by women. Some must have emptied their province of every marriageable noble female. No wonder the hall was so crowded! Alcandhor stifled a sigh of pity for the poor, young Laird.

He took his place on the Laird's right at the main table with Sarinna next to him, giving nods of greeting to the other lords. Only eight were present, by settings marked. The lords of Estan, Valeshon, Andethon, and Beshalon were absent. The latter three he could understand; their provinces were most distant, but Estan should be here. Great Bells, were they still bickering over which noble of their clan should be appointed lord?

Krendhal returned Alcandhor's nod with a cool incline of his head. Tadhrol of Taladar Province gave a crooked smile in welcome from down the table on the opposite side. Alcandhor did not miss the added silver in the lord's dark blond hair and the increased lines in his face. Surely, it had not been so long since he had seen his old friend? Rildhran of Tathelon directly across and Vendhal of Ranshalon next to him both nodded in greeting. The other lords present were new, having come into their positions on the recent death or exile of their predecessors when the siege ended. Their nods were polite, but he needed not sense to be aware of their wary curiosity.

The wives of the established lords met his gaze with varying amounts of wonder and amusement, their eyes invariably straying to his throat. Years of familiar acquaintance with them warned him that before the evening was over these matrons would be demanding details of how he came to be unmarried.

Lorwith of Pashelon Province, accompanied by a lady, hurried to his place at the table between Krendhal and the new lord of Lantral, squeaking an apology and patting the elaborate braids in his long blond hair. Alcandhor ground his teeth that no proof had been found to charge that lord with treason.

The Laird spread his arms. "Thane Alcandhor and Lady Sarinna, welcome. I am honored to introduce our new provincial lords. Lord Irdhith of Lantral Province, escorting Ashill, lady of Lantral clan." The Laird gestured to the tall, broad-shouldered man to Alcandhor's right, beyond Lorwith. He had at least Haladhon's height, with pale blond hair braided away from his face and falling to his waist. The Lantral heritage shone in his blue eyes, icy despite his smile, all too similar to the piercing eyes of his uncle and former lord, Zantith.

Pride and ambition both were strong in this one; he would have to be watched. He bowed to Irdhith, who displayed much deference in returning the courtesy to the Thane of the Rangers. The lord's eyes glinted as they fell upon Sarinna. A prickle of warning coursed down Alcandhor's spine, but surely his sister would not be vulnerable to such rakish charms. Ashill, was buxom, and fixed Alcandhor with a winning smile, her gaze resting on his throat. He felt like groaning but kept his expression bland.

The Laird indicated the man across from Irdhith. His pinched face and long nose lent him the appearance of the beach fowl called a piperbird. The woman with him was as heavyset as he was thin. "Lord Perdhal of Nelatan Province, and his wife, Lady Madinn."

Perdhal bent in a stiff, formal bow. From what Alcandhor could sense, this man had a small, petty mind. Another to be watched.

The Laird nodded to the lord to left of the Nelatan lord. "Lord Gilendhar of Keladar, and his wife, Lady Lerill."

Gilendhar was as fleshy as his odious predecessor. Were his political leanings and greed similar as well? He had met the man many times, a silent shadow in the background of his first cousin, Lord Paltor.

For that matter, did he hate the Rangers with the same passion Paltor did? Lerill curtsied with deference that came from her heart. Her face had hard lines in it, but her grey eyes shone with benevolence. He would fain know her story. Alcandhor's gaze followed as the Laird's hand moved toward Pashelon's lord.

"Rastill, lady of clan Esch'ala is the escort of Lord Lorwith."

Lorwith rubbed his hands together in nervous habit, bobbing a bow as the woman curtsied. Lady of a minor noble clan and only given the designation of escort? She was likely Lorwith's legal mistress. How many did he have, yet no wife? Ch'shalna clan would be called on that, but as always, the other clans did as they pleased.

"And this evening I have the honor to escort the lovely Felara, lady of Ranshalon clan, and Lord Krendhal is graced by the presence of Sotara, lady of Pashelon." The Laird glanced about the table. "Have I made all the introductions?"

"I believe everyone else is already acquainted, Your Grace," Krendhal said.

The Laird lifted his chin and then sat. All the guests followed suit, and the food was served. Not too soon, as Alcandhor's stomach rumbled.

"So, Thane..." Irdhith broke off a piece of bread. "You tell me truly that yon dark one is an Elder?" He nodded toward Ch'shalna clan's table.

Alcandhor paused in lifting his spoon. "Aye."

"How know you this for certain? Saw you him come through the portal?" The young lord's tone mocked, but he let the slight pass.

"As a matter of fact, the chiefs did."

Recognizing the imminent danger in Sarinna's sweet-as-nectar voice, Alcandhor bent over his soup to hide his mirth.

"Perhaps you would like to visit Zaidhron, Lord Irdhith," she said, "and see the places of the Enaisi for yourself."

A hush fell over the table. He glanced up to see almost everyone gaping at them. "Is there a problem?"

The Lantral lord glared at him as if he were a simpleton. "You will allow your sister to extend such an invitation, when your duty has always been to guard the secrets of the Elders?"

Alcandhor kept his tone even, ignoring the derision in the young noble's voice. "Our duty is to guard their edifices and structures, aye, milord, but not to hide them. The Portal Complex has ever been within our reach and you are welcome to visit and receive a tour."

The Laird nodded. "Aye, 'tis true. Thane Saldhor took me there when I was a lad. 'Twas most remarkable. Although the long climb up the mountain was exhausting." His eyes shone. "But to see that portal working, and not an empty frame—I would fain trek up there again to see that!"

"Perhaps Mattan would give a demonstration." Alcandhor ducked his head while grabbing a hand loaf from the platter to cover his smile.

"But would you not be afraid some of us might try to learn how it works?" Irdhith asked.

With a grin, Alcandhor broke off a piece of the bread. "I have studied for years but my knowledge is useless. Only the touch of an Enaisi can activate any of their devices."

The young noble took a bite of crust, looking thoughtful as he chewed.

"Tell us of your new Second at Table, Thane." Tadhrol's smooth, rich voice carried easily. "She is your niece? Valdhor's daughter?"

"Aye." Alcandhor dropped a piece of bread in his soup. "He Trained her well. She is a good fighter."

"I would fain see that," the Lantral lord said, laughing, and popped a morsel of crust in his mouth.

"Perhaps you would match her, Lord Irdhith?" the Laird asked. "I have seen her fight, but would fain watch again."

Irdhith stopped mid-chew, then quickly swallowed. "Fight a tiny lass as that? I could snap her in two!"

The Laird, Alcandhor, and Sarinna all chuckled, and Krendhal smiled.

"I would fain see you try," the First Minister said, an eyebrow lifted in amusement.

The arrogant lord's gaze darted from face to face. "You mock me," he finally said.

"Nay," Krendhal said. "Do not underestimate her. Accepting a lass as Ranger, and later as Thane, will take some adjusting to my thoughts, but not because I doubt her abilities." One corner of his mouth lifted in a wry smile. "I have prejudices to overcome."

"Thane?" chorused several lords.

Alcandhor studiously spooned soup as the Laird said, "Tam is her father's heir to Thane."

His sister leaned close and whispered, "You are enjoying this too much, brother."

He almost choked, and Sarinna slapped his back as Irdhith sneered, "That lass will be Thane?"

"Aye, when she comes of Age," the Laird said, bristling. He glared at the Lantral lord. "And I back her."

"You ask much of us to back a woman as Thane," said Perdhal, his small eyes narrowing.

"It is much for me to back you new lords, considering your

predecessors killed my father and plotted to kill me."

Alcandhor shot the lad a chastising look as the table fell silent.

Krendhal cleared his throat. "That was not meet, Your Grace."

"Perhaps not well-worded, but the fact remains that this is something that needs to be addressed." Tadhrol leaned back, glancing at the new lords, his upper lip curling slightly in what could pass as either a smile or sneer. "I admit to doubts about loyalty as you are all kin to the deposed lords."

"That is understandable," Irdhith said, face red, his tone less taunting now. "But we swore an oath of loyalty to both Laird and Thane when we took lordship of our provinces."

"The oath of the previous lords meant little. Only time can determine if your vows carry value," Rildhran said. "Just as time will determine whether we will back that lass as Thane."

Alcandhor pulled slices of roasted herdbeast onto his plate while peering past Krendhal to regard Lorwith out of the corner of his eye. The man's nervous habits made it impossible to tell if he were affected by the conversation, but within he warred against fear, struggling to maintain a calm façade.

Perdhal peered down at the Laird. "As Lord Krendhal said, your words were not meet, Your Grace. I had no love for Cardhal, and no involvement with his politics. I simply want my province to prosper."

The Laird's blue eyes glittered, despite the pink hue in his face. "I do not apologize for my statement. If not for the Thane and that lass, whom you all are so ready to dismiss, I would not be alive. If near-death and gratitude give me a quick tongue on their behalf, then so be it." His gaze rested on Irdhith. "And I will have proper respect from all of you when you address the Thane."

The lords inclined their heads.

"And Thane, I expect you to demand respect of these lords."

"Your pardon, Your Grace. I gave Lord Irdhith lenience as he is so very young."

Alcandhor sensed the bristling of the Lantral lord, who was not actually all that young, having what, twenty-four or twenty-five years? He schooled his expression and ignored the humor from Sarinna, giving intent interest to the Laird.

"If he has wit to be lord, then he has wit to understand respect. And know that I demand respect toward that clan which has taken oath to serve us at the cost of their own lives."

All the lords at the table again bowed their heads.

"It would appear," Rildhran said, "that you have truly stepped into your role as Laird."

"Aye." Gilendhar leaned back in his chair, his cheeks puffing out. "But be aware, young Laird, that we have not come to trust you yet, either. You are not even of Age. We could easily call Question and have your cousin set as Laird in interim, or permanently."

The Laird's face flushed, and Krendhal flashed a triumphant smile. "Indeed. My cousin is young and passionate in his idealism, and not wise in how to deal with provincial lords. I, however, am a cynical old kinchou, who cares nothing for any of you, or your posturing."

Randhal shot an indignant glare at his First Minister. "Aye, you have said I should show less tolerance—"

"And you should, Your Grace! Scrutinize their trade and internal laws. Look into their dealings, and arbitrations. If you cannot oversee the provincial lords with a firm fist then perhaps you should not be Laird yet."

Alcandhor hid a smile as Gilendhar heaved himself up straight. "Now wait! I am still in the throes of changeover from Paltor being lord. 'Tis not a quick swipe of the arm to bring changes. We need a clement hand as we take on our roles."

Irdhith snorted. "Have you dropped the ridiculous surcharges for the coal sold from your mines? Or looked into the large pockets of those overseeing the shipments of that coal to other provinces?"

Gilendhar's face reddened. "I–it is being investigated."

"I daresay," Irdhith said with a sharp laugh. "Nay, we all have much to order from our previous lords, and I think our young Laird would be more gracious than his cousin to us. I, for one, do give full support to the Laird."

Alcandhor winced. Krendhal had not been subtle, but the Lantral lord made him seem circumspect by comparison.

"This is not the conclave chamber, Lord Irdhith," Perdhal said. "We do not give a public vote."

The young noble's square jaw set. "True, but I publicly state my position—I have nothing to hide."

Tadhrol gave a quiet chuckle, but his voice belied humor. "Nay, you crow your endorsement of the Laird thinking we have not the intellect to see the pretension you display with such vulgarity."

Irdhith shot to his feet, chest out, but the older lord merely leaned back with an evil grin, his thumb brushing against his fingertips. "Sit you down, boy. I am too old for such posturing. Be aware that we lords do speak our own mind most cuttingly, and if you cannot absorb offense as well as you give it, you will not be respected."

The Lantral lord reseated himself, glowering.

"So, my dear Thane," Shalinn, Tadhrol's wife, said, breaking the silence. Her eyes cut around the table before settling on Alcandhor with a mischievous sparkle, "you must know we women are all curious about this missing necklet of yours."

He hoped his grimace passed as a smile. "Aye. It was inevitable."

"Then thwart the gossip and give us the details, and we can circulate the truth of the matter."

Sarinna gave a low chuckle, and he shot daggers at her.

"Shall I tell them, brother?"

After a slight hesitation, he stated, "I put out Aleta."

"Good," Shalinn said.

Rildhran's wife, Kylinn nodded. "Past due time, too."

Shalinn pointed her eating knife at Alcandhor. "Now you can set about finding yourself a good woman."

"And if I left it in your capable hands, I am certain you would have a new wife chosen, enh?"

Waving a hand to indicate the Great Hall, Shalinn exclaimed, "From this lot? My dear Thane, nay! Choose a good woman from Ranger clan. One who understands your ways."

Alcandhor snorted. Bells, did she think the women at Zaidhron were any better than those here? They desired the Thane, not the man. "And if my choice is to not choose?"

Kylinn *tsked*.

Vendhal's wife, Turill, gave a mournful shake of her head. "Men just do not know what is best for them, do they?"

Although Alcandhor might not know best about some things, on this subject the best thing was to keep quiet. He applied himself industriously to the meat and tubers on his plate as the women talked of marriage. The other men at the table displayed the same wisdom as well.

Chapter Nineteen

After the meal, servants cleared the tables and carried them away while the nobles congregated in small groups. Randhal eyed Mattan, who naturally garnered much attention. With Felara on his arm, Randhal approached the cluster around the Enaisi with smugness, having already met and spoken with him privately. They all turned toward him, bowing, then resumed their conversation.

"You expect us to believe that?" Irdhith was asking.

Mattan gave an unconcerned chuckle. "It bothers me not what you believe, milord. I answer not to any of you, but to my Thane. And to the Laird. The vows I took then still apply now." He gestured to a tapestry hanging to one side of the estrade. Shock struck Randhal like lightning— had this man truly lived back then, as he claimed? Was he represented in the tapestries?

"And if you are an imposter then that vow is meaningless, is it not?" Perdhal asked.

"I would fain reaffirm my vow. If my Thane and Laird desire it."

"It might be wise to do so, to set minds at ease," Krendhal said.

Mattan gazed at Randhal. "Your Grace?"

"It shall be addressed at conclave, once all the lords are here."

Shalinn joined them with a curtsey. Despite her hair starting to grey and fine lines about her eyes, the lady was still attractive. *If only I could find a lass with such poise and graciousness as this slender matron.* But then he remembered that Lord Tadhrol's wife's tongue could cut swifter than a well-sharpened knife. She smiled at Randhal's escort. "My dear, these men will discuss politics all evening, it is acceptable to excuse yourself if you grow bored."

Glancing at Randhal, Felara said, "I would stay."

Shalinn lifted her shoulders in a slight shrug. "As you wish. But do not let them catch you yawning." Her eyebrows raised as she met his gaze. Why did Randhal get the impression that the Taladar lady did not approve of Felara? He himself thought nothing of her save she was fairly pretty and rather quiet.

"Speaking of which," Gilendhar adjusted his surcoat over his bulk, "I understand your cousin is urging you to wed as soon as possible, to continue your clan, Your Grace."

Randhal's face warmed. "Aye. It is my duty."

The Keladar lord nodded. "Considering how Viltara has dwindled

189

due to several calamities, it would be wise. Have any caught your fancy yet?"

How could his face grow still hotter? Stars, his ears burned. "Nay." He inclined his head toward Felara, having learned through a recent very embarrassing experience that one always gives mention of the lady on one's arm. "There are many beautiful ladies here which turn my head, such as my lovely escort this evening, but I have not yet even thought of choosing."

Vendhal cleared his throat. "You should choose soon. 'Tis your duty not only to your clan, but to all of us. We must have an heir from you."

Irdhith gestured to Felara. "Considering the situation, you might be wise to invoke Clan Law, and take several wives and mistresses. Viltara needs to build itself."

"I have suggested that to the Laird myself, but he has resisted the idea." Krendhal shot a piqued glance at Randhal.

"Have you chosen a wife yet yourself, milord?" Mattan asked.

His First Minister straightened with an indignant expression. "Pardon?"

Randhal bit his lip to hide his smile; he had wanted to ask the same question but lacked the courage.

"Aye. As second to the thane of Viltara clan, it is also your duty to build it up."

"I–I was married. She died of the fever that swept through several years ago. As did our two children and grandchild."

"That is not what I asked. You need heirs as well as the Laird. You should consider one wife at least."

"It has been suggested that I consider marrying again." Krendhal's eyes flicked momentarily at Haladhon, who stood behind the others, grinning. "I suppose I should give it serious thought."

The tall Ranger caught Randhal's eye and gave an impudent wink. Again, his face grew warm, and he glanced at Felara, who also blushed. "Can we suspend our discussion of such things. There is a lady present."

"No need," she murmured, curtseying. "I...will leave you men to talk of...politics. With your permission, Your Grace?"

Randhal bowed, grateful for her departure, but what might halt the conversation now? The solution approached in the persons of Tam and Marcalan. Things should be livelier and more fun now.

"Bells, what said you men to drive away a lass with such high ambition?" the prankster asked, with a broad grin.

The nobles all burst into laughter.

Vendhal chortled. "Now, how know you that my cousin has such high ambition, enh, Ranger?"

"Stars, milord, is there one unmarried lass in attendance who has not high ambition?"

The Ranshalon lord lifted his glass. "A point."

"You seem unperturbed for her sake, Lord Vendhal," said Tadhrol, a smile twitching on his lips.

"I admit 'twould be a political boon for my province to claim such alliance with Viltara, but be not fooled by her demure matter. That lass has the claws of a ballan, and I would feel pity if this poor lad were stuck with her."

"'Tis a warning for more than our Laird." Marcalan chuckled. "I see quite a few of you do not wear necklets."

"You can jest about it, since you find yourself wearing one now, you rascal," Randhal said. "And considering Tam is intelligent and possesses common sense, how did you ever convince her to marry you?"

"'Twas my ineffable charm and striking handsome looks, Your Grace."

His friend rolled her eyes, but her husband just tugged her hair, grinning.

The lords all smiled, save Irdhith, who stared at her with an inscrutable expression. "So you are the lass who would be Thane, enh?"

She craned her neck to gaze up at the tall lord. "I am the lass whose uncle would have her be Thane. I am content to be a Ranger."

"Conclave vowed Valdhor's heir would be Thane," Alcandhor stated as the two continued to lock eyes. "The idea is new to Tam, and she is not yet comfortable with it."

"I have heard you are able to fight," Irdhith said.

"Aye. And you would fain match me, no doubt," Tam replied, mimicking Irdhith's slightly sarcastic tone exactly. Bells, but his friend had grown much saucier since he last saw her.

"No doubt."

The crowd of nobles quieted as neither one would look away. Tam was stubborn, but this new lord was tall, muscular, and intimidating. Would she give in first? It would not bode well if she did. Randhal struggled against the urge to fidget, holding his breath.

Irdhith inhaled, almost a gasp, and broke away from her stare, his gaze scanning them all. He cleared his throat, red creeping up into his face as he looked again at Tam. "I shall look forward to matching you, Lady Ranger." He bowed and retreated.

Tadhrol snorted softly, as several of the nobles murmured under their breath. Randhal grinned at her, and she raised innocent eyebrows in return. Bells, she was becoming like Marcalan!

"Tam, I would have a word with you, if my ministers and your husband will give us leave."

"Certainly, Your Grace."

The two walked a distance away. "I wish to impose upon our friendship. I hope you will not think me too presumptuous."

"What is it, Your Grace?"

"I...I am in a strait." He licked his lips. "I cannot avoid marriage, but I fear what I will marry."

"Ah, you wish me to sense for sincerity."

Randhal nodded, biting his lip.

"I would be honored to do so for you, Your Grace. I can understand your concern. I have remembered what you told me about never knowing who was truly your friend. I cannot imagine marrying and finding it was for ambitious purposes, not love."

Randhal sagged. "I cannot hope for love. I have not the time nor luxury for it. But I do hope for a lass that at least, well...likes me somewhat, instead of only thinking of marrying the Laird."

"I shall do my best, Your Grace."

"I thank you, Tam."

~*~

Mattan stood at the edge of the estrade, watching the dancers weave in intricate patterns. For a people not given to aesthetics, their creativity frequently demonstrated itself in subtle but beautiful ways. Unlike the Enaisi, who expressed themselves in flamboyant art forms which, too often, he found aggrandized to the point of banality.

"Will you not dance, Ranger Chief Mattan?" asked the Laird, stepping up next to him.

He bowed, smiling. "My apologies, Your Grace, but these are very different from the style of dances I remember, and I am not familiar with them."

"Perhaps some of the young ladies would care to instruct you."

The innocent look on the Laird's face made Mattan chuckle. "Wish you me to play marriage merchant?"

The lad's face grew red. "Nay, but every garden needs judicious weeding, does it not?"

"It has not been the policy of Zaidhron to weed Laird Hall's gardens, has it?"

"Nay, Ranger chief. But I do throw myself on your mercy."

Mattan laughed, bowing. "I am honored. For such a worthy cause, I shall constrain myself to learn these dances, Your Grace."

"You have my gratitude, sir." Returning the bow, he beckoned a page over and whispered to him.

As the young attendant announced quietly to the ladies that Ranger Chief Mattan was in need of partners to teach him the current court dances, the Laird murmured, "I do feel it is deceitful."

"Your Grace, I do not consider it deceitful to use my abilities to merely sense for honest affection and weed out those with a mercenary bent. I would imagine you have already asked for Tam's assistance also. It rests with you whom to choose from those that survive the weeding."

The Laird smiled sadly. "If only I did not have to choose. I feel I am too young, but I know Lord Krendhal is correct. My family needs heirs. And if I choose well, perhaps marriage will not be so disagreeable."

"Indeed, Your Grace, marriage can be much more than just 'agreeable.'"

"Did you find it so?" the lad asked, his expression eager, then he dropped his gaze. "Forgive me for asking such a personal question, sir."

"No need, Your Grace. I do not mind talking about Tarnill. I loved her deeply, and she, me. I know love cannot be your first consideration, your duty forbids it, but still, you may find companionship, and perhaps love will follow."

Several young women stepped forward and, catching Mattan's attention, curtsied.

"Excuse me, Your Grace, but I believe you have some ladies daring enough to dance with an Elder." He bowed, whispering, "Wish me good fortune!"

The women's intentions quickly became clear. They were more interested in whether Mattan could be counted on to recommend them to the Laird—or the Thane, unsurprisingly—than in helping him learn the dances. He politely endured, then withdrew to stand again near the lad, who, after dancing with quite a few ladies as well, had also retreated to the estrade.

"Your Grace, I found nothing but weeds," he murmured. "I am sorry."

The Laird nodded and shrugged. "I begin to wonder if I must simply choose from among the weeds."

"Do not give up hope, Your Grace."

Alcandhor approached, and all three bowed. Such strict courtesy these people had; so very different from his own people's customs.

"You seem perturbed, Your Grace."

"We are discussing weeding gardens, Thane," the Laird replied.

At Alcandhor's confused frown, they both grinned.

"I have agreed to do a little 'weeding' for the Laird," Mattan explained, his eyes darting quickly to the nearby ladies.

"A commendable endeavor," he said in an acerbic tone. "You are wise, Your Grace."

Anxiety exuded from the lad, and Alcandhor must have sensed it as well because he smiled ruefully. "Do not let my jaded viewpoint affect you, my Laird. You are not the fool I was, and I think you will not make my mistake."

"It is not that, Thane," the Laird said. "I need not be able to sense to see you are grieved. You are my friend, and I worry about you."

"I wear a cloak of my own weaving, Your Grace," Alcandhor said, "but I thank you for your concern."

"How fares the discussions you have had with the nobles this evening, Thane?" Mattan asked, hoping to distract both leaders from a subject that was only going to deteriorate. Alcandhor's deep wounds and bitterness about marriage and women were not what the Laird needed to be exposed to right now.

"It is, as usual, mostly well-disguised, polite sparring among the established lords." Alcandhor crossed his arms and rolled his eyes. "However the newly appointed lords are more wary, and not sure of themselves. They are allowing themselves to be swayed by their elders, and seem suspicious of Ch'shalna clan."

"Even with the evidence that your clan still has the strength of the Enaisi?" the Laird asked in honest astonishment.

"Now, that annoys me," Mattan said, crossing his arms as well. "Your people have used the intermarrying with mine as a way to 'prove' Ch'shalna clan had the right to be the peacekeepers."

"Aye, because of the special abilities it gave them," the Laird said.

"But why has that become a factor?"

The Laird frowned in thought. "I know not. It just has always been thus."

"It does not follow your laws, Your Grace," Mattan said.

"Traditions being followed rather than our laws," Alcandhor murmured with a wry smile.

The Laird stared at the Thane, a slow grin spreading. "And based on that tradition, our people have been questioning your clan's right as peacekeepers."

Mattan shook his head in exasperation. "Ch'shalna clan's authority is established by your oldest laws from before you settled on this planet. Yet, on Teledhar as well as this one, your people have continued to look for ways to contest those laws and that authority. I do not understand this."

"It is fear," the Thane said. "Despite our vows to serve, the nobles know the potential threat my clan could be. As they were on Teledhar. By all accounts, the last king on that world had an evil bent."

Mattan ignored Alcandhor's side glance; he was not going to get into a history lesson about King Janadhan of all people.

The Laird nodded in agreement. "It truly is wrong!" He spread his hands. "Fear controlled may be good, but what we have seen is out of control. I would fain have your advice on how to help quell these fears and put our nobles back to the proper tasks of administrating their provinces rather than advocating rebellion."

The two Rangers exchanged glances.

"There is no easy answer, Your Grace," Alcandhor replied.

~*~

Across the hall, Krendhal watched the two most important men of their world and the alien who was allied with Ch'shalna clan, as they stood on the lower section of the estrade, earnestly engaged in conversation. Both Ranger chiefs had their arms crossed, and the Laird was gesturing emphatically as he talked, his expression displaying agitation.

Lorwith walked up next to him. "What think you they are saying to our impressionable young Laird, Lord Krendhal?"

Raising an eyebrow, he considering the Lantral lord. No proof of treason had been found to implicate him, but he would not turn his back on the man, figuratively or literally, since the traitors had stabbed the previous Laird in the back. Their intention had been to murder Krendhal as well with the claim *he* killed the Laird, and they had to slay him in defense. If that plot, plus their planned ambush of the Thane and chiefs of Ranger clan, had been successful, it would have left the traitorous lords in control of their world.

Was this lord a traitor as Alcandhor claimed, betraying his conspirators and destroying any evidence of his own guilt? Had Lorwith indeed been in on the plans to have the Laird and Krendhal murdered? If so, could they ever find proof? And how did one treat a peer who might have been plotting against one's own life? Carefully, for certain.

With a silent exhale, he inclined his head at the pale noble. "I would say, Lord Lorwith, that if you wish to know what they are discussing, you should join their conversation."

"I imagine they would stop talking if I approached."

"Let us find out, shall we?"

Lorwith swallowed, his eyes flitting from Krendhal to gaze at the three men on the estrade. "Aye. L–let us join them."

195

His countenance carefully dispassionate, he accompanied the fretful lord across the Great Hall. As they drew near, he could hear their conversation.

"And you have nothing of these conflicts among your own people?"

"I did not say that, Your Grace. My people are as prone to conflict as yours, and tend to congregate into their own factions according to ideologies. But it does not cause the sort of problem that you have, because our structure is totally different. Your society depends on the whole working together and—" Mattan turned as the two lords stepped onto the estrade and bowed to them with a grin. "Lord Krendhal, Lord Lorwith, join us. We were discussing the differences between the political and societal structures of our worlds."

"I–I know nothing about your world, though, Ranger Chief Mattan."

"Neither do we, Lord Lorwith," Alcandhor said with a chuckle. "Mattan has been trying to explain things to us, and either we are incredibly dense, or he is an inadequate instructor."

"My thanks," the alien retorted with a mocking bow.

Krendhal frowned with sincere interest. "You were saying our political structure depends on unity, Mattan."

"Aye."

"But does not any system of government require unity?"

"By the Bells," a female voice broke in, "can you men talk of nothing else?"

The men all turned to see a wryly smiling Sarinna standing before them.

"This is supposed to be a social event, not a forum for political discussion." She stepped up onto the estrade next to her brother and curtsied. The men all bowed.

Krendhal smiled in dry amusement. "Lady Sarinna, for the lords, a social event *is* a forum for political discussion."

Hands on her hips, Sarinna asked, "So you eligible men will continue to stand here while the Great Hall is filled with ladies who wish to dance?" She looked from one to the next, an eyebrow raised. "I think I can state authoritatively for all the ladies present that we are flattered we rank second to such intriguing conversations."

"Do not take it as personal insult, Lady Sarinna," Krendhal replied. "Remember, we are on the edge of many changes, and—"

"Please, milord." Sarinna lifted a hand, her mouth quirking up. "There is no need to explain the events of our world, I am cognizant of them. I understand there are weighty matters that loom before you; is that not why our Laird called the impending conclave?" Sarinna's expression softened as her eyes lit on the lad, and she inclined her head. "Granted it is customary to have conclave to ratify a new Laird, and to honor him. But the immediacy of this conclave expresses urgency, and with the siege and trials that just took place, one would be a fool to think custom dictates this occasion."

As she turned to Krendhal, the intelligent spark and independent spirit in her eyes arrested his attention. What a strong, handsome woman! By both moons, if only she were not Ranger clan.

Her mouth tipped in a saucy smile. "And I do not take *personal* insult, my lord, but you see, I am not the only lady in the hall who stands idly while you lords gather in your little groups. I live in a world of men, and it vexes me not, but most of these ladies are very discordant, although they hide it well beneath propriety. I can sense it."

Krendhal raised his eyebrows. So the sister had abilities of the Enaisi, as did her brother? Was that why the Thane brought her instead of his mother, so she could mingle among the lords and glean attitudes? Nay, or why would she openly state thus? A mystery, those of Ranger clan. So forthright. Or so it seemed.

Mattan glanced around. "She is correct. There is strong disaffection through the Great Hall."

Alcandhor crossed his arms. "And you said nothing?"

"I presumed it was the antagonism between various lords and the noble clans, not from ladies who have been slighted. But now that I am consciously probing for the source of the discontent, I can state Sarinna is correct. Much of it is from the ladies, not the men."

With a sigh, the Thane said, "I think a wise decision might be for us to suggest to our fellow nobles that dancing is recommended over political debates for the evening."

"Does that mean you will actually dance, love?"

"With you, perhaps," he said, grinning.

"Oh nay, my dear Thane." His young cousin pointed at Alcandhor. "If I must dance, you must dance."

The man opened his mouth as if to dispute the Laird, then closed it with a martyred expression. Krendhal wanted to laugh but settled for a small smile at seeing the Thane submit to a boy's whim, even the lad was their Laird. He turned to Alcandhor's comely sister. "I am ever one to be a good example for the lords. Lady Sarinna, may I dance with you?" He held out his arm.

Sarinna's face lit up. "I am honored, lord." She put her hand on the back of his and he led her to the dance floor.

~*~

197

After uncounted dances with various nobles, all with intentions of mining for information about Mattan or Tam or Alcandhor's views on a variety of political topics, Sarinna felt a headache building. Was it too early for her to make excuses and flee to her suite? She sipped her wine with thoughts of shedding the dratted, fashionable gown and shoes, and reclining in private. She could claim she was exhausted after the long journey...

"Lady Sarinna."

She turned, her dutiful sister-of-the-Thane mask sliding into place. Lord Irdhith bowed. "Are you retiring for the evening?"

"I was thinking of it, aye."

"But the night is young. I only had one dance with you. Shall we return to the floor?"

"I thank you, Lord, Irdhith, but I am not inclined to dance, just now."

"Perhaps a walk then? I would fain come to know you a little better. After all, we are close neighbors, are we not?"

That was true. Lantral's provincial hall was but a four-day journey, as was Laird Hall. If he were truly an honest lord, a new friendship might be forged between Lantral and Ch'shalna. Aye, he was young, postured a great deal, and was ambitious, but that need not mean he was disloyal, only that he was a typical, overbearing noble.

"Where should we walk on a night chill as this, Lord Irdhith?"

"'Tis rather cold to stroll outdoors, true, although the Bells are clear and beautiful on such a night." He looked around at the ceilings. "And the hallways seem not suited to two people who wish to...become acquainted, but we have not much choice, have we?" He held out his hand with an inviting smile, and Sarinna could sense a banked-down passion as she tentatively set her hand on his.

It had been such a long time since a man had shown her any interest. Aye, she had at least a decade's years on him—although with her Enaisi heritage she did not show her age, and he could not possibly be serious, but still, his attention was a compliment. She smiled up at the incredibly handsome noble and murmured, "Nay, we have not many choices."

"At least these hallways are more comely than that of my hall. I understand Zaidhron is also built of this extraordinary white shimmerstone?"

"Aye, it is."

"And what does the sister of the Thane do in your city?"

"There is no particular duty, except to play matriarch of the clan when the need arises."

"Which is why you are here?"

"Aye. My mother did not wish to make the journey. She says her age is against it, but 'tis not true. She just cares not to travel. But my appointment is Steward of Zaidhron."

He turned to look at her. "You are city steward, lady?"

"Aye." Sarinna hoped she hid her irritation at his surprise.

"Forgive me, I mean not to..." He stopped, flustered, and it amused Sarinna to see such a tall, strong man embarrassed. "It is just that most noble ladies I have met could not take on such a position."

"Do your ladies not study, milord?" she asked, not able to hide a smile at his discomfiture.

His lips twisted. "I suppose, but I cannot say what. But I understand the women of your clan are not pampered as ours are."

"We live a different life, milord. We study, and we work. Our lives are one of service not luxury."

Irdhith frowned. "That is a fundamental difference between all the other noble clans and yours. I cannot comprehend this attitude of not being served or waited upon. We do our service in caring for our people. Why inundate ourselves in menial tasks when they can be so easily done for us?"

"Think not we have no servants in Zaidhron, Lord Irdhith. But they are there to facilitate the smooth operation of the city, not to wait on us when we are able to care for ourselves."

"An interesting viewpoint. Tell me more, milady."

Sarinna looked up into his gleaming blue eyes and smiled as they continued down the hallway.

Chapter Twenty

Hoping he did not look as sleepy as he felt, Randhal entered the arbitration chamber. He should not have invited the Ranger chiefs to his solar after he made his escape from the Great Hall, but Bells, they were such fun to be with!

He stifled a yawn and blinked at the man standing next to the scribing table, sleeves rolled up as most scribes were wont to do. He looked familiar, with his wide-set eyes and light brown hair streaked with blond. Had Randhal seen him before? Aye, if he was not mistaken, this was the scribe who, during the siege, recorded the conclave concerning Tam being heir.

"Your Grace," he said with a bow. "My name is Maradhor."

With his broad shoulders and muscled forearms, he looked very much the Ranger but not a scribe.

"I thank you for assisting us, Maradhor."

"It is an honor to serve."

The traditional response. Well, the man did not know him, so he would use a formal reply. He sat at the arbiter's table and took a deep breath to ready himself for the petitions.

"Ranger, I do have a request."

"Aye, Your Grace?"

"This is new to me. I have studied the forms and laws, but I have little experience in actual arbitration. If it seems I am...struggling or unsure, that you not hesitate to offer help."

"It is not meet to do thus, Your Grace."

Randhal held up his hands. "I ask not that you offer advice on the decisions themselves, but you could suggest me questions to see that I am not forgetting a point of protocol. I have no father or other tutors at this time. Lord Krendhal is arbitrating as well, so he cannot assist me."

"It is not the place of a scribe to say anything, milord."

"Bells, man! This is why I suggested we ask for Ranger scribes when we realized ours had been found to be among the traitors. Beyond knowing you know the points of order and the law, I trust your clan. Must we go over this?"

Maradhor frowned, twirling his quill in a nervous fashion. "Your Grace, I do understand. It goes against my training but I will endeavor to assist in points of order if I see the need." He hesitated. "But what of the people who are wary of Ranger clan? They may think I am influencing you."

"They have been told we are short of scribes. If they want their petition heard by me, they will endure my conditions."

The Ranger inclined his head. "You are the Laird."

~*~

Lord Tadhrol crossed the bailey after a hurried breakfast. Yells of encouragement quickened his pace. Stars, had the match started before he arrived? He forced his way between bodies into the guards' training hall, trying to get a view of the contest between the Ranger lass and the new lord of Lantral Province. Irdhith wore no shirt. The girl, of course, did. A quilted tunic of a material that wicked sweat and kept modesty.

Her size compared to his appeared comic; his uncommon height made Tam seem but a child.

Tadhrol wiped his brow. Why was the training hall always so airless and hot? Even when only a few men worked out it was thus.

Several Rangers, arms crossed, whispered next to him.

"He is getting steamed."

"Aye, and not from the heat in here," the other muttered. "He cannot get a point on her."

Low chuckles rippled among the onlookers.

"She is too tiny to find a strike point on."

"Aye."

Tadhrol hid his smile. He had to admit, the lass was a wicked fighter. She had given Irdhith several good thumps, but he could not touch her; she was too quick. His training obviously had been with large, brawny men. She seemed almost to be taunting him, buzzing about him like a blood fly, landing blows, then whisking away before he could counterattack.

If her intellect held as sharp as her physical skills, she would make a good Thane. Tadhrol inwardly winced at the thought. A female Thane. Would people accept such unconventionality? Her uncommon beauty and youth made it impossible to think of the lass as a Ranger, despite watching her best Irdhith.

Lantral's lord puffed like a bellows, face red, his skin gleaming wet, sweat flowing freely. Even now he postured, flexing his well-muscled chest and arms. Tadhrol snorted softly—did he think that would intimidate her?

Tam's hair hung damp, but she was not out of breath, and her eyes gleamed with an almost feral light. She stalked her prey, but lightly, playing with it, not moving in for the kill. Yet.

201

Irdhith grunted with effort, but she easily sidestepped his kick, blocking his second and then counterattacking with a series of punches and kicks of her own. She danced back as he cursed aloud.

"Call the match," someone called. "Before she knocks you out of your trous."

Irdhith's face darkened in fury. He charged at Tam with wild kicks. As she counterattacked, he snatched her wrist, pulling her off balance.

Jeers rose from the men watching, but the lass twirled under his arm, twisting out of his grasp.

"'Twas not mentioned you wished wrestling as part of the match," Tam said in a light tone, as one instructing an errant child. "It is not meet to grab during a bare-handed match unless it is agreed to."

"I care not what is agreed to. I only want to get hold of you, lass."

Hoots filled the air.

"Careful, milord," called someone from the safety of the crowd. "Her husband might object!"

Tadhrol glanced around for the impertinent Ranger she had married. What was his name? Marcalan? He stood on the far side of the circle, arms crossed, chuckling with a smug expression.

"Stick to the rules you agreed to, milord, else I will use what I need to fend you off, not just these few simple techniques."

Laughter thundered through the hall as Irdhith glowered, his eyes casting about at those heckling him, then glaring at Tam with open hostility.

He charged her again, his kicks and swinging punches only meeting air. He dove at her then, and caught her by the hair as she skipped out of his reach. He hauled her back, and although thin-lipped, her face did not show fear or alarm. She dropped as a dead weight and twisted about, pulling Irdhith down, then in moves almost quicker than Tadhrol could see, her fist and leg snapped out. The Lantral lord sank to his knees with a burbling moan, hands covering his groin as blood ran from his nose.

Tam rolled up and assumed a fighting position. Amazing lass!

Tadhrol chuckled at the sight of the proud cockerel so humbled. He glanced about the hall as Irdhith called the match. What did the other lords think of the fight? Perdhal's mouth gaped. Gilendhar openly sneered at his fellow lord, but would he be so scornful if he had to face the girl? Rildhran pinched his lower lip to hide a smile. Vendhal caught his eye and winked, grinning. Lorwith he did not see present, and he knew that Krendhal and the Laird were both in arbitration. What a shame to have to miss this.

The lords' opinion of Irdhith was no secret, and he won no new friends from his behavior today, but Tadhrol would have to ask later what his fellows thought of the feisty little Ranger lass.

Amid cheers and congratulations to Tam, Rangers knelt to assist her downed opponent. Not a single noble approached to help him, not even lesser ones from his own province. Ah well, if Irdhith's only shortcoming was the arrogance of youth, he would learn soon enough. Tadhrol hoped that was all it was; he had had his fill of despotic ambitions from his fellow lords.

With an awkward stumble, Irdhith rose to his feet and bowed to Tam, a sweat cloth still pressed against his bloody nose. He did not meet her eyes however. As he straightened he met Tadhrol's gaze, his jaw set in stubborn defiance despite the pain he was in.

Tadhrol shook his head in amazement at the poor fool's willful pride. Aye, the cockerel had some hard lessons to learn.

~*~

Some petitions had been easily dealt with, and a few, dismissed. The last was difficult, and the Laird rubbed his forehead, wishing he had the witnesses in front of him instead of just their written testimony. He glanced at Maradhor as he reread the petition, trying to decide what to do. The Ranger gave a subtle shake of his head.

Randhal looked up, decision made. "I understand it is an inconvenience, however, I wish to speak to the witnesses personally. Nelatan is our neighbor and the travel time is not that much."

"Why aren't their sworn statements enough?" the petitioner, Gandin, demanded.

Randhal glared. "This is how you speak to the Laird?"

The man's eyes widened, and he bowed. "My pardon, Your Grace. But...why aren't their statements enough?"

"I have questions I would put to them that are not covered in their written testimony. You brought this petition, do you not wish to do all you can to have judgment decided in your favor?"

"But who will bear the costs of their journeying, Your Grace?" asked Gandin.

"Whomever bears the costs of judgment, will pay their expenses for journeying, as is custom."

"It–it will take time to send word and have them journey here."

"Aye. I will allow reasonable travel time, and to set personal and business affairs in order before journeying. Two lunations."

"Yes, Your Grace."

"So be it. If there are no more petitions scheduled for this morning, we are adjourned."

Those in attendance filed out.

Randhal waited a moment, then leaned close to the scribe. "What think you? Was it a good answer?"

"Aye." Maradhor grinned. "And if I read people correctly, Your Grace, I would wager Gandin never returns."

"Why say you that?"

"This petition had not a good feel." Maradhor shrugged. "I cannot say on, I just have learned from experience over the years. After some time, you will have a sense of it. I think perhaps you have a good instinct as you did not accept the sworn statements without question."

"My thanks, Ranger. I feel at my limits from some of these petitions."

"You are doing well, Your Grace."

Randhal smiled, then stood, and stretched. "We finished a little before luncheon. What plans have you, then?"

The scribe rose, gathering his notes. "I must find time to recopy all of these today. But other than that, and instructing your guards in sword fighting, my day is free."

"You are an instructor as well?"

"Aye, I am a sword master."

"Bells, I knew that not. When will you be working with my guards?"

"This afternoon. I also hope to get some barehanded matches in for myself as well."

"I may come and watch. I have some small skill with a blade from lessons with your Thane, but I am so out of practice that I wager I could be beaten by a young Trainee as my father frowned upon such training."

"Work out with us, then, my Laird."

"And have my guards see how badly I wield a sword? Nay."

"We can work out privately. Just the two of us, if you wish."

Randhal grinned. "I think I would like that. Let us get some wasters and find an unattended chamber."

~*~

After luncheon, Randhal wandered to a window facing the south of the bailey rubbing his shoulder, sore from his practice with Maradhor. The meal had been dominated by tales of the thrashing Irdhith had taken that morning. If only he had been there to see it!

Some ladies walked outside. With the sunlight shining down on the glass, they likely could not see him. When they stopped to watch guards training, and Randhal had a chance to look them over. Most seemed a frivolous lot. Some were pretty, a few beautiful, but he wanted more than comeliness. His life had been one of loneliness and propriety, raised by tutors. He desired a companion, a friend, and he hoped, love as well. But Mattan and Tam both had said that most of the ladies' feelings were set on attainment of a goal, not romance at all. Randhal had no illusions that some lovely lass would just fall in love with him, but it would be nice to find one who at least was interested in more than the accomplishment of marrying the Laird.

He had to admit that they probably looked upon him as being just as cold-hearted. Randhal must marry soon, and not because he wished it, but because his cousin and First Minister demanded it. He was to select a wife as one would choose the best breeding stock—one who could give him strong, healthy babies, but he must be careful, as choosing from the wrong clan could weaken, not strengthen, Viltara's position with the nobles.

What a disgusting scenario.

One pretty girl stood a little behind one of the 'weeds' as Tam, Mattan, and he had named them. She must be a servant, because she was very deferential to the weed. Randhal *tsked* to himself—he really must not think of these women so negatively, or it might display in his speech or actions.

His eyes were drawn to the lass, who picked up something her lady dropped. The weed—*woman*—snatched it from her, and the girl scurried back. If only he could see her more closely. He bit his lip and decided; he would take a stroll in the bailey.

Once outside, Randhal feigned interest in the drills his men performed, but from the corner of his eye, he saw the ladies flutter, drawing closer. The guards fared well; they lined up in pairs, doing set routines with each other, to practice sidestepping and disarming an opponent.

One of the Rangers overseeing the training saw him and bowed. Randhal gestured the man over. "I see good progress in these men, Ranger."

"Thank you, Your Grace. Some will be ready for duty soon, working alongside us. Your senior guards," the Ranger said, referring to the ones that survived being imprisoned during the siege, "have been training with us too, honing skills and learning new ones."

"I am pleased." And he was. Those men had been willing to die for him. He wanted them as well trained as possible and kept in essential positions throughout Laird Hall. "I thank you for your diligence. Please continue."

The Ranger bowed and returned to the matches. Knowing he had to eventually acknowledge the ladies, Randhal took a deep breath and turned. They curtsied, and one stepped forward. He acknowledged her with a nod. Although she was pretty, he deemed her unattractive; her eyes had a set to them that was decidedly hard, and the lines around her mouth already pulled downward as if she were more used to frowning and finding fault rather than smiling.

"It is good to see Your Grace. You have not been about the hall much."

"Many concerns keep me busy." He inwardly winced; that sounded curt.

"But surely you must take a little time for yourself, Your Grace?"

"Occasionally." He glanced past the woman in an attempt to see that one girl. She stood in the back, her head down. Hang it! He wanted to know what she looked like, although why, he knew not. If she were a servant, and it was likely she was, he dare not think of marrying her—not with such upheaval among the nobles. They would all consider it a slap in the face. But perhaps she was not—he must find out! Should he be bold, march over, and ask who she was? Nay, not if she might not be a noble's daughter.

His frustration mounted—and what was this inane female chattering about?

"—should find time to walk around your hall more, Your Grace."

He inhaled and forced a smile. "Indeed. It is a splendid idea. Why do you ladies all not accompany me on a turn around the bailey?"

"But I meant inside the keep!"

He lifted his arms to indicate the clear blue sky. "A walk outdoors is so invigorating. I have found it so especially since having to journey in the wild with Rangers."

The lady gawked at him. "Walk the bailey? We would all be exhausted, Your Grace. And today is most chill, almost wintry."

He forbore asking why they were outside in the first place if it was that cold. "Aye, but we are all dressed warmly, are we not? Why should a walk from say, here to the west end of the bailey cause exhaustion?"

Her mouth pulled down. He looked past her to the others. "What say you, ladies?"

They exchanged glances of distrust at each other and at him as if he were mad. He suppressed the urge to laugh. None wanted to give up the chance to be near him and try to catch his eye or leave him in the company of the other females, but neither did they wish to walk the length of the bailey. How pampered were these noble women? 'Twas not that long a distance.

Before any of them could answer, Haladhon sauntered over, bowing first to Randhal then to the women. The ladies curtsied, several blushing or giggling at him.

"Greetings, Your Grace! I see you are out for a stroll this fine afternoon." Haladhon's green-grey eyes twinkled with mischief. "Stars, what an advantage being Laird—would that I could have such a beautiful entourage."

"From what I understand, Ranger Chief, you do."

Haladhon chuckled, then catching the eye of one of the females who stared with open adoration, he winked, causing her face to turn bright pink. "So, Your Grace, may I join you, or wish you to keep all the enchanting ladies to yourself?"

"It is tempting to keep all this beauty to myself, but it would be very selfish." He considered adding that Haladhon was in need of a bride too, but thought that might not only insult the women, but the Ranger as well. Not that he cared if the ladies were offended, but he did not want his friend angry with him.

"Very generous, I thank you, my Laird." Haladhon bowed. As they walked, he said, "Now, I know I will not keep them all straight in my muddled mind, but would you ladies please tell me your names?"

Haladhon made a game of forgetting their names, and had them all laughing at his feigned confusion, but Randhal saw a purpose to his ploy; by the time they were at the west end of the bailey, both men knew each of the ladies' names. Including the pretty one. She was a minor noble's daughter from Ranshalon, the youngest sister of three. Her name was Arala, and she seemed very nice. He would have to have her checked out by Mattan or Tam to see if she was a weed.

But in the meantime, he had to admit that he enjoyed the women's company as they responded to Haladhon's jesting and playful flirting. They relaxed, not thinking about trying to catch the eye of the Laird so much, or at least were somewhat distracted from their hunt.

"It is still early afternoon, Your Grace, and we are all chilled from our walk. Think you a nice tea might not put warmth back into our bones?"

"An excellent idea, Haladhon." Randhal gestured for them all to enter the Great Hall. Once inside the antechamber, a servant rushed over, bowing.

"We would like hot tea and some varied refreshments served to us," he said.

From behind the herd of females, Haladhon looked around in exaggeration, and gave a slight shake of his head. Not in the Great Hall? He thought quickly. "We shall be in the first level dining hall." The servant bowed and scurried off. Randhal smiled at the ladies. "It is unused at the moment and more private."

Haladhon shot him an approving grin and a subtle wink.

Randhal allowed that the smaller chamber kept everyone more at ease than would have the Great Hall. And they did not have to worry about any others intruding on them. If nothing else, he was learning to be just a little more comfortable around women by watching Haladhon's example. He treated them all as if they were—what? Not sisters, nay, he flirted outrageously with them, but he was so carefree. Not fearful at all. Randhal had not been around females, except servants, which did not count as he had never talked with them, save to give orders. He could still see and hear his father lecturing him that it was *not done* to talk to servants.

His father... The man seemed to fare badly with women. His first wife and three daughters died of a fever, then when he remarried, his second wife died only a few years after his only son and heir was born. So Randhal had no mother, sisters, or female relatives.

Of course, Viltara fared badly in general. Within the last fifty years several fevers had reduced his clan to only a few families. The only males left in the line were a few minor landholders that lived in the northern part of their Province. He thought it ironic that his clan had dwindled, as had various of the other noble clans, yet the Rangers had continued to flourish. No wonder so many feared them. Was their proliferation because they were not indulgent as were other nobles, but more hardy, surviving sicknesses such as these outbreaks of fever with fewer deaths? Or perhaps Enaisi blood gave them a strength to ward off illness?

Ah well, it was useless speculation. The sad truth was, he was required to find a bride and start producing heirs to build the clan. Young ladies were less intimidating with the engaging Haladhon around. But still, it did not change the fact they looked at Randhal as if he were a prize to be contended for. Nothing mattered to them—not his looks, personality, interests, only that he was Laird.

When the tea was over, he and Haladhon excused themselves. He ran after the tall Ranger who was hurrying down the hallway. "Where are you going?"

"To the training hall, Your Grace. Most of the Rangers are there, matching and working with your guards."

"I would fain watch." He felt his face grow warm as he realized he sounded like a child begging for a sweet.

Haladhon grinned. "Forget you that you are Laird? You need no permission. Come, Your Grace, and see how the guards' training goes."

As they crossed the bailey, Mattan called to them, and they waited for him to catch up.

"Going to match?" he asked, grinning.

"Aye. Where have you been?"

"Several lords wished to ask me questions. I believe they fear my people are going to invade and take over." He chuckled. "I hope I have put their fears to rest."

"Probably not," Haladhon said. "But there is not much you can do about it."

"Nay, but it is one more excuse to distrust Ranger clan," Randhal grumbled.

Mattan lifted his shoulders in resignation, his smile broadening. "Heard you about the match this morning?"

"Aye. Sorry I was to miss it," Randhal said.

"Aye." Mattan gave a mournful shake of his head. "It was glorious, I hear."

"You were not there, either?"

"Nay. I seem to have developed a bad habit since returning to your planet, and it has affected my sleeping pattern."

"Oh, and what is that?"

Haladhon chortled, and the alien glared at him. "I have been enjoying the company of my new friends too much, Your Grace."

"I understand not what you mean."

"He has gotten tipped back almost every night since arriving, Your Grace," Haladhon said with a wicked chuckle.

"And who has been my drinking partner most evenings?" Mattan shot back.

"Do you find it necessary to drink to enjoy your friends?" Just how different were the Enaisi from their own?

"Nay." A remorseful frown flitted across his dark features. "I give a bad impression, I fear. It has been so long since I have been here, that each day feels like a celebration, and I end up overindulging."

"Aye, but it was worthy entertainment watching Alcandhor strip the covers off you this morning in an effort to wake you." His eyes twinkling, Haladhon elbowed Mattan. "You should have heard him, Your Grace. He moaned he was dying while 'Candhor rolled him out of his bedding. We finally left him on the floor amid his blankets, snoring."

Randhal laughed in spite of himself. All the stories and legends of the Elders but this one seemed as one of them, not some astonishing godlike being. Did Mattan blush under his dark skin? Bells, how amazing!

The Enaisi held up a hand. "Enough! You will have our Laird think me a lazy sot."

Haladhon snorted, while Mattan grinned at Randhal, winking.

The heat and humidity hit them as they entered the training hall. Every man was stripped to the waist, and the doors and windows to the bailey all open wide despite the cold weather.

"Stars." Haladhon grimaced, taking off his cloak and hanging it up. "You can almost see the sweat rise and hang in the air from these men."

Mattan frowned. "It should not be this way."

"It is ever thus, especially on the south side of the hall, Enaisi." Randhal pointed at the walls. "This is part of the curtain wall, and the only windows are on the north side. The training halls and range kitchens fare the worst."

The Elder shook his head. "Nay. This is wrong." He gave a low, throaty chuckle. "So much for automated systems that need no oversight or maintenance. Excuse me, Your Grace. I must attend to something." He bowed and left.

Randhal turned to Haladhon questioningly, but the tall Ranger only shrugged.

Before long, the Rangers cajoled Randhal into joining them in easy matches, learning simple techniques. His cloak and surcoat he removed, and soon perspired so heavily he took off his tunic as well.

Several matches later, he held up his hand and retired to a bench, grabbing at a sweat cloth. A slight breeze cooled his face, and Randhal straightened with a frown. Rangers and guards stopped matching and stared about them, murmuring to each other or exclaiming their surprise. The air now circulated, and the humidity dropped noticeably.

Haladhon laughed. "I think our Enaisi is tinkering with something beyond our ken. Stars, how extraordinary!"

"What else of this hall know we nothing about?" Randhal asked in astonishment.

Shrugging, Haladhon wiped his neck and chest with the sweat cloth. "Ask, my Laird. I am certain Mattan will show you, unless it falls under those things he has taken vow not to reveal."

"But has he not revealed this by his tinkering?"

"A point. Perhaps I can convince him to show me what workings go on behind the walls at Zaidhron. I know there are things hidden."

"I knew that the water and waste systems used in this hall, yours, and Estan's, as well as Lairdton's Ranger Hold, were built by the Enaisi, but I knew nothing of this."

"We shall have to pry the information out of him, my Laird. But for now, shall we continue to match?"

Before he could agree, Tam and Marcalan entered, and Randhal excused himself to talk to his friend. He wanted her to try to find out more about that girl, Arala.

Chapter Twenty-one

Alcandhor strode across the bailey, cloak flapping in the chill wind, his eyes dark. Randhal halted, as did Haladhon, Mattan, Maradhor, and several other Rangers walking with them.

"Someone is going to bear brunt," the tall Ranger murmured.

As Laird, Randhal knew he was beyond almost any direct reproach the Thane could give, but still, the years that Alcandhor had been his tutor left an impression, and he found himself dreading he was the target.

"I wager I am the mark," Mattan muttered.

The Thane would upbraid an Elder? Aye—his eyes bored into Mattan's, his voice cold as he stopped in front of him. "Word is spread that the Enaisi has used magic to bring cool air to the training hall."

The alien met the Thane's gaze with a chuckle. "You should not listen to idle rumors, Thane. I just repaired a malfunction in the air circulation system for the south side of the curtain wall."

The set lines in Alcandhor's face relaxed. "Ah." He looked at those gathered. "And you will all help spread word that the Enaisi merely fixed a device and that no magic was involved, enh?"

They grinned as they chorused their agreement. The Rangers barracked called farewell and headed to their quarters while the rest continued on toward the keep.

"So tell me, what did happen?" Alcandhor asked.

"The hall was steaming hot, as usual," Randhal replied, "and Mattan said something about it not being right and rushed off. Before long, cool air began to blow in the training hall. It was the most remarkable thing I have ever seen."

Haladhon chuckled. "You mean that you felt, do you not, Your Grace?"

"Aye, that too. But I do vow that I could see a haze dissipate. I thank you, Mattan."

The Enaisi gave an exaggerated bow. "I am honored to serve."

At the traditional response, Randhal smiled and rolled his eyes.

"Ready to get dressed for tonight, Alcandhor?" Haladhon asked, opening the side door.

The Thane groaned. "I know not what I dread more, the clothes or the banquet."

"Come, is it that bad, Thane?" Randhal asked. "Surely, spending your evenings discussing politics with hard-headed nobles who have no

212

interest in anything but their own gain at worst, or maintaining traditions merely because that is what is comfortable at best, is a bright point of each day here, enh?"

"Not to mention the moon-eyed women who are contending for high-ranked nobles without necklets," added Haladhon with a melodious giggle.

"Stars," muttered Alcandhor as they ascended the back stairs, "just remember we are all in that category."

They stopped by the Thane's door, and Randhal bowed to them. "I will see you tonight."

The chiefs bowed in return, but straightened at the sound of running. Tam, already dressed in her formal garb, nearly slid on the smooth floor trying to come to a halt rounding the corner. Her arms flailed for a moment as she almost fell, then she somehow turned it into a bow.

"What has a Ranger in need of such haste?"

"Looking for you, Your Grace. I–I have the information you requested."

Randhal felt his skin warming. Flicking a gaze to the chiefs, their grins told him they knew what was going on.

"Let us go to my solar, so you can give your report."

"I hope 'tis good news," Haladhon called, his mocking laugh following them down the corridor.

"What did you discover about Arala?" He asked, opening the door.

"What women do with their time is something I cannot comprehend." Tam wrinkled her nose.

Holding up a hand, he said, "One moment." He turned toward his bedchamber. "Holnin?"

The older man that had been his manservant since he was a boy appeared and bowed.

"Is my bath ready?"

"Almost, Your Grace."

"I will be in momentarily."

The man inclined his head and disappeared, and Randhal returned his attention to Tam.

"Now, what do you mean about what women do with their time?"

She crossed her arms, tipping her head. "What purpose is needlepoint? At least if she were learning how to sew clothing I could understand it."

He shrugged. "I know not anything about needlepoint. But what about Arala?"

"I think she is not for you, Your Grace. I am sorry."

"But why? Is she a weed, also?"

213

"Nay. But she is younger than she appears. She has only thirteen years." Her mouth pursed. "Stars, she has more figure at thirteen than I probably ever will have!"

Randhal's face grew hot. "Bells, Tam, your husband must be quite an influence for you to talk thus."

"I blame it more on Haladhon." She waved an arm with a dismissive sniff. "But 'tis true. I have the look of a stripling lad more than that of a lass."

What did one say to a woman who talked ill of her looks? Haladhon's advice came to mind—when in doubt, compliment a lady. Randhal employed it. "But you are very pretty, Tam. You have such pretty eyes." Bells, could he find no word other than pretty? What a clumsy effort. "An–and anyway Marcalan seems not to mind," he added, hunching his shoulders at such a lame reply.

Dimples flashed in Tam's cheeks. "Thank you. And nay, my husband likes me fine, skinny as I am. But back to Arala. She talked to me a little as I used the pretense of wishing to know more about needlepoint. She is not of marriageable age, so was only allowed to come as lady's maid for her older sisters so they would appear to have servants. She felt it would probably be her only chance to ever visit Laird Hall. She thinks not of you as a possibility for marriage, but only as the Laird. I asked her what she would think if a noble took a second look at her, and she whispered she was enamored of a young man back home."

"Too young," he groaned, "and already smitten with another. I begin to lose hope."

"Do not, Your Grace. That is why I was seeking you—I found a flower or two, or at least I think they are not weeds."

"What?"

"I shall wait while you dress for the banquet. I can show you who they are when we go down for the meal."

"But where is Marcalan?"

"Tormenting several nobles in the Great Hall. Lords Perdhal and Gilendhar stopped him to ask about me. Now they cannot escape." She giggled.

"Oh, by both moons! I wonder what he is doing to them?"

She tipped her head with a blank expression for a moment, then her face brightened, her golden eyes shining. "He has been telling them stories. He started subtly and is slowly making them more and more ridiculous, wanting to see how long until the lords realize he has duped them."

Randhal's mouth gaped open. He closed it. "You know what he is doing?"

"We both have Enaisi blood and so bonded when we married. We can share thoughts just a little."

"By the Bells and both moons!" He stared at his friend. What else could she do? She seemed almost an Elder herself, so strong were her abilities.

"Your Grace?"

Randhal turned. Holnin waited at the door of his bedchamber.

"Wait here, Tam, while I bathe and change. I do not meet the lady I escort for the evening until I arrive in the Great Hall. Lord Krendhal is arranging everything so I will not appear to play favorites."

Tam's brow creased with concern, but he shook his head. "I am resigned to my fate, my friend. Fret not about me. I shall be back shortly."

~*~

Randhal came out, dressed, hair freshly combed and braided, and ready for the banquet to find Tam looking out a window.

"Ready to show me some flowers?" he asked.

She turned with a small smile. "I hope they are flowers, Your Grace. I do worry for you."

"I thank you. Let us go down before I am reproached by all the nobles for not being punctual."

They walked down the main staircase into the Great Hall and casually toward his table when Tam spun sideways as they passed a group of ladies. "See over my shoulder?"

"Aye," he replied, with a quick glance in that direction.

"Earlier, they called me over to ask about you, since it is well known we are friends. They wanted to know your thoughts on marriage."

"My thoughts?"

"Aye. I saw no reason to lie, so I told them that you do not feel it is right to be pressured into marriage, yet you have a responsibility to your clan and our world. I also told them that you wished you could wait for romance, or at least to find a friend in the woman you would marry."

"What did they say?"

"There were various responses. Most openly scoffed the idea of romance. Some seemed pleased that you were interested in more than 'breeding stock.' Your pardon, Your Grace, their words not mine. Several expressed a similar opinion to yours, they wished they could have romance, or companionship, but knew with their positions they most likely would be married off to other nobles' sons to strengthen ties between provinces. One said she would not marry unless for love. She has the green ribbons on her gown. The one in the dark blue, the one with the two colors of green in her gown, and the one with all that ridiculous braiding in her hair were the ones who were sympathetic."

"This is most interesting. And they were sincere?"

"One can feign emotions, but do they know of my abilities to sense? Are they that clever?"

"They might be."

"Then shall I find Mattan?"

Randhal gave her a fond smile. "I think I shall have to make some decisions on my own, my friend, but I thank you." He glanced at the women again. "Perhaps I have found this evening's dancing partners."

"I wish you good fortune, Your Grace. I never understood what marriage was growing up, but now that I am married, and have seen happy and unhappy marriages, I wish to help you. You are my friend."

"My thanks, Tam. You know, you are the first person near my own age that I ever could call friend. I have called the Thane and Haladhon friends for several years, but there are no others. All are tutors, counselors, ministers—no friends."

"I am honored, Your Grace. And you were my first friend as well. Other than Uncle and Haladhon."

They shared a smile.

"We have a few things in common to build upon, do we not?" he asked.

"Aye. We both understand loneliness and heavy responsibility at a young age. But where I have a whole clan to turn to, you have only one cousin, and he is, I fear, for all good intentions, too old and settled in certain traditions to be able to be as a father or mentor to you."

"I do have one other now, as long as the Thane allows me to borrow your great-uncle. Lamadhel has been as a father to me these last weeks. I am coming to love him."

Tam smiled. "He is a good man. I am happy you have found a friend in him."

"He and Nadinn have been fresh air in this fusty hall. And Lord Krendhal listens to Lamadhel because of his age, where he might disregard the Thane, and listens not to me at all."

"He thinks because Lamadhel is old he is more wise?"

"It is said that age brings wisdom. That is what I am told, anyway. In the case of Lamadhel it is true."

Tam tipped her head with a thoughtful frown. How endearing it was.

"I have never thought in terms of age and wisdom," she murmured. "I suppose that one has more experiences to draw upon when older so it has certain reasoning, but I have met many old people who seem to lack the sense of a babe. I will have to ask Uncle and Mattan about this."

Randhal chuckled. "You had best join your table for now and ask later. I must let Lord Krendhal introduce me to the lady I am escorting."

He bowed to the female Ranger chief. Watching her walk away, he tried to muster some feeling of joy instead of dread at the thought of escorts and dancing.

~*~

Sarinna stood on tiptoe but did not see her brother or the other chiefs. Or the Laird. 'Twas not that late, but perhaps they had all retired for the evening. She hoped Alcandhor had gone to bed early. Ever since they left Zaidhron he said he slept little, and it showed in the strain around his eyes and mouth. He had mentioned a dream that harried him.

She scanned the Great Hall once more. Other than her kin and the Laird, few had left.

Lord Irdhith remained, although he stood by himself, too proud to bend. Some openly mocked him, and he had not the grace within himself to laugh with them.

His eyes narrowed as she approached. "So, do you come to gloat, too?"

"Nay, milord. You seemed lonely."

The sneer on Irdhith's face faded, replaced by a doubtful frown. "And you care, Lady Sarinna?"

Still so guarded. For all his devastating looks and pride, and dominating attitude, he was afraid. What did he lock away under his arrogant façade?

"It is difficult to change the way one thinks, lord. And you learned a misperception very publicly and in painful way. It is perhaps understandable that some of the nobles have given you grief over your match with Tam, but notice the Rangers have not."

"Not openly."

"Not at all." Sarinna's lips thinned as she met the chill of his blue gaze.

The ice in his eyes melted as he gave a grudging nod. "Aye. I have not heard or seen anything from any Ranger. As you say, 'tis the nobles who have taunted me."

"Yet despite their doubts of Tam's abilities, none had the courage to even offer to match her. You, at least, did that." Sarinna's eyebrow arched as she continued her gentle lecture. "Once you saw she was more than she appeared, you could have called the match. That was your error was it not? Your pride was wounded, and that sparked your anger?"

"Aye." Irdhith's lips tipped up. "You are very perceptive, Lady Sarinna."

"It comes from being a spectator in life, milord."

"A spectator? Why say you that?"

With a blithe shrug, Sarinna replied, "A widowed sister of the Thane is not the center of things. She sits to the side, watching life go by." She brightened her smile, determined the bitterness rising in her throat would not choke her tonight. Not with a tall, handsome man who thought her attractive. She could dance, laugh, and forget for a time how lonely she was.

Irdhith's blue eyes pierced, and she suppressed a shudder at both his look and his fervor as he spoke. "You should never merely sit, watching, Lady Sarinna. You are like a rare gem, cast in a corner. You merely need to be brought into the light, blinding everyone with your beauteous radiance."

Hiding her astonishment that a noble obviously given to rugged training could be so smooth-tongued and poetic, she laughed at patter she would have expected to hear from Haladhon.

Irdhith's brows gathered like a storm cloud. "Why do you laugh, Lady Sarinna? Think you I am insincere?"

"Nay. It is joyous to be complimented so well. I do not often hear it."

He regarded her for a long moment, then held out a hand. "Lady Sarinna. Walk with me again."

She hesitated before putting her hand over his. "Let us dance first, milord. I have not often the chance to dance."

His smiled deepened as he led her to the floor.

Chapter Twenty-two

Maradhor finished the match and straightened, panting. He glanced over to see Sarinna near the door of the training hall. Alcandhor, stripped to the waist as all the other men, sauntered over rubbing his face with a drying cloth. She smirked. "Cannot use your sleeve now, can you, brother?"

The Thane grimaced. 'Twas an old jest, known to all, her scolding him for using his sleeve to wipe his face as would an untutored child.

"And what are you doing here?" Alcandhor returned, grinning. "Do you enjoy watching sweaty, bare-chested men fighting?"

"I came to deliver a message." Her gaze swept the room as she gave a coy smile. "But I might stay and watch a little."

"Ah, and what is the message?"

"I did not say it was for you."

"Oh." Alcandhor stared at her for a moment, then grinned and winked. "Think you one of these men might be bold enough?"

Sarinna laughed. "Bold fighters, aye, but as I have said before, none have ever approached me."

Maradhor's eyes narrowed. Did she imply what it seemed?

"I cannot believe no Ranger has ever tried to catch your eye," Alcandhor said.

She shrugged, smiling. Maradhor threw the drying cloth on the floor and turned to find a match partner. Cordhan. Perfect.

~*~

Maradhor left the training hall. Upon seeing Sarinna, he changed his course to intercept her, calling her name. She turned and smiled, but it faded as he neared.

"So no man has ever tried to catch your eye, enh?"

Sarinna frowned. "You heard that?"

Teeth clenched, he leaned toward her. "All the dances I asked for, all the walks in the bailey you refused me. Was I not good enough to consider? I was dismissed without a thought?"

"Stars, Maradhor! Nay, your attentions were not dismissed because I thought little of you, but because I thought too much of someone else. And alas, that was not to be."

His anger cooled—just a bit. "Then why did you not say thus to your brother? Why tell him no man tried?"

"Because...stars, you know him. He would pester for details, and I hold them private. Surely, you can understand that." She put her hand on his arm. "I am sorry, Maradhor. Truly. I hope...surely after all this time you do not still...?"

He shook his head. "I spoke of the past. I killed what I felt for you. It took a long time, but it is dead. I think of you only as the sister of the Thane. And a friend. But when I heard you say what you did, my pride was wounded. Sorely wounded."

"Take not my petty deceptions personally. I only attempt to keep Alcandhor from prying, as brothers are wont to do. I do regret I hurt you. But truly...we are friends?"

Maradhor allowed himself a smile. "Aye."

He bowed and turned for the barracks. Sarinna could sense, she must know he still held resentment. Hang her. Hang all women!

Knees tucked up next to her, Sarinna stared out the window, not bothering to wipe away her tears. She had truly hurt Maradhor, and he deserved better. A Child of the Enaisi who can sense should know such things, yet she never realized how deeply he had once cared for her; a woman blind to all except the one she wanted and could not have.

"Lady Sarinna?"

She jumped with a quiet gasp at Irdhith's voice. She had thought the curtain over the bench seat would hide her from anyone passing in the hallway. Before she could turn to the Lantral lord, he said, "I apologize. I see I have intruded on a private moment. I shall leave."

"I–it is all right, Lord Irdhith. I should not have stopped here but gone to my suite."

"What is distressing you, Lady? Is there any way I may be of assistance?"

Sarinna shook her head. "But I thank you."

He hesitated, and she managed a smile. "Perhaps a walk with a friend is better than sitting alone and mulling over past wrongs."

"Past wrongs?" Irdhith asked, holding out his hand.

"I caused a friend heartache. I think he may never forgive me."

"How could anyone not forgive you, dear lady?"

Warmth shone in Irdhith's blue eyes. What a balm his attention was to her. Perhaps she was being foolish to let her head be turned by the fact that a man so incredibly handsome as well as so much younger was attracted to her—yet not so foolish as to think he was completely sincere.

But right now she cared not.

He clasped her fingers and brought them to his lips. Aye, she needed this.

~*~

With a sigh, Randhal exited his solar and faced his cousin in the hall. Krendhal's expression indicated some severe disapproval. Nothing new there.

"You take a chance, Your Grace."

"How so, Lord Krendhal?"

"You sit, tucked away with Rangers, giving the lords reason to think you plot with them."

"Bells, 'tis only a game of backhand or two to aid in digestion after that extravagant luncheon! Why not join us?"

"It is not meet that you spend your time in your solar with only Rangers as guests, Your Grace."

"They are my friends. They will be gone soon, and I wish to enjoy their company."

"The other nobles are not pleased that you lock yourself away with the Rangers. Did you think no one would notice that you and they disappear late in the evening? And now afternoon as well?"

Randhal sighed. What might he do to keep the lords from being offended? "Then send word that tomorrow at the second hour past luncheon that I am inviting the lords of the provinces to my solar."

"Instead of the Rangers?"

"The Thane will be asked since he is the head of his clan, but that is all. It will be a time of relaxing and learning of each other, with no politics to be discussed. I would make friends, or at least build a more friendly atmosphere, if possible, with my ministers. How does that sound?"

Krendhal arched an eyebrow. "Your Grace, I will do so if that is truly your wish, but the lords do not necessarily wish to become friends with you."

Randhal threw his arms out. "Then what do they want?"

"The Laird must be careful that he not only is impartial but appears thus as well. Close personal relationships could possibly sway judgment."

"So I am not allowed any friends? Nay, I will not shy away from those I care about because it might offend someone." He crossed his arms. "Perhaps the lords might consider making a few friendships themselves instead of political liaisons."

Krendhal drew up, haughtier than ever. That look intimidated Randhal, especially since his cousin had been one of his tutors, but in the past few weeks he realized he truly was Laird. He could now tell Krendhal what to do. So he did not let on any discomfort, but met his First Minister's gaze straight on. "If there will be nothing more, Lord Krendhal, I have friends awaiting me in my solar to play backhand. Amend the invitation. Any who wish to join us are welcome after luncheon."

Krendhal gave a stiff bow, his eyebrows arched high. Randhal blew out a loud sigh when the minister had gone and re-entered his solar.

Before long, a knock at the door halted their game, and Krendhal entered, bowing. "Excuse the intrusion, Your Grace. But cousins have come to honor their new Laird—Bandhran and his family."

The Rangers all rose, and Alcandhor grinned at him, clapping him on the shoulder. "You have few cousins, Randhal. Enjoy them."

As his friends filed out, he met the stern set of Krendhal's face with his own, chin raised. "I will allow a touch, and for my kin and friends to call me by name in private."

Krendhal bowed. "Your Grace."

Randhal spread his arms. "I wish you would call me by name as you did when I was a lad."

"You are my Laird now."

"I am still your first cousin, once removed. I would fain have a cousin who is my counselor, rather than a counselor who happens to be a cousin."

Krendhal looked down for a moment, his lips pursed and brow furrowed. "I am old, Your Grace. Do not expect me to be able to toss off the teachings and traditions I have held my entire life."

Randhal nodded, his shoulders sagging. "Show them in, Lord Krendhal." He turned to his servant. "Holnin, have refreshments brought."

He quickly reviewed his cousins' names in his mind, hoping he made no mistakes when introduced.

~*~

Maradhor entered the Thane's suite and glanced around. What reason would Alcandhor have to summon him? He hoped it was not over what he said to Sarinna. The Thane stood with an expansive smile. "Ah, cousin. I have a pretty problem, and you are just the man to solve it for me."

Maradhor eyed Alcandhor with suspicion; he knew him well, and that grin was dangerous. "And what may that be, Thane?"

"The Laird has cousins visiting. They are landowners from the east. The eldest daughter has no escort for the banquets, and since his clan has no males of suitable age in attendance, he has asked if a Ranger would be her escort."

Maradhor stared at Alcandhor in disbelief. "Why me?"

"Because you are older and unmarried. Most of the unmarried Rangers are too young to understand the respect and the responsibility of the task of escorting a noble lady."

True. Maradhor cringed imagining Baidhrol or Loch'alan as escort. Stars. But why their clan? "There are nobles from other clans here. Why does it have to be a Ranger?"

"Because that is the Laird's request."

Maradhor thought fast. "But I have no attire for a banquet."

"The Laird has said if we have no spare garments among the chiefs for you, that he will guarantee Laird Hall's tailors will have you ready in time for tonight." Alcandhor grinned. "Which is good, because I think your shoulders are even broader than Haladhon's. Although I imagine the tailors are not happy with the situation given mere hours."

Maradhor sighed in resignation. "I suppose this request from the Laird is an order from you, sir?"

Alcandhor frowned. "If you truly do not wish to escort Atinna, lady of Viltara clan, I will find another—somehow. The only other older, single Ranger available is Haladhon, and I refuse to give him this task."

Maradhor's mouth twitched as he fought a smile. "Indeed? And why do you not escort her yourself?"

Alcandhor glared at Maradhor, but his pursed lips gave away his own struggle against the humor of such a ridiculous situation. "I already am escorting a lady. I have given escort of Sarinna to Haladhon, as I am escorting Aliss, the maiden sister of the landowner cousin, Bandhran. Lord Krendhal has escort of a widowed aunt. The man brought his whole household." His disgusted expression changed to a pleading one. "I cannot have a woman on each arm, can I?"

Maradhor did smile then. "If you can suffer through it, Thane, then I can."

His cousin returned the smile with relief.

~*~

Maradhor was amazed—and dismayed—at how quickly the tailors had prepared garments for him. The Rangers in the barracks hooted as he dressed for the banquet, and his scowls did not deter them.

As he laced the suede azure jerkin, Loch'alan waltzed over, grinning. Maradhor glared at him. "Leave off, Loch'alan."

The young Ranger blinked, looking too much like his brother at that moment. "Have I said word one?"

"You sound like Marcalan."

The Rangers laughed as Loch'alan huffed. "No need to insult me."

"Then leave off."

"Why the dark face, cousin?" Baidhrol asked. "Is escorting a lady such onerous duty?"

Maradhor did not answer. The jerkin now laced, he grabbed his cloak and stormed out.

As he neared the chambers of Atinna, he wondered how old she was, what sort of a person—stars, not a giggling woman, please—and how much inane conversation she would expect him to make.

He knocked at the door, and a servant answered.

"I am escort for Atinna, lady of Viltara."

She nodded and stepped back. He entered, swallowing. A slender lass, not having more than perhaps fifteen or sixteen years, stood there, her silvery blonde hair braided across her head, and cascading down her back in soft curls. She was pale, almost wan, her eyes a light blue, and had nearly Maradhor's height. Her blue gown accented her eyes. She was no blinding beauty, but she was not unpleasing to the eye. At least there was that, he thought as he bowed. "Atinna, lady, I am Ranger Maradhor, and have the honor to be your escort this evening."

She curtsied and set her hand on the back of his without a word.

Good. Perhaps she would not jabber the whole evening until he was wearied of hearing her voice.

~*~

She was indeed quiet, and Maradhor had to bend close to hear her answers several times when asking if she wanted refills of her wine or wished more food served.

When the meal was over, and they left the table, he asked, "Do you wish to dance, lady?"

She shook her head. "Thank you, nay."

Maradhor stifled a sigh. At least dancing would be better than standing there next to her all evening. Now what was he supposed to do with her? He glanced over to see Alcandhor escorting his lady to where the Laird and Krendhal stood, talking with other relatives.

"Shall we join your family, lady?" he asked, holding up his arm. She nodded, her fingers lightly touching the back of his hand.

For most of the evening, he spent his time silently standing next to the lass as she listened to her cousins discussing various mundane matters and conjecturing on whether rumors of a fever in Nelatan were true. He could be in the barracks, jesting and talking, playing kingsmen, or in the training hall, matching. In silent frustration, he ground his teeth.

Later, as he returned with a glass of wine for her, she gave him a shy smile. "I thank you for being such a gracious escort, sir."

Maradhor inclined his head. "I am honored to be escort to such a lovely lady." It was a standard reply, except for adding she was lovely. She was, more or less, and it could not hurt to say something nice.

She blushed. "We have not really talked all evening."

True, he tended to be fairly taciturn, but between still feeling the sting in his pride from Sarinna's comments earlier and being ordered to be escort, he supposed he had been more quiet than usual. He tried to smile. "Nay, we have not."

"Tell me about yourself."

"There is not much to tell, lady. I am a Ranger and a scribe."

"Where are your bounds?"

"I live at Zaidhron. But sometimes am sent to the Scribe School at Kentin, to instruct students."

"Do you stay with my cousin Lord Krendhal at the provincial hall, then?"

Maradhor shook his head. "Nay. I stay in the Ranger hold near there."

"Oh, aye. I suppose you would." She turned pink. "Silly of me."

What could he say? It was silly, but he did not wish to insult her.

"Do you visit your cousin Lord Krendhal or the Laird often?" he asked in an attempt to keep the conversation going.

"Nay. We children have never traveled much, and father is too busy to visit himself."

"So this is your first time to Laird Hall then?"

She nodded. "And probably the last time. It is a grand place, is it not?"

"Aye, it is. Have you been given a tour?" He mentally kicked himself for asking. Now it would be only proper to offer to give her one himself if she had not.

"Nay."

Stars. "I would be honored to show you around. Perhaps tomorrow, after luncheon?"

She smiled shyly and nodded again. Stars. He made himself smile back at her.

She requested to return to her chambers to retire for the evening,

225

and Maradhor was never so relieved to return to a barracks as he was that night. As he entered, many of the Rangers jumped up.

"What was she like?"

"Was she pretty?"

"What was it like being in the Great Hall for a formal banquet?"

Maradhor held up his hands, rolling his eyes. He strode to his cot and plopped down, unlacing his boots. "She was young, pretty, and did not talk much. The food was good, and the discussions were boring."

"Oh, come, cousin, tell us more of her," begged Baidhrol.

He sighed—loudly. "She had perhaps sixteen years, was tall, slender, blonde, and very shy."

"Did you kiss her?" asked Loch'alan, his eyes twinkling.

With a glare, he spat, "You are too much like your brother. Nay, of course I did not kiss her. I was escorting her, not trying to gain a necklet."

"Would you?"

"Would I what?"

"Try to catch her eye."

Maradhor was tempted to throw a boot at the irritant. "Nay."

"Why not? Stars, Maradhor, will you never consider marriage?"

"That is my business."

"I would back away from that subject, Loch'alan," master bowman Bardhal said in a quiet voice. Marriage was the one topic Maradhor avoided and most of the Rangers had wisdom enough to have learned that.

It grew quiet. He nodded his thanks to Bardhal, and the Ranger inclined his head with a small smile.

Baidhrol however picked up a thread of the conversation. "Besides, you simpleton, Rangers cannot marry into Viltara clan, remember?"

Maradhor lay back in his cot, stifling a groan. Would they ever leave off?

"Oh, aye, that is true." Loch'alan snorted. "Stars, what a bore then. No wonder you did not try to flirt."

He closed his eyes, wishing he could close out the conversation as well. "It is a bore listening to you prattle, Loch'alan."

"What else have we to talk about?"

Maradhor pushed up onto his elbows. "You have good rank. Let it slip that you are Ninth at Table and I wager you could walk away from Laird Hall with a wife."

Loch'alan gaped as Maradhor flopped onto his back again.

"A wife? Why in the name of both moons would I want a wife?"

"Why would I?" He draped an arm across his eyes, hoping the

young cockerel would leave off. He heard a quiet slap and whispering. When the conversation began again, it was about tomorrow's duties and the weather.

Chapter Twenty-three

Maradhor glanced over at the lass as he explained the various chambers along this section of hallway—the conference halls, the law library, and archives. Finally he asked, "You are so quiet, lady, am I boring you?"

Atinna looked up, surprised. "Oh nay, you are not, Ranger. I...I just am...distracted."

He inclined his head, and they walked in silence toward the near staircase. "The next level is mostly bedchambers and suites."

"Aye." She kept peeking up at him and after ascending the stairs, finally asked, "Ranger, may I confide in you?"

Oh, not that. "Certainly, lady."

"I...I have been unsettled because I am to be married to my cousin upon our return home. It is why I am so distracted. I cannot sleep or eat."

"You are not happy about your marriage?"

She shook her head. "Our clan needs to...to grow, so it was decided by our fathers that we should marry. Build the clan's blood strongly in our line."

Maradhor nodded. "Clan first."

"I am coming to loathe that phrase. It is used as a precept to force people into conduct they would not otherwise willingly engage in."

"We do have Clan Laws."

She whirled to face him. "Where is it written that we must blindly obey for the good of the clan, sacrificing our own happiness?"

Maradhor shrugged. "The principles of Clan Law are for preservation of the clans, which can mean self-sacrifice. At least we do not do as we did on Teledhar. You may not know, but children were often taken from their own parents and given to another family in their clan to strengthen loyalties to clan and break that of individuals to their families."

"Would that we still did! I am tired of hearing how I must obey my father—and the law." A slender hand wiped her wet cheek. "I am sorry. I am not good company. Perhaps I should return to my chamber."

Pity filled him, probably her tears were to blame. "Lady, walk with me." He held out his hand, and after a moment, she placed her palm on the back of it again. He stared straight ahead as they strolled along the hallway. "I was fortunate to be born, raised, and to continue to live at Zaidhron. It houses so many families that I cannot begin to count them. I have seen the lives of many of those families, and wish to share some thoughts."

"Please."

"I know of a man and woman who married for love, yet years later, theirs is a cold, lonely life, as they became selfish and grew apart. I rarely see words pass between them." He grimaced at bitter recollections of his parents, and murmured, "They live together, but alone."

She said nothing so he continued, "Yet I know of a man and woman who married simply because it seemed a suitable match between their families. But they took pains to care for each other. I remember him telling how he returned from journeying, and she had a hot bath ready, then rubbed his sore feet while he ate. He would surprise her by doing little chores for her, or bringing her tea when she was resting at the end of a busy day. Over time, love grew between them." He smiled in thought of many doting scenes between Edhron and his wife. "Now they are old, but so in love that they cannot be near each other without holding hands, or touching tenderly."

Maradhor stopped and turned to meet her gaze. "Lady, if he is a good man, and you care for each other's needs with tenderness, love can grow. You are not necessarily 'sacrificing' for your clan."

Her blue eyes grew icy. "And if he is not?"

Maradhor hesitated. How did he ever come to be in the position to give advice to a young lass? "'Tis difficult. But we still can choose to find happiness within ourselves, it is not completely dependent upon others."

"You...have given me much to think about. I thank you. I wish to return to my chamber now. Will you be my escort again tonight?"

Maradhor inclined his head as an answer. He had no choice in the matter, but would not hurt her feelings by saying so. She curtsied, and he bowed, then watched her until she rounded a corner out of sight.

~*~

"Still worried about your upcoming marriage, lady?"

She nodded as he whirled with her to the music. They separated, then crossed wrists to twirl in the opposite direction. "I have thought of what you said, and I am trying, truly I am, but the dread of it will not leave."

"I am sorry."

"May I ask a personal question?"

Maradhor had been waiting for it. It was asked him all the time. "Aye, lady."

"Why have you never married?"

"It takes a man and a woman for marriage. There is no woman."

"But...why? You are handsome. Why has no woman set her skirt for you?"

"When I was young, I was not only in Training as a Ranger, but also studying to be a scribe. I held off the idea of marriage at that time. Then, I found I am not one who knows how to charm a woman and gain her eye. So here I am."

"So you never were in love?"

He considered how to answer. "I was. Once. She did not love me."

"What did you do?"

The music ended. He held up his hand to escort her off the floor. "What was there to do? I could not make her love me. So I just forgot about her and went on with my life."

"Are you ever lonely?"

"Who is not, at times?"

Atinna turned to look at him, her pale blue eyes steady. "Ranger, will you answer another question for me?"

"If I can."

"How does one know one is in love?"

Maradhor pursed his lips. "That is hard to say. Would you get the same answer from any two people if you asked that question? Is it passion, or something more?"

"I know not."

"Nor I." He gestured to the confections table. "Wish you a sweeting, lady?"

She shook her head. She had eaten little that evening and was going to make herself ill at this rate. "You should try to eat."

"I know." She looked down. "I just cannot..."

"Is there another man? Is that why marriage to your cousin is so abhorrent to you?"

"Nay, I–I just feel nothing for him. And growing up, he was always unkind to me."

An amusing thought flitted through Maradhor's mind, and he chortled slightly before he could stop himself. Atinna stared at him with wide eyes.

"Forgive me, lady, but it came to me that if you could catch the Laird's eye, it might forestall your marriage to your cousin."

The lass turned even whiter, if that were possible. "The Laird?"

Maradhor smiled, gesturing around the Great Hall. "Why think you all these single, noble ladies are in attendance? They have all set their skirts for him."

"My poor cousin. I can sympathize."

"Perhaps you could sympathize together."

With a wry expression, Atinna replied. "I think not, Ranger."

He grinned in lieu of an answer, and her face slowly softened, her lips tipping up. "Are you teasing me, Ranger?"

"If I thought you could be persuaded, I would be in earnest."

"How could I do so to my father who has signed a betrothal contract? Besides, I know not my cousin. We are strangers."

He leaned close and whispered, "Ah, but that could be remedied."

"You *are* teasing me. Thank you."

"For what?"

"Making me smile. For one moment, I had forgotten about Tirnin."

"Tirnin?"

"My betrothed."

Stars, her tone was bitter saying that word. He felt sorry for her. Leading her to the confections, he said, "Try, lady. If you faint from hunger how will that reflect on your escort? Would you see me in stocks?"

Her blue eyes gazed earnestly into his. "You are teasing me again?"

What sort of person was she to not understand jesting? Or was she raised in a home without humor? "I am trying. But you should eat something."

The corners of her mouth twitched. "I will try, Ranger. So as to keep you out of stocks."

He smiled at her attempt at a jest. That was better.

~*~

Alcandhor waited in the council chamber with his chiefs. Conclave could not start; they awaited lords from several provinces. What purpose did their Laird have in calling for this meeting?

They all bowed as the two lords of Viltara entered, and then everyone sat.

The Laird folded his hands. "I have moved the conclave back again. Two weeks. Naidhar of Andethon Province still has a ways to journey, and we await the arrival of Dardhal of Beshalon, and also Mirdhol of Valeshon. I know it is an imposition. The nobles seem to be bearing it well, with little complaining."

"An imposition?" Haladhon's eyes twinkled. "My dear Laird, please impose as you desire."

The Laird smiled over at him, one eyebrow cocked.

Mattan leaned over, replying in a feigned whisper, "It is the suite, my Laird."

"Very pleasant things, suites," Marcalan with a smug wink at his wife. Tam elbowed him, her face turning pink.

The Laird chuckled, then turned to Alcandhor. "I understand you had determined to go to Estan, Thane."

"Aye, with Tam and Marcalan."

"Perhaps this would be a good opportunity. You could assess the situation, meet with Stendhar, the noble who is claiming lordship of Estan, and report back."

"That would be ideal."

"This Stendhar, who is he?" asked Eladhrel.

"Second cousin to Batrig, I believe," Alcandhor replied.

"Second cousin, one time removed," Krendhal said with a condescending smile, but his eyes twinkled.

Alcandhor inclined his head. The Viltara lord would ever spar with him, but it seemed now, at times, more convivial than antagonistic.

Haladhon frowned. "I do not favor the idea of you going alone, Thane."

He rubbed his eyes, wishing his cousin would not continue to harangue him on the subject. He knew what he was doing. "I will not be alone. Tam and Marcalan shall be with me."

"You know what I mean, Thane. It is not wise to journey into Estan at this time. And you plan on going with only two Rangers as guard."

"Tam is worth many Rangers, cousin."

Haladhon sighed and leaned back with a scowl. "I still like it not."

~*~

"Maradhor!"

He and the guard he matched both straightened and put fists over their hearts. From the door of the training hall, a guard called, "Someone here who wishes to speak to you."

Atinna stood at the entrance. Stars. Maradhor grabbed a drying cloth and wiped the sweat from his face and chest. Did he excuse himself to dress or go directly to her? Being stripped to the waist in the presence of a lady was not proper, but she saw him thus at the moment anyway. He draped the cloth over his shoulders—it was not much for modesty but it was the best he could do. He approached her and bowed. "Lady."

She gazed up with red, puffy eyes. "I would say good-bye, Ranger. You have been kind, and I wanted to thank you."

"You are leaving?"

Atinna nodded. "My father has received disturbing news of some sort, and we are going home at once. He has talked of me marrying right away when we arrive."

"I am sorry. I know you have dreaded this."

"Thank you." She curtsied and hurried off.

Maradhor sighed. Poor child. As he sparred, his mind kept straying to her. She nearly made herself ill just at the thought of being forced to marry, how much worse the actual event, and after? Would she even survive? Gritting his teeth, Maradhor focused on his opponent.

~*~

Across the training hall, Haladhon strode over to Lamadhel, wiping his face with a drying cloth. "I am calling Question on the Thane."

His uncle frowned. "Why?"

"He should not journey to Estan."

"Stars, Haladhon, you do not let go, do you?"

"Nay."

"He has sight and has seen that he must go to Estan. You cannot stop him."

"I can by calling Question. Given the state of that province right now, he is reckless to consider it, and he has not slept well since we left Zaidhron. His mind is addled."

"Leave off, son. Think you any of the other chiefs will back you? You know we all give leniency when he has sight."

Haladhon threw down the drying cloth in a fury and stormed out.

~*~

A voice called hoarsely.

Malkim turned, gripping his sword hilt, as a man ran into the camp. Tevsen. A servant of Estan Hall and a spy for his Royalist faction. The man bent over, hands on his knees gasping for air.

His hand dropped from his weapon, and he squinted in the light of the torches. "What news?"

Tevsen gulped and panted, unable to speak. Malkim ground his teeth, waiting.

Finally the man was able to gasp, "The Rebels have captured Stendhar and his new wife. They say they will kill them if we don't agree to their terms and their rule."

Malkim spat on the ground. "Stupid man! Journeying without adequate guards! We'll move at first light to try to find trace of him." His lip curled. "And his charming bride." He tossed his tea out in an arc and went to the fire for a fresh mug. "Tell me again what you know of Stendhar's plans."

"Not much, really. He said that Batrig used to prowl around the hall, obsessed with finding secret places of the Elders. Stendhar told me several times about their magic and of the powers they wielded. Batrig talked of a special key of the Elders that was the only way to open those secret places and used to say that when he had overthrown the Rangers he would get such a key. Stendhar hoped to find one when he got to Laird Hall."

"Now, wait. How did Batrig find out about this key?"

"He had ways. I suspect it was *her*."

"If that is so, then we do need her. Where is the key kept?"

"It is said the Thane wears one."

Malkim paced back and forth. "What would Stendhar give if we could provide him with a key? He'd be even more our puppet."

Tevsen snorted. "Do you intend on storming Laird Hall and capturing the Thane, then?"

Malkim scowled at his spy. "Watch your mouth. If we can rescue Stendhar, perhaps *she* can offer a suggestion."

Chapter Twenty-four

All eyes followed Alcandhor and his two Ranger chiefs along a street in Polli, the town situated a day's journey between Estan's provincial hall and Laird Hall, and most of the stares were not friendly or curious but antipathetic.

The barely veiled animosity upon entering a tavern needed not be felt—from all sides they received baleful glares and scowls.

"Uncle, if we stay, I fear we will have to fight before long."

"Where else shall we find rooms, Tam? 'Tis the same all over Polli. Or should we sleep in the woods, where they might try to track and attack us there?" Attempting to be more light-hearted, he added, "Besides, your father may have raised you in the high mountain wilds where you grew accustomed to sleeping on cold, hard ground in the snow, but I prefer a warm bed."

"I did not realize it would be this hostile. I understand Haladhon's concern now."

"We shall be fine," Alcandhor muttered.

Marcalan's reproachful gaze over top of her head bespoke he was in agreement with his wife and Haladhon. "Far be it for me to disagree with my Thane, but three chiefs, and one of them a lass..." He glanced about as they sat at a table. "This is not good."

"We have survived worse, cousin."

The serving woman, her face drawn into hard lines, approached and crossed her arms. "Rangers don't normally come here. They aren't welcome."

Alcandhor smiled, sending calming feelings to her. "Do you wish us to leave? We only want a meal and rooms for the night."

She blinked, hesitating. "I–I will ask."

After an animated exchange behind the counter, the innkeeper strode over, scowling. "I don't want trouble."

"We simply wish food and a place to sleep." Alcandhor kept his demeanor passive as he sent to the innkeeper as he had the serving woman.

The man eyed the three of them for a long moment, then grunted. "You pay in advance. You have Estan coin or do you expect me to take Ranger money?"

Since the currency was identical, save the stamp of province on the back—or in their case the stamp of their clan—the point was obvious.

But such bias was expected. "I have both, sir."

"Estan," he demanded, then glanced at Tam with a frown. "How many rooms?"

"Two." Alcandhor reached into his pouch and took out several coins. "Is this sufficient?"

The innkeeper gaped. "Three silver moons? Are you jesting with me? Or bribing?"

"Neither." Alcandhor kept his expression bland. "I know not the rate of exchange in this province. Is that fair for the rooms and meals?"

The man frowned, staring at the money for a long moment. Finally he took one coin. "I have no use for Rangers, but I am an honest man. I can't cheat you."

"I thank you, sir." Alcandhor inclined his head.

"I will have your meal served to you." He stalked off.

"You are as sly as ever," Marcalan whispered, his eyes twinkling.

Keeping his face dispassionate, he dropped the coins into his pouch, despite his desire to grin at his cousin. "I will get our drinks."

"What sense you?" he murmured to his niece after returning with their ale and her tea.

Tam cupped the steaming mug with her hands, her voice low. "Anger. Distrust. And they are not happy the innkeeper is letting us stay. This does not feel good, Uncle."

After the serving woman set dishes on the table and left, Alcandhor said, "We cannot let ourselves be intimidated. The innkeeper had the choice. He could have told us to leave, and we would have respected his wishes."

"But you manipulated him," she whispered, leaning forward, her face anxious. "You sent to him."

"I did not sent to him to manipulate him, only to set his mind at ease that we were not here to purposefully bring trouble into his tavern."

"Our presence is going to bring trouble, though, you know that," Marcalan said softly.

"Aye, and he knows it too, but he still chose to let us stay. Dislike of Rangers notwithstanding, he is an honorable man. We must do our best to not allow trouble to start."

"And you will leave that to Tam?"

"If necessary. Between the three of us we can all send peace through this room to try to disarm tension somewhat. I would rather have her disable would-be troublemakers using strong sent emotions than have to fight them physically."

"You are trying to deliver a unmistakable message, are you not, Thane?"

"Call me not by title. They know we are chiefs if they have an eye, but they need not know exactly which chiefs we are." He paused. "What message think you I would convey?"

"That Ch'shalna clan still possesses the strength of the Enaisi."

Alcandhor's lips tipped in a slight smile. "I am more interested in enforcing that we still possess the right to be peacekeepers. 'Tis a message that needs to be communicated clearly. I hope tomorrow that we will find the newly proclaimed lord of Estan Province in his provincial hall. I wish to impart the same understanding to him as well."

"Last word was that all the nobles of Estan are there, and the hall is in an uproar as they do not all accept Stendhar as provincial lord. They are feuding." Marcalan shook his head in dismay. "We walk from one battleground to another."

Alcandhor scrutinized the somber Ranger. "You are still not your usual jovial self. What is wrong? Still adjusting to the bonding?"

Marcalan shrugged, sighing, and Alcandhor nodded in understanding. "And it is more difficult for you than her as she has much stronger abilities."

"It does not hinder my ability to carry out my duties."

The serving woman approached with a tray and placed steaming bowls of stew on the table, as well as a platter of meats, a large bowl of roasted vegetables, and a loaf of bread.

They were not far into the meal when Tam, not looking up from her plate, murmured, "I sense anger rising."

"Send peace," Alcandhor ordered, doing so as well.

"It is not helping," Tam hissed after a few moments.

Voices at the counter rose, and he put a hand over Tam's, whispering, "Be ready," then stood.

"You know we don't want them here," one man said to the innkeeper.

Alcandhor stepped up to the counter but before he could say anything, the innkeeper glared at him. "I don't need your help. I won't have you drawing your swords and bloodying my place!"

Holding out his hands, palm up, he said, "I simply wished to get more tea for my niece."

The innkeeper's mouth snapped shut, and the men arguing with him blinked, obviously not expecting that reply. The innkeeper quickly poured tea.

"My thanks." Alcandhor picked up the mug and turned toward his table when a hand grabbed his arm, almost spilling the tea. He ignored the discourtesy.

"Why is that lass dressed as a Ranger?"

"Because she is a Ranger."

"Since when do women Train to become Rangers?"

"She is currently the only female Ranger."

The man stared at Alcandhor, confusion mingling with his hatred and anger.

"How can a lass be a Ranger? Women cannot fight as men can."

Alcandhor kept his voice reasonable and even. "She can."

"This is some jest, yes? Look at how small and young she is, yet you would have me believe she can fight? Why do you dress her as a Ranger?"

"Because she is a Ranger."

"There has been talk of a lass who is a Ranger, Gadrik," a voice called over. "One was seen at the nobles' trial at Laird Hall."

"What would you know of it, Lenton?"

"My cousins were there. I heard the story."

Alcandhor returned to the table, as Gadrik replied, "Oh, I forgot, since then you have changed your tune about the Rangers, haven't you?"

"The Thane and the Laird both were just to my cousins. How can I find fault with that?"

Gadrik sneered, marched over, and glared down at Tam. "Are you a Ranger?"

Tam looked up with aplomb. "Aye, sir, I am a Ranger chief and Second at Table in Ch'shalna clan."

The man stared at her in open disdain, pointing at Lenton. "You're the one he has told us about that was at the trial?"

"Aye."

"How did you come to Train as a Ranger?"

"My father Trained me."

"Who was your father?"

"Valdhor, son of Thane Saldhor."

Gadrik licked his lips, glanced around the room, then asked, "Would you fight me, girl?"

"Why should I?"

"To prove you are a Ranger."

"Rangers do not fight to prove anything, sir. We fight to protect others and to defend ourselves when needed."

Her answer filled Alcandhor with pride, but he dared not take a moment to relish it; he must keep his attention keen.

Gadrik's face turned red. "You're just coming up with excuses. What if I threaten you then?"

"Here now!" The innkeeper strode over to the table. "They aren't starting anything!"

"Taking their side, now, Niklas?"

"I will have peace in my tavern!"

"Then you should have told them to leave!"

"Rangers need to eat and sleep as anyone else, and they paid me good money in advance. You leave them be!"

Gadrik sneered at the three Rangers. "You Rangers need him to take your part, do you?"

"It is his tavern." Marcalan's level voice had no trace of his usual teasing lilt. "In here, he is law."

Laughing, the man shouted to Niklas. "Did you hear them? You are the law in here, they say!"

"Leave off." Lenton stepped closer to the table. "You are the one causing trouble."

"Do you hear this?" Gadrik shouted, swinging in a circle, arms wide. "Do you hear these two siding with Rangers?"

Several men grumbled, but most called for the man to be quiet and leave off.

"We come in here to relax," called one, "not to fight."

"Go back to your ale and let them alone," another chimed in. "They aren't bothering us."

"But they are Rangers! They are our enemy!"

The hateful words tore at Alcandhor's heart. In a soft voice, he asked, "Why?"

Gadrik spun about, and Alcandhor rose and faced him. "Why do you consider us enemies?"

"You crush us under your feet," the man snarled. "You cheat us, and you lie to us." He thrust his face into Alcandhor's, teeth clenched, voice low. "You steal from us."

Keeping his demeanor calm, he met the man's gaze, ignoring the challenge implied by the man's face being so close to his. "Tell me how. Give me facts, situations, petitions."

"So you can haul us before a court and take more from us? Throw us in stocks or cells for defying you?"

"I am not from Estan, and know not what happens here. But I can seek justice for you if Rangers have not treated you fairly. Tell me what has happened to you that you are so bitter? If it is within my power, I will make it right."

Gadrik glared, slowly straightening to his full height, never breaking his gaze. He spat in Alcandhor's face and stormed out of the tavern. Gasps filled the room; Tam and Marcalan shot to their feet.

Alcandhor held up a hand to stay any action, then turned for the back of the tavern, his expression set. Niklas, face pale, ran ahead to point out where the wash room was.

When he returned to the common room, the place had gone silent. It stayed that way, and they were left to eat in peace.

Tam leaned forward. "Uncle? Why are you so sad?"

Alcandhor stared at the bread he pulled apart. "That man is so filled with hate. He cannot think clearly because his heart is eaten up with bitterness. How many more are beyond reasoning, Tam? How far has this province strayed? Can we pull it back or must there be war before it is done?"

Neither Ranger answered him. Soon they finished their meal, and Alcandhor asked the innkeeper if they could be shown to their rooms.

When he was settled into his bed for the night, Alcandhor stared into the dark. How could the turmoil in this province end peacefully? Time moved slowly as he went over all the troubles assailing him. Sleep finally came, and he awoke, startled, from a hand on his shoulder.

"Thane, it past time to rise." Marcalan stood over him with a concerned expression.

Stars! He had slept in? And someone entered his room without his being aware of it? He threw back the covers with an imprecation and grabbed at his clothes. "What is the time?"

"Past the start of day's thirteen."

"Stars, we should have eaten and been on our way! Why did you not wake me sooner?" He pulled on his trous.

"Tam thought you should be allowed to sleep a little."

"'Tam thought,' enh? She thinks not like a Ranger then. We have duties and—"

"She sensed you all through the night, as did I." Marcalan crossed his arms. "You slept not, and your worry was keen. You have not slept well in days, and I need not tell you how that slows the reflexes and wit. We need a Thane with an alert mind."

Alcandhor clenched his jaw to keep his temper and mouth under control. "Where is Tam?"

"She is ordering breakfast. It should be on the table by the time you have readied yourself." Marcalan bowed himself out, and Alcandhor glared at the door and snatched at the laces as he tied his jerkin. How dare they not wake him!

By the time he joined them at the table, his fury had abated somewhat. The light snowfall on their journey toward Estan Hall cooled his temper even more, and the two chiefs were both quiet, giving him time to consider a new worry. Marcalan was not being Marcalan, and that was troubling. He was too quiet, not jesting. How long would this adjustment to bonding take?

"You need not be anxious," his cousin said, interrupting Alcandhor's thoughts. "I can feel what Tam does even more acutely than before, and we both strongly sense your worry for this province. I am slowly learning to separate such emotions and keep them from making themselves so intensely a part of me."

The younger Ranger's normally blithe face was careworn, a dismaying sight. Marcalan smiled, some of the twinkle coming back to his eyes. "Why, Thane, one would think you enjoy my little pranks and jests. Worry not, soon I will be back to my lightsome self."

Alcandhor snorted, but relief filled him at hearing the slight lilt to Marcalan's voice.

The snowfall grew heavier than a mere dusting through the morning. Would it end up a deep snow slowing their arrival at Estan Hall?

Shouts, cries of pain, and the clashing of blades ringing off each other echoed from the nearby woods. Alcandhor drew his sword, elation swelling that his shoulder was healed and he could fight full on once again. He and his two chiefs rushed toward the sounds to find a skirmish between Rangers and one of the factions.

Wading into the fray, Alcandhor took down one attacker after another easily, but then several of them broke and ran; Alcandhor pursued them, crashing through the trees and brush, slowly gaining on the scofflaws. He skidded to a halt, realizing too late they had not been fleeing but running for aid as he came upon a band of several dozen men.

They all drew swords and advanced on him with evil grins and snarling expressions, but then something sharp cracked the back of his skull, and he dropped to his knees in the snow-covered mould of the forest floor. Everything went black.

~*~

"Where is Uncle?" Tam stood, sword in hand, after the fighting stopped.

Marcalan looked about, as did all the other Rangers. He felt Tam's panic and forced himself to fight her hysteria threatening his own emotions. "Can you sense him?"

"Nay."

Marcalan turned to the other Rangers. "Where is the Thane?"

They all shook their heads.

"Search for him. Look for tracks, signs..."

The Rangers scattered. He sheathed his sword and put his hands on his wife's shoulders. She clutched at his arms. "I cannot lose him!"

"You are Second at Table." He forced her to look him in the eye and used their bond to help her gain control. "You must think as a Ranger, not as kin."

He lived a moment in her mind and heart, as she remembered her uncle pulling her away from her father's body, reminding her she was a Ranger, had duties, and no time for grief. She closed her eyes and called to Mattan.

Marcalan heard not only her thoughts, but the Enaisi's reply: *I sense him not, Little One. It does not mean he is dead, he may be unconscious.*

"He may be wounded and unconscious," she called to the Rangers. "Search diligently."

~*~

"He must have been taken captive," Marcalan said some time later as they all gathered again. "If he were dead or injured, we would have found him." He met his wife's eyes. "We must continue on with the mission. It must come first."

Tam's jaw set. Marcalan matched his own will against her stubbornness and her fear. After a moment, she turned to the Rangers. "Keep searching. They cannot have gotten far with him, and they had to leave tracks. It should not be hard to follow in the snow."

"The snow is falling much heavier and with more wind," one Ranger replied. "It will soon cover any tracks."

"Then search quickly!" She whirled to glare at Marcalan, but determination not anger drove her. "*We* will continue on, but *they* will continue to look for our Thane, now, before the trail is lost."

He bowed, seeing her as Second in Table, not his wife, for the first time; she was willing to do her duty when her heart clearly desired to stay with the search. But his heart was heavy as he knew, and she must too, if she would admit it, that the fast-falling snow and whipping wind worked against their needs.

~*~

A messenger wearing a tunic banded with Ranger clan colors came down the road early that afternoon, running as he could but trudging through many areas of deeper, drifting snow. He stopped before the two chiefs, gasping out their names, as he bowed. Despite the cold, he was sweating, his cloak thrown back over his shoulders.

"What news?" Tam asked.

"Rebels have captured Lord Stendhar and his wife. As the Thane has ordered the drums not be used to relay messages between northern Estan and Laird Hall, I am sent to bring news."

Marcalan held out his waterskin but the messenger shook his head.

"My thanks, but nay. I have water. I must continue."

As he ran on, Tam asked, "What do we do now?"

"As our runner says, continue. They are not disposed to like Rangers at Estan Hall, but they might allow us to assist in the search for their lord. Either way, we need to be there to assess the circumstances." Marcalan put an arm around her, feeling her apprehension for her uncle. "I cannot promise he will be fine, Tam, but I know our Thane is resourceful, and a fighter. He also seems to have the Maker smile on him more than any other Ranger I have ever known. Remember his recovery from the ambush? You cannot surrender to fear or despair."

She nodded, blinking back tears. "I wish I could see, or sense him..."

"I know, Love-ling. My heart is torn as well. But duty lies before us."

Chapter Twenty-five

Alcandhor woke, his head throbbing and body shivering. He lay on the ground next to a tree, his hands tied behind him, snow falling heavily, covering him. He fought to clear his mind.

A loud argument nearby added to his headache.

"You wanted bargaining pieces, you have more than you realize. Don't you know who that is?"

"I don't care. You should have killed him."

"Fool! That is the Thane!"

"And you would know, would you, Faltin?"

"Yes, I would! I was in the tavern in Polli last night, and he was there with the Ranger-lass that everyone has been talking about."

"The one who was at the trial at Laird Hall?"

"Yes, and he called her his niece," Faltin said. "Everyone knows the claim that she is Second at Table and her uncle is Thane."

"Not 'everyone' knows," sneered the first voice.

"Leave off and think, Kaltar! We have the Thane. What will they do to get him back, hey? We have leverage now with both the nobles and with the Rangers. We have the advantage."

"I want proof of who he is before doing anything. But how to find out?"

"If you want to know for certain, take him to where we hold Stendhar."

"Yes." Kaltar's voice was happier. "That would do it. But we have to move fast. Rangers are likely tracking us since we have him."

Alcandhor wondered how all this worked into the foresight he had of this mission into Estan. Being captured by Rebels had definitely not been something he had seen. They gave him no chance to fight or flee; another blow to the head brought unconsciousness again.

He woke to find he was propped against a tree near a fire, and he ground his teeth against an even worse headache. It was night. The men eating around the fire glanced at him but did not offer him food. He shivered, contemplating what he might do, when he heard Mattan in his mind.

We have been worried.

Alcandhor inhaled sharply. Stars! How could he answer the Enaisi and tell him what had happened?

I can hear your thoughts. Do you know where you are?

Rebels have me. I know not where.

I can estimate the location. I will tell Tam.

Alcandhor shook his head, then grimaced at the pain. *Tam must continue the mission.*

Rangers track you. She and I can help narrow the field of search.

Nay, these Rebels also have Lord Stendhar captive. Rescuing him should be the primary objective.

I will relay that message. But now, I feel that you have been injured. I am able to heal you.

Alcandhor resisted the urge to smile, despite his circumstances. *I cannot stop you.*

The headache slowly eased, and he closed his eyes. *Thank you.*

I will let you know what Tam and the others report.

Amazement and relief flooded over him. In the days when their people first colonized this planet, the Enaisi were with them, helping in ways such as this. And it created the legends. Now, he was in the midst of such tales as he had been told as a child.

Oh, he had no doubt that his chance of survival was not great; a fit of pique by a Rebel, the decision that he slowed them down, or that his presence endangered them because Rangers undoubtedly were tracking them, could mean a swift death. But still, he had been able to talk to Mattan over a distance of two days' journeying, and he had been healed of whatever wound had caused the agonizing headache!

~*~

Night fell full before Tam and Marcalan reached Estan Hall. 'Twas also built of shimmerstone, but not as large as Laird Hall. The white stone reflected the flickering light of the torches, giving the appearance that the lower part of the wall was aglow.

Guards at the gatehouse drew swords.

"Do not advance," the one called. "State your business."

Remember, Love-ling. Patience. Calm.

Tam lifted her chin, determined to behave as her uncle would deem correct. "I am Tamissa, Second at Table in Ch'shalna clan, and this is Marcalan, also a Ranger chief. We request to speak to whichever noble is in charge of Estan Hall."

"I am ordered that no one is to gain entrance to Estan Hall for any reason."

"Can you not announce us and—"

"No. I am under orders." The guard hesitated. "Come tomorrow and you may be able to seek an audience." He was worried, and frightened, and not just of the two Ranger chiefs standing before him. Tam could almost feel sorry for the man, and it helped temper her response.

"We will return in the morning. I would suggest when your watch is over that you mention to someone that Ranger chiefs were here offering aid in your search for Lord Stendhar. You may find that you receive different instructions."

Holding her anger in check was much easier with Marcalan's help. He said nothing, but his pride welled at her comportment as they turned away from the gatehouse. Her husband guided her through Vindel, the town contiguous to the provincial hall, and to the Ranger hold.

As they approached the gate, Rangers on guard stepped out, but at Marcalan's call drew back, bringing their fists to their hearts. Aye, her husband was well-known in this province.

Once inside, Tam noted casually the darker stone—not shimmerstone—of the small keep then skimmed the faces of the men, not knowing which one might be the steward. "Where is Ranadhor?"

An older man, silver-streaked blond hair caught back to the nape of his neck in a thong, stepped forward. "Here."

"I am Tamissa, Second at Table. What news?"

"There has been no change in Estan Hall's status since the messenger left this morning. Did he pass you on the road?"

"Aye. I have further news." Tam paused to take a breath, hoping she could keep her voice level. "The Thane is missing. He has been taken captive by Rebels."

Every Ranger in the hall stood, several calling out or gasping aloud.

Tam lifted her chin. "I know the general area where he is being held. I wish to send a band to rescue him and Lord Stendhar, who is also their prisoner."

Ranadhor's blue eyes glinted. He turned, pointed to two Rangers, lifted a finger, twirled it, and clenched his hand. Men scattered.

"Two bands totaling thirty Rangers will be ready momentarily, Second at Table."

Tam nodded.

"Evening meal is long over, but there is still food available for those on second watch. Sit you here at a table by the fire and warm yourselves while I see you are brought something to eat."

Tam sat on a bench, weariness overtaking her. She pushed back the hood of her cloak, enjoying the heat radiating from the fireplace, wiggling her almost numb toes to get some warmth into them.

Marcalan put an arm around her, and she leaned against him, not caring what the Rangers thought of her needing his comfort. She was lost without Uncle. Now she could see the truth of what Mattan had said about familial bonds. She had one with her father, aye, built over years and oh, so deep. He had cared for her needs, taught her to survive, and Trained her. He had been her life, all she knew until the Thane came.

But the bond with her uncle was different. It had not been built over time or existed for years, but somehow it ran as deep, and unlike the bond with her father, this one was filled with love, and so intense, as between a father and daughter.

And she hurt.

Marcalan's love enveloped her, and she closed her eyes, letting herself float for a moment in their entwined emotions.

She sat up, blinking, when Rangers placed plates, utensils, bowls of soup, platters of meats and breads before them, along with two large cups of steaming tea.

Tam tried to push away the troubles that vexed her while she ate; food and sleep were necessary if she were to think clearly—was it just this morning she had chided Uncle about this very thing?

Ranadhor stepped close to the table. "The bands are ready, Ranger Chief Tamissa."

Tam turned, lifting her legs over the bench seat to face the men. "This may seem very odd, but I am going to attempt something with the help of the Enaisi, Mattan, who has come back to reside on our world. He could sense the general area where my uncle was when he last spoke to him in his mind." She paused as she saw the Rangers exchanged glances in disbelief. "Mattan will be able to show you where to begin your search. It will seem frightening, as any new thing does, but try not to fear. This is something that our ancestors used as a matter of course."

"Second at Table," one said hesitantly, "what do we do?"

"Merely stand firm. I will simply sense you all, and Mattan will be able to use that to...to pass from my mind to yours to give you a map of where to search. Does that explain it more clearly?"

The men exchanged uncertain glances, although no one said anything.

"It will not be an invasion of your thoughts," Marcalan said, "just a placement in your mind of a picture. A place. It is more accurate than any description we can give you."

Ranadhor glanced at his men with an apprehensive expression. "You have experienced this, Marcalan?"

"Bells, aye." Her husband grinned, winking at Tam.

Tam smiled slightly at him, then sensed the men and called to Mattan. Using her as a conduit, the Enaisi sent the images and feelings of where Alcandhor had been to the Rangers.

Almost as one, they inhaled sharply, their eyes wide.

247

"This is where he was when Mattan was able to speak to him in his mind, not over an hour ago," Tam said. "They have probably made camp for the night so you should be able to find them and get our Thane back safely. He told Mattan that these Rebels also hold Lord Stendhar captive, so you have two duties. You will search for and secure the lord's release as well. Any questions?"

The Rangers were all silent, save one who softly replied, "Nay, milady Ranger."

"Then you have your orders. Go."

They bowed and filed out the door. Ranadhor sat down across the table as Tam turned around on the bench to continue eating.

"She has taken on her duty as Second at Table well for a wild mountain lass, has she not?" Marcalan quipped, rubbing her back.

The hold steward glanced at her, then at Marcalan. Tam frowned. "Why do I feel disapproval from you?"

"It is just that he speaks and acts so familiarly to you, Second at Table."

"Oh stars, call her Tam. Just as you call our Third at Table Haladhon."

"It is difficult, Marcalan, as I know she is the daughter of Valdhor, and now have seen for myself her Enaisi abilities."

"Bells." Marcalan rose, taking off his cloak. "She is just a Ranger as we are."

Tam felt Marcalan's question in her mind and gave a mental nod to him as her mouth was full, so he took her cloak off her too, and strode to hang them on pegs near the one hearth.

Ranadhor gasped and exclaimed, "Stars, Marcalan, what has happened?"

Tam straightened in alarm. The hold steward stared open-mouthed at Marcalan, who burst into laughter. Of course! Ranadhor could not have known he was married.

"What this little thing?" Marcalan touched the necklet as he sat down. "Tam slipped it on me when I was unconscious. Devious, she is, trapping me that way."

Tam slapped his chest with the back of her hand. "I told you to stop telling people that!" She looked over at the hold steward. "I think I need not tell you to pay him no attention."

Marcalan giggled and kissed her hair.

"Eat, vagabond," she ordered.

"Aye, milady," he replied with mock contrition.

"And what about your jerkin?" Ranadhor asked. "It shows a chief's status."

"Because of my marriage." Marcalan leaned forward, cutting his gaze one way and the other, as if to check for eavesdroppers before sharing a secret. "I have discovered, cousin, the one way to increase one's status—find a female Ranger who is a chief, and marry her."

"Stars, Marcalan," the man remarked with feigned disgust, "only you."

Tam smiled. "He has a penchant for the incredible, does he not, cousin?"

Ranadhor's eyes twinkled. "Indeed."

~*~

Alcandhor heard men approach their camp, then saw a man and woman, both bound, brought over by the campfire. They had been gagged, but now those were removed. The man was quiet, but the woman screamed obscenities and tried to lunge at one of the men. Alcandhor recognized the shrill voice—Aleta!

"Quiet, woman, or I'll use this knife on your face," hissed the man who dragged her back to her place. She sank to the ground as he let go of her, staring at the blade in his hand.

Another man came over and pulled her head up by the hair. "Do you know that man?" He pointed over at Alcandhor.

Her face twisted into a sneer. "That nothing! That weak, worthless excuse of a man! What do you want to know about him?"

"You do know him then?"

"Of course. He was my husband, if you wish to call him that."

"So he is the Thane?"

"Are you deaf? Didn't I just say so?"

He backhanded her across the face, knocking her into the snow-covered ground. He marched over and grabbed a fistful of Alcandhor's jerkin.

"So you are the Thane, after all, hey? One thing after another seems to go my way. First them, now you." He let go and glanced at the nearby men. "You take no chance with him. You know how fiercely Rangers can fight. You don't give him the chance to get free, do you understand?"

No umbrage or anger filled him that a woman he had loved, that had borne him three children, was being treated thus. Was he that callous? Had he died inside that much?

She slowly struggled to sit up, blood on her face, but still she displayed no remorse and no comprehension of the gravity of the situation, indeed, her expression was one of contempt. She snarled,

"Don't you know who I am?"

"You are a cheap trull who needs to learn some manners," Kaltar spat. "And if you don't shut your mouth, I'll—"

"How dare you talk to me that way!"

Alcandhor would put no unspeakable act past these men, and horror gripped him at the thought of any woman being subjected to their base desires. It was useless to warn her, but he had to try. "Aleta, do not say on. It is folly."

"Shut up! Shut your fatuous prating! You don't tell me what to do any more." She sneered at the leader of the Rebels. "No man tells me what to do!"

"You think so?" Kaltar pulled her to her feet, crushing her against him, roughly kissing her throat, and fondling her body through her clothing. She screamed obscenities and threatened him, but he just laughed, shoving her back against a tree, trapping her.

A signal call came from the dark, and Kaltar dropped her unceremoniously to the ground, drawing his sword. "If we begin to lose, kill our hostages."

A band of men rushed into their camp, and Alcandhor's guards ran forward to fight. He rose, watching while struggling to work the ropes loose that cut into his wrists. Who were these attackers? Not Rangers. Most likely Royalists.

The man now considered the lord of Estan Province lay on his side, sobbing quietly. Aleta stared around her, stunned, as if she could not grasp what was happening. She tried to stand, but with her arms bound behind her back, and the long skirt, she could not. She writhed along the ground, as if to crawl away through the snow.

Despite his feelings, Alcandhor's duty demanded he protect those two, or die trying.

The fighting closed in; the Rebels fell before their attackers. Kaltar turned from the battle and ran at Stendhar, sword raised, but Alcandhor dove at the Rebel, his shoulder ramming into the man's stomach, knocking him onto his back. Kaltar scrambled for his fallen sword, but Alcandhor landed solid kicks to the man's head and chest. He drove his last strike to Kaltar's face with all his strength and knew without sensing he had dealt a fatal blow.

He twisted on the ground to fend off another Rebel, crosscutting the man's legs, then as the man fell, he rolled, gained his feet, and kicked at the arm of a second who was bearing down on the lord. He only partially succeeded; Alcandhor's kick ruined the aim and kept the sword from running Stendhar through but the noble screamed as the blade pierced him.

"Hold!" called a voice.

Alcandhor turned and faced a sword to his chest.

"He is a *Ranger*," the man with the sword growled.

"He is the *Thane*. I want him alive."

"As you wish, Malkim."

Alcandhor sighed, resigned, as a broad-faced man swaggered into the firelight with an evil smirk, weapon still in hand. New captors.

"So. How fortunate. Parnel, you have some knowledge of healing. Tend our Lord Stendhar." Malkim eyed Alcandhor. "I have been told you have a special key, Thane. Where do you keep it?"

Alcandhor stared at him without expression, although he was curious where this man got his information and why he would want the bio-crystal key. Malkim raised as hand to strike him, then seemed to think better of it, lowered his fist, and turned to Aleta, whose bonds had been cut. "Woman, you know Ranger secrets, don't you?"

She brushed her hair out of her face, cutting her eyes at him with suspicion. "Why do you want to know?"

"I want an Elder's key. Where does he keep it?"

Aleta seemed to consider the question. "Why should I tell you?"

"I just saved your life, woman. I could change my mind. Stendhar I accept as provincial lord. There is still dispute over the validity of your recent marriage." He glanced over at the noble, lying on the ground, moaning in pain, then pointed his sword at her heart with a savage grin. "You are expendable."

She licked her lips and swallowed, eyeing the blade. "Around his neck."

Malkim clawed at Alcandhor's throat and chest, ripping the shirt, although the jerkin held.

"It's not here! Where is it, woman?"

"If he's not wearing it, I don't know where it could be. Perhaps it got lost in the fighting."

Malkim's eyes narrowed and he jerked Alcandhor to his feet. "Where is it?"

He met the Royalist's gaze in silent defiance. Rage distorted the man's visage, and Alcandhor braced, knowing what was coming. Malkim drew back and struck him with the hilt of his sword.

Chapter Twenty-six

I lost contact, Mattan thought to Tam. *He must be unconscious again.*

But why can you not sense him when he is unconscious or sleeping? You first contacted me while I was sleeping.

He is not as strong as you are. I could not contact him through the portal, only you, remember? I have not time to explain it all. I will keep trying to reach him.

Tam looked at her husband, sitting on the bench next to her, his own grief as well as heartache for her welling from him. "I wish I could behave as a lass and cry," she whispered.

Marcalan put his arms around her, and she let herself curl into him for a moment.

Ranadhor frowned. "Are you feeling well, Tam?"

"Mattan has lost contact with Alcandhor," Marcalan said.

The steward's face became impassive, even as worry grew in him. He came over and sat on her other side. "Our Thane is strong, stubborn, and resourceful. We must hold to that."

She nodded and straightened, determined to act like a Ranger. "Do you think they will let us have audience with whoever is in charge, since Lord Stendhar was captured by Rebels?"

"I know not. Estan Hall's policies change daily. 'Tis easier to tell which way the wind will blow than to predict what Estan Hall will pronounce."

"We will find out tomorrow," Marcalan said.

"Why do you not both rest?" said Ranadhor. "And if word comes of the rescue, I will call you immediately."

Tam met her husband's gaze and reluctantly nodded. "It makes sense. We must be rested for the morning."

They followed the steward along a hallway and up stairs. Tam frowned at her surroundings. "This Ranger hold is laid out much differently than the one in Lairdton. 'Tis a small keep."

"Lairdton's is unique. It is more of a barracks than a hold, but we know not why that is. This one is more traditionally built." Ranadhor stopped in front of a door. "Here are chambers for you. Marcalan has been here before. He can show you where the priv and washing rooms are."

Tam tried to smile. "My thanks. Night's rest."

The steward bowed. After the door closed, her husband held out his arms and Tam dove into them, finally able to let the tears flow. "I am so afraid. I cannot lose him!"

"He was still alive earlier this evening. We have to believe he is all right."

"He trusted me to keep him safe, and I betrayed that trust."

"How could you know he would run off, chasing Rebels?" He sighed. "It is not like him to do so. I cannot comprehend why he would do something so foolish."

"He has been on the edge of rationality for quite some time. He barely gets any sleep, and his emotions keep him in turmoil. I have been very worried."

"I know. So have all of us who know him well. Haladhon was against his coming here. He wanted to call Question on his decision, but Lamadhel talked him out of it."

"Lamadhel...why?"

"He said the Thane knew what he was doing, and that we should not get in the way of what was meant to be." Marcalan sighed. "Haladhon was livid when he spoke to me of it. But Lamadhel was right."

"I do not understand. What was Lamadhel talking about?"

"When the Thane moves as decisively as he has about Estan, then he has seen something. No one stands in his way when he is following sight."

Tam bit her lip, looking up into her husband's blue eyes. He was so much older than she, and at this moment, she was glad of that; she needed his steadying influence and his faith in their Thane. She wanted to bolt out the door in a frantic search for her uncle.

He tightened his embrace. "I would not let you."

"You must feel you married a child at times." She squeezed him around the ribs, resting her head on his chest.

"So must you."

Tam smiled at the lilt in his voice; despite her worry she could not resist the amusement she felt from him. "At times."

He chuckled quietly, swaying slightly as he held her, resting his chin on the top of her head. "Only at times? Then I need to try harder."

She raised her eyebrows, her smile broadening as she looked up again at him. "You want be thought of as a child?"

"You mean I am not?"

She tipped her head. "Aye, Prankster, I think you often are."

She could feel the smile on his lips as he kissed her.

~*~

Elendhar pulled a robe around him and followed the servant who had called him.

He entered a bedchamber to see his father being tended by a healer. He rushed over and gazed down at Stendhar worriedly, then up at the Royalist leader standing near. "What happened, Malkim? How did you find him? How did he come to be injured?"

"Rebels had him and they had captured a Ranger as well, milord. As we fought to free your father, the Ranger worked loose of his bonds and attacked him. We tried to stop him but your father was sorely wounded despite our efforts. I am sorry, lord."

Fists clenched, Elendhar growled, "You dispatched the Ranger, then, Malkim?"

"No, milord. He is their Thane. Despite the temptation to kill him, he is a valuable playing piece and as our prisoner, gives us an advantage."

As enraged as Elendhar had been at his father for putting out his mother for that wench, Aleta, simply because of the ties and knowledge she claimed, and for her beauty, he still loved his father. He would see him avenged. "Where is he being held?"

"In a bottom cell."

"When it comes time, I want to be there when that by-blow of a Ranger is killed."

"As you wish, milord."

~*~

Malkim sneered from his seat as Aleta entered the chamber. "What do you want? Are you concerned for your husband's health?"

The trull swept to the bed without answering. She stared down at Stendhar, her face impassive. "Will he live?"

"Not likely." Malkim laughed. "What will you do then? Seduce the son?"

She whirled, eyes flashing.

"You know he will have you thrown out of the hall, and his mother reinstated as proper widow of his father."

"I married Stendhar! He cannot!"

"Oh, can't he? He will be lord of the province, and he detests you. Rightly so, in my opinion. You had better hope the son is as easily enamored of your brittle beauty, wench, if you wish to keep the title Lady of Estan."

"How dare you!"

He snorted, looking her over; thin for his tastes, but fine for a quick tumble. "Get out of here before I decide to find out if you're worth tossing a wife out for."

Aleta took a step toward him, hand raised, but he stood, leering, and she rushed from the chamber.

Malkim laughed again.

~*~

Alcandhor awoke to find he was still bound, and in a damp, dark place. He closed his eyes and opened them but saw no difference. He listened carefully. He could hear water trickling nearby. He ached all over. But why? He remembered being hit in the face, but the familiar soreness that came from bruises assailed his body. Was he beaten while unconscious? He twisted a little to let his fingers feel the ground beneath him. Flat stone floor. A cell? But where? He could not be certain, but the most likely place was Estan Hall. He could not imagine how he ended up there, but as unconsciousness slowly took him over again, his last thought was, *this is not good.*

~*~

Tam sat bolt upright in bed as Mattan mentally shook her awake, Marcalan only a moment behind her.

He is alive. He was awake for a few moments, but fell unconscious before I woke enough to talk to him.

Where is he? Tam asked.

I could not focus quickly enough to tell. I am sorry. Sleep now. I will call if I learn anything more.

Thank you. Tam felt Marcalan's arm steal around her. She burrowed into his chest, trying to pull strength and comfort from him as they cuddled.

"How can Mattan sense for the Thane while asleep?" Marcalan asked.

"I know not," Tam murmured tiredly.

"I begin to wonder about their abilities. Can they do even more than what they reveal to us?"

Tam sat back up. "Do you doubt Mattan's sincerity?"

"Nay, but he has said there are limits on what he will allow himself to do."

"I had not thought of that. But surely he would not let Uncle die if he could save him."

"If it would involve breaking our laws, I think he might."

Tam looked at Marcalan in the glow from the fireplace. "Why do you say such things? What has brought this to your mind?"

"I know not. It was just a thought, a feeling I had just now."

Tam stared at him, alarmed. "Do you sense something? Or see something?"

"Nay, Love-ling. I do not think so. Do not fear for our Thane. He is alive. We will find him." He pulled her to him as he lay back down and wrapped his arms around her as she clung to him.

She closed her eyes. "I hope so."

~*~

Marcalan felt Tam's ire rise as they waited at the gate of Estan Hall. Breaking a path in the deep snow the entire distance had been a slow trek, and now they stood, shivering, while word was taken to whoever was in charge. He had no doubt the delay was calculated.

Finally, a thin-faced man with small, close-set eyes came out to see them, bundled heavily against the cold. He did not even bow to them. "I am to deliver a message: Thane Alcandhor is our guest. We will exchange him for an Elder's key. You have ten days to produce one, or you will not see him again."

Tam glared at the man, and Marcalan could feel her trembling rage. She took a step forward. "Think you we can be coerced? If our Thane is not returned—"

Marcalan grasped her shoulder, sending peace to her. He met the messenger's gaze and said, "Tell your masters to think twice about this course of action. Rangers will not capitulate to ransom demands, but we will respond to threats in a manner not likely to be appreciated."

"I shall deliver your answer." He stepped back inside, and the gate slammed shut.

Tam turned and clutched at Marcalan's arms with a sob.

We are watched. Control, Love-ling.

Tam took a shuddering breath and nodded.

"Let us hurry back to Ranger hold," he said, "and contact Mattan. Through him, we can make plans with Haladhon on what to do next."

"I have already told Mattan, and he agrees with you."

Marcalan smiled grimly. His wife and that alien certainly facilitated communication.

The trampled, packed snow leading to the door of the hold told of the return of the bands of Rangers. Stomping the snow off his feet once inside, he nodded to the men filling the hall, taking off their heavy cloaks and shaking snow off near the fireplaces and central hearth.

Ranadhor walked over. "What news?"

"Estan Hall claims to have Un—the Thane, hostage."

"They want the Enaisi key to secure his release," Marcalan said, "that is, if we believe them."

"Oh, they have the Thane, that is certain. Our men found the place the Enaisi had shown them, but they were not there. There had been a battle in that spot, with dead Rebels left behind. Our men followed the trail straight to Estan Hall."

Marcalan shook his head. "I meant, if we believe they would truly release him after given the key."

Ranadhor hesitated then nodded. "This is dire. They have the Thane, and we have no way to rescue him. Not in Estan Hall."

Marcalan frowned. Both Laird Hall and Estan Hall had tunnels as secret methods of escape. He was not certain why; perhaps Mattan could tell the history at some time. "They would know and be watching the tunnel entrance, would they not?"

"There is no tunnel entrance. Batrig had it filled in."

"What?" Marcalan clenched his fists. That had been his private hope. "Why?"

"Batrig was a strange man. He often talked of enemies conspiring against him, even as he planned conspiracies of his own. He could not defeat the white stone of the tunnel, but he could fill it in, and he did."

Marcalan groaned. "Stars! We could have used that to get in, find the Thane, and leave without being seen."

"Even if it were open, how would you do that?" Ranadhor asked. "The guards would know of it."

"With Mattan's help, it would be possible. But it is immaterial now."

"What can we do then?" asked Tam.

Ranadhor shook his head. "I know not. Even if we wanted to give them the key, where could it be found?"

Tam glanced at Marcalan, then said quietly, "I have it." She reached inside her shirt and pulled out the alien crystal, dangling on its chain. Even in the well-lit chamber it glowed brightly. A hush settled over the hall. Tears in her eyes, she whispered, "I would fain give it to them for Uncle, even knowing he would not have me do so, but I...I know they mean not to give him back."

"Foresight?" asked Marcalan.

"I know not. I just know. They do not mean to let him live."

"I would concur," Ranadhor said. "It seems folly to us to think of killing the Thane, but I have been steward of this hold for a long time and know how many of these Royalists think. And Stendhar hates the Rangers, and the Thane especially, as Batrig did."

Tam breathed in sharply, and Marcalan put an arm around her, sending to her to calm her down and try to reassure her. "We will find a way, Tam. We must! Come, sit. Let us have some hot tea and you can discuss matters with Mattan."

Tam gave a dull nod, and Marcalan led her to a table.

~*~

Randhal fell into the chair, staring ahead, oblivious to the people in his solar.

He saw a merry face, felt hands tickling him. Strong arms over his, showing him the proper way to swing a sword. Earnest smoke-blue eyes boring into his as the rough, low voice taught him the law. A comforting hand on his neck, offering comfort and support. A furrowed brow, worry lines. A smile. A gentle laugh. Smoldering coals for eyes in a face hardened by anger.

Randhal's father had not been one to disregard tradition, but he did not like children or teaching. What was easier than to turn over tutelage of his son to the man who knew more of the Law than any other alive, even if he was young and son of the Thane? So Randhal became Alcandhor's pupil. And in more than just learning the Law. Alcandhor had become the youngster's mentor, a surrogate big brother. Randhal knew he cared for the Thane, but this news made him realize how deeply he loved the man.

"Your Grace? Are you all right?"

Randhal looked up at Krendhal. Even now, despite the look of concern, his cousin remained aloof. Who would touch him now with Alcandhor gone? Who would ever see beyond the Laird? Was it possible for a heart to be sucked out of a body, yet still live? His father's death had been a hard blow, but this one felt it would destroy him.

Without replying, Randhal dropped his head, not seeing the carpet beyond his clasped hands. He could not cry. He was Laird. He was used to loneliness. He would just have to become used to being alone as well. Totally alone.

He shook himself at his selfishness. Stars, these Rangers in this chamber with him were all kin of the man. And here he sat, feeling sorry for himself. He looked up at Sarinna. She was composed, although pale. Haladhon had circles under his glazed eyes. He was not handling this well. That was natural, being raised as brothers as they were.

He took in the drawn expressions on all their faces.

"There must be some way to free him," he found himself saying.

"We see no chance of doing so." Lamadhel crossed his arms. "Estan's tunnel was filled in by Batrig, and there is no other way into the hall."

Eladhrel nodded. "They state they will exchange the Thane for the key. Tam told Mattan she senses they will not honor that. And at any rate, Ranger policy is not to bargain. Not even for our Thane." His voice cracked on the last two words and he cleared his throat, averting his eyes.

"Is there anything I can do? As Laird there must be something."

Lamadhel shook his head. "They do not accept the authority of the Rangers or of Laird Hall, Your Grace."

"Can we besiege them, as we did this hall?"

"I would expect that if we tried," Lamadhel said, "the skirmishes and fighting between the besiegers and the Esteni would erupt into widespread violence. And with the recent siege of this hall, I would wager other halls have become more judicious in stocking provisions, at least those in certain provinces."

"So what are our choices?"

Haladhon's voice came from the corner where he sat, a harsh, ragged whisper. "We have none."

Randhal's own voice fled then, his throat thick, and he swallowed hard.

"The lords need to be told," Krendhal said.

"Aye." Lamadhel stood. "Shall I see to calling a meeting of the lords, Your Grace?"

Randhal lifted his head slightly as he whispered, "Aye."

A swish of material, then Sarinna sat, her soft hand lighting on his arm. "Come, Your Grace. Let us eat something."

Choking back a sob, he shook his head.

"He would want it."

Aye, he would. He would expect Randhal to be Laird. To make him proud. To do his duty. It took several breaths but finally he was able to reply, "You are correct. Thank you, Lady Sarinna."

He stood, holding an arm up to his mentor's sister, wishing he had her strength and resolve. She placed her fingers on his hand, her grey eyes bespeaking approval, and together they walked to the sideboard laden with food.

Chapter Twenty-seven

"What is being done then, about the treason and about the Thane being captured?" Irdhith's blue eyes snapped as he glared around the lords' chamber that afternoon.

Randhal carefully considered his words. "It is an internal matter, involving Estan, Laird Hall, and the Rangers, doubly now that we know they hold the Thane."

Irdhith shook his head. "It involves all of us. Even if Estan was not my neighbor, this treason concerns us all."

His face grave, Krendhal rumbled in a low voice, "That is why the Laird has called this meeting, to inform all of you. But what action can any of you take? It is the Laird's decision on how to proceed, and the Rangers to carry out his wishes."

"And what do the Rangers say of all this?" asked Gilendhar of Keladar Province. His brown eyes focused on Haladhon, the highest rank of his clan present. Did the noble harbor animosity toward them as did his late cousin, Paltor?

"We have met with the Laird and are considering our options," the tall Ranger chief said. "No decisions have been made yet."

It was reassuring somehow to see Haladhon in control rather than in benumbed grief. The man's attitude helped Randhal to maintain a façade of calm and appear as Laird not the fearful, sorrowful boy he truly was inside.

"Will you consider advice from the lords of the provinces?" asked Tadhrol of Taladar, his stern gaze flicking between Randhal and the Ranger chief.

"We will fain listen to any advice, lord," Randhal said, inclining his head.

Tadhrol rubbed his thumb across his fingertips. "Can you not bargain for the Thane's life?"

"We dare not, although it grieves me deeply." Haladhon frowned, staring at the table. "We are trying to devise a rescue, but Estan Hall is a fortress, as is Laird Hall."

It was silent for a long moment, then Tadhrol let out a slow breath, his expression compassionate. "How fare you, Ranger Chief? The Thane is your close kin and friend."

"It is hard, milord." Haladhon stared at his hands.

"You know not for certain if he still lives, is that not right?" asked

Lorwith of Pashelon.

"We do know he is alive, Lord Lorwith. He is wounded, bound, and in a bottom cell. He has not been fed nor been tended to in any way."

"How know you this?" the Pashelon lord exclaimed, disbelief on his face. Although whether of the Thane's treatment, or the Rangers knowledge of it, Randhal was not certain.

"The Enaisi, Mattan, has been in mental contact with him."

Tadhrol sat back, nostrils flared. "They would treat a man so?"

Haladhon was grim. "They are, milord."

"But can we do nothing about that?" Vendhal of Ranshalon Province slammed a fist on the table. "That is unconscionable!"

"We can do little, we have tried sending notice that if he is not properly treated, we will not accede to their demands." Haladhon spread his hands. "They will not open the gate, and the written notice left at the gatehouse is still there, untouched."

Lorwith frowned. "But you stated you will not give them what they want."

"They know that not, lord. It could buy us time to try to devise a rescue by declaring that we must send word to Zaidhron and wait for someone to journey to Estan with a key." Haladhon sighed, staring at the table. "If they would listen."

Tadhrol's knuckles whitened. He reminded Randhal of a viper preparing to strike. The lord leaned forward, his voice low, menacing. "We can make them listen. Estan is my northern neighbor. I can set patrols and close the borders, allowing no crossing or trade until Estan releases the Thane and returns to the Laws of the Enaisi. And I can order all whose ships claim my province as home to avoid Estan's harbors as well." His gaze swept the table, his eyes piercing. "We provincial lords all can publicly decry their actions, and demand proper treatment for the Thane at least, if not his immediate release."

Vendhal nodded. "We only touch at the corner, but I can do the same. Let us call a scribe and put our names to paper, not only in setting sanctions against Estan for their actions but to condemn them for holding the Thane and their treatment of him. We will let our world know we all stand solidly behind the Laws of the Enaisi, our Laird, and the Rangers. We will not allow any province to supercede our laws."

"Do you call a vote then, Lord Vendhal?" asked Randhal.

Irdhith shifted in his seat, frowning. "While I am in agreement with this, I wish to point out that I do know Stendhar somewhat, and he may take our notice of declaring sanctions negatively, and be driven to violent actions. He could decide to kill the Thane now."

A hush fell over the chamber, and Randhal's stomach turned.

Vendhal's mouth dropped open. "Then what do we do?"

"Postpone voting on sanctions is my suggestion." Irdhith gestured toward Haladhon. "Give the Rangers a chance to consider how they may rescue their Thane."

The tall chief shook his head morosely. "There is not much chance of that. Not given the short time Mattan says the Thane has to live. He is...failing quickly."

"If you know he is still alive, we must hold on announcing sanctions against Estan," Irdhith said earnestly. "You Rangers seem resourceful. Or perhaps your Enaisi will have an idea."

Krendhal drew himself up. "That is not sound. We already know the Royalists intend to let him die. Sanctions might make them reconsider releasing him, or at least force them to give him proper treatment."

"Aye. I agree. Without action he is dead," Haladhon said.

Tadhrol rubbed his thumb across his fingertips. "Sanctions might offer him a chance." He drew in a quick breath. "Nay, Irdhith, I disagree with your assessment. We must impose the sanctions now. Your Grace, I call for a vote." He lifted a hand indolently toward the tall lord. "And do not say on. I am inclined to believe you are more worried about the trade lost between Estan and Lantral than about Stendhar moving with unwise haste against the Thane."

Stars, but Tadhrol did speak his mind cuttingly!

Irdhith shot from his seat. "Say on and see what it cost you, old man!"

"The only thing it will cost is your position. We mince no words here, cockerel, and threats of violence against each other can be cause for judgment by your peers and removal as provincial lord." Tadhrol's lip curled in what could only be called a malicious smile. "Now sit you down, boy."

With deliberate slowness, Irdhith seated himself as the Taladar lord continued: "The cost of closing borders to Estan is a reality, but if we rely on each other, we may find we can all lessen the hardship of the lost trade."

Perdhal of Nelatan looked from Tadhrol to Krendhal. "What of ships that would land at Estan's harbors? That increases my ships' journeys to go past Estan to Taladar. And in treacherous waters." His eyes narrowed. "I think you do this to steal Estan's sea trade, Tadhrol."

Krendhal leaned back with a disgusted grimace. "The treacherous waters are all Nelatan's and around the Forbidden Peninsula, which your ships must needs navigate, so do not feign hardship on that account. Estan's North Port's harbor supplies much to Viltara Province. If a blockade is enforced for an extended time, it will affect my province greatly."

Perdhal's lips thinned, and he looked at them all down his long nose. "I need not agree to this embargo."

"Just remember, Perdhal," Tadhrol said, lounging in his chair, his mouth curved in a vicious smile. "Your province is north-most and has only Viltara as a direct neighbor. What if Krendhal closed borders on you? And what if the Rangers set their ships to blockade your harbors?"

The Nelatan lord stood. "They would not dare!" He stared at one face then the next, until finally he sat down with a defeated look.

Randhal glanced about the table. "If there is no more discussion, then let us put it to vote. Do you impose sanctions, aye or nay?"

All the lords save Gilendhar, Perdhal, and Irdhith promptly voted aye. Randhal's heart drummed in worry that they would not all agree to the sanctions. This one thing might be the only chance to save the Thane's life. Gilendhar did not border Estan, so his vote was not as important, but Irdhith and Perdhal were essential. *Vote aye, please, vote aye!*

Perdhal licked his lips, his eyes flitting between Gilendhar and Irdhith, then he gazed at Krendhal for a long moment before he said, "Aye."

Gilendhar sucked a tooth, then finally shrugged, muttering, "Aye."

Irdhith pulled himself up straight, scanning the lords. He lifted his hands. "Aye."

"So be it." Randhal said, hoping he hid his relief. "Let the paper be readied and your signatures put to it. We shall send it by runner and announce it by drums." He gazed about the table. "Any other concerns or questions?"

"I–I have a concern," Lorwith said, lifting a finger. "If you enforce this...this siege of Estan Province, it traps your men as well, including two Ranger chiefs. They would be unable to call for assistance in a hostile province."

"We could call them all out, and leave Estan without arbiters and peacekeepers, but that is not our way," Haladhon said. "Our people know how to care for themselves."

"Could you not send in more Rangers?" asked Krendhal.

"We could. And might, if necessary, to protect our kin. But the Rangers posted there need to be allowed to try to handle whatever situations occur as much as possible. Rangers are not warriors, but peacekeepers. We will only wage war if Estan were to declare it on us first."

Krendhal's eyebrow arched. "Have they not already done so?"

"The Royalists led by Lord Stendhar, aye, but Estan Province as a whole, nay." Haladhon tapped his knuckles on the table. "And we might find that Estan will not back these Royalists, not in a confrontation that puts the entire province at odds with all the other provinces, and Ch'shalna clan as well."

"A good point, Ranger Chief." Vendhal nodded.

Lorwith looked around. "Wh–what shall become of Lord Stendhar? He shall have to face trial, shall he not?"

"Aye." Randhal spoke in as commanding a tone as he could. "He has already broken Enaisi law by declaring independence, which is treason. And he keeps the Thane hostage for ransom, which leaves no doubt as to his fate once captured."

The chamber was quiet for a few moments, and Randhal hoped that the lords truly took to heart his declaration.

"What know we of Stendhar's family?" asked Tadhrol. "Are they all truly Royalists, or could some be faithful to us?"

Randhal liked that noble more with each comment he made, but dared not let it show. He had just asked a question that forced the lords onto the side with Laird Hall, the Rangers, and the Laws of the Enaisi. And these new provincial lords, Irdhith, Perdhal, and Gilendhar, were all kin to the lords who had been traitors. Who knew what their, and Lorwith's, real opinions and motives were? Some might be Royalists, who wished autonomy and to rule their provinces without any outside interference, which could lead to a destructive dictatorship. Others might, like their predecessors, wish to not only rule with impunity but want to claim more, although was that a dream any of them could harbor with all that had happened? The Rangers had shown they could quell such treason and now they even had an Enaisi to help.

If only he were older and wiser. He felt so untutored; he should not even be Laird. But Krendhal and Alcandhor had both insisted that regardless of age, he must take the mantle, as evidence that despite the traitors' attempts, his family still held power.

Randhal was brought out of his musings as his First Minister replied to Tadhrol's query about Stendhar's family.

"I know not." Krendhal looked at Taladar's lord, then around the table. "I do not know Stendhar's family well, nor any of their leanings."

"It is irrelevant." Irdhith leaned back in his chair. "We cannot ascertain anything of his family until Estan is brought into compliance and her leader ceases his mad bid for power."

"Aye, and mad it is," Vendhal stated.

"Hopefully the sanctions will bring Stendhar to his senses," Tadhrol said.

Irdhith shrugged his shoulders. "We shall see."

~*~

"You seem to have changed in attitude, Lord Irdhith," Haladhon said as they left the council chamber together and walked down the hall.

"Have I, Ranger Chief?" Irdhith smirked.

Haladhon kept his face neutral, although he wanted to punch the smug expression off the cockerel lord's face. "You had leanings that favored Zantith's thoughts on provincial governing, and concerning the Rangers, too."

"I did. I have not hidden that fact. But in my bid to become lord of my province, I swore fealty to the Laird, and renounced any intention of overthrowing the Laws of the Enaisi. I saw the futility of trying to wage a war, covert or overt, against the Rangers, which is more than I can say for these Rebels and Royalists in Estan."

"So you merely acquiesced to the inevitable and do not truly honor the Enaisi's laws?"

Irdhith stopped and crossed his arms. "Find one point in which I honor not the laws, Ranger Chief. I am lord of my province, and will do my best for what is my domain. And what I see is that working in union with Rangers is beneficial. Besides, I have found another reason to think well of Ranger clan." He paused before continuing, a victorious gleam in his eyes. "If you will excuse me, I have the honor of being a lady's escort this evening. As her brother is captive, I doubt she will wish to join the banquet, but I am certain she will be in need of comfort."

Haladhon stepped closer to Irdhith. "Your intentions had best be honorable toward her."

Irdhith's lip curled in a sneer. "What do you know of honor, Haladhon? Your exploits are well known, and the fact you continue to wear a jerkin cause many to doubt the veracity of Ranger clan."

Haladhon did not acknowledge Irdhith's statement. He set his jaw, speaking through clenched teeth. "She is my first cousin, and is as sister to me. Since her brother is missing, I claim Right, Irdhith. Just remember that."

"She is a woman grown, Haladhon, and needs not her honor protected by you." His blue eyes pierced. "My intentions are very honorable, though, I will tell you that. If she will have me, I will make her my lady."

Haladhon shook with such jealousy and rage he could not even reply as the tall, handsome noble strode away.

~*~

His eyes staring blankly ahead, Haladhon barely registered the presence of his uncle, cousins, and their wives in the Thane's suite with him and Mattan. None of them joined the banquet in the Great Hall. The gathering had the feel of a death vigil.

A knock caused everyone to tense. "'Tis Sarinna," Mattan said, rising to answer the door.

"Poor child," Nadinn muttered.

Haladhon rose as his lovely cousin appeared in the doorway. Irdhith was with her. He met the challenge in Irdhith's eyes with a dead stare, then lowered his gaze to Sarinna's pale face, and held out one arm. She rushed to him like a small child to a parent and let him wrap his arms around her.

"I had to be with all of you. I could not stand it anymore. Lord Irdhith has been kind, but I wanted to be here."

Haladhon closed his eyes at her open vulnerability, so rarely seen. His lips brushed the brown tresses on the top of her head as he held her.

"I thank you for your solicitude, Lord Irdhith," Lamadhel said, bowing.

Irdhith returned the courtesy, his gaze sweeping the chamber. "Call upon me if I may be of service in any way."

Haladhon ground his teeth at the insinuating cockerel. Irdhith's blue eyes flicked at him, a smirk twitching at the corners of his mouth. Only the fact that Sarinna was in his arms kept him from attacking the fulsome noble. Aye, one day he would have the privilege of knocking the inbred by-blow topside down, not only for his unctuousness, and his presumption about Sarinna, but for using this tragedy to try to ingratiate himself with Ch'shalna clan.

As the door closed and the Rangers were alone, Haladhon directed Sarinna to a divan, sitting next to her. Mattan brought her a hot cup of tea. Her hands shook as she accepted it.

"Have you eaten?"

"Aye. Lord Irdhith insisted." She looked up at Mattan. "Any news?"

"Nay. Well, the Laird has already had the sanction signed, and a runner has been dispatched to Estan with the drums also sending the message, but that is all."

Sarinna's chin trembled as she lowered her lips to the cup. After a sip, she gazed up at her kin. "How fare all of you?"

"As you are, my dear," Cariss murmured.

Sarinna gave a shuddering sigh and nodded. She stared ahead, her voice low. "I know I shall survive this, but I cannot see how yet."

Haladhon agreed, but kept his thoughts to himself as he tightened the arm around her. For all his strength, his resourcefulness, he could not save the man he loved dearer than brother.

Chapter Twenty-eight

Elendhar eyed the men posted along the hallway. How many of the guards in Estan Hall were Royalists? Most of them, he would wager. Were there many left who regarded the Enaisi's laws as they should? He had not pondered the politics of it much, but he had not thought the Royalist viewpoint prudent. For each province to be independent, and have no Rangers to keep the peace—that did not sound wise. As he put his hand on the door latch, he remembered the Ranger that had tried to kill his father. His upper lip drew back. If that is what Rangers were, perhaps the Royalists were right, after all.

He entered the bedchamber. Stendhar was awake, seemingly, but fevered, muttering, his head rolling back and forth. He brushed the damp hair off his father's face, then gave a questioning look to the healer sitting next to the bed.

"He doesn't seem to be aware we are here, lord. He hasn't been lucid once. The cold and the wound have done him in."

Elendhar shook with anger. "Curse that foul Ranger! Why would he strike down a defenseless man?" He looked over at Malkim, standing in the corner. "What are you going to do to that by-blow?"

"He is bound in a cold, bottom cell and will stay there till he rots. The guards are wagering how long he will live."

"What mean you?"

"Just what I have said. He is bound. He cannot care for himself, even to get a drink or relieve himself. He is not being fed. Wish you to wager as well?" Malkim grinned maliciously.

Elendhar stared at him, swallowing his disgust. He wanted the Ranger dead, but he could not see making sport of it. He hoped his face did not betray his repugnance. Malkim would pounce on that. He sat down, wondering when the insanity in Estan Hall would stop. He wished the Royalist were not there, watching him watch his father.

Stendhar quieted, finally, and Elendhar stood, fearing the end was near. He did not wish to see it; he had never seen death. "Let me know of any change," he murmured to the healer.

Malkim joined Elendhar as he left the chamber. "I need to speak with you."

They walked toward Elendhar's bedchamber. What might Malkim wish to talk to him about? The man frightened him. How did he ended up in this predicament? His father had insisted he accompany him to Estan

268

Hall to watch and learn. Stars, he would not come of Age for another few lunations, and knew nothing of politics. He felt he betrayed his mother by leaving her, but he had to obey his father. In how many more ways would his world fall apart?

Once inside his chamber, Elendhar turned to the Royalist leader. "What would you say?"

"You know you will be lord of Estan Province—likely by day's end, don't you?"

Elendhar scowled. "Can you not pretend sorrow over my father, at least?"

"I am more interested in other matters," Malkim said, laughing. "Have you thought of the direction you will take as lord?"

Torn between hysterical laughter and rage, Elendhar took a breath to calm himself and shook his head. "Two lunations ago, the thought never entered my head that I would be other than a cousin to Estan's lord. And a minor cousin at that. One hardly ever at court." He sat down, avoiding Malkim's gaze. "But I know what direction to take. Worry not. You are the true ruler of this province, not my father, and not me. I may not have an understanding of all the laws and politics, but I understand that he who wields the sword is in control. If I thought to gainsay you, I would be dead, or joining that Ranger in the cells."

Malkim chuckled, but it was not a happy sound. "You are wise for one so young."

If only he had the courage to at least try to stand up to the Royalist, but he did not. He knew Malkim was skilled with a sword and eager to use it. Elendhar sighed. *It is a horrible thing to know you are a coward.*

~*~

A voice whispered to Elendhar as he walked down the hall. He turned to see a fearful face peering out from a barely opened door. It was one of Malkim's men.

"What do you want?"

"Lord." The man inclined his head. "My name is Kirtin. I wish to speak to you privately."

Elendhar glanced up and down the hallway, then slipped into the chamber and shut the door. "What is it?"

"I am not a friend of the Rangers, milord, but still I do not like to see a man unjustly accused. Not even a Ranger."

"What mean you?"

"The Ranger we hold in the bottom cell? He did not strike the blow to your father. He tried to defend him from Rebels."

Disbelief froze Elendhar, but why would this nervous man lie? "You are certain?"

"I saw it myself. And now he lies bound in a bottom cell, wounded. He is unable to care for himself, even to get a drink."

"Why do you tell me this?"

"One of my complaints against the Rangers is that justice wasn't served. Lies were believed, and the real villains weren't uncovered."

"So you would pay this Ranger the favor of clearing his name, despite your antagonism toward his clan?"

Kirtin grimaced, straightening his shoulders. "Malkim will have my throat cut if you tell, milord, but he wishes the whole world to think the Thane killed Lord Stendhar and use your grief and vengeance as an excuse to wage war on the Rangers and rid our province of them." He lifted his chin with a proud glare. "I am a Royalist, and want Ranger Clan gone, but I have a clear grievance against them and don't like using deception and excuses. Isn't truth enough? Do we have to use lies?"

Elendhar frowned. "What think you I can do? Know you not I will merely be his puppet?"

Kirtin nodded. "Yes, but I just thought you should know. You seem to be an honest sort, milord, if you don't mind me saying so. You're in a hard place, and not in the position to do much against Malkim, but, well..." The man shrugged, a gesture of hopelessness. "I just thought you should know."

Elendhar smiled sadly. "My thanks. Now let us hope we leave this chamber carefully, and are not seen."

Elendhar tossed and turned, unable to sleep, his mind on the Ranger in the bottom cell. Bound and cold. Finally he got up and dressed. He could not do much for the man, but perhaps...perhaps he could do a little.

~*~

Elendhar's heart pounded as approached the cells. The guard straightened.

"I wish to see the Ranger."

"Malkim has given orders that no one enters, milord."

Elendhar remembered the imperious tone his cousin, the late Lord Batrig, had used. Could he control the quavering of his voice and sound like a man accustomed to giving orders? "Because of this man, my father lies dying. I will see him for myself. Now. Or I will get Malkim myself and bring him here to give the order."

The guard hesitated. "Just this once, milord." He unlocked the door, and took a torch from the wall.

Elendhar stared at him, fear choking him. "What are you doing?"

"Escorting you, milord."

Elendhar snatched the torch from the man, hiding his trepidation behind feigned indignation. "Do you fear a bound man will attack me? Or do you fear I will help him escape as a reward for attacking my father? I will see him alone."

The guard shook his head, his mouth open.

"You may be Malkim's man, but remember I am lord of this province, or will be when my father dies."

"Yes, milord."

Once in the cell and with the door closed, Elendhar leaned against the wall, relieved he had gotten this far. He put the torch in the bracket on the wall, then pulled out his knife and knelt by the Ranger.

The man was unconscious or sleeping. He cut the ropes, then went to the corner where water trickled into a basin and then further down a tiny sluice to the priv where it drained out. He brought water over, cupped in his hands, and splashed it in the Ranger's face, then a second time, hoping some dribbled in the man's mouth.

"Wake, Ranger, please," he hissed softly.

The man grimaced, then his eyes flew open. He stared at Elendhar with a wary expression.

"I have only a few moments, Ranger. I brought food." He pulled out the pouch and set it down. "When Malkim finds I have been here he will order the guards not to let me in again, I am sure. He may come in to see how you are. Keep the ropes handy to make it appear you are tied. I...I do not know to tell you to hide the food though."

"My thanks." The Ranger's hoarse voice cracked.

Elendhar stared at the man as he staggered to his feet, and slowly made his way to the basin to gulp water. "I wish I could do more for you, Ranger. They mean to let you starve in here. I cannot do anything against Malkim. He rules this place. But I could not bear the thought of a man bound and left as they did you."

The door slammed back, and Elendhar jumped, his heart hammering as Malkim strode in followed by guards. Several went to the Ranger, swords drawn as if afraid the weakened man would attack, while two others dragged him over and retied his bonds, then ran the ropes through a ring in the wall.

Malkim snatched a handful of Elendhar's shirt and pulled him close. "If I didn't have a use for you, I'd put you in a cell next to the Thane and let you rot as well." He shoved Elendhar back, so he fell against the guards. "Take our provincial lord to his bedchamber." Malkim leaned close, sneering. "If you cause any more trouble, I will gladly slit your throat myself. Do I make myself clear?"

After the guards delivered him to his chamber and locked him in, Elendhar collapsed on his bed, his heart still pounding wildly, wondering how long Malkim would need him alive. Only then did he realize the Royalist had called him provincial lord. His father was dead. He sobbed quietly in the dark.

~*~

I am sorry, my son, Mattan's voice murmured in Alcandhor's head. *We are discussing matters. They claim they will free you if we give them the key.*

They have no intention of freeing me. My noble friend said they intend to leave me locked in here to starve.

That is our belief, too.

Under no circumstances let Tam give them the key. She will be frantic, but must be made to obey.

I will send that message on.

A thought came to Alcandhor. *What of the tunnel?*

Batrig had it filled in.

The last spark of hope left Alcandhor.

My children! Alcandhor's heart ached, dying within him. Not only would he not be home for winter solstice, he would not be coming home at all. *My children...*

Mattan sent no conscious thoughts, but his presence remained with Alcandhor so that it seemed the Enaisi was actually there, grieving with him.

~*~

Tam clutched the key in one hand, her eyes searching Marcalan's, begging him to agree. "I have to try."

"You cannot give them that key."

"But if I do nothing, Uncle will die!" Tam's voice broke, and she clenched her jaw to stop tears. This was not how a Ranger should be reacting.

"You yourself said you knew they had no intention of releasing him even if they got the key. And Mattan told you what the man who sneaked into the cell told the Thane. They intend on just leaving him there. You cannot use the key to bargain with!"

"I can use it as excuse to gain access." Tam's voice broke and she took a breath to calm down. She had to sound like a reasonable Ranger, not a hysterical lass. "If I get in and tell them they will not get the key unless I see him—"

"You know that will not work. Their instructions were explicit. The key will be left. No one will be allowed in Estan Hall."

"But Marcalan—"

He put his hands to her face, his eyes filled with tears. "Think you I grieve not? Know you how dear he is to me? My heart is torn to shreds knowing what is happening to him. But I will not allow you to go to Estan Hall. If they were to let you in, you would only become another hostage or worse."

"But how can I do nothing?"

"'Tis our Thane's orders. And as much as it breaks my heart, I know he is right."

Tam's resolve broke. She collapsed into her husband's arms, weeping uncontrollably.

~*~

Lamadhel gripped Haladhon's shoulders and shoved as hard as he could. "I said, sit down!"

Surprisingly, his tall nephew obeyed. He pointed a finger. "You do no one any good ranting and cursing. Think you we feel any less because we are not carrying on as you are?"

Haladhon's eyes pleaded. "I want to go to Estan, Uncle."

Lamadhel met his gaze evenly. "Tam has said nay. She is as Thane now. And from the last word Mattan gave us, Alcandhor agrees. You, of all of us, he wants not there. You will try to storm the hall single-handedly and get yourself killed."

"Why is Tam suddenly as Thane when she has but fifteen years? It should come to me in interim."

Lamadhel blinked in disbelief. "You want Thaneship?"

Haladhon scowled. "Nay. But why is it given her?"

"Alcandhor likely gave it to her knowing what you would do as Thane right now. We can have conclave vote on whether you become interim Thane when—" Lamadhel stopped and Haladhon's expression crumbled before he dropped his head.

He watched his nephew breathe hard, fighting to keep control. Finally he looked up, tears brimming in his eyes. "Who is counseling her? Marcalan?"

"All of us, through Mattan."

Haladhon dropped his gaze. "I have given no thought to her. How is she doing through all this?"

"She is taking it hard. She keeps begging to go to Estan Hall, to try to get inside using the key as bait for entrance. Marcalan is finding it difficult to keep her at Ranger hold. Mattan joined her mind to Alcandhor's for a little while, but it did little to ease her."

"And Alcandhor?"

"Mattan gave you his latest message, did he not?"

Haladhon laughed, tears on his face. "He told me not to grieve. To remember the fun of our youth. Curse him! Curse them!" He jumped up and Lamadhel clasped his shoulder, but he twisted away. "Leave off! I cannot sit while he is dying!"

"Haladhon! Where are you going?"

"I know not!"

Lamadhel closed his eyes as the door slammed. He sank into a chair and kneaded his hands together. At least Haladhon had not said a word of blame. If he had not stopped Haladhon from calling Question on Alcandhor going to Estan, perhaps his nephew would not be bound and left to starve to death.

~*~

Elendhar knew there was not much he could do but pace his chamber. He reviewed all the circumstances and wondered if his father would be alive if it were not for that wench, Aleta. She had been the one who pushed Stendhar to accept lordship of the province. She had been the one who seduced him and blindly led him into this political fray.

The betrayal and hurt on his mother's face when she received notice she was put out as Stendhar's wife ripped at his heart. He would not have her brought here, not with Malkim in control, but she would be restored to their family manor.

And Aleta. He would take care of her, too.

He rang the bell and told the servant he wished to speak to Malkim.

When the man finally made an appearance, Elendhar said, "I have two orders as lord of this province."

Malkim barked out a scornful laugh. "Do you?"

He squared his shoulders and lifted his chin. "Aye."

"And what are they?"

"I want that wench Aleta out of this hall. Now."

Malkim grinned. "That is one order I had expected you to give. Any further instructions concerning her?"

"Nay, I merely want her out of this hall and out of this province."

Malkim chuckled. "And the other order?"

"I want my mother reinstated as the proper widow of Stendhar, and she is to be restored to our family manor."

Malkim gave a mocking bow. "I am happy to oblige you, my lord."

Elendhar might be powerless to do anything else, but at least he had done something for his mother.

~*~

Mattan entered the solar and bowed to the Laird. Lamadhel sat in a chair, elbows on his knees, head in his hands.

"You wished to see me, Lamadhel?"

The chief raised up, his face drawn. "Haladhon is missing. I think he is on his way to Estan."

"Great Bells!"

"You need to inform Tam. They must watch for him and keep him from going to Estan Hall. All he will do is cause his own death." Lamadhel gave a ragged exhale, shaking his head. "I have never understood Haladhon. But he is very impassioned, and his love and loyalty run deep. He is half-crazed."

"I will tell Tam."

Chapter Twenty-nine

Mattan stared ahead at nothing. Should he disobey his Thane? What would Alcandhor do to him? What if he ordered him to leave Elyria? He could imagine no worse punishment. He had already seen Alcandhor's commitment to the letter of the law where it concerned things of advanced technology. The Thane would not be forgiving. But if he did not act, his son would not last long. Bound, he could not reach the water in the cell. He was dangerously dehydrated, and being a physician Mattan knew all too well the suffering Alcandhor was going through, even without sensing him, and that he would soon die.

Tam's hysteria over her uncle when she contacted Mattan telepathically burned in his heart, increasing his own heartache.

Sarinna, although she hid it well, was almost as frantic, and now Haladhon had left. Mattan harbored no doubt that the tall Ranger would do something drastic if the Thane were not rescued before he arrived in Vindel. Alcandhor need not suffer, and his family should not have to suffer either.

Mattan stood, decision made. He wanted to say good-bye to the Rangers, but if they suspected, they might stop him, even though it would cost Alcandhor his life.

Soon after he had arrived on the planet, he had checked the maglev system out of sheer habit, and had found it still had power and the structure of the rails and tunnels were sound. He would need them now.

It was late, well into night's thirteen. The perfect time. Centuries ago he had helped the architects design Laird Hall, and had forgotten none of its secrets. Once on the ground level, he strode to the maintenance entrance. Sensing and finding no one near, he pressed the touch-pad and slipped inside as the door silently slid open.

The lift swiftly took him to the subterranean levels. Only a very fine dust covered the panels in the maglev car he entered. His fingers flitted over the controls, double-checking not only the instrumentation but that the rail and tunnel were clear and the structure sound. In moments he was on his way to Zaidhron. The front light lit up the tunnel before him as the car rushed ahead.

About a half hour later he arrived and hurried up to the portal level. Hesitating a moment, knowing he could not go back once he crossed, he activated the portal and stepped through to Anatai.

Several of his colleagues looked up in surprise as he entered the lab.

Treyor came over, his eyes bright. He spoke in Teldheri, gazing at Mattan in awe. "Look at you, dressed in Ranger garb—although it's changed somewhat in style. How is it there? When may we visit? Is my accent very bad?"

"You might be welcome, but after I do this, I may not." His lips twitched in a slight smile. "Your accent is faint to me, but their language has shifted. You will adjust easily."

Treyor followed Mattan into the infirmary, frowning. "What's wrong?"

"I am breaking every rule of the Teldheri to save the life of the Thane."

"Why? What's happening?"

Mattan told his friend as he collected medical supplies and stuffed them into a bag. He did not need much—just enough to stabilize Alcandhor so he could bring him back to the Portal Complex to care for him. He dare not attempt it in the cells, as guards might come in and see him, and that must be avoided. He was interfering too much as it was.

"But you are trying to save his life. Why would he not be grateful?"

"The law is more important to this man than his own life. I hope I am not too late."

"May I come with you?"

Mattan hesitated then shook his head. "Best let me do this alone. But in case I have trouble, I will call to you through the portal. You can bring more medical supplies, if necessary."

"What are you going to do with him once he is recovered, and awake?"

"I know not. He will not wish me to return him to Laird Hall or Estan by way of the maglevs, yet to appear suddenly at Zaidhron would cause many questions as well."

"You obviously haven't thought this out. Wait and let's talk—"

"I have no time! He is dying." Mattan slung the bag over his shoulder.

"But—"

"Nay! I must leave now." He met his friend's worried brown eyes. "Wish me best, both for his life and for me." He paused then whispered, "If only we could pray."

Treyor's brow furrowed. "I don't know if the Maker listens to us, but I will pray anyway."

~*~

Mattan set the maglev to Estan Hall. After arriving, he took the lift to the ground level, sensing for anyone near before opening the hidden access door. Once in the hallway, he crept forward toward the stairs that led down to the cells, wishing there was a secret way instead of having sneak about. Before turning the last corner, he sensed ahead. Two guards stood at the entrance.

He considered options, then decided if he was going to break rules, he might as well break them all. Ismari would have approved; she had always broken the rules. But it bothered Mattan to do so. Lyric and Logic, but he had no Lyric to balance him anymore. No time to think of that. He took a deep breath, concentrated, and sent—and both guards slumped into unconsciousness. He was glad Alcandhor could not see this; he would begin his questions again about the extent of Mattan's abilities.

He grabbed the keys, ran through the door, and down the stairs. He sent to the guard in front of Alcandhor's cell and took his key, too.

Once inside, he cut the bonds from his son, grateful that his medical training inured him to odors such as those that permeated this dank cell. He gritted his teeth in anger at leaving a man tied and helpless, unable to care for himself. Such behavior was a rough echo of the old Inta'ai faction. Mattan fought down nausea at the memories the comparison evoked.

The severity of the Thane's condition clenched his stomach—hang it, Alcandhor had deteriorated faster than he expected! He applied a pressure spray of electrolytes and carried him over to the basin. He dribbled water in the unconscious man's mouth but not much made it past his swollen tongue and lips. Trying again, he used his mind to force Alcandhor to swallow. The sensation of thick dryness filling his own mouth choked Mattan, but he persevered until coolness trickled down Alcandhor's throat.

He lifted his son in his arms and hurried out of the cell and up the stairs, his one thought to get to the maglev. He reached the back hallway on ground level but before they got to the hidden door, he found a dozen men facing him. By the foul Krahassha, he had been so concentrated on Alcandhor he had not sensed ahead!

"What have we here?" asked a broad-faced man with an evil grin.

Mattan could not disappear with Alcandhor now—he must interfere in events even more. He glared at the one who spoke. "I am an Enaisi. I came to rescue my Thane."

"I am Malkim," the man sneered, "and I would like to see you try."

Mattan sent pain, driving all of them to their knees. At their cries and groans, more guards appeared, and stared at the sight, mouths open. Mattan could not handle them all; he sent to Malkim, then the others, one by one, until they all sprawled unconscious on the floor. The newly arrived guards still stood frozen, gaping at the men at their feet.

"If you wish not to join them, then help me. I am an Enaisi from Ch'shalna Clan, and am here to set this hall in order. I need a chamber, and broth for my Thane. You will send for your lord, and you will send for the Ranger chiefs at Vindel's Ranger Hold—they are named Tamissa and Marcalan. Malkim is to be put into a cell. Any who do not obey me, will end up like this." Mattan nodded to the men on the floor.

The guards exchanged glances. Faces hardened, three of them advanced on Mattan, and he drove them down with pain. If only the rest of these men would react with wisdom; his arms and back ached from carrying Alcandhor, and he taxed himself having to keep his mind focused on so many people at once.

Reading their thoughts, he found mostly confusion and fear. "Be quick or you will be on the floor, too," Mattan ordered.

A guard stepped forward. "This way, Enaisi. Shall I carry him for you?"

Mattan shook his head, and as he followed, he read the man's mind in case of duplicity. "Do not forget, Rostin, I wish to see the Ranger chiefs, and your lord."

Use of the man's name did what he intended; the guard turned and looked at him in amazement. "I–I will see to it, Enaisi."

The man was sincere. He was not pleased, but filled with awe and fear, and he was a follower. He would fall in line behind whoever was in power, and for now, that was Mattan.

Rising anger and purpose from the guards following them up the stairs gave Mattan warning. Over his shoulder he called each guard's name, and said, "You will end up in a cell near Malkim if you try to attack me."

Rostin stopped, scowling. "Fools! Take the others to cells as the Enaisi ordered. Alert the hall that the gates are to be opened and send for the Ranger chiefs. Go!" He continued up the stairs. "Malkim's suite is near, Enaisi. I'll take you there."

"I thank you, Rostin."

In moments, Mattan laid Alcandhor on a bed, and the guard left to order broth brought and to fetch their lord.

Mattan applied the pressure spray again, then sensed his son. This was not enough. He rushed to the washing room and returned with a cup of water. Lifting Alcandhor up, he tried to trickle the water in his son's mouth. That was not sufficient—he needed intravenous fluids. There was no choice. He called out mentally to Treyor, telling him what to bring.

Mattan could do little to stabilize Alcandhor using empathy—he must be rehydrated. And fast. He doubted Treyor could get there in time.

A man arrived, clutching a robe around him, his dark hair tangled and eyes heavy with sleep. He was young, perhaps only just of Age. He stared at Mattan in disbelief. "It is true? You are an Elder?"

"Aye. You are the provincial lord?"

"Aye. I am Elendhar, son of Stendhar." The man tore his gaze from Mattan to look at Alcandhor. He walked toward the bed, his face lighting up. "Is he all right?"

"I know not. You are the one who came to the cell to try to help the Thane?"

Elendhar nodded, fear flitting across his features. "Is it true Malkim is in a cell?"

"Aye. He can no longer threaten you."

The lord exhaled, closing his eyes for a moment. "How did you get in? How did one man take power away from Malkim?"

Mattan shook his head with a wry smile. "It was not my intention to interfere in this matter. I merely tried to sneak in and rescue my Thane before he died."

"Batrig was right then? There are secret ways in and out about which only the Elders knew?"

"You have more important things than that to worry about right now. You had best decide whether you are a Royalist or rightful lord of this province."

The young man threw up his hands, his frustration and sincerity apparent even without sensing him. "I was not political at all until weeks ago. I know not what to think—not about politics or where I stand on them."

"Then let me advise you. The lords of the other provinces are gathered at Laird Hall and have already signed an agreement imposing sanctions against Estan Province, closing borders, blockading the harbors, and allowing no trade, if you do not agree to abide by the law. If the runner has not yet arrived with the dispatch, he will soon."

Elendhar blinked, swallowing. "I...think it would be wise if Estan complied with the law."

Mattan nodded, then looked down at his Thane, worried at what he felt from him, tipping the glass to Alcandhor's mouth. This time some seemed to go in, and automatic reflex caused him to swallow without Mattan's help.

The young Esteni lord cleared his throat. "I fear I shall get little sleep this night. I had best get dressed—I understand guests are arriving shortly."

"Aye. Ranger Chiefs Tamissa and Marcalan."

Elendhar bowed and left.

Mattan leaned close to Alcandhor and whispered, "Live, my son."

Moments later, he heard Treyor: *I am coming.*

Hurry. He kept trickling water in Alcandhor's mouth, wishing he had brought more medical supplies with him. Perhaps he should have just left with him anyway, even with witnesses. Would that be any worse than what he had done?

A servant carried in a small kettle and hung it on the fireplace crane. Mattan sensed her for insincerity, but found nothing.

"Sir? The fire is burned low in here. Shall I tend it for you?"

"Aye, please. Then have a taste-tester sent in."

The lass stared at Mattan. "That is not necessary, sir."

"My Thane is in a hall that has declared war on our clan. Shall I not take precautions?"

She hesitated. "I will have one fetched at once." She curtsied and fled out the door.

I am below Estan Hall.

How did you get here so fast?

I didn't wait. I thought you might need help, and it would need to be immediate.

Mattan sighed in relief, and brushed the hair from Alcandhor's face. "Another few moments, my son."

Treyor soon rushed into the chamber, holding out a kit. Mattan grabbed it and set the pouch against Alcandhor's arm, tapping it quickly into the vein.

"Did you bring more?"

"In my bag. This is the Thane?"

"Aye. I hope I did not wait too long. He cannot die, Treyor." Mattan's voice broke.

"You care so much? But you have not been here enough time to form attachments."

"If you met him, you would understand."

Treyor put a hand on his shoulder. Mattan relaxed a little as warm waves of sympathy washed over him.

"As soon as he is stabilized, we can get these filthy clothes off him and bathe him."

"He has acute kidney injury," Treyor murmured.

"We shall see how he does with the fluids and electrolytes, and then perhaps we may have to do a little healing."

"You're weak. Have you been doing more healing since that time through the Portal soon after you made contact?"

Mattan waved a hand in dismissal.

Treyor muttered a foul word. "You nearly died! If we had not—look, if this man needs healing, I'll do it, do you understand me?"

Mattan sighed. "Aye."

Treyor stared down, fists on his hips. "What manner of men would do this?"

Mattan's voice held bitterness as he replied, "Our manner of men."

Treyor squeezed his shoulder but said nothing as just then the servant came in with the taste tester. Elendhar came with them. They stopped as they saw the newcomer.

Mattan glanced at his friend, who regarded the three Teldheri with amusement.

"You are an Elder, also?" Elendhar whispered, staring at Treyor.

"Lord Elendhar, this is another Enaisi, Treyor. He has come to assist me in trying to save the Thane."

"Welcome, Treyor, sir. Anything Estan Hall can do to help, please let me know."

Treyor smiled. "Thank you."

Feeling Tam's approach, Mattan warned Treyor: *Prepare yourself.* His friend frowned in puzzlement.

A gasp made them turn. Tam and Marcalan stood in the doorway, his niece's mouth open in joy and astonishment.

She looks like Ismari!

Mattan paid no heed to Treyor. Tam flew to the far side of the bed and crawled over next to Alcandhor. "Uncle!" She knelt next to him, caressing his face, then looked at Mattan in fear. "Is he dying?"

"I think not. I hope not. I am doing all I can."

Tam kissed Alcandhor's forehead, murmuring she loved him.

Marcalan walked slowly over, eyeing Mattan and Treyor, then at the pouch on Alcandhor's arm. "What have you done?"

Mattan sighed. "What I had to. I know the penalty."

Marcalan closed his eyes, shaking his head. "The Thane will not forgive you."

"I know, but I could not let him die."

"Does Haladhon know?"

"I told no one."

Tam looked up, tears in her eyes. "Thank you, Mattan. I know Uncle will not be happy—"

"That is an understatement," Marcalan muttered.

"—but I thank you. I know not what I would have done if he had died."

Marcalan walked around to the side of the bed, and sat by his wife, rubbing her back. "She was inconsolable with grief, knowing we could do nothing."

Is she Ismari's daughter?

Mattan managed a smile. "Treyor, meet Tamissa and Marcalan, two chiefs of Ranger clan. And aye, Tam is Ismari's daughter."

Tam wiped her eyes, and smiled briefly at Treyor, then bent over her uncle again.

Alcandhor slowly stabilized, to Mattan's relief, but he knew the Teldheri would need something substantial to reassure them so he felt Alcandhor's pulse and smiled. "Stronger."

Treyor nodded. *Stars, she looks like Ismari! How hard is this for you?*

Seeing her eases the grief a little, knowing some small part of my Lyric lives on.

Treyor squeezed Mattan's shoulder again, and sympathy wafted over him.

Tam looked up at them. "He will be all right?"

"We should know once he wakes."

The taste tester still stared at the two Enaisi. The maidservant stood with him, looking around with uncertainty, wringing her hands. These poor servants had gone through many upheavals and must wonder day by day what master they should obey.

Mattan nodded at them. "Lord Elendhar is your master now. Do his will."

The young lord hesitated, his expression as uncertain as both servants. "Do whatever the Enaisi says. The Thane must regain his health."

"See to the broth, and the fire," Mattan said.

Marcalan straightened, his eyes grave. "We must talk."

Mattan sighed, glancing at Treyor. *Watch over the Thane. And those servants as the broth is tested. Did you bring the carbohydrate-electrolyte compound?*

Yes.

Add some to the broth after it is tested.

Treyor nodded.

Once on the far side of the chamber, Marcalan crossed his arms, frowning and biting his lip. "I understand why, and you will find no one who is more relieved that you acted than me, but do you truly comprehend what the Thane will do?"

Mattan grasped Marcalan's shoulders. "Aye. I do. And the fact that I did not slip out with him secretly as I wished, but instead was forced to interfere with events is going to double his ire."

"You can be brought before conclave for this. You can be disowned,

Enaisi or not."

"I know." Mattan dropped his gaze. "And I think I know Alcandhor well enough to know he will do exactly that. And likely order me off the planet."

"It will be difficult for Tam."

They both turned to see her still kneeling on the bed, leaning over her uncle. Mattan sighed. "I know. But it would have been more difficult if she had to watch his dead body brought up from the cells."

"I think she could not bear that, not on top of the other grief and changes in her life in the past few lunations."

"It was close. I was almost too late." He crossed his arms. "I should have done it when he was first imprisoned."

"He would have fought you. Stars, you had to wait until he was unconscious."

Mattan smiled despite his dread. Marcalan was right about that.

Chapter Thirty

The drum message rolled in, announcing that its rightful lord now controlled Estan Hall, and that the Thane had been released. Shouts, whoops, and cheers echoed through the training hall thunderously, as Rangers jumped, shouted, pounded, and clouted each other.

~*~

Alcandhor became aware that something warm and tasty trickled into his mouth. He swallowed and more followed. Ah, it felt good. What had happened—why he was so weak?

The cell! His eyes flew open, and he struggled to sit up. Tam pushed him back. "Lie still, Uncle, and sip this."

He sank into the pillows propping him up, gazing at his niece while drinking the delicious liquid. She knelt on the bed next to him, her golden eyes shining with adoration. He tried to speak but his throat hurt. He cleared it, swallowed again, then in a hoarse whisper managed, "How did I get here?"

Tam's smile broadened. "You need to rest and gain your strength. We can answer your questions later."

"I will have them answered now."

"Stars, Thane, barely awake and you are giving orders?"

Alcandhor turned his head to see Marcalan sitting back in a chair, legs stretched out and crossed at the ankles.

"How did I get here from a cell? How did you both gain entrance to the hall?"

"The healer does not want you worried with...worries, Thane. You are supposed to rest. All is well. Estan is under the rule of her rightful lord, Elendhar is his name. Tam is as Thane, and her first order was to have all draperies in Zaidhron replaced with new ones that were embroidered with bright, garishly colored flowers, and our jerkins are to be replaced with brocaded tunics of lavender with paned sleeves. So you see, you have nothing to worry about." Although his expression was one of perfect ingenuousness, his blue eyes sparkled with mischief.

Alcandhor gave a loud sigh, belying the fact he was overjoyed to hear Marcalan sounding like Marcalan.

Tam rolled her eyes and held out the cup. He took another sip.

"Now tell me what happened?"

285

The door opened. Mattan hesitated before entering, doubt and trepidation emanating from him. Breaking into a broad smile, he strode toward the bed. "You are awake. Good."

Alcandhor frowned at the Enaisi's fleeting fearfulness. What was he hiding?

Mattan squeezed his hand, then stepped back. "We have been very concerned about you."

"Have you indeed?" The alien averted his gaze, and Alcandhor pushed: "What is it?"

"Uncle, the healer says you should rest and not be bothered with worries—"

"Hang the healer! I want answers!"

Mattan almost fidgeted, although he was trying very hard to appear composed. *It works both ways, my dear Enaisi. I can sense you as well as you can sense me. What has you so unnerved?*

The last time he had talked mentally to Mattan, the alien had relayed messages to his kin at Laird Hall for him. But Laird Hall was two days away. His eyes narrowed. "How long has it been?"

Mattan's shoulders stiffened slightly. "Since what, Thane?"

Alcandhor strove to sit fully upright, slapping away Tam's hands as he glared at the Enaisi. "It is a two day journey. Have I been in this bed two days?"

The alien hesitated before replying, "Nay, Thane."

"Lie down, Uncle!"

"Leave off, Tam!"

Marcalan rose and walked over. "You need rest, Thane. This can wait."

"It cannot—"

"It can wait," his cousin repeated in a slow, deliberate voice. "He is not going anywhere, and neither are you."

"Do not presume to tell me my duties as Thane, Ranger Chief. This is a breach of the law."

Mattan held his hands out, palm up. "Thane, I expect you to address this, but not now. You need to rest."

"I will address this when I please, and that is now!" Alcandhor lifted the blankets to throw them off but realized he wore nothing and clutched the covers tightly to himself. "Where are my trous?"

Tam crossed her arms, her chin set. "In the wardrobe. And if you want them, you will have to get them yourself."

Alcandhor's face warmed with both anger and embarrassment. "Has everyone gone mad? I am well enough to rise and see to my duties—"

"Not until the healer says you are," Tam said.

"Then get the healer in here."

Mattan sighed, fists on hips. "I am here. You are to rest and continue to drink that broth and water. You may eat if you feel hungry. Since my presence is only causing you aggravation, I will leave. You are under Tam's care."

"Hold, Ranger Chief Mattan—"

The Enaisi strode out, and Alcandhor pounded the mattress as the door slammed. He glared at Tam. "I want my trous."

Marcalan chuckled. "Bells, how grand. You are both cut from the same piece of stubborn cloth. This should be enjoyable."

"Leave off, Marcalan. I am not in the mood. Did you know he was going to do this?"

"He told no one. But I, for one, am very glad he did something." Marcalan leaned forward, his blue eyes warm and sincere. "It is good to see you alive and roaring, my dear cousin, when we had no hope."

Alcandhor sighed. "I understand, believe me, I do. But the law is strict. I have to call Question. He has to face conclave."

"He knows, Uncle. But he loves you so much he cared not what happened to him."

"What can happen to him, Tam? He has only to disappear through the portal and go back to whatever life he has there. He does not face what you or I would. Even if disowned—what does that truly mean to him? He has his own world, his own family." He pointed toward the door. "He comes here, has no regard for our laws, and does what he pleases. I will not have it."

"You will have to not have it later, my dear Thane," Marcalan stood up, "because for now, all you are having is rest. And something to eat if you feel ready. All you have had is broth so far—Tam has poured it down your throat steadily since we arrived. There is a meat stew by the fire. Wish you a bowl?"

"Give me my trous, and I will get myself a bowl."

Tam pursed her lips, an eyebrow raised. "You will be up and doing too much if we let you have your trous. You need rest. Marcalan can fetch you stew."

Alcandhor crossed his arms. "And if I need to use the priv?"

"Do you?"

"Aye."

Tam went to the wardrobe and took out his trous. Alcandhor reached out for them, but she dimpled and flitted backwards, holding them out of reach. "I shall be back in a little while."

"Tam!"

She slammed out, and he stared at the door in astonishment.

Marcalan burst into laughter. "Oh, cousin, she is quick."

With a scowl, Alcandhor swung his legs over the side of the bed. "Remember, you married her. The day may come you will not appreciate that quality." He paused before standing to let a wave of weakness settle and disperse.

"She loves you dearly, cousin, and almost lost you. Think you she will not be protective of you now?"

Alcandhor snorted. Could he stand? Aye. His eyes flicked to Marcalan, but his cousin averted his gaze—to give him the semblance of modesty or to seem not to notice that he faltered before rising?

Back from the priv, he edged onto the bed and covered himself. Marcalan handed him a bowl of stew. Stars, he was hungry.

"Thane?"

Alcandhor paused, spoon in the air.

His cousin's voice was soft and serious. "Do not be heavy-handed to those who love you."

He finished chewing and swallowed. "You think to lessen my wrath against Mattan, is that it?"

Marcalan sighed. "It is not just him, although what it can hurt to thank him for saving your life is beyond my ken. What about Tam? Have you said word one to her except 'where are my trous?' What of the rest of us? Will you plunge ahead, growling about calling conclave and getting back to duties, not caring that we simply want a moment to enjoy that you are alive?"

Chastised, Alcandhor stared at the stew. "Deep thoughts from a prankster."

"Aye. I blame it on Tam—she is a bad influence on me. My reputation is ruined day by day."

Alcandhor's heart eased at the familiar lilting voice. "I will try to be less heavy-handed, you rascal."

~*~

Alcandhor woke to find he was alone. A glance out the window told him it was daylight, but with the snow swirling, he could not say for certain whether early or late in the day. How long had he slept? He threw back the coverlet and strode to the wardrobe, pleased that the weak feeling had left. His clothes had been washed and neatly hung. That brought to mind his state in the cell. Stars, who had cleaned him up? He snatched the trous from the bar at the angry thought that someone had to care for and wash him like a babe, then dismissed it from his mind; he had more important things to be concerned about.

As he strapped on his knife, a knock sounded at the door.

"Come."

Haladhon entered, face pale, and took a ragged breath.

"You came against orders? You and Mattan both defied me, enh? What did you plan on doing when you got here?"

His tall cousin shrugged. "I just had to come."

"So should I call conclave on you for disobeying me before or after calling conclave on Mattan for his breach of our laws?"

"Do what you will, Thane."

"Right now my will is to see Lord Elendhar. Then I wish to get back to Laird Hall. Once there, I will see about calling conclave." Haladhon's dolorous expression tugged at Alcandhor's heart as he remembered Marcalan's words, and he slapped a hand on his cousin's shoulder. "Come, you vagabond. Join me."

The lines on Haladhon's face smoothed out, and he gave a tight smile.

The guards outside Alcandhor's chamber glared at him but did not move. They were not there to keep him prisoner, obviously. "Would one of you men be able to tell me where I may find Lord Elendhar?"

One stepped forward. "I will take you to him."

No title—not Thane, not sir, not even Ranger. No empathic ability was needed to detect this man's animosity. Stars, what must they do to rebuild trust between those in this province and the Rangers? Alcandhor could start by showing politeness. "I thank you."

They followed the guard into a chamber where the provincial lord sat at a table strewn with books, documents, and papers in several piles.

"Lord Elendhar. This man wanted to see you."

Elendhar stood and walked to the front of the table. "Kirtin, really, you must use proper respect, regardless of your feelings, or I cannot keep you as hall guard."

With a sigh, the man muttered, "Yes, milord. The Thane wished to see you."

"Thank you." The lord looked at Alcandhor, his green eyes shining. "It is good to see you well. Please, sit down here with me."

Alcandhor gestured to his cousin. "This is my Third at Table, Haladhon, Lord Elendhar."

Haladhon bowed. "I understand we owe you a debt for trying to help our Thane, lord."

Returning the bow, the noble said, "The one you should thank for that attempt is Kirtin." He nodded toward the guard. "Despite his dislike for your clan, he told me that Malkim had lied to me. That you had not been the one to deliver the wound which killed my father, but had tried to defend him."

Alcandhor faced the glowering guard. "I thank you for your honesty. But why do you have such feelings for my clan?"

Kirtin glanced at his lord, who nodded. He sneered, "Your justice is a dung heap. My family has no home because of Ranger 'justice.'"

Another claiming corruption in his clan. Perhaps this time he could get answers. He crossed his arms and raised his chin. "Tell me."

"My neighbor wanted my land. I would not sell, but he had money to buy what he wanted. A forged document and false witnesses who would state I had sold the land to him and then refused to leave it. Rangers came and threw us out of our home. We lost everything! And I...I lost my family."

Alcandhor suppressed his indignation and anger for this man's plight. His claim of unjust treatment might not be true, but he was not acting; he honestly felt he had been cheated. "When did this happen?"

"Last year."

"Did you not file a petition to have the matter looked into?"

"The Rangers who threw us out said that my neighbor had the papers to prove he bought the land, and there was nothing that could be done. We left. My family is staying with her father. He thinks me a fool for losing my land and will not let me on his property."

Alcandhor spun to Elendhar. "Lord, give this man paper and pen, please. Kirtin, I want all the names, dates, the parcel of land, everything you can think of. I will have this searched out."

"Garton is rich!" Kirtin threw up his arms. "He has the forged papers. What can be done?"

"Much. You should have gone to the nearest Ranger hold, or if you trusted not the local Rangers, called petition to your lord, the Laird, or to me. It is your right. Now write down all you can remember. We will find the truth."

As he sat to write, Kirtin's hands shook. Alcandhor raised his eyebrows at Haladhon, who nodded. They needed no words; his Third at Table understood he was to take charge.

Alcandhor turned back to Elendhar. "Lord, we need to discuss how to resolve such situations. Perhaps tribunals can be set up in each district and ward, where people can bring petitions."

"Thane, I am new to this. I have not—"

Alcandhor quickly put a finger to his lips, then nodded at the guard, still writing out details.

"We will discuss this matter fully, Lord Elendhar. I know you are a man of compassion, and that eases my heart. I hope we can be allies in bringing about peace in your troubled province."

Elendhar hesitated then inclined his head, and they waited for Kirtin to finish writing. Finally the man stood, blowing on the paper to dry the ink, and handed it to the Thane.

Alcandhor took it by the edges and passed it to Haladhon. "My Third at Table is going to personally look into this matter, Kirtin. If you have been wronged, we will have it set right."

Kirtin's lips thinned, but he nodded.

"I wish to speak to the Thane alone, Kirtin," Elendhar said. "You may go back to your post."

Haladhon and Kirtin left together. Elendhar sat down, and gestured Alcandhor should, too.

"I apologize for stopping you from speaking a moment ago, Lord Elendhar, but I feared you were going to admit you had doubts about yourself. That is not wise to do before subordinates. They need to believe in you."

"I–I understand, but the truth is, I know not what I am doing. See you all these books? I have been trying to study, but I am drowning in a sea of words and laws I cannot comprehend." He threw his arms out with an expression of futility. "I cannot be lord of Estan."

"That is your decision. You can step down, and let another take your place. Who would be lord then?"

"I know not. My father was chosen because he was of a similar mind to our late cousin, Lord Batrig, and detested the Rangers. But I am not closest cousin. There are others who could contend me for title."

"And what say you of the Rangers, Lord Elendhar?"

He smiled. "I have been a spoiled child, Thane. I had no interest in politics. I know not what to say of Rangers, or tribunals, or how to help a young man get his land back."

"What are your interests, then, lord?"

Elendhar chuckled, turning pink. "Strategy games."

"My pardon?"

"Games like kingsmen, backhand, recall." He frowned, his voice soft and sad. "My father used to say I was a daughter not a son because I did not follow a man's interests. I never did learn to use a sword well. So you see, I have not much to recommend me as lord of Estan."

"You have compassion. You are interested in finding the truth of matters and of people, without prejudging. And if you are good at strategy games, I would say you have a quick mind and would be able to learn what you need to know. One of your first important decisions is to name counselors. But choose wisely, as their advice can either make your province strong, or destroy it."

"My friends are all as I am. They would have no advice for me. My kin are mostly of Batrig's mind. Whom do I choose?"

"You may ask for recommendations of the other provincial lords, the Laird, and even from me. Although I doubt if many in your province would appreciate my suggestions."

Elendhar shrugged, looking miserable. "I am in Hillsdown."

"Come to Laird Hall, Lord Elendhar. The lords are gathered there, and you can ask advice of them. You are not the only new lord, you know."

"That is how my father was ambushed."

"How did that happen? Did he not have an escort of guards?"

"Aye, but they were obviously inadequate to the task."

"Or secretly working for the Rebels. If you journey to Laird Hall with my Rangers, I can guarantee your safety, lord."

"I think I will do that, Thane. I may decide not to be provincial lord, but I think I should talk to the other lords before making that decision."

Alcandhor nodded, pleased, and gestured to the books stacked on the table. "Perhaps we can spend some time plowing through these tomes together."

A relieved smile spread on Elendhar's face.

Chapter Thirty-one

"This noble is a viper," Haladhon muttered as they passed the gate.

Mattan raised his eyebrows and glanced behind at the six Royalist guards accompanying them to Garton's hall. "You have met him?"

"Nay. But Marcalan has. I need not his opinion though. Look at that timman he has chained by the gates in the deep snow. The poor beast is half-starved and has old wounds. He has treated it brutally to make it savage. That says enough."

"A point." Timmeni unlike their distant lizard cousins, the ka'gua, attacked only when hungry, injured, or protecting their own in the wild. When captured young and raised by men, they responded to love and gentle training with fierce loyalty. Such cruelty was unnecessary.

The door opened, and Haladhon said to the wide-eyed servant, "We are here to see your master."

The man backed up with a bow. Mattan let his mind flitter through the hall as they stomped their feet and shook the snow off their cloaks. Garton hid in a nearby chamber, curious and fearful as to what would bring both Rangers and Royalists to his home.

Mattan suppressed a grin at the emotions of the cowardly noble; this was serious, and he needed to appear grave. "Lord Stendhar is dead. We are here on the word of his son, Elendhar, who now claims heirship as provincial lord." Not the whole truth, but enough of it to draw the greedy coward out.

Haladhon's eyes twinkled with approval as he pulled off his gloves.

"That little snot?" A voice boomed. Garton heaved into view from a side door. "I was closer kin to Batrig than he was. What does he want from me? A promise I will not go to clan conclave and oppose him?"

"Nay, sir," Haladhon said. "He has sent us upon receiving a petition from a man by the name of Kirtin who claims you stole his land."

Glancing at Mattan with open curiosity, he wheezed, "Kirtin sold it to me over a year ago. I have a note of sale, and the deed is registered in the archives."

"May we see the note of sale?" Haladhon asked.

Garton snorted. "Come this way."

They followed, listening to the noble mutter about upstarts who try to buy loyalty by heeding useless petitions. Haladhon winked at Mattan. The guards crowded into the chamber behind the Rangers as Garton riffed through piles of papers. The exertion of the walk had Garton's breath coming in quick pants.

"Here." Garton held up a document. "Note of sale with both our signatures."

Haladhon read it, his brow wrinkled. "Strange. I have the petition written and signed by Kirtin and the signature here bears no resemblance to that one."

Mattan pursed his lips to hide his smile at his tall son's innocent confusion over the disparity.

"Ridiculous," Garton spat.

The guards drew close, suspicion and anger growing. Haladhon handed their leader, Barsin, the note of sale and pulled the petition out from his jerkin.

"The Ranger is right," the Royalist said, holding both papers.

"You cheating by-blow!" exclaimed another guard, glaring at the noble, his hand on his sword.

"Wait now!" Garton backed up against the table.

"He needs to be taken to a cell," Haladhon said, putting his arm out. "Your lord has commanded you to see justice done. Hold him while we investigate this matter."

"Do you think we trust you to look for evidence, Ranger?" asked one guard.

"He showed us the difference in the writing, you blind kinchou," Barsin said. "And besides, he has an Enaisi with him." He inclined his head to Mattan.

"Enaisi?" Garton's eyes widened.

"Yes, Enaisi," Barsin sneered. "They have come back, and will make everything right!"

The other guards murmured agreement. By both moons, surely none of these men were Worshippers!

Panic rose in the fat noble, his thoughts scurrying to the Rangers who had taken bribes and protected him. Now, he feared the arrival of an Enaisi had changed that. Mattan dug deeper for those Rangers' names. Good. He would give them to Haladhon later. Not that this knowledge would constitute evidence, but it would be a start in order to dig for proof. He concentrated his thoughts on justice, not his dismay over corrupt Rangers.

"Take him to the cells," Barsin said. "I will go with the Ranger and the Enaisi."

Garton bellowed, and the five guards grunted under his weight as he resisted, but they prevailed and dragged him from the chamber.

"Where to now?" the Royalist asked.

"The archives," Haladhon said. "I want to see the signature on the new deed, and the old one."

As they journeyed back to the town, he nudged Haladhon's mind, hoping, since he had not mindspoken to the Ranger in the past, that the sensation would not be too unsettling. After several blinks, the tall chief turned, eyes wide.

Mattan nodded. *Aye.*

An ironic smile flitted across Haladhon's face.

I know the names of the Rangers who helped Garton. How shall we proceed? Just think your answer.

Haladhon huffed, his brow wrinkling. *If they hear of Garton being taken to a cell, they may panic and run. We need to hold them, but how? Your knowledge cannot be used as proof.*

I can tell Tam. She can see that stealthy watch is kept over them. But do you think they will run when we have no evidence against them? It would be admission of guilt, and put the clan in hunt for them as Rogue.

I know not. 'Tis said the guilty flee, fearing pursuit when none exists. Nandhal ran without proof.

Aye, that is often true. I will inform Tam.

~*~

Mattan took the deeds from the archive keeper while sending peace to Barsin. "Calm, man. I understand your rage, and share it, but we must proceed carefully with this investigation and anger leads to rashness."

The Royalist bared his teeth. "You tell me you didn't know this was going on, Feltor? You're a liar if you do! Deeds are to be signed in your presence!"

Mattan put a hand on the man's shoulder. "Rangers are on their way here to assure the records here are untouched until further investigations can take place. We will find the truth, and those guilty will be punished. You have my word."

Barsin blinked and swallowed. With a hesitant nod, he stepped back. "Since you've given your word I'll leave off, Enaisi. Where do we go next?"

Mattan gestured to his tall son.

"To talk to Kirtin's wife," Haladhon said. "But not until the Rangers arrive." His glare fixed on Feltor. "'Twould be convenient if documents disappeared. And the keeper as well, enh?"

Mattan needed no mental touch to know of the archive keeper's guilt. Feltor's ashen face gave him away. Alcandhor would roast him if he found out how much he broke the law by intruding upon minds, but this investigation must be thorough. He plucked not only Garton's name and that of the Rangers who helped him, but of others who had bribed Feltor. Being of weak will, he would break easily and reveal all.

The culpable Rangers were a worry. Their Training and discipline would make it hard to get the truth out of them. But dare he invade their minds or exert his will upon them? If anyone suspected, it would overturn their trial. Best leave the investigation to the Rangers.

~*~

"What now, Enaisi?" Barsin asked, pulling his hood close to his face against the biting wind as they left Kirtin's father-in-law's home.

Mattan shook his head. "That is for Ranger Chief Haladhon to decide."

"But you are a chief as well, and an Enaisi."

How ironic and amusing to witness such blind trust considering the past. At least the man did not seem to be a Worshipper, although at times his attitude came close. "Aye, but I am not in line of command. I merely go in case assistance is necessary."

Barsin turned to Haladhon. "So what will you do now that we have Kirtin's wife's testimony to back his?"

"A wife's testimony is not much thought of, as it is assumed she will corroborate her husband's, but the fact she and her father-in-law have been told of others who claim to have this done to them, gives us cause to examine Garton's doings more thoroughly." Haladhon grinned. "What say you to teams—Rangers and Royalists investigating together, as we did today?"

Barsin stopped to gape at the tall Ranger, then a smile twitched on his lips. "I think it would be a good idea."

Haladhon clapped a hand on the Royalist's shoulder. "I hoped you would think so." He leaned close. "Personally, we make a good team, you and I, enh? Even with an Enaisi tagging along."

Mattan snorted in feigned indignation. Haladhon winked at Barsin, whose open mouth slowly spread into a grin.

"Know you a good tavern?" the tall chief asked. "I think our fruitful efforts today deserve an ale as celebration after we report to the Thane and Lord Elendhar. Or considering the weather, hot spiced wine."

"Yes, I know the best in Vindel. I would be happy to take you there."

One strand of trust had been spun today. Good.

~*~

Alcandhor opened the door to his suite in Estan Hall. A strange voice, filled with frustration, spoke in Enai. "...still finding those damnable plasma pockets the Krahassha left almost every time we send a probe down. The electromagnetic fields play havoc with them. We have been able to accomplish so little, and I had such high hopes—"

Across from Mattan sat another Enaisi, slight grey in his hair, wearing garments such as Mattan wore when he first arrived. The alien stood and bowed. "Thane."

Caught between the joy of a second alien being there and rage knowing that he could not have gotten to Estan without using technology forbidden by their laws, Alcandhor clenched his fists.

Mattan rose. "This is Treyor, Thane. He only came at my urging."

"That does not excuse discarding our laws."

This new alien bowed again, his expression one of confusion. "How did I transgress, Thane?"

His accent was thick, as Mattan's had been the first few days. Alcandhor blinked at his seeming sincerity, and empathically he detected no deceptiveness. "You used the maglev to get to Estan, did you not?"

Treyor shrugged. "Yes, of course."

Alcandhor's mouth dropped open, and Mattan raised a hand. "You see? In our time, your laws were not as they are now. Prudent use was allowed."

"It is not thus now. He may not have known, and I would then have cause to perhaps absolve him, but you have not that excuse, Mattan. You and I have discussed how the law has changed."

"Nay, *you* told *me* it had changed, and that the Complex had been closed off. That is not a discussion. And it is not what your ancestors wished."

"I will not debate this with you. Not now."

"You mean never! Your missing books are all in our library. They are there for your use. And other things your ancestors meant—"

"Enough!" He stepped closer, locking eyes with his dark ancestor.

Behind him the door opened, and Haladhon groaned. "Stars. Leave off, 'Candhor!"

Alcandhor whirled, pointing a finger. "You stay out of this."

"I will not."

"So you will not back the law in conclave?"

"I think you should not bother with a conclave."

"Have you gone mad?"

Haladhon pulled a sealed missive from his jerkin. "Read this and you may ask that question again—of all the chiefs."

Lips thinned, Alcandhor broke the seal. It was a declaration, written in Maradhor's impeccable handwriting, signed by all the chiefs, stating they did not favor calling Question on Mattan and requesting a review of the laws forbidding use of ancient technology in light of the return of the Enaisi to their world.

"How...how did this come to be signed by all the chiefs when some are here, and the others at Laird Hall?" Alcandhor whirled to Mattan. "You used the maglev!"

"Actually, Thane, I did," Treyor said.

"At the bidding of your Second at Table," Haladhon added.

"What conspiracy is this?"

"'Twas Marcalan who set this in motion," his cousin said. "He knew how adamant you are about the law, and foresaw trouble. He discussed it with Tam, then they both went to Mattan about it. He discussed the situation with Lamadhel—"

"He what?"

"Via telepathy," his ancestor added quickly. "I forbore using the maglev again—"

"Yet you did not stop your friend from using it!"

"That was Tam's request. Not mine."

"How does she order Treyor? He is not a Ranger."

The new alien shouldered Mattan aside. "We took vows to your king, and later to your first Thane and Laird, but none of them involved being forbidden to use our own devices or technology. Indeed, up until the time we left, access was still possible, and used—mostly by us, but also by your people."

"Our laws have changed!"

"Only because we left, and because somehow knowledge was lost." Treyor leaned close to Mattan and said, "I suspect your sister and Ashani were behind that, but what their reasons were, I can't say—"

"Do not try to stray the conversation from the matter at hand."

"The matter at hand, Thane," Treyor said, "is that you—rightly, I'd say—restricted access and use of advanced technology and of anything you could not deem safe. But now, we are here, and can restore what has been lost, and, as we did before, suggest and guide."

"Our history indicates that when we colonized here we sought to eschew those ways and that knowledge. Live a simple life."

"And you have done that! Your ancestors would be so proud!" Treyor grinned. "I think even Avadhron would approve, and he rarely approved of anything."

The two Enaisi exchanged grins. Alcandhor fought back a smile, remembering the holographic image he saw years ago of his formidable, collateral ancestor.

"But," the alien continued, "that doesn't mean that they didn't allow innovation and invention."

"You are asking much."

"Which," Haladhon said, "is why the chiefs have asked for conclave to review this entire matter."

"And what about you, enh?" Alcandhor asked. "You disobeyed my direct order."

Inclining his head, his cousin murmured, "I shall take whatever punishment you decide, my Thane."

"We shall discuss that later."

Haladhon bowed.

"And as to you..." Alcandhor planted his fists on his hips, contemplating Mattan. "I shall wait until we have conclave."

"I thank you, Thane."

Chapter Thirty-two

"Then if our disfavor is—at least temporarily—set aside, please sit and chat with us, Thane. I would like to know you better."

Alcandhor acquiesced, seating himself near the fire. Treyor wordlessly handed him a steaming cup. Nodding thanks, he sipped it, then as warm sweetness rolled over his tongue, he gazed up in amazement. This was not tea.

The two aliens chuckled.

"My apologies, Thane," Treyor said. "I did not think to warn you. It is a drink favored among our people, and I brought some with me. Let me steep some tea for you."

Alcandhor shook his head. "Nay, this is good. I was just surprised. This is not a plant grown on my world, though, enh? I could drink this often."

"Your ancestors considered introducing it, but instead bartered our people for it."

"Aye. I knew there was limited barter off-world. But why not introduce it? If something as invasive as sweet creeper was allowed, why not this?"

"Sweet creeper was an accident." Treyor grinned. "Or so Ismari said. But this only grows in very tropical climates. It was best grown by us and bartered as you had no colonies or provinces in a climate suitable at the time."

"We might now. Tathelon and Beshalon are both very hot climates, and there are southern settlements beyond them, as well."

The two Enaisi exchanged glances and then slowly nodded. "It may be possible. We shall have to look into it."

Alcandhor smiled and sipped the strange, sweet brew again. Stars, it was good. "What is it called?"

"Tepyn."

"I have one on Tam, now," Alcandhor said with a chuckle. "Or has she tried this already?"

"Nay. But if she is like her mother, she will adore it, enh, Mattan?"

Mattan gave a nod, his smile fading. "Aye," he whispered.

Treyor dropped a hand on the other's shoulder again. "I apologize. I should not mention her."

Mattan shook his head. "Nay, I must face it. I just...it occurred to me that she never again had the chance to drink tepyn. I have wondered what her life was like here all these centuries." He took a deep breath. "I cannot let myself dwell on such things."

"No, it's not healthy." Treyor's dark eyes met Alcandhor's with a hard glint. "Has this fool been drinking like a sot, Thane?"

Alcandhor resisted the twitching of his lips. "Aye, he has."

Treyor gave a knowing nod as Mattan pointed a menacing finger at him. "Now, look—"

"Give me no indignation, just your promise you will stop—"

"Give me no lectures, Treyor. Despite the joy of coming home, I miss my old friends. More than I thought I would. And my Lyric is gone! I am coping the best I can." Mattan's voice broke, and he dropped his head into his hands.

Alcandhor watched his ancestor, his heart aching. From his limited understanding, an incredibly strong bond existed between the twins. He knew not what he would do without Sarinna. How much worse for Mattan then?

For so long he had thought the Enaisi possessed of such great wisdom because of their astounding knowledge. But this man was as flawed as any of them, and struggled with the same vices and weaknesses. And the same pain.

He sipped the hot drink, letting Mattan grieve in silence. Treyor refilled Alcandhor's cup and gave one to his friend. He pulled another chair over and sat, squeezing Mattan's shoulder. "Better?"

Mattan gave a nod. "Aye. Thank you."

Alcandhor turned to Treyor. "So, will you stay with us as well?"

Treyor's lips twisted in a wistful smile. "I wish I could. Since Mattan is playing truant concerning his pet project, I doubt he will let anyone else do so."

"You can certainly spend a day here, though, can you not?"

Mattan snorted, and Alcandhor was relieved to see the sparkle returning to his eyes. "Stars, Treyor, watch him," the alien murmured. "He will convince you to stay permanently if you are not careful."

Hoping his expression was not too eager, he asked, "Will you stay? Just for today?"

Treyor glanced at Mattan, then nodded. "Another day or two will not hurt."

Alcandhor leaned back in his chair with a satisfied sigh, blithely sipping the tepyn.

~*~

Elendhar hesitated, glancing around the arbitration chamber. "What

301

do I do?"

Alcandhor pointed to the table. "Be certain the scribe is ready, that is very important. The investigator, which in this case is Haladhon, gives summation of his report, which may include but is not limited to, witness testimony, reports, and physical evidence. Then the accused may speak on his behalf, ask for any witness or evidence to be brought forth in order to rebut, or call for his own evidence or witnesses. Throughout this, you take your own notes, jotting down questions, points made, contradictions—anything you might think is important or wish to refer to.

"The scribe's duty is to record the literal happenings, yours is to interpret evidence. And do not hesitate to stop testimony to continue writing, or ask questions. You are the arbiter and command all that happens in this chamber. Do not be bullied by an investigator, witness, or the accused. You have the right to adjourn to review any laws that you think might pertain to the case."

"I am in Hillsdown," Elendhar said, sinking into the chair behind the table, "even though we have reviewed proceedings to familiarize me with them. I have never even seen one trial."

Alcandhor smiled. "As we would do for a lordling being trained for his duties, so we shall do for you. I shall sit with you, and shall handle the proceedings, but you shall write your own notes, and make the final judgment."

"If Garton does not want a Ranger involved in the proceedings, what happens then?"

"Since he can ask for no higher arbitration from either your province or my clan, he would appeal to the Laird himself."

"By the Bells! Which would mean the Laird himself would read my judgment!"

Alcandhor threw back his head and laughed. "The Laird is younger than you, milord."

"But he has studied the law for years, has he not?"

"Worry about it if Garton appeals, milord. But I think you would find the Laird sympathetic. After all, he began actual arbitration only a lunation or so ago himself."

Elendhar closed his eyes with a sigh, then met Alcandhor's gaze with a nod. "I suppose I am ready."

~*~

Alcandhor stood behind Elendhar and found he enjoyed watching the lord arbitrate. At first he spoke little but wrote copious notes. Before long, he began to ask questions and review testimony. His mind, ever bent to strategy games, treated this as one.

Twice Alcandhor had to reprimand the noble for disrespect to his provincial lord. The third time, Elendhar rose.

"Garton, I am well aware I am newly confirmed as provincial lord, but you will honor this position, or I will have you removed."

"You cannot try me if I am not here!"

"You can review the transcript of the investigators' reports and write your rebuttal. Is that what you wish?"

"Th–that is not legal!"

"Ah, but it is," Alcandhor said, fighting a smile.

The noble's mouth fell open, and he stared at both men for a moment, then sagged in the chair.

Garton's witnesses and evidence did not hold up under scrutiny, and he slumped lower in his seat as the trial continued.

Ranadhor, present at his Thane's request, had listened to the proceedings his eyes narrowed and lips thinned. The two Rangers called by Garton to give testimony shuffled in nervously, glancing about but avoiding meeting anyone's eye. Both claimed they had merely been called in to witness the document, and later to evict the reticent Kirtin, who, they said, changed his mind.

"If events transpired as you state," Elendhar began, "then tell me how you could have witnessed signatures which have been proven to be forged?"

"We...we were not aware the man who signed was not Kirtin," the one mumbled.

"Not aware? You claim to have witnessed his signature in the presence of the archive keeper, and did not notice it was not the same man you forcibly evicted from his lands?"

"We...did not remember what he looked like," the second one stated, glancing up to meet the lord's eyes, then he looked at Alcandhor and his face flamed. He dropped his gaze.

"I find that hard to believe," Elendhar said. "You Rangers are Trained from early on to be diligent in noting details and remembering them, yet you did not remember Kirtin?"

They shook their heads, and the young lord leaned back with an exasperated expression. "By the Elders, you would still deny complicity in front of your Thane?"

The second Ranger's face grew more suffused, but neither said on.

Alcandhor touched Elendhar's shoulder, and the lord asked the question given him before the trial began: "Did any other Ranger know of your involvement in these schemes, or profit from them?"

The men wagged their heads in denial, still staring at the floor.

"You will answer aloud, and you will tell me the truth!" Elendhar ordered.

"Steady on, milord," Ranadhor said. "They have given their reply."

"Have they indeed?" Elendhar banged a fist on the table. "Look at me. Both of you! I wish the truth."

The one Ranger lifted his head and swallowed. His eyed flicked to his hold steward and then to Alcandhor. He muttered something.

"What did you say?" the lord asked.

"It was Ranadhor. He knew. Garton paid him as well."

"What? How dare you!" Vindel's steward straightened, uncrossing his arms, fists clenched.

Alcandhor nodded to the Rangers standing guard by the door.

"Thane, you cannot believe these men! They are lying to divert their own guilt!"

"Unfortunately, Ranadhor, I already knew the truth." Alcandhor nodded to his men. "Remove him, and both Rangers."

When they had been escorted out, he turned his attention back to the trial before him.

The mountain of evidence grew, making Garton's last attempt to squirm out of the accusations ludicrous even to him, and he dropped his head into his hands, defeated.

Elendhar adjourned to review precedents before giving sentence.

~*~

Twirling a quill, Elendhar shook his head. "What shall I do? I am in Hillsdown about sentencing."

"You have precedents before you, milord," Alcandhor said. "And he has more trials ahead. His schemes are coming to light, and those of several of his kin as well. This is not the end for him. And I have a feeling the more we dig, the more putrescence we shall uncover, not only in both our clans, but in others as well."

"Aye, but you stray, cousin." Haladhon crossed his arms. "Strictly speaking, Garton owes Kirtin a home, since he demolished the cottage on Kirtin's land. You might consider some recompense for the loss of two years' crops as well as the cost to have a new home built."

"Two years?" Elendhar frowned. "They were only off the land a year."

"And what of that year's crops, milord? Kirtin had to pay his wife's father for his family's keep. He lost the cost of the whole crop."

"Aye. He owes two years' crops. And a home." Alcandhor said.

Haladhon grinned. "Garton can pay the cost for Kirtin's family to rent a home until his is rebuilt as well. What think you, milord?"

Elendhar smiled. "I think 'tis an honest recompense." His expression grew somber. "What about your men, Thane? Your hold steward. To find such a trust was broken."

"Aye. We must scrutinize Ranger dealings in this province now, not only to assure no others have committed crimes, but to display to the Esteni that we expect and maintain the highest standards from our Rangers." He nodded at Haladhon. "I will set my Third at Table, who is also Chief of the Elites in charge of the investigation."

His tall cousin bowed, no glimmer of humor in his eyes at accepting such a task.

~*~

After sentencing, guards escorted Garton back to his cell. Kirtin sat with a shocked expression. Only Alcandhor, Haladhon, and Elendhar remained.

"What is the matter?" Haladhon asked.

"I cannot believe it. When my home is rebuilt, I can go get my family."

"Nay. Garton will be paying lease until your home is built." Haladhon grinned. "The guards tell me there is a nice place to let not far from here, near the edge of the town. Say the word and it is yours. Today."

With a stunned expression, Kirtin murmured, "I have a home? I can bring my family back?"

Alcandhor smiled sadly. "If you had gone to Ranger hold that day—"

"But Rangers were the ones who threw us out!"

"Then if you trusted them not, to your district arbiter. Who is he?"

"Faldon," Kirtin said.

"And he is Garton's nephew," Elendhar murmured.

Alcandhor pursed his lips. "Then you go up—to your provincial lord, or to me, or to the Laird. You have the right, man!"

Elendhar rubbed his forehead. "Thinking of Faldon...it makes me wonder if we need new district arbiters. And to let it be known that anyone with grievance should come to them. But whom do we appoint then? I have a feeling I could trust you Rangers, but my people would not."

"It would not be wise, lord." Alcandhor was privately pleased. Elendhar had said 'my people'—a sign he was starting to consider himself provincial lord. He was a good man, and with some instruction and study, would be an honest, compassionate leader. "You may find some advice from the other provincial lords. Perhaps Kirtin, after moving his family home, might consider working with several of your guards and a Ranger or two to collect petitions and begin looking into matters."

"Me? I was a farmer before I became a Royalist fighter. I don't know anything about the law."

Alcandhor shrugged. "You are honest. That is a basic requirement of an arbiter. Laws can be learned."

"Aye," Elendhar said, "you would have the zeal to see that justice is done. I trust you. Will you help me? Help our people?"

"But I am a commoner. An arbiter must be from a noble clan."

"Not true," Alcandhor said. "For high arbitration, aye. Because it would come to this hall. But for town or district arbitration, locals may be appointed, regardless of clan."

Kirtin shook his head. "I have to go bring my family back. And I don't even know how to care for them. I have nothing left. I can't just go off and leave them. They would have no food, nothing."

Haladhon sat on the table's edge. "Think, man. You are receiving recompense from Garton. The documents are already sent to his clan's accountant for implementation. And if you become arbiter, you will draw a salary from that. It would mean some travel, but your family would be cared for."

Looking away with an uncertain grimace, Kirtin replied, "I must think about it."

"Why not think about it as you bring your family back? I can go secure the lease, then you can bring your family there. Your wife's father's home is not far. Just south of Vindel. You could be there by nightfall."

The guard gawked at them.

"Why stand you there?" Elendhar waved his arms. "Go get your family!"

Kirtin grinned and ran for the door. He turned. "Thank you!"

Haladhon laughed as the guard ran out. "Stars, it is times as these that I love being a Ranger. Did you see his face?"

Chapter Thirty-three

Alcandhor bowed the young lord and Kirtin into his suite.

"You wished to talk to us, Thane," Elendhar asked.

"Aye, sit." He handed them each a mug and watched as they took a sip.

"By both moons, what is this?" the noble exclaimed.

Laughing, Alcandhor sat across from the pair of Esteni. "It is called tepyn, milord. The Enaisi brought it with them. Hopefully, soon we will grow it ourselves. Is it not delicious?"

Kirtin glanced over at the dark-skinned aliens sitting to one side as Elendhar replied, "It is good."

"What are your plans, Thane?" the noble asked.

"I would ask that of you. I need to depart for Laird Hall tomorrow. Would you be able to journey with me?"

Elendhar hesitated. "I fear traveling. If I leave, even just to go to Laird Hall, what might happen? I have cousins who already wish to overthrow me, despite a vote of confidence as provincial lord from the majority, and some Rebels who refuse to back me. I may return to civil war."

"That is a possibility. But you will be but two days away, and drum messages can relay any news or commands you would give to your people."

"Aye. And I know I need to confer with the other lords, and be present for the conclave, but so much is happening here. If only I had someone to set in place while I am gone."

"Why not Kirtin? He is trustworthy and backs you."

The guard shot to his feet, eyes wide. "You are mad!" He grimaced, glancing at Elendhar. "Your pardon, Thane. But I couldn't possibly—"

"Is not Lord Elendhar considering you as an advisor?"

Kirtin scowled. "Yes, but—"

"Have you set any others as advisors, milord?"

"Not yet. I wanted folk from various crafts and clans, so I could not have claim made I only listened to nobles."

"A sound thought." A notion flitted through Alcandhor's mind, and he smiled. "Lord Elendhar, what do your people think of the fact we now have Enaisi in our midst again?"

"Thane, what are you scheming?" Mattan asked, a wary tone to his voice.

He ignored the Elder, his eyes on the young noble, who in turn gazed over at Kirtin. "What do you hear about the Enaisi? How do the people view them?"

"Everyone is in awe. I am, too."

Alcandhor's grin broadened. "Milord, what think you of setting Kirtin as vice-regent while you are away, with an Enaisi as his advisor?"

Mattan stiffened, pointing a finger at Alcandhor. "Now, wait! You cannot just appoint people to tasks without consulting them!"

"Have I appointed anyone to anything?" At the realization his innocent protestation sounded much like Marcalan, Alcandhor blinked, appalled, and cleared his throat. "I am merely suggesting. Any appointing is Lord Elendhar's duty."

"But I'm not a noble! How can I be appointed as vice-regent?"

Elendhar laughed. "Know you not my family was not a major noble clan centuries ago? We rose in prominence through appointments and were eventually taken as associated clan of the provincial ruling clan, Jonasel. Why think you Estan is the only province not named for their clan? When most of Jonasel was killed in that foiled revolt, my ancestors were appointed as provincial leaders and the province renamed Estan, though I know not why."

"It was the original name of this area in the Enai language," Alcandhor said. "The renaming of the province was to remind our people to be mindful of Enaisi's laws and obedient to their rulers." He snorted, leaning back and crossing his arms. "'Twas a futile effort, I would say."

"Not at the time, or for many years afterward," Treyor said. "I recall the attitude here. Some were repentant of their rebellion, others wary of their new lord. It was ticklish. Remember, Mattan?"

"Aye, but not as you do. You were more involved in the politics in Estan than I was."

Alcandhor's chair banged back as he stood, his gaze locked on Treyor, his mind whirling in feverish delight. Stars, how could he have been so blind as to not realize that just as Mattan was the same Mattan of old, this was the same Treyor. The one who had been advisor all those centuries ago for Estan Province!

Mattan rose, one hand out as if to ward Alcandhor off the other Enaisi. "Now, wait. I know that look, Thane. Do not even think—"

"Leave off, Mattan! 'Tis Treyor's choice if he wishes to remain and help."

"We have the project on our world, Alcandhor! He has a duty there."

Treyor pulled on Mattan's shoulder. "A little time here will make no difference at this point in the project. And Dassel is in charge in the interim anyway. Stars, this is where I wish to be as much as you, man! If I can stay and be of service—"

"Is he your master, Treyor?"

Both Enaisi stopped and blinked at Alcandhor.

He looked from one to the other. "I know not your ways. Is Mattan your lord, or thane? Your master, by whatever name you call it?"

Treyor ran a hand over his short, black hair, glancing at Mattan with almost a guilty look. "In a way, yes. He is head of our science council, and this project is our main concern at the moment."

Alcandhor fell back into his chair, despondency settling like a heavy blanket on his heart. "Then 'tis not a matter of discussion after all. I apologize. We shall have to find another alternative..."

"No, no," Treyor grabbed Mattan's arm. "Please, Mattan. Let me stay!"

Mattan exhaled sharply. "Stars, if I gave the word, the lot of you would descend on this planet, would you not?"

"Yes, and why not? Our hearts are here, you know that. Please, Mattan!"

"I will not let the project come to a halt."

"We may have no choice anyway. The high council—"

"I have leverage to keep the project alive despite the high council's objections! Leave off that topic, it gives me indigestion."

"As it does us all. Dassel will not disappoint you, you know that. Please, let me stay!"

Mattan averted his gaze, licking his lips. He gave a reluctant nod, and Treyor grabbed his shoulders, giving him a wild shake as he laughed. He turned to Elendhar, eyes bright. "May I serve you and your people, Lord Elendhar? If not as advisor, then in any way? Any way at all?"

"Will the Esteni accept an Enaisi as a person of authority?" Mattan settling into his chair and crossing his arms.

"That is a question," Elendhar said, looking at Kirtin. "What say you?"

"I cannot speak for all, but I would accept an Enaisi."

"Why?" asked Mattan.

Kirtin stared at the Elder in puzzlement before giving a slow shrug. "Because you are Enaisi."

"That is not an answer." Mattan leaned forward, his gaze piercing. "Why would you trust an Enaisi?"

"Because you are Enaisi," the man repeated. "You are off-worlders, the ones who brought us to this planet. You saved our people. Why should we not trust you?"

Treyor snickered, and Mattan slumped lower with a groan.

Alcandhor grinned. He knew their history and why this was so humorous. Laws had been made over time restricting Ch'shalna clan because of their Enaisi blood. Fear was rampant at one point, despite lack of proof of any animosity or schemes by the aliens. It had been a source of bitterness to both the Enaisi and the Rangers.

Now, a commoner stated an opinion that had been always been professed by both his clan and the aliens—that they cared for all the Teldheri, not just Ch'shalna clan.

"I am part of Ranger clan, Kirtin," Mattan said. "Do you not notice that I wear the jerkin of a Chief?"

Kirtin grimaced, his face turning bright red. "Yes, sir. But you are not a Ranger. I mean, you are, but you aren't. If you understand me."

Trying to hide the smile twitching on his lips, Alcandhor said, "Perhaps you should pose the question, Lord Elendhar. Ask your guards and the people here in Vindel what they think of an Enaisi as an advisor here in Estan. That should give a good indication whether the idea is sound."

"Aye. 'Tis an thought." Elendhar grinned at Kirtin. "See to it, will you? Gather some men and have them go about the town and hall."

Mattan gave a sharp laugh. "If they do not think well of one of my people being advisor, you may find a mob outside this hall, milord."

"We shall see, Enaisi."

~*~

Alcandhor entered the new provincial lord's solar and bowed. "Have you made a decision, milord?"

Elendhar nodded, his bearing more authoritative. Alcandhor smiled; the young noble gained confidence by the hour, it seemed.

"Aye. Since my people seem to agree it is a wise course, Kirtin shall be vice-regent in my absence, with Treyor as his advisor. The Royalists seem to be appeased by the way Kirtin's petition was handled by the Rangers, and by the presence of the Enaisi. Some of the Rebels are skeptical but are willing to wait and see what changes will occur now." A disgusted expression crossed his face. "However, others are still fighting."

Kirtin chuckled, scratching his chin beard. "It's strange to see Royalists and Rangers working together in bands to flush out the Rebels." His smile faded. "And you will be here as well, Ranger Chief Haladhon, for this investigation into whether other Rangers have been guilty of crimes?"

"Aye. I must return to Laird Hall for a short time by my Thane's command, but I have sent for several Elites from Zaidhron. When they arrive, we shall undertake the task."

"Good. Not that there might be more Rangers who are guilty, but I trust you to be honest in your duty."

Haladhon inclined his head at the new vice-regent.

Alcandhor turned to the young lord. "So then, Lord Elendhar, are you ready to journey with us to Laird Hall?"

Elendhar sighed, shaking his head. "I have family arriving in a day or two, and I wish to bring them with me. But that delays you to wait for me. Why not go on ahead? I can join you when my sisters arrive."

"They are coming then? That is good "

"Aye. My mother will not come. She despises that our family got involved in all this, and still is grieving my father's death, even though...even though they were not together at the end."

"My condolences again on Lord Stendhar's death. And the circumstances of your parents' marriage ending."

"I thank you. I regret the day that particular cousin came back to Estan Province."

"Regret ever follows her, and misery as well." Bitterness rose like bile in Alcandhor's throat at the thought of Aleta. "I pity anyone impolitic enough to take up with her and her schemes."

Elendhar bit his lip, hesitating, then said, "At least she is gone from here. Whatever trouble she is causing, it is not in this province. I have sent word out she is considered outcast from my clan."

"I doubt she will return to mine," Alcandhor murmured. Did she care about her children at all to ever seek them out? He looked at Elendhar, taking a deep breath to clear his mind of acrimony and remorse. "Your escort to Laird Hall will be both your guards and Rangers, then?"

"Aye. I will not allow what happened to my father to happen to me."

"Rangers will not allow it, either." Alcandhor stood and bowed. "We will see you at Laird Hall in a few days." He could feel trepidation in Elendhar and he smiled, adding, "And milord, I would wager that if you can survive the lords' conclave, you will be able to handle being provincial lord."

Elendhar's surprised expression gave way to a grin as he returned Alcandhor's bow. The chiefs all bowed, then followed Alcandhor out.

~*~

The cold blasted through Alcandhor. Never was he so glad as when they reached Polli that evening. He wanted to stay in the same tavern, to compare and assess the reactions now.

The Rangers all stayed bundled up as they entered. The innkeeper came forward to greet them, bowing. Alcandhor pushed back his hood a little, unable to smile if he wished; ice encrusted his moustache and chin beard.

"Take a table near the fireplace, Rangers. I shall have hot food and drink brought to you right away!" He bowed and hurried off.

Marcalan vented a quiet chuckle as they moved to stand by the hearth. Before taking off their cloaks, the Rangers warmed themselves in front of the fire. Alcandhor fumbled getting his gloves off, his fingers numb and stiff. Stars, did ice even cake on his eyebrows? His eyes felt raw and he blinked, not rubbing but placing his hands over his face for a moment. No good, they were nigh frozen too.

The chatter and loud talk had died down upon their entering. Now, it slowly started again. Alcandhor strained to hear anything that was said, his eyes darting about in surreptitious assessment. The mood was not as ambivalent as last time, but curiosity ran high.

"You wanted to know," a man shouted. "Rangers are here. Ask them."

Alcandhor turned, blowing on his hands, and patting them over his mouth and chin to get the ice off his facial hair. One man sitting at the next table stared openly at them, another was red-faced, his eyes lowered. The other three gave nervous glances one to another.

"Did you wish to ask something?" Alcandhor said. "Please, do so. We will answer if we can."

The loudmouth's gaze raked over him with suspicion. "It's said Elders are back again."

"Aye. 'Tis true."

"And that one appeared by magic at Estan Hall and rescued the Thane."

Alcandhor's lips twitched. "'Twas no magic, but aye. One came to Estan Hall, followed by another."

"How? How did they get there then if it wasn't magic?"

Alcandhor shrugged. "They know secrets we do not."

The men all stared at him. The loudmouth again spoke. "Not even you Rangers?"

"Aye."

"Why? If the Elders are part of your clan, why would they keep secrets from you?"

"Not all of us are Ranger clan, only me—now," came Mattan's voice from behind him. "And there were things that your ancestors did not wish revealed. We are merely keeping the promise we made to them."

Loudmouth pushed his chair back and stood as they all stared, mouths gaping open. Alcandhor wiped his moustache and chin beard, now wet instead of frozen. Mattan shook out his cloak and hung it on a peg next to the fireplace, then turned to face the table of men, eyebrows raised with an expectant expression.

The leader strutted toward him. "You truly are an Enaisi?"

Mattan shrugged. "Aye."

"Why were your people gone for so long and why have you come back now?"

The innkeeper brought over a tray with a large pot and cups. He set them on the table slowly, listening to the conversation. Which was more unusual—being served their drinks or the innkeeper's honest interest?

"We were attacked and had to lock down the portal to protect your people. Our leaders just now gave permission to open the portal again."

"But it has been centuries! What attack would bring us danger for so many years?"

"It was the danger at first, but later caution on the part of our leaders. They did not wish to open the portal again at all. 'Tis a long story, and very political. I am certain you have had your fill of political disputes. I am just pleased that the portal is open again, and that my people are still welcome."

Alcandhor moved past Mattan to hang up his cloak, then sat, smiling over at Haladhon, who winked. Marcalan took Tam's cloak for her, whispering something in her ear. She gave him a quick kiss and seated herself.

"They say an Elder is at Estan Hall," one of the other men said, his eyes darting to each of their faces, "and will be an advisor for our new provincial lord."

Alcandhor listened to Mattan's reply as he poured a cup of tea for himself.

"Aye. His name is Treyor. He will be advisor to Lord Elendhar for the present, and also to vice-regent Kirtin while Lord Elendhar is in Viltara for the lords' conclave." Mattan bowed to them. "Please, do excuse me for a little while. We have been journeying in the cold, and I am in need of some hot tea to try to put warmth in me. Perhaps we can talk later?"

The men muttered, their expressions more confused than antagonistic as they turned back to their own conversations.

"You put yourself in for it now," Marcalan whispered. "They will expect more answers from you before the night is out."

"Aye. I don't mind."

"At least they did not ask for proof that you are truly an Elder. You must get so tired of that."

"It is more tiring when people treat me as some sort of god. That I cannot abide."

Haladhon chuckled. "Just let them see you get tipped back. That should solve the problem."

Mattan shot daggers at the tall Ranger. Alcandhor hid his smile in his cup of tea. As his cousins and niece snickered, the innkeeper brought over a platter of meat. The serving woman carried over another platter of various vegetables and bread.

"In this biting cold I knew you'd want some hot tea, but would you also like ale perhaps?"

Ah, what a change in attitude from their last visit! And now, the innkeeper himself waited on them. "Aye. Thank you."

"You would not think it is the same tavern," Tam murmured. "Can so much have changed in such a short time?"

"'Tis my charm," quipped Marcalan. "Either that, or someone spiked the ale."

"I would put my wager on the ale," Haladhon replied.

Marcalan spluttered in mock indignation. Too cold and hungry to banter with them, Alcandhor speared slices of meat and pulled them to his plate, then a large portion of the roasted vegetables. Pins jabbed his toes, and he wiggled them in his boots, resisting the urge to stamp his feet; at least some feeling had started to come back.

He sipped his tea, enjoying the heat cupped in his hands, while sensing the room. Aye, it was a very different atmosphere. Listening to the quiet raillery of his kin as he ate, Alcandhor felt at peace. What had he accomplished in Estan? Nothing. Not directly. But events had conspired, through the Maker no doubt, to bring at least some ease to the turmoil in this province. He sent up thanksgiving for such a blessing. Perhaps tonight he could truly sleep.

Chapter Thirty-four

Although not quite dusk as they passed the gatehouse, the torches had been lit, and their light added a warm glow to the scene before Alcandhor. He entered the bailey and bit back a moan, glaring at the chuckling Mattan. All the Rangers at Laird Hall and from Lairdton's Ranger Hold lined up at attention on his right, hold steward Capalan at the front. On the left, stood all the Laird's guards.

Alcandhor stopped, knowing it was expected, and at a signal, every one of them saluted him. He gave an answering bow and continued across the bailey. He would find out whose idea that was and wring his neck! Stars, what had he done that was worth such a tribute? Allowed himself to be captured? Aye, that was a worthy action. He grimaced in disgust.

As he neared the antechamber, Sarinna stood in his path, a heavy cloak wrapped tightly against the cold, tears in her eyes. As he reached out, she dove into his arms, murmuring her love for him, how worried she was, and how he should not be so reckless, did he not know how much they all loved him?

He just held her, his gaze going to his uncle, Eladhrel, Andhrel, and their wives who waited nearby. Finally she let go of him, and he kissed her gently on the cheek. "Why do you all not go to my suite, and we can have time alone instead of in front of the whole of Laird Hall?"

Lamadhel's blue eyes gleamed too brightly as they all turned about and preceded him inside.

As before, Galran, Master of the Guards, stood at the antechamber entrance. He bowed. "Glad to see you, Thane. We were worried."

Alcandhor managed a smile.

"After you have rested, the Laird bids you visit him in his solar."

"Thank you, Galran." Alcandhor needed no rest, but a hot cup of tea and a few moments by a hearth would be welcome as he enjoyed the reunion with his family. He stamped his feet and slapped his gloved hands together, glad that the snow and wind had eased from the dreadful weather of the day before.

Nobles bowed as they crossed the Great Hall to the main stairs. Strange that the Laird was in his solar instead of here.

The new steward, Weltin, ran Laird Hall efficiently, and Alcandhor appreciated that never more than now; he knew that he would find his bed freshly made and fires roaring in the hearths. The man proved himself to be an excellent replacement for the traitor Vitran.

He had barely opened the door to his suite when Sarinna pulled him inside and threw her arms around him again. Before she even let go, Cariss and Amilla hugged him, weeping. The outpouring of affection was wonderful but embarrassing. The men were not much less restrained, however, and he endured many thumps on the back and embraces from his cousins and uncle.

When they finally released him, Alcandhor hung his cloak near the fireplace and stood close to the warmth, pulling off his gloves. He placed them on the mantelpiece and turned with an appreciative inhale at the laden sideboard.

"Sit." Cariss pulled a chair near the hearth while Eladhrel and Andhrel dragged a table over so they could all eat next to the fire. Sarinna set a heaping plate in front of him, as the others sat.

"Stars, Thane," Marcalan quipped, "you should get captured more often, at least when I am journeying with you. I have never seen our kin give such solicitous service!"

Sarinna slapped the rascal on the shoulder, and he yelped in mock pain. "Quiet, scamp, or this hot tea will find its way down your shirt instead of into your cup!"

"You would threaten a Ranger Chief, woman?"

Sarinna tweaked his ear, causing him to yelp again. "More than just threaten, now behave!"

Marcalan muttered about being put upon while they all chuckled. Alcandhor had to admit it was good to be with kin again. It was good to be alive.

~*~

Randhal opened the door himself, and Alcandhor wondered what Holnin thought of such improprieties from the Laird as the servant left the chamber, allowing the two leaders to be alone.

Tears welled in the lad's eyes. "I wanted to privately greet you, Alcandhor. To tell you—" He choked and turned away. "I apologize. I have been trying to learn to keep my emotions in control as is proper for the Laird. But I knew if I greeted you in the Great Hall as you arrived I would bring embarrassment to us both."

"We are in private, Your Grace—Randhal."

Tears spilled down the Laird's cheeks. "When I thought you were—when I..." He stared at the floor, his voice soft. "Is it wrong to say at times I feel I love you more than I did my own father?"

Alcandhor paused before replying, wishing he could vent, wishing he could say, no, it was wrong for your father to shuffle you off to tutors and never take the time to be a father. Instead, he put a hand on the back of the Laird's neck and gave him a shake. "Never apologize for what you feel. It is only how you react to your emotions that might be inappropriate."

The Laird managed a short laugh. "Still being my teacher?"

Alcandhor grinned. "And your friend."

A knock at the door caused them to exchange resigned smiles. After rubbing a hand over his face, the Laird answered it.

"What is it, Holnin?"

"I apologize, but your cousin Bandhran is here and seeking an audience with Your Grace."

The Laird frowned. "Did he not just leave with his family some days ago?"

"Yes, Your Grace, but he has returned. He is, if I may say so, rather piqued."

Randhal exhaled slowly, then rubbed his forehead. "Give me a few moments more with the Thane, Holnin."

"As you wish, Your Grace." The servant bowed and pulled the door shut.

Alcandhor clasped the Laird's shoulder. "Duty ever calls. I shall see you later, my friend."

The lad muttered, "I wished to say so much..."

"No need. I can sense, you know. And believe me, it is reciprocated." He opened the door, pretending not to notice the Laird wiping a hand across his eyes.

Holnin inclined his head, murmuring, "Thane," before entering the chamber.

~*~

Randhal fell back into a chair with a sigh, taking time to gather his composure. Finally feeling ready, he took a deep breath, stood, and nodded to Holnin.

Bandhran stormed into the chamber, Atinna following, shoulders drooping and face pale.

His cousin bowed in a careless bob, a mere formality. "Your Grace, since you are the thane of our clan, I would have you intervene and annul our cousin Tirnin's marriage to some commoner."

"Your pardon?"

"You heard me," Bandhran sneered. "His father and I signed a marriage contract for him and Atinna several years ago. But the boy has married behind our backs."

Randhal drew himself up, his jaw set. "Is this how you address your clan thane and Laird?"

The man's mouth worked silently. Finally, he found his voice. "I beg forgiveness, Your Grace. I–I am overcome by the situation. All our plans for this marriage, and all for the good of the clan..."

"The good of the clan? Tirnin's father is Baylor, is he not? Whose lands are adjacent to yours?"

"Well, aye, Your Grace, but—"

Randhal snorted. The good of the clan, indeed! "If Tirnin is married, I will not interfere."

"But Your Grace, we wished to strengthen the blood line of our clan."

"At the moment, we are all simply concerned with continuing it. It must grow, not dwindle further. Atinna, do you wish to have me claim Right for your broken heart? It is proper that Tirnin compensate you at least for the breach of contract."

The lass stared at him in surprise, her voice soft. "I had not thought of that, Your Grace. I know not what to say."

"I signed the contract, Your Grace," her father said. "Payment should come to me."

"She is of Age. The contract reverts to her."

Bandhran stood with his mouth open. Was he that ignorant of Clan Law, or did he think his clan thane was? Randhal suppressed a curl of his lip. He should retain the appearance of being impassive.

His offensive cousin blinked, and slowly his features took on a sly expression. "Your Grace. Since my daughter is now free from her previous betrothal, you do realize that she is eligible—"

"Father!"

"Quiet, girl."

"But Father, I wish not to marry—" she paused, blushing, and curtsied. "Your pardon, my Laird." She turned to her father. "But I wish not to marry him."

"You will marry whomever I say, or you will be cast out of my house!"

Atinna's eyes filled with tears. "I shall not, Father."

He raised his fist, but Randhal stepped forward, interposing himself between them. "Bandhran, leave. Now."

The man stood, back rigid, staring at Randhal with an expression of disbelief. He spun to Atinna. "So be it. You no longer have a home." He bowed and stormed out.

An awkward silence hung in the air for a few moments before

Randhal held out a hand to his cousin with a small smile. "Come. Be not concerned. Sit and talk with me."

"A–about what, Your Grace?"

He led her to the divan, and they sat.

"This is my solar. The one place I am just me. In here we are merely cousins. You are Atinna, and I am Randhal. We have something in common besides blood, you know."

"What is that?"

"We both know what it is like to be forced into marriage." He sighed and leaned back. "Stars, if my father had been different, realize you that we might have been raised knowing each other? Been playmates as children? I have no kin my age that I have ever been friends with."

"I am sorry, Your Grace."

"Randhal. Please. In here, call me Randhal."

She bit her lip.

"What is it, cousin?"

She ducked her head. "I mean no offense, but I was serious when I said I did not wish to marry you."

"Is that what you think I am...oh, Bells, no! I merely wish to be kind to my cousin, and perhaps make friends. Stars, if you are not interested in marriage either, then I have found a secret ally to whom I may complain about my situation. One who will definitely understand. So," he paused, gazing at her earnestly, "will you call me Randhal?"

The girl murmured, "I will try to remember."

He smiled and leaned close, whispering, "So how did you feel about your betrothal?"

Atinna closed her eyes, as if grimacing in pain. "I dreaded it. I thought I should die having to marry him. He is three years younger and has always been hateful to me."

"Three years younger?"

"We are the oldest of our families. My father would not let me think of marriage. I was to wait for Tirnin."

"Bells! So now you are free. How does that feel?"

"It is wonderful, yet, where can I go?"

"Am I not your clan thane?" Randhal asked, grinning. "It is my responsibility to care for you since your father has turned you out. He cannot keep you from claiming the contract price Tirnin must pay, so you will not be in straits financially. And until you decide what you wish to do, you can stay here."

"Here?"

"Aye. I would ask if you have plans, but it is too sudden, I know."

"I was a birth attendant back home. And have studied to be an herbalist. Father would not let me study further to become a healer. But perhaps I could find a position in Lairdton as attendant or herbalist?"

"Bells, aye, that should be no problem. We shall have to look into that for you. But for the moment, we need to get you settled in here." He frowned. "We have had more nobles arrive, and I think the suites your family used are now taken. No matter. We shall find chambers suitable for the cousin of the Laird. Come."

What, by both moons, was happening now? Maradhor arrived at the Laird's solar door, as ordered, and was let in. The Laird came to him, smiling.

"Ah, my good Ranger. I hope you mind not that I asked to see you."

"Your Grace?"

"I appreciate that you were escort for my cousin Atinna when she was here before, but I did not wish to assume you would automatically want to resume that duty again. I would escort her myself, but Lord Krendhal wishes me not to have any lady on my arm save those I might choose to marry. He could escort her, I suppose, but it seems unfair to her to have such an old man as escort, cousin or not. So what say you? Do you mind? If you do, I can find another."

Maradhor's mind whirled. "A–Atinna is back, Your Grace?"

"Aye. And she is staying at Laird Hall for the time being."

"But she was to be married."

"It did not happen." The Laird rolled his eyes, shaking his head. "Would that I could be so fortunate." He blushed. "I should not bother you with my problems, Ranger, I apologize. I simply wished to ask if you would mind being escort again."

Maradhor hesitated. What was going on?

Eyebrows raised, the Laird waited, and Maradhor took a breath. "She seems very timid, and since she is already acquainted with me, it might be easier for her if I continued as escort. I mind it not, Your Grace."

The Laird grinned. "Thank you."

~*~

Maradhor knocked on the door, and Atinna opened it, smiling, color in her face now. The dread of that marriage must have truly weighed on her heavily.

"Why were you given this suite, lady?" Maradhor asked as he

walked her toward the main staircase.

"The one my family occupied has been taken by nobles that arrived from one of the provinces. The Laird thought it would be better if I had a suite near the Rangers, rather than in another part of the keep. He trusts you Rangers so much."

"For my part, I will do my best to guard that trust." He glanced over at her. "I understand your marriage will not take place."

Her smile widened. "Tirnin married behind our fathers' backs. I was never so happy. Father raged about frighteningly like a rabid ballan. He dragged me back here to make the Laird annul Tirnin's marriage and force him to marry me. But the Laird refused. Then Father began to suggest that the Laird consider marrying me."

"By the moons, that was bold!"

"Aye. But the Laird grew angry and told my father to leave. I am not welcome in my family home anymore, so the Laird, being clan thane, has said I can stay here."

"I would say that is a definite improvement. So is the Laird interested in marriage to you?"

Atinna blushed. "Nay."

They were silent until they reached the main staircase, then he carefully held her hand, instead of letting it rest on top of his while descending, in case she tripped on her gown, or had a misstep.

He had to admit, she stepped daintily and with poise. If a man were only interested in something soft and feminine, Atinna would make a fine wife. But he could not see such a timid thing being wife to a Ranger. Would she pine, not eating or sleeping, while her husband was gone, as she had done over the dread of her impending marriage? And what if her husband was killed? He thought of Sarinna, who was strong despite her grief when her husband died all those years ago.

Nay. Atinna, no matter how comely, would not make a good Ranger wife, and even if so, it was not allowed. He set his jaw, and closed his heart. He would not allow himself to notice her looks anymore.

Chapter Thirty-five

News about Estan Province—from reports of another Enaisi mysteriously appearing, to the new provincial lord soon journeying to Laird Hall, the excitement of the Thane's capture and rescue, and the strange fact of Royalists and Rangers actually working together—along with the worried talk of the fever in Nelatan dominated the discussions all evening. Maradhor wearied listening to it, and Atinna soon did too, asking that he take her back to her chamber.

They did not speak ascending the stairs. Voices and laughter floated up behind them. The Laird, the Thane, and some of the chiefs overtook them. Marcalan called his name. Stars. What would the prankster have to say about this escort duty? He had been able to avoid the rascal all evening.

The Laird hurried toward them. "Maradhor! Atinna! How fortuitous! We are retiring from the banquet for our own private party to celebrate the Thane being safe. Please, join us." The Laird took the lady's hand. "Come, cousin!"

Maradhor followed the procession down the hallway to the Laird's solar. Stars. He had hoped to get back to the barracks soon.

Once they entered the chamber, the Laird pulled off the white surcoat, the sign of Lairdship, with a quiet whoop and threw it across the room, grinning. The chiefs all settled onto various pieces of furniture, laughing. Ha, this was obviously not the first time they had all gathered here. Haladhon sprawled in an overstuffed chair, Tam sat in another, with Marcalan on the floor in front of her, leaning back against her legs. Mattan relaxed on a settee.

Platters of food filled the sideboard. The Thane and Laird turned over glasses at the wine table. Maradhor blinked in disbelief. The Laird had no servants in attendance?

"What shall you have Atinna? And Maradhor?" called the young lord.

The lady sat stiffly on the edge of a settee. "Wine," she whispered, and Maradhor strode across the chamber to get it for her.

"Bells, sit you down, man," the Laird said. "I will bring your drinks over. What is your preference?"

"Wine for the lady."

"And you, Maradhor?"

He eyed the keg at the end of the table. "Ale, Laird."

Marcalan hooted. "Ah! We need to list the rules for our guests."

"Aye, we must," the Laird said, grinning, holding out a tankard. "The first rule is that no titles are used. Only names."

Maradhor took the ale, staring at the lad, incredulous. He would be expected to call the high lord of all the provinces by name?

"Second rule is, that there is no rank," Haladhon said.

"And Alcandhor and Randhal serve the first round of drinks. After that, we serve ourselves," Mattan added.

The Laird pointedly handed the glass to Atinna himself, with an elaborate bow. Maradhor seated himself next to her, and her noble cousin sat on her other side.

"You see, I have to be the Laird at all times outside this solar. I have never had a moment in my life to merely be me. So whilst my friends are visiting, we steal away for a little while to be just friends. No rank, titles, or formalities. Just kin and friends." His blue eyes implored. "And now, my cousin, I actually have you, of my own clan, here to share it with, and on such a grand occasion as celebrating the safe return of our Tha—of Alcandhor." He paused, then in a softer voice asked, "Can you understand?"

Atinna nodded with shy smile.

"Just behave yourselves a little since we do have a lady here with us," Tam said.

The Laird stared at her, frowning. "You do not count yourself?"

"Nay. I am a Ranger."

Alcandhor chuckled. "That is ever your reply. I thought once married you would think of yourself as both a woman and a Ranger."

Marcalan giggled. "I can attest she is a woman."

Tam blushed, prodding him with her foot. "I cannot deny I am a woman, but I think not of myself as a lady. I do not braid my hair or wear gowns. I am Ranger Trained."

Haladhon raised his tankard. "And all who have matched you have the bruises to attest to that." He sat up. "Oh, say, did you see Lord Naidhar of Andethon tonight when he saw our Second at Table? Stars, his eyes bulged out this far!"

"Many of the lords have that response upon first seeing Tam. They know not what to think of a Ranger lass." Marcalan leaned back, grinning up at his wife. "I remember my first reaction when I saw her."

Tam arched an eyebrow. "Aye, and I felt it, though I knew not what it was at the time."

"Oh, and what was it?" Marcalan asked with that insufferable innocent blink of his.

Tam blushed, and Haladhon laughed. "That tells the story. Stars,

Mar, she had you from moment one, enh?"

Her husband chuckled, hand over his heart. "I had never seen anything so beautiful—this amazingly lovely lass, wearing trous and wielding a sword. I was smitten."

"I had wondered." The Laird smiled, pointing a finger at Marcalan. "You ever had your eye on her."

"It is your turn now," Marcalan said. "Found a lass you enjoy looking at?"

The Laird groaned and threw a pillow at him. "Leave off, you rascal!"

Laughing, the prankster tossed it back. Maradhor gulped his ale to hide his shock.

"What say you, Maradhor?" Haladhon asked.

He glowered at his cousin. If he was going to ask about marriage, Maradhor would skin him.

"What was your thought upon first seeing Tam?"

Exhaling in relief, he smiled across at the lass. "Stars. I know not where to start. I was scribe in that first conclave and wondered if the Thane had gone mad, but she has proven herself. But she does seem to turn everything topside down."

"Aye, she does seem to." Haladhon raised his tankard toward Tam with a grin.

Mattan pointed with his glass at Maradhor and Atinna. "You two were sneaking out early as we were. Discussions of Estan boring you?"

Maradhor hesitated, glancing at the lady, who turned pink and nodded.

The Laird snickered. "Oh Bells, cousin, if you think you are bored, try being Laird. I cannot get away from such discussions. I begin to have them in my sleep!"

They all laughed.

"It will be worse when the conclave begins," Alcandhor said.

Mattan stood and walked to the wine table. "Ah, but then at least they can all focus the topics at hand, instead of asking us the same questions over and over." He filled his glass, then turned. "I, for one, am tired of answering."

"You would not if you had not interfered—"

"Ah, you agreed to drop that topic, 'Candhor," Haladhon said, his voice hard. He rose and walked over to the table, casting a reproachful glance. Alcandhor held up a hand in apology. Maradhor's gaze flitted between his Thane, the Enaisi, and Haladhon. What ever was that about?

Tam got up, grumbling, "Stars, you are on the edge of breaking rules." She smiled across the room at Atinna. "Wish you something to eat? The confections are delicious, but there are also some other foods here."

The lady hesitated, then rose and joined Tam. Maradhor studied the difference in two women. Both were slender, but Tam was much shorter, and had not nearly the figure Atinna did. It had been a long time since he had thought of women's appearance or had compared them. Stars. What was Alcandhor asking? "Thane?"

"Ah!" Marcalan laughed, tossing a pillow at Maradhor. "Broke a rule!"

Maradhor rolled his eyes and tossed the pillow back. "Pardon. 'Alcandhor.' You were asking?"

The Thane grinned. "What think you of the banquets?"

Stars. How could he answer? If he said they were boring, the lady might take it personally.

"They are...interesting. The nobles, your pardon, Your Grace, er, Randhal, but most of the nobles seem very taken with themselves."

"I would find the whole thing boring except for Maradhor."

He gaped at Atinna. She rarely spoke without prompting. The lady smiled at him as she nibbled the edge of a sweeting.

"Oh?" Haladhon looked at her and then at Maradhor in interest. Too much interest. Marcalan did, too. Stars.

"He makes a game of pretending he knows what people are saying and tells me."

Marcalan threw his head back, laughing. "Bells! We used to do that all the time as striplings. It was such fun. We would watch the chiefs talking together seriously, and we would tell each other what they were saying: 'Oh, the herdbeast tonight was underdone, and I have such indigestion,' or 'Oh, I split my trous, keep me next to the wall,' or—"

"Used to do that?" Haladhon snorted. "You still do, you scamp! What sort of things was he telling you, Atinna?"

Her face turned pink. "Just silly things."

"Tell us."

She looked at Maradhor imploringly. "They...they might be considered improper."

Marcalan hooted. "Our dear Maradhor? Improper? Never!"

Atinna blushed bright red. "I only meant, that to jest about the nobles might be considered improper."

"Bells, it is just us, and no nobles present. Say on, please." Marcalan looked at Maradhor. "Or will you tell us?"

"You know the game. It was just the usual. For example, Lorwith shifts nervously from one foot to the other so I would make comments that his cobbler had erred in measurements." Maradhor put on a thin, high, whiny voice. "Stars, my boots are pinching so tight. Oh, my dear Lord Irdhith, think you I could possibly say something to that cobbler? I am a mere lord after all. Think you he will listen to me?"

Everyone roared.

The Laird wiped his eyes as he got his laughter under control. "Great moons, you sound just like him. My compliments."

Haladhon pointed at Marcalan. "I thought you had a talent, but he puts you to shame. Very good, cousin!"

Atinna lifted a hand. "But wait. Please, tell them Lord Irdhith's reply."

Maradhor shrugged slightly, then lowered his voice, and lifted his head in the arrogant way the Lantral lord did. "Bells, you simpering fool. If he does not fit you properly, simply put the fellow in stocks for a week. And on second error, have him hung."

"Oh, this is frightening." The Laird stood and walked to the wine table, shaking his head. "You have him too close."

"It was a favorite pastime of striplings, as Marcalan said. Except Valdhor. Stars, he was ever being jested about."

"Aye, I cannot imagine my father ever playing such games."

Alcandhor groaned. "The only game he ever played was Rangers'n'Rogues. At least with me. And I was always the rogue. He would chase and thrash me."

"Aye," Maradhor said. "I remember one time Zandhral and several others pulled him off you as he was too enthusiastic in his efforts. You were about six at the time, I believe."

"Enthusiastic? Aye, there is a good word for it." Alcandhor chuckled. "I do seem to remember you playing your game back then. You do it very well." He sat up straight. "Oh, Bells, aye! I remember one time you did it to my father. He was talking with someone, and you made up what he was saying, then discovered Lamadhel was behind you. Stars, you turned white!"

Maradhor snickered, nodding at the memory. "That got me scullery duty for a day. Disrespect to the Thane."

They all laughed.

Alcandhor approached the sideboard, grinning at the Laird. "So how goes the weeding?"

The lad grimaced ruefully, and the Thane laughed.

Maradhor looked from one to the other. "Weeding?"

Alcandhor nodded toward the Laird as he picked up a plate. "Our young friend has managed to acquire allies in trying to discover which ladies might be, hmm, shall we say, more sincere, rather than simply interested in marrying the Laird."

Maradhor nodded in understanding. "Weeding the garden, so to speak?"

"Exactly." Alcandhor picked up an item and frowned. "What in the name of both moons is this?"

Tam peered at it, wrinkling her nose.

The Laird walked close and bent to gaze at it, too. "It is a delicacy from Nelatan, I am told. It smells like fish, and looks like—" He snickered. "I cannot say what it looks like with ladies present. Are you brave, Alcandhor?"

The Thane eyed it then put it back. "Not that brave. Anyway, as I was asking, how goes the effort?"

The Laird shrugged.

Tam shook her head. "There are not many who are not weeds. Randhal has been trying to catch the attention of the ones we have found who are, well, not weeds."

"Which is difficult to do, as I do not fain pretend interest when it is not there. And they probably feel likewise." The Laird walked back over to the settee and plopped down. "Stars, I wish I could fall in love. Then it would not seem such a burden."

"I can verify that marrying when you are in love is no burden." Marcalan smiled at Tam, who dimpled at him.

Maradhor's parents had loved each other once from what was said, but it had grown cold years ago. Love was no guarantee a marriage would be happy. It took work. And strength. Self-absorption hindered both of his parents from giving effort, admitting mistakes, or forgiving.

"Hopefully some girl will catch your fancy," Haladhon said.

The Laird rolled his eyes. "Bells, they all catch yours. You just do not pay attention."

"I give full attention to not paying attention." Haladhon nodded in finality, lifting his tankard, his eyes twinkling.

Atinna returned to the settee, her mouth set in a fashion Maradhor recognized as fatigue, her expression pleading. He rose. "Excuse us, but the lady wishes to retire."

The men all stood, bowing as they wished her night's rest. She smiled gratefully at Maradhor, putting her hand over his.

Once at her door, he bowed. She stepped close, looking up with those blue eyes. "Thank you for being such a wonderful escort."

"It is a pleasure, lady."

She did not move, and Maradhor became aware of how close she stood. Disturbingly aware. He swallowed and quickly backed away, then bowed again. "I will see you tomorrow evening, lady."

Her face fell. He was in trouble; she was becoming attracted to him.

Stars. And he could not just stop escorting her.

After her door shut, he closed his eyes for a moment. What could he do?

~*~

Haladhon tossed back his ale. "Stars, two have gone. We are not going to call night's rest yet, are we?"

"It is getting late." Alcandhor filled his tankard and sat down. "Some of us are not as young as we used to be."

"Oh, come, do not think of retiring already." The Laird grinned. "Surely we can find something to talk about."

Haladhon snickered. "How about the two that left?"

"Aye," Tam said. "What say you? Shall they be a match?"

The Laird shook his head. "They cannot be."

Tam frowned. "Why not?"

"Ranger clan and Laird clan cannot intermarry."

Her mouth opened then closed again, her eyes on the Thane. "Is this true?"

"It has been that way for a long time. The two most powerful and influential clans marrying into each other has not been allowed to happen in many generations."

"Stars," she whispered.

"What is it?" asked the Laird.

"She loves him. And he has feelings for her."

"Oh Bells! This is not good." The Laird sighed. "Should I have him replaced as escort?"

Alcandhor took a deep breath, frowning. "Not yet. Let me think on this."

Haladhon shifted and sat up, breaking the silence. "We cannot end the night thus. What say you we sing something?"

"What?" asked the Laird.

Haladhon grinned.

Chapter Thirty-six

"Nay, nay! Wait. I have it now. Shall we try it again?" The Laird's face flushed, and his eyes sparkled.

Alcandhor gestured compliance, grinning at the lad, then they all began once more:

He roared the 'keeper t'fill him up,
Then tipped it back and drank the cup.
He belched an' then he hit the floor
And rolled himself right out the door.

The Laird laughed. "Stars, what a song. I think that will never be sung at court."

"I agree," Alcandhor said with a chuckle. "But there are many more verses."

"Are there? Such as?"

Haladhon raised his tankard. "Oh, I know quite a few."

"Sing on, then!"

"As my Laird wishes." His tall cousin inclined his head, then began:

Across the room I stood entranced,
The girl gave me a second glance.
I thought that I might have a chance
As, smiling, she asked me to dance.

I gave a proper little bow,
Then danced we in the tavern crowd.
And bold I was as I allowed
Her hand to slip inside my—

"Haladhon!" Tam's voice was sharp.

The tall Ranger stopped and blinked. They all roared with laughter.

"Stars, Tam, the next verse is even better."

"Perhaps we should go back to the first verse," she ordered, one eyebrow arched at her cousin. What a change from when Alcandhor first met his niece! He grinned at her peremptory attitude.

"Aye," the Laird said, face red.

They sang again. The second time through, the door opened. Lord

Krendhal walked in with a displeased expression. "I apologize, Your Grace, but I knocked and received no reply, yet I could hear the singing."

Marcalan giggled, and Tam back-slapped him.

At a signal from Alcandhor, the Rangers all rose. "Perhaps we should call it night's rest."

The Rangers filed out past Krendhal, each one bowing to him. The Viltara lord met Alcandhor's eyes, and his lips thinned, but he said nothing.

Even with the door was shut behind them, they could hear the Laird. "Bells, Krendhal, what was so important you could not wait until morning? We were having such a good time!"

"The singing could be heard down the hallway, Your Grace. It is not befitting—"

The Laird's voice grew louder and more shrill. "I care not!"

Alcandhor motioned them all to leave.

~*~

Sated after luncheon, Haladhon opened the door to his chamber to hear Sarinna's light, alto laugh floating down the hallway. He peered around the jamb to watch her curtsey to Irdhith before entering her suite. Haladhon pushed the door to until the Lantral lord swaggered past around the corner. Rage built in Haladhon, and he marched to her door and banged on it.

Sarinna's skin seemed to glow and her eyes shone as she answered. "Haladhon!" Her smile faded. "What is it?"

He stormed in and, as she shut the door, he thundered, "What can you see in that strutting cockerel?"

Sarinna stared at him, open-mouthed. Crossing her arms, she replied in a low, almost menacing voice, "You are jealous? How dare you."

Haladhon hesitated, licking his lips. "You are as a sister to me, and—"

Her short laugh chopped off his reply. "It is only the two of us, Haladhon, leave off." She lifted her chin, her eyes hard. "There are many things left unsaid between us, and it is best kept that way."

"He will only hurt you."

"You would know, would you not?"

Her cutting tone made him wince, but he had to warn her about that inbred by-blow. "Sarinna, Irdhith has plans. He only wishes you as—"

"Leave off, Haladhon!" Her eyes darkened. "I want to hear nothing about Irdhith. Especially not from you."

"But Sarinna—"

"Please, leave." She strode to the door and yanked it open. "Now."

He hesitated before stomping out. The slamming door punctuated the end of their conversation. Grinding his teeth, Haladhon headed for the training hall to vent his frustrations.

~*~

Arbitration kept Maradhor's mind busy all morning, but at luncheon the younger Rangers again harassed him about Atinna. He stormed off to the guards' training hall, hoping to rid himself of his anger, both at them for their taunting, and at himself for slowly losing the struggle of becoming infatuated. Her face as she stood close to him, her eyes begging him to kiss her, haunted him. He must conquer his feelings!

Maradhor threw himself into the workout. Haladhon came in, his countenance as stormy as Maradhor felt. They faced off and buffeted each other solidly until Alcandhor arrived and took the tall Ranger off to the far end to practice with some of the guards. Maradhor went to work on the body pell then, striking it as hard as he could, over and over.

"Great Bells, cousin, what did the pell ever do to you?"

Maradhor glanced up, breathing heavily, blinking the sweat out of his eyes, to see Loch'alan grinning at him.

"Leave me be. I am in no mood for your mouth."

"Are you that enraged that you are falling for a woman?"

"Leave off!"

"Why not admit it? You know you are."

Maradhor slammed a fist into the pell as he grunted. "I am not." He glared at Loch'alan, straightening. "And if I did want to get married, it would be to a woman not a child. Someone with strength in her to be the wife of a Ranger, not a timid maid who cannot handle the problems of life."

With an embarrassed grimace, Loch'alan glanced past Maradhor. He turned to see Atinna standing near the doorway. She blushed bright red, whirled, and ran out. He grabbed the thoughtless clod by his jerkin. "You knew she was there! Yet you urged me on, angered me, knowing I would say something that would hurt her?"

"I thought you would admit you loved her!"

Maradhor shoved the Ranger back so hard he lost his balance, hit the pell, then fell to the floor. He snatched his shirt and jerkin and strode out, still soaked with sweat, hoping to find the lady.

~*~

Maradhor knocked, waited, and knocked again. Atinna answered, eyes red, and before she could shut the door, he stopped it with his palm. "Lady, I came to apologize. Please."

"You said all you needed to."

"I said most of it in anger, in response to my cousin's taunting. You understand not the endless teasing because I have never married. It is a sore spot with me. Lady, please let me explain."

"You think me a child."

"You are half my age, lady. How shall I think of you?"

Her blue eyes glinted like ice. "I am a woman grown."

Maradhor stifled a sigh. A woman's age was not a topic one discussed if one wished to live a long life. This he knew from growing up with many female cousins. "You look young, lady. Have I erred?"

"On many things."

"I apologize."

"Thank you. Now may I close my door?"

"Lady—"

"I wish to shut my door."

Maradhor's brows raised at her imperious tone. He removed his hand, and the door slammed.

~*~

No one said a word as Maradhor readied for the evening. Loch'alan avoided him. He hurried to Atinna's door. Her servant answered and replied she was not attending the banquet that night.

"May I speak to her, please?"

The woman shook her head, and the door shut in Maradhor's face. He stared at it a moment, considering whether to knock again. Finally, he went to a chair down the hallway and sat. He doubted there was any way to mend the rift he had created, yet, what he said had been the truth. He would not consider marriage to a child such as her even if their clans were allowed to marry. He liked strong women, and this lass, who let herself become sickly by not eating or sleeping over the former betrothal, was not strong.

He loathed returning to the barracks. He could cadge a meal in the barracks' dining hall or even the range kitchen easily enough, but he was not hungry at the moment. He sat, staring at her door, wishing by the names of both moons that he knew what to do.

~*~

Accompanying Irdhith to the estrade of the Great Hall, Sarinna heard Perdhal say, "I understand Lord Elendhar is setting out for Laird Hall tomorrow."

"Aye," the Laird replied. "He should arrive two days hence, hopefully in time for that evening's banquet. It is opportune, too, as the conclave is due to begin day after that. Since the other lords have all arrived, I had not wished to postpone again."

"Good. Get it started and done with." Perdhal gave a derisive sniff, glancing about the Great Hall as if it stank. "I, for one, will be happy to return to my province. The hospitality here is not what I would have expected."

"I would think you would fain stay here, considering the illness that is spreading across Nelatan," Irdhith said.

Sarinna put a chastising hand on her escort's arm. Did he have to antagonize at every opportunity? She turned to Perdhal before the Laird could reply. "Have you truly found it so inhospitable, milord? I have never seen this hall more accommodating than during this visit. I am certain any problems or complaints you have would be received gladly by the hall steward." Sarinna gave him a charming smile. The Nelatan lord swallowed his sneer with an uncertain frown.

She turned to the Laird, whose eyes twinkled at her. "Weltin seems to be doing very well as your new steward, Your Grace. He is to be commended for restoring order so quickly when the siege ended."

"I will pass along your observations. It is high praise indeed coming from Zaidhron's steward."

Sarinna smiled, turning to Perdhal. "How badly is your province faring, lord? Is the fever sweeping through severely?"

"It has not been this bad in many years," he said, frowning. "But you know the drums as well as I, Lady Sarinna. You know how it is spreading, and that it is heading for this province."

"I know not what private messages you might receive that are either worrisome or comforting compared to what is sent on the drums. Have you enough healers and herbalists? Can Zaidhron lend assistance?"

"And is it contained?" Irdhith asked, worry evident on his face and in his voice.

"Nay, it is not contained, despite our efforts. That wretched fever blasts through every so many years killing often as not, but aye, Lady Sarinna, at the moment, our healers are managing. You are gracious to offer. My thanks."

"Indeed, I have found the Lady Sarinna ever gracious."

Sarinna smiled at Irdhith's flattery, although it wore thin. His intentions were to buy friendship with Zaidhron through her, of that she had no doubt. He was attracted to her—she did not even need empathy to be aware of that. To be so admired had been soothing at first, but now she wished she had a true friendship with him, not one filled with ulterior designs. She was as guilty as he, though, so she could not fault him.

The conversation turned to other matters, and Irdhith excused them both. He seemed especially attentive this evening. After several sets of dances, he asked her to walk with him again. She stifled a sigh. He was never forward—well, not since the first night when she made certain he was aware of his limits, but the conversations were repetitious. He claimed to want to know more of Ranger clan, their ways and views on matters, but always ended up countering anything she said. It had become circular and tiresome.

This evening though, she sensed something different about him. An anticipation as well as a rise in passion. Her guard went up just a little as they walked the second floor hallways. He gestured to a bench seat in an alcove. Sarinna held her gown with care as she sat and then folded her hands, waiting.

Irdhith sat next to her, his blue eyes gleaming even in the dim light. "Lady Sarinna, I hope you have enjoyed these days and evenings in my company as much as I have enjoyed yours."

With a slight, confused frown, she responded, "Aye. Very much so, Lord Irdhith."

"Please, I would fain have you just call me Irdhith." Before she could reply, he boldly took her hands in his. "Lady. Sarinna. I–I have become enamored of you, and I...I wish to ask you if you would honor me by becoming my wife."

She straightened, pulling her hands away. Enamored, indeed! Was this his thought of how to firmly fix a good position for himself with Ranger clan? By both moons, did he think her a fool? "Lord Irdhith, this is not meet. I have made you no necklet nor given you reason to think we have more than friendship. Perhaps your clan does things in a different manner, but Ch'shalna follows the old ways, and a marriage offer is a woman's prerogative."

At his stormy expression, she took a deep breath. Stars, but her rash reply had been too blunt. How could she best deflect his attentions with tact and grace? She did not wish to make him Ranger clan's overt enemy over personal matters. She leaned forward, placing a hand on his. "Forgive me. Your proposal took me by surprise. But you must know it is not possible. Clan Law restricts the women of my clan with Enaisi blood from considering marrying outside Ch'shalna. And even if 'twere possible, our children cannot inherit from their fathers, but must be raised as Ranger clan. I could give you no heirs."

"What? That is nonsense!"

"It is not nonsense, it is the law."

He stood, glowering. "Does your clan so strongly protect your Enaisi blood? Such superiority you have, enh? I shall call conclave on this ridiculous law!"

"But it is Clan Law and cannot be changed."

"We shall see. Night's rest, milady." Irdhith stooped in a stiff bow then strode off, leaving her sitting alone in the dark.

~*~

"Maradhor?"

With a start, he blinked up at his Thane, then glanced around bleary-eyed. He had fallen asleep in the hallway? Stars.

"Are you all right, cousin?"

He rose, shaking his head. "I need to get to the barracks. I am sorry, Thane."

"Sorry? What were you doing sleeping in this chair? Why were you not at the banquet?"

"Atinna...erm, she decided not to attend tonight. I sat here after I found out, t–to think about a few things, and must have fallen asleep."

Maradhor did not like the knowing look he received from the Thane and the others. Stars. Haladhon would have quite a bit to say at the first possible moment from the grin on his face.

"Get you to bed, cousin. You may do your thinking tomorrow."

Maradhor bowed and strode off, cursing under his breath at both women and knowing cousins.

~*~

Maradhor scribed for the Laird the next day, which gave him the perfect opportunity. He rose from his table when arbitration ended. "Your Grace?"

The Laird turned with a smile. "Aye, Maradhor?"

"I think it would be best if you found another escort for your cousin."

"Oh?"

Maradhor took a deep breath. "I gave insult to her, Your Grace. Not intentionally, on my honor. But nonetheless, she...is not happy with me."

"Ah." He smiled again. "So that is why she was absent last night. She sent word she was not feeling well." He crossed his arms. "Let me think about it, and I will let you know by afternooning whether to dress for the banquet."

"I thank you, Your Grace."

As Maradhor left the arbitration chamber, he heard his name called. He turned to see Krendhal approaching him. He inclined his head. "Lord."

"I have heard a rumor."

"Aye?"

"It is said that you and Atinna are...becoming romantically attached."

Maradhor stared in astonishment at the Viltara noble. "May I ask the foundation of this rumor?"

"You two talked and laughed together quietly the night before last. It seemed very...private. Intimate. You and she left early, yet she arrived not at her chambers until quite late. Then yesterday it is said you two quarreled."

A slight smile quirked Maradhor's lips. "A quarrel is necessarily part of courtship?"

Krendhal's eyebrow lifted even further. "Is there truth to this rumor?"

"Nay, milord. The facts are correct, but out of context. I will elaborate only on what might cause shadow to fall on the lady's reputation. We left early as she wished to retire, but her cousin, the Laird, invited us both to his solar. We have an entire chamber of Rangers and the Laird to attest I was not bringing ruin to the lady's name."

Krendhal brows drew down.

His arms spread, Maradhor replied, "Milord, hall gossip is notoriously unreliable. I have never said nor done anything to cause or encourage such to be said. I am merely her escort."

"I hoped that was the case. I had to ask. It is not common knowledge, because it has not been an issue for many years, but marriages between your clan and mine are not allowed."

Maradhor frowned. "Perhaps this is not common knowledge among other clans, but 'tis taught in Ranger clan. I am aware that there can be no attachment between the lady and myself. And as I said, I have merely been her escort."

Krendhal bowed to Maradhor, who returned it. As he strode away, he clenched his jaw, fighting the ache in his heart. He had not wished to marry her, and would no longer be her escort in any case. It would be easy to forget her.

Chapter Thirty-seven

Maradhor entered the training hall, and Tam rushed to him. "Cousin, I wish to speak to you."

With a smile, he asked, "About what?"

She gestured, and he followed her to a corner so they could have relative privacy. "About Atinna."

His smile faded. "What about her?"

"Did you know that marriage between our clans is not allowed?"

Maradhor sighed in disgust. "Aye, I am aware of that. What has it to do with Atinna? If you think we are romantically involved, you are mistaken."

"You and she have in love."

He stiffened. "You are mistaken."

"Cousin, I can sense. You may fool others but not me. She loves you very much. And although you fight it, I know you love her."

"What right have you to interfere?" Maradhor hissed. "Simply because you can sense does not give you the right to jump into people's lives."

Tam flinched. Stars, he should not have spoken so harshly, she was merely still a child in many ways. "I apologize. I seem to say too much lately. Forgive me."

"I do. I know how you are hurting. I am sorry you feel I am intruding. I...I only wished to help."

"Even if what you say is true, if I did love her, I could not marry her. And even if I could, I would not. She would not make a suitable Ranger's wife. She has not the strength necessary."

"She is young, and has been sheltered. How know you what strength she has in herself?"

"And what know you of finding strength, daughter of Valdhor?"

The set of Tam's chin reminded Maradhor of her father. "I had to find much strength in myself since leaving Pashelon. I still do. It is hard. I lost my home, my garden, my father, all this is new to me. If I had not the love of kin through this, I know not what I would do. Who does Atinna have? Was there anyone for her to confide in about her former betrothal? Is there anyone now? Who will she turn to when she discovers she can never marry you? She must make a life for herself, away from her close kin, unless her father relents, and without the man she loves."

Maradhor crossed his arms; he did not want to hear this.

Tam put a hand on his arm. "You can fight through this, although it will hurt. But can you be so callous to her? Think you what this will do to her?"

He knew. She would stop eating, and make herself ill as she did over that betrothal. Stars. He could not bear that. Maradhor went to a stack of drying cloths and snatched one, thinking. Tam followed him. "What will you do then?"

"What can I do? I cannot continue to be her escort, even if she would want it."

"What mean you? Why would she not want you as escort?"

"She overheard me saying something unkind about her, and will not speak to me or see me. Perhaps it is best. Seeing each other is not wise."

Tam frowned. "Are you certain?"

Maradhor nodded. "I shall talk to the Thane. Perhaps he could send me away. It would be better for her."

Tam shook her head. "I do not think that is wise."

"I think it is. Your pardon, Tam. I shall speak to him now." He crossed the training hall to where Alcandhor matched a guard. As soon they finished, Maradhor tossed a drying cloth to his Thane who grinned as he caught it.

"Waiting to match me, cousin?"

"Nay, I have a request. May we talk for a moment?"

Alcandhor nodded, and they walked to the side. "Thane, I would like to be sent to the scribe school in Kentin."

The Thane scrutinized him. "Does this have to do with Atinna?"

Maradhor scowled. Did everyone know? "Aye."

"We have need of scribes here."

"Jonadhan is here. He can take my place."

"This is sudden."

"Aye. I think only of the lady. I feel it would be easier on her if we were apart."

"I cannot say I know what is best," Alcandhor said with a grimace. "But I will consider your request."

Maradhor stepped closer. "Please, Thane. You know not what she..." He licked his lips as he tried to think of how to explain. "She was betrothed to a man against her wishes by her father. She was pale and ill from lack of food and sleep. Tam says she loves me. What shall she do when she discovers we cannot marry?"

Alcandhor rubbed his hands across his eyes with a moan. "I am sorry."

"She will forget me faster if I am away. For her sake. Please."

The Thane hesitated then nodded. "Tell Jonadhan to report to me.

You may leave for Kentin in the morning."

Maradhor sighed in relief. "Thank you, Thane."

~*~

Randhal meandered along the corridor. What could he do about his cousin?

"Your Grace."

He turned with a smile at Alcandhor's voice. "Thane! May I ask a question?"

"Most assuredly."

"When does one's duty as clan thane end, and friendship as well? When does it become meddling?"

Alcandhor crossed his arms, with a disgusted expression. "Ask Mattan. Or Haladhon." He lifted a hand and shook his head with a rueful grimace. "My apologies. I could not say. Friends and kin often intrude into private matters. Whether it is meddling or welcome advice is the opinion of the recipient."

Randhal made a wry face. "That is not helpful."

"Have you asked Lord Krendhal for advice?"

"Oh Bells, nay! I...I think I will muddle through it on my own. I must learn, must I not?"

"Aye." Alcandhor glanced past the Laird to the far door in the hall, Atinna's suite. Randhal found himself flushing as the Thane gave him a knowing look and dropped a hand on his shoulder. "'Tis not an easy task. It might interest you to know that Maradhor has requested to leave Laird Hall. He is going to the scribe school in Kentin."

"Because of her?"

"Aye. He told me he thinks it would be easier on her if she did not have to see him."

"I feel for them."

"As do I. He still will not admit he has feelings for her. I know not which is worse."

Randhal nodded, then a thought occurred to him. "What of our need of scribes?"

"We have another scribe here to take his place. His name is Jonadhan."

"There is that, then." He glanced back at her door. "I must see to her having a different escort, and I suppose I should tell her he is leaving, should I not?"

"That would come better from him."

"Is he coming to see her, then?"

"I doubt it."

"He would just leave without saying anything to her?"

"Knowing Maradhor, aye."

"Then I shall tell her. And Thane, I would not give orders to your men, especially regarding something personal, but since it is my cousin, perhaps you could let him know I do expect proper etiquette from him in this matter. Leaving thus with no word to her would be most inappropriate."

"I will advise him."

"I thank you."

They bowed, then Randhal approached Atinna's door, inhaling deeply as he knocked. The maid answered with a curtsey.

He swept in to find Atinna sitting in a chair by the window. "I will speak with my cousin alone." He waited and after the servant left, then said, "I am sorry to intrude, but I had need to speak to you."

"About what, Your Grace?" she asked, rising.

"Bells, must we go through this again? Can I not be Randhal to you in private?"

She dropped her gaze. "I will try to remember."

He gestured to the chairs. "Let us sit." He had been trained for many years by tutors and instructors to not fidget, but he was sorely tempted. This was so new to him. He stared over at her, unsure how to begin. "I am here to tell you that I will be appointing a new escort for you."

Her face paled. "But why?"

"Maradhor has requested it, and he is leaving."

She shot to her feet, round-eyed. "Leaving? Why?"

This was going to be difficult. Randhal took her hands and nodded that she should sit again. "He...he knows you have feelings for him, and well, you see, you cannot marry."

"But why?"

"It is law. There can be no marriages between our clan and Ranger clan."

"Why?"

Could the lass ask nothing but why? "It was made law ages ago, by the nobles who feared what could happen if alliances were made between our clans."

"But what could happen?"

Randhal stared at her in amazement. "Do you truly not know?"

She shook her head.

He took a deep breath, then thought perhaps a concise explanation would be more appropriate than one explaining the complexities of the power balance between the clans. "Marital alliances between our clans could cause influence or pressure to be put against either the Thane or the Laird, or their counselors."

"Think you I could influence you, cousin?"

Randhal smiled. "Actually, nay. But that is not the point."

"Then what is?"

"That such influence could be possible."

She stared at him for a few moments, then looked at her hands. Her voice trembled. "So I...I would be foolish to make a necklet for him, then?"

"I am sorry."

"Think you I could be excused from the banquets, Your Grace?"

"It would not be proper. I have given thought to who might be a suitable escort."

She rose with a slight sob and went to the window. Randhal followed her worriedly. "I truly apologize. If I had known there was affection between you, I would not have had him continue as escort."

"I have made the necklet already," she whispered, clutching the draperies with one hand. "I did not know we could not marry."

What could he say? Before he could reply, she continued, her words fast, voice thick. "I had ripped apart the one my father had me make for Tirnin. I started on one when we began our journey back here. I knew then I would refuse to marry Tirnin even if you did annul his marriage. I would refuse anyone because I knew I loved Maradhor. Then yesterday, I heard him say he thinks of me as a child, and that I am not strong enough to be a Ranger's wife. I–I was hurt, and despaired for awhile, then thought I might change his mind eventually, but now, I know not what to do." She turned to look at him, her eyes brighter blue with tears in them. "I am lost."

Randhal was tempted to tell her to live up to her clan, but he remembered the countless times that had been his father's response when he had told him he wished for playmates or was lonely. His father had been of the mind that personal considerations were not important, only clan obligations. He had seen a different viewpoint from the Thane, that the individual should be considered as well. He swallowed his irritation at her helplessness and self-pity, but knew not what to say or do. There was no solution except for her to forget Maradhor.

How did one comfort a crying female? What would the Thane do? That he knew. He stepped toward his cousin and touched her shoulder. She leaned toward him, and he let himself embrace her. She clung to him, sobbing aloud. He just held her.

~*~

From his chair in the hallway, Alcandhor waited. The Laird come out of Atinna's chambers, his face troubled. He rose as the Laird walked over.

"How do you handle such things as clan thane?"

Alcandhor smiled. "I have both Taniss and Sarinna to help." He eyed darted to the smudged shoulder of the Laird's white surcoat. The Laird glanced down and shrugged. "She cried. I..." His face turned pink.

The Thane gave a slight smile. "It was the best thing you could have done for her. I take it she will not be at the banquet tonight?"

"How did you know? I had intended on insisting, but she begged and I could not see demanding it with her in such a state."

Alcandhor clapped a hand on the Laird's shoulder. "I am often teased that I know little about women, and," he leaned close, whispering, "it is true." He grinned but it faded. "But there are a few things I do know. It is best if she is allowed to grieve a little."

The Laird nodded. "Will Maradhor be telling her personally that he is leaving?"

"Aye."

The Laird frowned and turned away, then waved his arms angrily. "Bells, Thane, it is all foolishness! Why should not two people in love be allowed to marry?"

"That is a question for the nobles. They ever distrust my clan. And yours, too."

"Aye. Imagine if we became cousins through their marriage. The nobles would cry about our duplicity and schemes for power so loud the Bells in the nebula would hear it!" Steel blue eyes met Alcandhor's. "How do you deal with it? How have you kept from knocking heads off?"

A twitch threatened the corners of Alcandhor's mouth. "Any inappropriate actions or words of mine will be remembered and brought up at the most inopportune times, Your Grace. Knowing this helps me to think and react calmly."

Exhaling with deliberate slowness, the Laird nodded. "Good advice, as usual. I thank you."

Alcandhor bowed. "I will see you at the banquet then, Your Grace?"

The Laird groaned. "Aye. I wonder who I am escorting tonight." He bowed. "I suppose we shall see soon enough." With a morose expression, he walked away.

~*~

Maradhor approached Atinna's door with dread. What scene would the child make when he told her? He knocked and bowed when she answered the door. "I wish to speak to you, lady."

She opened the door wider, and he glanced inside. "Is your maid here?"

She shook her head. "The Laird said you were going to come, so I told her to leave. I know it is not proper, but I thought we should speak alone."

Stars. What should he do? Go for a servant, or one of the chiefs down the hallway? Nay, it would seem he was running away. He sighed and, with reservations, entered, but kept one hand on the latch, keeping the door from shutting completely.

"I wished to apologize again for offending you, lady. And to tell you I will be leaving in the morning. I am to teach at the scribe school in Kentin."

She nodded, looking down. "I know. The Laird told me."

He stared at her in amazement. "He did?"

She nodded again. "He also told me that we could not marry."

Stars. "We have never discussed marriage, yet he talks to you of it?"

"He knows how I feel. He said you did, too."

"I–I thought you might having feelings for me, lady."

She gazed up with a pleading expression. "And you, Ranger? What do you feel?"

He frowned. "What can my feelings matter?"

"They matter to me. I will be bold and tell you I love you, even though we can never marry. Will you tell me how you feel?"

Maradhor glanced about the chamber. He wished he had not come. "I only came to tell you good-bye, lady."

She stepped closer. "Please."

He ran his tongue over his dry lips as he backed up. "This discussion is fruitless."

She glared at him, then spun and crossed to the window. "Is your pride so important you cannot admit you care for a child? A woman too weak to be a Ranger's wife?"

Stars. Here it started. "I will not get into some pointless argument with you. Is this what I would face if we *could* be married? A woman who would nag and prod me?"

She turned, her eyes filled with tears. "I just want to know if you love me, as I love you. Would it wound your pride so much to give me that little bit of salve for myself?"

So calmly she stood. Had she so readily accepted it? She was beautiful, he finally admitted to himself. Why did she have to push him to this? To think of things better left alone. Things better left unsaid. He had felt such an ache before, when he realized that Sarinna would never look upon him and see a suitor, a lover. Now, how could he deny his feelings for Atinna?

But—what was she going through? If he had to admit it to himself, then why not say it if it would ease her anguish. He took several breaths, then at last managed to say, "You have captured my heart...My Lady."

She smiled, tears running freely down her cheeks. "Thank you."

It was quiet for a moment, and finally he said, "I need to make preparations to leave."

Atinna paused, as if about to say something, then merely curtsied. Maradhor bowed and left.

Chapter Thirty-eight

Alcandhor's mood did not improve the next day or that evening. He stood at the side of the Great Hall, watching the lords and the ladies, wishing he were home with his children.

A servant sought out the Laird and whispered to him. Curiosity roused, Alcandhor casually made his way across the Great Hall. As he approached, Randhal smiled. "Lord Elendhar and some of his family have arrived and have been shown directly to their chambers. It is late, and they are cold and tired, so I am not requiring them to appear before me to be welcomed and pay their respects as is custom. Wish you to join me in welcoming them privately?"

With a grin, he inclined his head, whispering, "Anything to escape the Great Hall in the evenings."

"What is he like?" Randhal asked as they approached the suite.

Alcandhor knocked on the door. "I think you shall become fast friends."

A servant answered, and they entered. Besides the servant and Estan's lord, two young women, nay lasses, were in the chamber. Elendhar's sisters no doubt, with their black hair, green eyes, and slender stature. Alcandhor strode forward and clasped shoulders with the noble. "Good to see you, my friend. May I introduce our Laird?"

After they bowed, Elendhar lifted a hand. "And may I introduce both of you to my sisters, Marlinn and Analinn?"

The lasses curtsied, and Randhal bowed again, flushing. "My honor and pleasure, ladies."

"We have just finished dining, but perhaps you would care for some refreshment?" Elendhar gestured toward the sideboard.

As the Laird started for the table, the servant stepped forward, but Randhal waved him back. "Your journey was uneventful, I hope, Lord Elendhar?" he asked, fumbling and almost tipping the teapot. He hunched slightly, then straightened his shoulders and poured hot tea into a cup.

Alcandhor found himself caught between watching his usually composed friend and waiting for the Estan's lord reaction to a Laird who served himself. The Esteni stared with a confused frown as he answered, "Aye. But cold. I am grateful my province borders yours, and it is but a two day journey."

His face still pink, the Laird turned toward the sisters, nearly losing his balance. His tea sloshed over the edge and he quickly passed the cup to his other hand, then waved his burned fingers. "I hope you ladies did not find it too difficult."

The girls ducked their heads, smiling. "Nay, Your Grace," replied the younger sister.

"A–and what do you think of Laird Hall?"

Alcandhor stared. Randhal was not the type to stutter or be clumsy. What was the matter with him?

"We have not seen much of it yet," the one sister said, "but it is beautiful, as is Estan Hall. The white stone is remarkably pretty."

"Perhaps I could give you a tour tomorrow?"

"We have conclave all day, Your Grace," Alcandhor said, and when Randhal *tsked*, he added, "You might give them a short tour just before the banquet."

The Laird's eyes shone. "An excellent notion, Thane. Thank you." He took a step toward the older sister, staring at her. "Would you like a tour tomorrow?" He blinked and quickly turned to Elendhar. "I mean—I would be honored to give you all a tour."

Ah, the problem with the lad was the older sister. In his own regard she was not a beauty, but he did admit the long, black lashes framing her green eyes were fetching. He had not the abilities of Tam, but he let himself sense her and found a mixture of awe and shyness.

"A tour? That would be such fun, Elendhar!" the younger sister squealed, clasping her hands under her chin.

"Marlinn," her sister chided in a soft voice. "Such manners and in front of the Laird!"

"I–I mind not," the Laird said, too quickly. "It is tiring having to be proper all the time."

Stars, the boy was going to make a fool of himself. Alcandhor had too many memories of his own and would fain spare his young friend such embarrassment. "Your Grace, did you know Lord Elendhar enjoys games such as kingsmen and recall? He is very good at them, too."

The Laird's attention drifted to Alcandhor, then to Estan's lord. "Does he?"

"You shall have to play him."

Randhal's expression was of one in Hillsdown. By both moons, was the lad so far gone that fast?

"Is there not a cabinet in each suite that contains a variety of games? Why not play a game tonight?" Alcandhor scrutinized Elendhar. "Unless you are too fatigued after your journey?"

"Ah, nay. 'Twould warm my blood to play a good game of backhand or kingsmen."

The young men set up a game, and the sisters curtsied, Analinn saying, "Excuse us, but we would like to retire for the evening."

The Laird looked stricken but managed to bow. After the girls left, Alcandhor said, "I think I should find Tam, I have remembered a task she is to perform. Your Grace, may I speak to you a moment, please?"

Once they were to the side, he whispered, "Befriend the brother first. Remember, she is underage." Wide blue eyes locked on his as the Laird's face turned bright red. In a normal voice Alcandhor said, "I shall have Tam make the proper inquiries for you, of course."

Straightening with an understanding gleam in his eye, the Laird said, "Oh. Oh, aye. Aye, of course. Th–thank you for taking care of that for me, Thane."

Alcandhor smiled as the lad went back over to the table where Elendhar was waiting. "Do not stay up too late, my friends, as we do have conclave in the morning."

Once outside the door, he bent over, hands on his knees, and laughed long and low.

~*~

"Irdhith has been thundering for two days, but will not speak to anyone."

Alcandhor raised his eyebrows, pretending interest in the Taladar lord's gossip as they strolled along the hallway toward the conclave chamber. Tadhrol leaned closer. "I think it has to do with your sister."

"Indeed?"

"You did notice they spent no time together the last two nights?"

He had noticed but wisely refrained from asking Sarinna any questions that could shorten his life span. To protect himself from perjury, he rounded a direct reply. "I left early with the Laird to introduce him to Lord Elendhar."

"Aye, they arrived rather late. The weather has not been conducive to travel. I have not met the man, is he proud and ambitious as our Lantral lord is?"

Alcandhor smiled. "Nay, and I hope he stays that way. He and the Laird are both young, naïve, and idealistic. I think they might become friends."

Tadhrol let out his breath in a melancholy sigh. "By both moons, another like you? Just what we need in conclave."

His lips twisted in a smile. "Like me? Stars, think you I am young and naïve?"

The lord halted, glaring down his nose with a vexed expression.

"Compared to me you are still young, and aye, about some things you are still naïve, Thane. And idealistic?" Tadhrol smiled dryly. "Need I answer that?"

Alcandhor chuckled, and they continued on to the conclave chamber. Guards opened the doors. Glancing around, he quickly tallied that only Irdhith and the Laird were missing. The Ranger scribe Jonadhan sat at a side table, ready to record the proceedings. Stifling his pique at the reminder of Maradhor's situation, he made himself smile as he introduced Elendhar to Tadhrol.

Before the two had a chance to do more than bow, the tall lord of Lantral Province stormed in, snatched his chair out, and dropped into it, glowering at Alcandhor. Interesting. He met the cockerel's gaze with a calm, detached expression until Irdhith turned away, then he continued introducing the new Estan lord to his peers. Small talk filled the chamber as they waited.

"Do not tell me our Laird is going to be late to his first conclave?" Vendhal finally asked, snickering.

"Not at all." Randhal grinned, entering the chamber with Mattan on his heels. Everyone stood.

"This is a lords' conclave." Gilendhar pointed at the alien. "He should not be here!"

"Nay. Enaisi often attended conclaves ages ago. I have asked that he be present."

"Is that in the law?" asked Mirdhol of Valeshon.

"It is tradition," the Laird shot back.

"But it is not in the law?" Perdhal reiterated the question.

Alcandhor chortled. When they all gave him questioning looks, he responded, "The lords speaking against tradition and wishing instead to seek the law?"

Krendhal snorted softly, his eyes gleaming with amusement. "Indeed."

"It is not in the law, nor is there anything written in the law against it," the Laird said, his jaw set. "But it was the precedent set by our ancestors."

Mattan caught Alcandhor's eye and winked as he sat down. Did the Enaisi maneuver to be in conclave? If so, why? Was it foresight? Only the thought that he could do so later helped Alcandhor fight down the urge to grab Mattan, haul him out, and ask him.

Krendhal picked up the sheaf of papers and straightened them, then looked around. "I see all the lords are here, so shall we begin? First item of business is formalizing Randhal, son of Kandhal, as Laird of the Teldheri people. Is there any discussion?"

The Nelatan lord said, "He is a bit young. Four years under Age, enh?"

"Bells, is there any pleasing you, Perdhal?" asked Rildhran of Tathelon, brushing back his hair in irritation.

"I just wish to go over all the facts. His training, who his tutors were..."

Alcandhor sighed. He should have known even something as simple as officially approving their new Laird would grow into a lengthy debate.

~*~

Years of long, boring meetings and conclaves had taught Alcandhor one thing. It was possible to sleep with one's eyes open, keep one's mind alert enough to record what each person says, and rally with a reply or vote if necessary.

But when, after dealing with several mundane matters—which the new lords especially had to drag out to show they were doing their duty by examining every item in the minutest detail—Irdhith cleared his throat, Alcandhor instinctively perked up.

"Since this is my first conclave, I am not certain of protocol, but I have a matter to be brought before you lords."

"What is this matter, Lord Irdhith?" the Laird asked.

"There is a law that I have searched out, it was added to Clan Law, although that is supposedly not done. It prohibits Ch'shalna women from marrying outside their own clan if they have Enaisi blood."

Alcandhor held up a hand. "It does not specifically prohibit them from marrying, my lord, it merely does not allow offspring to be considered anything but Ranger clan."

The Lantral lord stood, his blue eyes ice. "Is your clan so superior you would keep all Enaisi blood in it?"

Mattan burst into laughter and continued for some time, despite the reproving looks he received. Still grinning, he finally wiped his eyes, leaning back with a sigh.

Irdhith glowered. "What is so humorous, pray?"

Mattan sat erect, smile gone, his eyes glittering black. "You!"

The chamber fell silent with Mattan's vehement one word answer. "That law was enacted despite the protestations of myself, others of my race, and Ch'shalna clan." He pointed at Irdhith. "It was you, lords like you, who forced this law to be added to Clan Law, although Clan Law was considered unalterable—never added to, or taken away from. Because you-did-not-want-your-clans-tainted-with-Enaisi-blood!" The alien spat out the last sentence, his dark eyes scanning the lords one by one, finally resting on Irdhith. "So do not speak of superiority to me. It was you Teldheri clans who claimed superiority over the Rangers and my people. I can still see the supercilious faces of the lords as they bellowed of keeping their heritage pure!"

The Lantral lord exhaled slowly as he sat down, his face red, his gaze averted.

"And pray, what is your interest in this Clan Law, Lord Irdhith?" Tadhrol asked with a casual air.

Alcandhor dared not glance at his old friend or let himself give in to the smile twitching his lips. That lord enjoyed baiting the newer lords, especially the young Lantral lord, too much.

Irdhith's eyes flicked toward Alcandhor, his voice low. "I had asked Lady Sarinna to marry me."

"Unfortunate," Tadhrol said, his tone still light. "You will have find another lady to pursue, now, enh?"

Irdhith stood, his eyes like icicles. "You do not ease up, do you, Taladar?"

Tadhrol leaned back with a smirk. "Tell me how your heart is breaking, Lord Irdhith."

"My personal life is not the business of this conclave."

"It is when you bring up Clan Law which keeps you from marrying," Gilendhar said with a low chuckle.

Red-faced, Irdhith slammed his hand on the table, but the Laird stood before he could say anything. "I think it is best if we adjourn for luncheon. We have more items on the docket for this afternoon, and a petition as well."

Alcandhor excused himself, hoping to escape before the lords could pester him about his sister and Lantral's lord. He wanted to see her about this matter and luncheon provided the perfect time.

Tadhrol's voice, still taunting Irdhith, could be heard in the hallway. "Perhaps next time you will not breach etiquette and force the question instead of waiting for the lady to offer a necklet. Or fear you no lady will ever offer one?"

Alcandhor quickened his retreat.

~*~

"This is such nonsense!"

Shrugging, Alcandhor picked at the foods on the sideboard, tasting some of this and that. He poured a cup of tea from the urn and took a swig. "Lord Irdhith gives a good performance."

"Of course, but he feels nothing for me. It is his pride and his ambition being thwarted that have him in an uproar."

"If you knew this about him, why did you continue to let him escort you?"

"He was solicitous and flattering. It made me feel young and pretty."

"By the names of both moons, Sarinna, what would make you feel you needed that sort of attention?"

"You would not understand." Sarinna swept to the window and stood looking out, hugging her arms.

Alcandhor's reply did not make it past his lips. She was right. Whatever her reasoning, he probably would not comprehend it. And considering the set of her jaw, if he tried to discuss it further, it would probably be detrimental to his health. Thane of the Rangers, and he feared his sister. He picked up a large leaf from the bowl of greens and heaped meat and the marsh grain kaduk into it as he sought a safe topic. He wrapped the leaf around the filling, tucking the ends in to complete the meat roll. "I think Randhal has found his lady."

Sarinna turned from looking out the window as he took a bite. "Oh?"

Alcandhor nodded as he chewed. "When Lord Elendhar introduced him to his sisters, he turned red and became not only fumble-tongued but almost fell over his own feet. He kept staring at the one sister—Analinn is her name."

Sarinna's eyebrows raised, her lips tipping up. "Interesting. And honestly, can you please not talk with your mouth full?"

Alcandhor swallowed, rolling his eyes. "The Laird is going to give Estan's lord and his sisters a tour of the hall before the banquet."

"Has he requested that he escort her this evening?"

"I know not, but he would discuss that with Lord Krendhal, not me."

"What is the lass like?"

Alcandhor shrugged. "You are asking me? Are you not always telling me I am hopeless regarding women?"

Sarinna chuckled. "Aye, and so you are. But did you sense her?"

"Aye. I detected nothing amiss."

"Have you talked to Tam?"

"Aye. But I know not whether she will have the chance to meet the lass before this evening."

Alcandhor scooped some roasted grain kernels, tipped back his head, and dropped them into his mouth. When he was through munching, he said, "I hope this afternoon is more interesting than this morning."

"That bad?"

Alcandhor snorted, picking up another handful. "They reviewed the Laird's entire life. The poor lad. Especially where his studies with me were concerned."

"But they did confirm him?"

He gave a low chuckle as he shook the kernels in his fist. "Aye. It was a choice of him or Krendhal, and our dear lord of Viltara had already let them know he would deal heavy-handed with them. 'Twas well done. He forced them to choose Randhal." He tossed back the kernels and chewed. With a sigh, he headed for the door. "Better get back."

Sarinna walked toward him. "Already?"

"I was stopped a dozen times on my way here. Questions about Irdhith and you, questions about Elendhar and Estan, even concerns about that fever in Nelatan."

"My poor brother. So put upon." She kissed his cheek and patted his shoulder.

His lips twisted in a wry smile as he walked out.

The lords trickled back into the chamber. Alcandhor took his seat, stifling a yawn. He had eaten light on purpose; he did not want to nod off in the middle of conclave.

"This afternoon's session begins with a petition." The Laird said. "If you will all take your seats, we may begin."

Chairs scuffed as the lords sat. The Laird nodded to a guard who escorted the petitioner in. Alcandhor's eyebrows rose when he saw it was Atinna. The paper shook in her hands.

She approached the table, her pale blue eyes flicking from one man to the next. She curtsied. "My lords. My name is Atinna, daughter of Bandhran, family Sirakan, sept and clan Viltara." The lass paused and swallowed before continuing, "I am petitioning that you allow a marriage between Ranger Maradhor and me, despite the lords' conclave law against marriage between our clans."

The lords murmured, and one hissed, "A bold lass."

"I–I will vow that there is no political gain or manipulation planned in wanting this marriage. We...we are in love."

"Think you that there is no manipulation involved in love?" asked Gilendhar.

"Like you would know what love is?" Rildhran asked with a snort.

"My lords, may we address the petition," the Laird said, his face impassive. Too impassive.

"You can get over love, child," Tadhrol said, his voice gentle. "But for your two clans to be so allied, it just is not wise."

Ah, so his friend was as infected with this ridiculous fear as the other lords? Bells. No matter. He rose, knowing he must address this.

"Do you really think that the Laird could be swayed in opinions by a cousin he barely knows? Or that I could be swayed by mine?"

A sharp laugh brought everyone's attention to Gilendhar. "Nothing sways you from your idiotic idealistic notions, Thane Alcandhor."

"Then what do you fear?"

"The setting of a precedent."

Krendhal lifted his hands in apology. "I feel for you, cousin. But this is about much more than one couple who wish to marry. There could be repercussions we cannot foresee."

Atinna licked her lips, her eyes seeming more blue from unshed tears, and when she spoke her voice was thick. "We will take any vow you wish. I plead with you."

Randhal cleared his throat. "Let you take a vote. Since it involves Viltara and Ch'shalna clans, the Thane and Lord Krendhal will abstain. How vote the rest of you?"

A chorus of nays came from the lords. The Laird sat, lips thinned.

The lass stood, silent, then gave a dignified curtsey. "I thank you for your time, lords."

Alcandhor clenched his fists on his thighs as she exited the chamber, head bowed but back straight. The lords continued to the next item without a moment's pause, and he ground his teeth that they could be so callous.

Chapter Thirty-nine

Atinna did not attend the banquet that evening, which did not surprise Alcandhor. If only there were some way to ease her pain, but the lass would have to work through that by herself.

The Laird danced with Analinn. Both blushed slightly, but wore happy smiles. That, at least, was more cheering. Tam stood across the hall, in a conversation with a group of Rangers and nobles, Marcalan beside her and, from what he could tell, pulling one of his favorite pranks.

Standing close to Elendhar, a hand at his side, he subtly pulled down on the noble's surcoat. The lord would occasionally give a slight tug, to adjust it around his neck and over his shoulders, then Marcalan would start again, waiting to see how long until Estan's lord realized it was not the garment askew.

At least his cousin had the sense to pull such a prank on a young lord who would not mind the game and such familiarity. He crossed the Great Hall, watching the prank unfold. Elendhar gave an irritated jerk on his surcoat, then glanced down with a frown. Marcalan met his gaze with an innocent stare. Alcandhor grinned. *One more time and he will be caught.* He pinched a bit of the cloth again, and the lord whirled. "Bells, Ranger, what are you doing?"

The rascal smirked, and the Rangers all laughed.

"Excuse my husband, Lord Elendhar," Tam said, "he has yet to learn to behave himself."

"So I see," the noble replied, a slow smile spreading.

Alcandhor got Tam's attention. She excused herself, leaving Elendhar to become more acquainted with Marcalan, or more likely, to become more acquainted with his pranks.

"Aye, Uncle?"

"I have not had the chance to ask you about Analinn."

Tam dimpled. "She is sweet and a bit unsure of herself. I think the Laird has good taste in women."

Alcandhor smiled. "Has she any feelings for him?"

"Nay. Nothing special yet anyway." She sighed, tipping her head. "It is difficult to explain what I feel from her. I think...she is afraid to like him because he is Laird, but she likes him regardless. She is very shy." Tam's eyes shone golden with her approval.

"Have you told the Laird?"

"I simply said she was not a weed. He will find out anything else he needs to know on his own."

"Such wisdom from one with only fifteen years," he said with a grin. "You shall make a good Thane."

An arched eyebrow was her reply. He gave her a quick hug across the shoulders, snickering, then nodded toward the gathering. "Better go see to your husband. I think he is up to something again already."

Tam turned with a sigh. "He really never does quit."

"But you would have him—"

"No other way," she chimed, finishing the sentence with him, rolling her eyes. "Aye. And he is scheming, I know the feeling. I had best get back before he causes trouble."

Alcandhor gave a low chortle as she crossed to her husband, looking more like a mother after an errant child than a wife. He was not certain which one to pity.

~*~

Conclave the next day ground on. Alcandhor noted that the Laird took his luncheon with Elendhar and his sisters, and went back to the Esteni suite with him for afternooning after conclave finished. Good.

That evening, Alcandhor wandered over to Mattan, whose expression was bland, although his eyes glinted with amusement. Alcandhor gazed at him expectantly.

"There is some unrest among the young ladies," the Enaisi said. "Not all, but some are very put out that the Laird's attention has been on Analinn since she arrived, and that he has escorted her two nights in a row and dances exclusively with her. Lord Krendhal on the other hand, is very pleased."

"Perhaps now he will look for himself, as you pointed out to him."

Mattan shrugged. "He is set in his ways."

"Aye, but he is also one who believes in fulfilling his duty. And one of his duties is to build the clan. I have many chiefs as my council, but the Laird only has one minister. Who will the next Laird have? It is only the two of them now." He shook his head and quaffed his ale.

"The Laird had better have many children," the Enaisi said with a straight face.

Alcandhor almost choked, then said, "Do not say thus in front of the lad. He is barely used to the idea of marriage, much less fatherhood."

Mattan nodded toward the dance floor. He twisted to see the Laird smiling at a laughing Analinn while he twirled her. "I would say he is becoming more used to the idea of marriage, and he had best become used to the idea of fatherhood as well, as it usually follows apace."

"Aye, that is true."

"What is true?"

They both turned to see Marcalan standing there, eyebrows raised in innocence. Too much innocence. But Alcandhor merely returned the stare in kind. "That fatherhood usually follows marriage quite closely."

His cousin's expression faded into a nervous swallow.

"Aye, Marcalan," Mattan said. "Who knows? It could be your turn next."

"Now that I look forward to," Alcandhor said, crossing his arms.

"Aye, just remember that as her foster-father, you are as grandfather to our babes. I cannot wait to call you Gran'fa."

Mattan chortled, and Alcandhor glared at the rascal, wanting to wipe that insufferable grin off his face. How did he always turn things around?

"Marcalan!"

Tam strode toward them, fists clenched, her countenance fierce. His cousin grinned and sketched a quick bow. "Excuse me, my kin. I must needs leave."

He hied away with Tam close behind. As she passed them, Alcandhor saw her hair had been braided in the back. Bells, he never did quit. At least he was getting back to being Marcalan. Then again, was that such a good thing?

~*~

"Maradhor? You have company."

He looked up at his fellow scribe with a scowl and wiped his face. He had been chilled earlier, why did the chamber now feel so warm? "I am reviewing the students' work from this morning. Who is it?"

Gardhen grinned. "I know not, but she is pretty."

She? "Pretty?" Maradhor stood, curiosity winning out. He arched his back trying to relieve the achy feeling. He must have been sitting for too long. No matter. He wanted to see who his guest was. He strode down the corridor toward the antechamber, and his heart plummeted at the familiar figure standing there. "Lady."

Atinna curtsied. "I will not stay but a moment. I only wished to tell you something."

Maradhor took a few hesitant steps forward, despising the heartache that welled up inside. Stars, but she was beautiful. "What is it, Lady?"

"I...I petitioned the lords to allow us to marry."

Taken aback that she would attempt such a thing, he stared at her open-mouthed before replying, "That was a bold move, Lady, but futile."

"Aye. But I had to try."

"Is that what you wished to tell me?"

She bit her lip, nodding, then curtsied as if to leave.

"Lady?"

She waited, an expectant expression on her face.

"You came a day's journey just to tell me that?"

"It was on my way. I am journeying north."

"North? For the Bells' sake, why? Fever is raging there."

"Aye. And I am an herbalist. I can help."

Maradhor stepped close, frowning, and took her hands. "Lady, 'tis dangerous. You could get the fever, too."

"Aye. I have had it, and nursed my family through it—we lost a brother and a sister to it. I know what could happen."

An icy feeling washed over him. "Is that why you are going?"

Atinna sighed, shaking her head. "Nay, but I must do something. This is what I know. I must keep busy."

He nodded, understanding. "All the best to you, Lady. I hope your heart finds peace and love."

She smiled, tears in her eyes, and he discovered his throat suddenly thick.

"I have found love, my dear Ranger. But I do hope to find peace." After another curtsey, she swept out the door.

Maradhor tried to swallow and could not. He went to the kitchen to request tea before returning to review the students' work.

The tea seemed to help at first, but then the papers swam before him, and he felt awash in heat. The pen fumbled in his fingers, and the inkpot tipped. The blackness spread—into nothingness.

~*~

"What do you mean, she is gone?" Alcandhor asked.

Mattan crossed his arms. "Just what I said. Atinna is gone."

"When?"

"Yesterday morning, from what the Laird surmises."

Stars, he should have looked into it when she did not appear for this evening's banquet. "Where?"

"I know not."

He eyed Mattan. "You do know."

"I have my suspicions."

"And what are your suspicions?"

"That she has gone to Kentin."

"But why? Why see Maradhor? It would only deepen the cut."

"Aye, but when one is in love, one often does not think clearly."

Alcandhor rolled his eyes at the truth of that.

"And I have a suspicion that wherever she is going, she is being followed. I had a strong sense of distrust from several lords concerning her. I would like to go to Kentin myself, just to make certain she is heading there. And to warn the both of them that they are watched."

"You see something?"

Mattan frowned. "I would not call it seeing..."

"You do not think they will do something foolish, do you? Maradhor would not break the law. I know him, Mattan."

"I know not. I only know I should go."

"All right. Leave in the morning." He grabbed the alien's arm. "But try not to meddle too much."

Mattan raised his eyebrows. "Meddle? Me?"

Alcandhor groaned.

~*~

Maradhor became aware that he was in pain. His joints, his muscles—what had he done to himself? Had he been in a fight? A wracking cough took him and he rolled on his side, shuddering chills sweeping through him. It was so hot! He tried to push off covers—he was in a bed? Coolness touched his face. Something wet against his mouth. A cloth. A cool, wet cloth. So good against his dry, hot skin and lips.

He tried to speak, but his throat hurt, and his mouth was too dry.

"Shu. Rest," came Atinna's voice.

Lady? He blinked a few times and managed to keep his eyes open. He opened his mouth again, but she shook her head.

"Do not speak. You have the fever. Try to sleep, it is the best thing for you."

He closed his eyes. When he opened them again, the room had darkened. His chest felt as if pressed by a great weight, and he tried several times before he managed to call, "Lady?"

A quick rustle of stiff cloth and she was at his side, her cool hands on his hot face. "Would you like to try to sip some water?"

He nodded and cool liquid trickled into his mouth. He licked his lips. "So hot."

"Aye. The fever is on you heavy."

Her voice was soft, but the lightness in it was empty. This was her worried voice.

"Not good?"

She hesitated, and he said, "The truth."

"You are very ill. The fever is not abating."

"Bad sign."

"Aye."

Cool hands on his cheeks and neck again. Was the room growing darker, or was it him? Atinna lit a candle. Her face was drawn, worried. She sat on the bed next to him, her hand chilled on his hot arm. Neither spoke as he struggled to breathe. After awhile he felt himself doze off...

His limbs were leaden and breathing almost impossible. He did not need Atinna to tell him his body still burned with fever. A cool cloth wiped his face, then was placed on his forehead. Water dribbled into his mouth. He managed to open his eyes, and she tried to smile.

"Not good?" he asked, his voice a hoarse whisper.

She shook her head, her mouth set, eyes haunted. That told him what she would not say. If only he had the strength and voice to tell her what he had not before. He licked his lips, and she wet them again, dribbling water into his mouth from a cloth. He swallowed, took a painful breath, and tried again to speak. "Love you."

She stood with a sharp inhale and turned away. Before long she returned and sat back down next to him. "Maradhor, I know you think me silly and childish, and I admit this is very silly, but...I made a necklet for you. Would...would you wear it? No one need know. Only you and me. I could say in my heart, 'My husband' when I...I remember you."

"The law..."

"No one would know."

Her beautiful blue eyes pleaded with him, and he could not make himself tell her no. He finally nodded, closing his eyes, too exhausted to keep them open. He felt the necklet going about his throat, then soft lips touched his. He drifted into blackness hearing her say, "I love you."

~*~

Atinna heard the knock but was not going to leave Maradhor for a moment. That might be all the time he had left. The door opened. She twisted in her seat next to the bed to see the Elder, Mattan, standing there, his face filled with sorrow. He strode around her to the head of the bed and placed a hand on Maradhor's forehead.

"He is not doing well."

"Nay," she whispered.

"There is always hope."

Atinna hesitated and then shook her head. "Nay. He is almost gone. I have seen it too often. 'Twould be foolish to hope now."

Mattan pulled over a chair, and sat, his hand on Maradhor's shoulder. "I shall stay with you awhile, if you do not mind."

She did, she had wanted these last moments alone with her husband, but how could she dare tell an Elder to leave?

They sat in silence, Atinna trying her best not to allow tears. Every so often, she took the cloth from his head and dipped it in the cool water. It was futile, but as long as Maradhor was alive, she would try to ease his suffering. An occasional glance at the Elder revealed little. He seemed content to sit quietly, eyes closed for the most part.

Yet again she rinsed the cloth in the little basin next to her and gently placed it back on his forehead, her fingers trailing along the side of his face and down to his chest. The sheet snagged on her hand and pulled away slightly. She stifled a gasp. *The necklet! Oh stars, surely he will see the necklet!*

She looked up at him, holding her breath.

"Nay!" he whispered. "Nay!"

She wiped her eyes, murmuring, "Please do not tell. It is a secret, only between the two of us. Because he is dying. I am not trying to make a claim as widow. I just wanted to be his wife. I will take it off before your clan claims the body."

Mattan closed his eyes with a sigh. How could such a dark-skinned man look pale? Yet this Elder did. He wiped perspiration from his face.

"Are you ill, sir?" she asked. That would explain the pallor and sweat.

"Nay. Be not concerned." His dark eyes strayed to Maradhor and then pierced hers. "And if he lives? What then?"

She shook her head. "I am an herbalist, sir, and have tended not only my family through the fever, but many others as well. I have seen how they fail as the fever burns up their bodies, and they lose the ability to breathe." She stopped and swallowed to control the tremor in her voice. "He has not much time."

Mattan sighed again, his brow furrowing. He leaned back in the chair with a quiet moan.

"Are you certain you are not becoming ill, sir?"

"Nay. I am just sick at the injustice served to you and Maradhor."

She knew no answer, and he said no more, just sat with her, watching the Ranger. His breathing seemed to ease a little; the last rally before he succumbed. Each breath brought dread that it would be his last.

Mattan stood and leaned close. "Are you strong?"

Atinna knew Maradhor's opinion. She was determined to prove him wrong, to prove she was worthy to be his wife, even if he would not be there to see it. "I am trying to be."

"You will have need to be strong, I think, before this is over. I will leave you two alone."

The door clicked shut, and she placed her hand on Maradhor's chest, waiting for the last breath to come, the Elder already forgotten.

Chapter Forty

A message drummed as Maradhor sipped broth, stating that he and Atinna were found guilty of conspiring against the provincial lords and breaking conclave law. They were to appear to face the lords when quarantine was lifted and then would be taken to the mines to serve their sentence. If they did not appear, they would be considered outlaw and hunted down.

Atinna paid no attention to the drums, as she did not know drum code. It gave Maradhor time to think.

Mattan knocked and came in soon after. "You heard?"

"Aye."

"What are you going to do?"

"With all respect, Enaisi, it is best if I say nothing more to you."

Mattan met his gaze, then slowly nodded. "Know that if you do need help, of any sort, I will fain give it."

"Despite the law, Enaisi?"

"I can be discreet."

"Indeed. But if you know nothing, you cannot be held responsible. And I know you have had enough grief with our Thane already."

Mattan bowed and shut the door.

Atinna leaned forward. "What is it?"

"Word of our marriage is known."

"What? How?" She straightened, gasping. "The Elder?"

"Nay. He is trustworthy in everything but keeping the law, from what I have seen."

Atinna did not share his humor, and his smile faded. "It matters not who. What matters is that is it too late to remove this necklet. And if we return to Laird Hall as we are ordered, we will be sent to the mines. While I could survive that, I know you could not, Lady. To save you, we must flee. But it is winter, and the Rangers will look for us. It will not be easy, and there is not a great chance we will succeed."

Atinna's hands flew to her face as he spoke. "Th–the mines? Why such a severe punishment?"

"I could not say, Lady, except that they wish to set an example that their decisions will not be disobeyed."

"But...the mines."

"Aye, Lady. It will be difficult and dangerous, but will you go with me?"

She put her hands over his, her eyes alight with love. "The Maker gave me a miracle and spared your life. I will not be separated from you now. But, where shall we go?"

"Let me think on that."

~*~

Alcandhor stormed toward the Laird's solar before the drums echoed into silence. The Laird met him in the hall, his face flushed and jaw clenched. "Did you hear that? What is the meaning of this?"

"I was going to ask you that, Your Grace."

"I am sending word to see all the lords in conclave chamber now."

He stomped off, and Alcandhor stood, eyes closed. He whirled and headed back to his suite, hoping to gather his wits and temper before facing the lords.

~*~

After some thought, Maradhor asked Atinna to have his friend Gardhen come in.

"It is good to see you recovering," the scribe said, shifting from one foot to the other.

Maradhor pushed up in the bed. "Sit and quit dithering. I know you heard the drums. What say you? Shall I go back and take the Lady to her death in the mines?"

Gardhen's face hardened. "It is an evil thing to send a woman there. Especially so fine a lady. But what can I do?"

Leaning forward, he whispered, "If you help, you could be found guilty of conspiracy."

His eyes boring into Maradhor's, the scribe repeated in a slow, even voice, "What can I do?"

Maradhor gave a small smile in gratitude. "Commoner clothes, all male, heavy for winter journeying, and as much journey food as you can acquire without arousing attention. I want not to see you indicted for assisting us."

A slow grin spread on Gardhen's face. "Gladly will I help. And worry not about suspicions directed at me. I know how to be subtle. When do you want them?"

"As soon as you can get them."

"You are not well enough to travel," Atinna said.

"I grow stronger by the hour. Worry not about me."

"But what about the danger of breaking quarantine?" she asked.

363

"We shall avoid people. We have to anyway." He looked up at his friend. "Please, bring us the clothes."

Gardhen nodded and left.

"What is your plan?"

"Lady, I am troubled for you, traveling in such weather."

"I walk much in all weather as birthing attendant and herbalist. I shall be fine."

Despite her assurances, Maradhor fretted. Was he only going to kill her by running to save her from death in the mines? He held out a hand, and she sat on the bed by him. Her expression softened, and she curled up, head on his shoulder as he wrapped an arm around her.

"Shall you be able to live in the wild, Lady? Away from all comforts? In a roughly built cottage, perhaps? Wondering and looking over your shoulder to see if they have found us?"

"If I am with you, I care not."

Maradhor sighed. She may not care now, however some day she might. Her love might turn to bitterness. But it was too late to do anything else.

~*~

"You what?" the Laird spat.

"We have the right to check on those we think might be about to breach our laws," Gilendhar said, his cheeks puffed out in self-righteousness. "What is so hard to understand about that?"

"How would your messenger even be able to find out about their marriage if it were secret?"

"The scribe school is not very secure, and they were all too willing to accept anyone who said they wished to help care for the ill. He says he looked in to see her sleeping with him, and that he wore a necklet."

"You have had your meeting in private, without the Thane or me present," the Laird said, shaking. "You have decided their guilt and passed sentence."

"It is not meet that you or the Thane be present for your own kin's—"

"It is not proper that you have a meeting behind my back!" Randhal's voice thundered, and Alcandhor's brows raised. He had never seen the lad look so adult. Or so angry. The other lords all fell silent, eyes wide. The Laird turned to Alcandhor. "You have been silent for the most part. What is your say, Thane?"

Alcandhor struggled to control his own rage. He met the Laird's gaze evenly. "I will prepare a statement. When I am ready, I will call conclave and have my say."

~*~

Worry in her eyes, Atinna said, "You should not be up yet."

Maradhor looked down at his lady, beautiful despite her disguise as a young lad. "I have done more feeling worse, Lady. We must leave while 'tis dark. Snow is falling, it can help hide our tracks."

"What if they guess where we are going?"

"Gardhen has said that he will betray me by stating that he overheard us talking of ships, and how we should head for North Port although Nelatan ports are nearer. With the inclement weather, the hazardous seas to the north, and the fever, the farther journey to Estan's harbors would be the smarter road."

"But how does that help us? A ship would be the fastest way to journey far. We did discuss that."

Maradhor smiled. "Aye, we did. But we are not taking a ship, Lady. Fear not. I know where we are going. You must trust me."

She pulled the warm cloak tightly about her. "I do. And I am ready."

~*~

Alcandhor brooded over his decision. He was torn but had discussed the ramifications with his chiefs. Lamadhel and Andhrel both assured him that his knowledge of the law was correct. Clan Law took precedence over every other law, even other High Laws—and the Laws of the Enaisi. Mattan might argue about the latter, but fortunately, he was not present.

He did not go to the banquet that night but spent the evening deliberating and praying that the Maker would give him wisdom and peace about his decision. In the morning he sent word to the lords to meet in the conclave chamber.

When they were seated, he stood and took them in, one by one. The lords all had wary expressions, some almost fearful, some suspicious. The Laird was expectant, and from the set of his jaw, still infuriated by the situation.

"We all here, save Lord Krendhal, are clan thanes. We have a dual duty, to serve our clan, and to serve our people. Your service is to your province, and mine to all of you."

Alcandhor took a breath and exhaled with deliberate slowness. "My clan is treated as a feral timman. A beast trapped and trained to protect you, but kept tethered out of fear. Laws were added to Clan Law, which as Lord Irdhith pointed out in his petition, is strictly illegal. More laws were added to lords' conclave law to restrict us, such as this law which forbids marriage between my clan and Viltara."

Alcandhor stopped, again, looking at each of them. "I call Question on all of the laws passed restricting my clan. I claim Right as clan thane to choose protecting my clan's interests over my duty to protect you. As protest over all these laws, I am ordering all Rangers to cease their peacekeeping duties in all provinces."

The lords stood, speaking all at once.

"You cannot do that!" shouted Vendhal.

"Feral beast is right!" Perdhal spat. "Just looking for an excuse—"

"How will we protect our people?" asked Rildhran.

Mirdhol waved his arms. "This is mad, Thane! You dare not withdraw your men!"

Alcandhor glared at them all as they continued to clamor while the Laird called for order. The lords gradually subsided and took their seats, and Alcandhor continued, "Until these laws are rescinded, and the charges and sentence against Maradhor and Atinna are revoked, there will be no Ranger protection or arbitration. This order will go into effect in three days. You have until then to answer. So be it."

Alcandhor bowed to the wide-eyed Laird, then strode out without acknowledging the other lords.

~*~

Alcandhor sat on the divan in his suite, staring blankly ahead. Had he done the right thing? This would give the lords reason to doubt his clan's faithfulness in being protectors and peacekeepers. It might undermine their authority and effectiveness. What would happen to their world if that occurred?

Elendhar had visited earlier to tell him that the vote had not been unanimous. He had voted against it; Krendhal had abstained. Despite the Laird's urging for the lords to acquiesce, the other lords all had voted to send Maradhor and Atinna to the mines regardless of Alcandhor's declaration.

"I know not what I can do, being a new provincial lord and not yet of Age, but let me know if I can be of assistance in any way."

"You will be putting yourself in opposition to all the other lords by taking a stand with me."

"Bells, they are not as fearsome as Malkim was."

They shared a smile, then the young lord left. Interesting that

Krendhal had abstained, Alcandhor mused, staring at the fire. Was it on the principle of the matter, or because it was his cousin being condemned? Certainly not pressure from his young cousin, despite rank.

Haladhon answered a knock at the door. "It is Lord Tadhrol. Wish you to see him?"

Alcandhor snorted. His old friend. "Wish it? Nay. I wish to see none of them. But aye, I will let him briefly try to persuade me."

"I hope do more than try, Thane," Tadhrol said, walking over.

Alcandhor did not stand. "You cannot. My mind is made up."

"But can you not see what you are doing?"

"Can you not see what you have done to my clan? My kin? My people?" He rose and strode to the sideboard to pour another cup of tea. "You kick us as chained pets, treat us like midden refuse. We have our uses, aye, but we must know and keep in our place." He slammed his cup on the table and spun around. "For the time we have been on this planet it has been thus. Yet forget you my clan's position? Who we are?" He met Tadhrol's eyes, his voice quiet yet emphatic. "Who I am?"

Tadhrol lifted his head with a sharp inhale. Good, he understood. Alcandhor narrowed his eyes. "I will not let my people pay the price any longer for your unjustified fears!"

"But Thane, your duty—"

"Aye, 'Thane.' I am thane. To my *clan*. My first duty is to my clan." He clenched his fist to his chest. "Clan Law is higher than any other, I need not tell you this. Because of your foolish fears, my cousin, my friend, my best scribe, an invaluable sword master, is sentenced to the mines. If that is not bad enough, a sweet lady whose only crime was to be in love is also sentenced, and you know for a certainty that it will kill her to toil in those mines."

"But they cannot be allowed to flout a decision by the lords. It would set precedent. These two deliberately chose to ignore our decision."

"As all of you deliberately ignored their declarations of love." Alcandhor threw up his hands. "None of this matters. You shall not change my mind, Lord Tadhrol. I cannot perhaps save those two from dying in the mines, but I will not stand idly by any more while my people suffer. For the first time in a thousand years, Ch'shalna clan thinks of its own first."

"Then a compromise. We will rescind the laws regarding marriage."

Alcandhor set his jaw. "All laws. No more restrictions. No more restricting whom my people may marry. No more mutilation of my kin when found guilty of breaking High Law. No more, Lord Tadhrol." Alcandhor chopped the air with his hand as he repeated the two words.

"No more!"

Tadhrol's eyes mirrored his fear. "Excuse me, Thane. I think we have nothing more to say to each other."

Haladhon raised his eyebrows as he shut the door behind the retreating lord. Alcandhor shook his head. His decision had also cost him any friendships he had with the lords. How far would the repercussions go?

Chapter Forty-one

"It is no bluff or idle threat. He means it." Tadhrol gazed about the chamber at his peers.

Irdhith shrugged, watching his fingers tap the table in rhythm. "Then let him make good his threat. We can create our own forces for keeping the peace."

Tadhrol stared at the cockerel, incredulous at such denseness.

"Are you mad, or simply a fool?" asked Vendhal. "It is not merely peacekeeping. Their duties are so broad and varied that it is unworkable to consider replacing them."

"Why?" Gilendhar asked. "Train men to fight, teach them the laws, and give them a bounds."

"And how long do we train them to fight?" asked Rildhran. "A lunation? Two? Seven? A year? And how do we enforce the peace and the laws in the meantime?"

Mirdhol jabbed the table with his finger. "The Rangers are effective because they begin Training as children. It is part of their regimen for their whole life. They begin to study the law as children, also. Their knowledge is keen and sharper than a blade."

"And you are forgetting also that they cull their Trainees and stripling Rangers." Krendhal said. "If they do not have the temperament and the self-discipline, their Training is not completed. It is not foolproof by any means, but for the most part, Rangers are above reproach. They cannot be bought or bribed. They truly live to serve. What trust would you put in men you hire and train in say, a year's time, to assume the duties that the Rangers now carry out?"

"Why have the lords not build up their own forces over time and eventually displaced them?" asked Irdhith. "Then we would be free of them."

Tadhrol waved a hand with a beleaguered sigh. "Nay. By the Laws of the Enaisi, all peacekeeping is Ranger Clan's duty."

"But they are threatening not to carry out that duty!" The Lantral lord slammed a fist on the table. "We must do something!"

"The Thane has the right by law to protect his clan. As do we all." Krendhal gazed about the table. "'Clan first' is what we all live by, is it not?"

Perdhal swept a hand over the table. "Those two renegades did not follow Clan Law. And he would just give them leave to flaunt their disobedience in our faces and make us a spectacle to be laughed at and not respected?"

"I would say you have done that yourselves," Krendhal said, "by sentencing them to the mines. And I would remind you that they did not break Clan Law, but one set down by a lords' conclave."

"Going to preen that you did not agree with that decision?" sneered Gilendhar.

"I merely state that no one in this hall, not other nobles, not commoners—no one, agrees with our decision. Disaffection is strong toward us. I feared this reaction. We have overstepped our bounds in our punishment of those two."

"They had to be made a strong example of!" Gilendhar spat.

"We chose too strong a punishment," Tadhrol murmured. "It has backlashed against us. Not only among the people, but the Rangers."

"I would not have thought the Thane would choose one Ranger over protecting our entire world," Rildhran muttered, sagging back into his chair.

"He is protecting not only his Ranger but a young lass. A lady of my clan." Krendhal grimaced, his brow furrowed. "He has attempted more for her than I dared to." He took a deep breath. "Nay, we have brought this on ourselves and only have one answer we can give."

"But we cannot accede to him. To them." Perdhal clenched his fists. "It would let them know they have power over us."

Tadhrol gave a short laugh. "Think you they know it not? The Thane reminded me today of that. He actually asked if I knew what his clan is." He paused, regarding them with solemnity. "And who he is."

The chamber fell silent.

In a soft voice, Rildhran said, "We need time to think on this. What say you all? Adjourn until tomorrow?"

The others nodded, and Krendhal said, "Aye. He said we have three days until his order to his Rangers goes into effect. Let us use that time to discuss this. I would not hurry a decision."

Tadhrol could only agree, although he only saw one possible way to vote.

~*~

Alcandhor gazed at the sullen, stubborn lords, his own heart heavy. He bowed and left. Did the fools not realize what they had just done? What they were forcing him to do?

The chiefs waited in his suite.

"Well?" Haladhon asked. "What did they say?"

Alcandhor slowly closed the door. "Tam, Tell Mattan to hasten back to Laird Hall. I wish him here."

"But he is in Kentin, which is still quarantined."

"I doubt anyone can stop him from going where he wishes, and I also doubt he is contagious. Ask him to be certain. If he says it is safe for him to return, tell him I wish him here as fast as he can journey. If not, you will have to relay our messages."

"Aye, Uncle." She closed her eyes, but opened them again. "He says he anticipated being needed here and is already on his way."

Of course. He would have heard the drums.

Haladhon leaned forward. "Thane, what did they say?"

Alcandhor took a deep breath. "Every provincial lord save Krendhal and Elendhar has refused to accede. They state they will raise their own forces to become peacekeepers. They wish to throw off the role of the Rangers."

His chiefs all gasped.

Lamadhel exclaimed, "That goes against all our laws, and the laws the Enaisi gave us when they ceded us this planet!"

"Aye. Breaking the Laws of the Enaisi could cause Mattan's people to rescind their agreement."

"But what could they do?" Eladhrel asked. "We are spread out over this continent, and our people are beyond number now."

Alcandhor gave a slow shake of his head. "The technology of the Enaisi is formidable. I know only a fleeting shadow of information from the past of this planet, but I know enough to know most of Mattan's people have no love of us. From what he says, the Enaisi fought alien invaders who came to their planet, a people who descended from the stars, if you can imagine!" He gazed about at his chiefs. "If they have that ability, what could they do to us? They could start a war to force our compliance or even kill us all. Many of them might even prefer the latter." He strode to a window and stared out. "I did not foresee this. I thought the lords would accede."

After a silence, Tam whispered, "What will you do?"

Alcandhor swallowed. In a hoarse voice replied, "What I must."

~*~

In the Great Hall that evening, Tam stood next to Marcalan. Two opposite moods conflicted. On one hand relief dominated as no new outbreaks of the fever had been reported since yesterday. But the Thane's ultimatum and the lords' response resulted in a wariness in most and outright fear in others. The lords avoided the Rangers, and Lord

371

Krendhal succeeded in convincing the Laird to forego private visits with his friends and mingle with the nobles for the entire evening.

Valiantly the musicians struggled to keep the mood light.

The double doors of the antechamber swung wide before the outer doors even had a chance to shut, admitting a gust of chill air through the Great Hall. Not waiting for the door-warden to herald his name, Mattan strode across the palatial chamber, his cloak billowing in his wake, oblivious to all the lords and nobles, aiming straight for his Thane. Even at a distance, Tam could see his eyes were not merely dark brown, but glittering black. The two men nodded to each other and marched silently up the stairs. She reached for Marcalan's hand, whispering, "What do you think they are talking about?"

"I know not, but I wager we find out soon."

Marcalan's prediction was accurate. Before long, a meeting called all the chiefs to the Thane's suite. When Mattan and Alcandhor finished explaining what was about to happen, Tam felt numb, unable to believe it. From the expressions on the others' faces, they couldn't either.

~*~

Entering the conclave chamber the next morning to see the smug expressions on the majority of the lords' faces solidified Alcandhor's resolve. So sure were they that they held with complete dominance and with impunity the tether around the neck of Ch'shalna clan? Or was it arrogance in thinking they could overthrow the Rangers?

Nay, not all of them. The Laird's eyes glinted with anger, Elendhar sat hunched in on himself, and Krendhal leaned back, eyes locked on Alcandhor—waiting? For what?

Jonadhan entered and took his seat at the side table. He picked up his quill and nodded.

Sensing his alien ancestor at his back, having his back, Alcandhor squared his shoulders, denying the clenching of his stomach. "Your refusal to acquiesce to my demands that you rescind the laws chaining my clan, and your threat to dismiss my clan as peacekeepers in defiance of the Laws of the Enaisi force me into a decision." He stopped, not wishing to say on. But he had no choice. He had never foreseen this. He had argued repeatedly throughout his life that this would never happen. Could never happen. The words of Zadhras came back to him: *One decision will come that will seem impossible to contemplate. You shall want to draw back from it, abhor even thinking it, but it is a decision that is yours to make. Thus it has been seen, and thus it shall be.*

And then there was the prophecy, which had given Alcandhor a ominous foretelling when he first read it:

Hail to the lesser one,
May his hair ne'er be shorn.
From the fire he shall rise,
And shall reclaim his bourn.

Lifting his chin, he stared at them all. "I make Claim. I take back all the power and responsibility of my true status and rank. All laws restricting my clan I pronounce void. The injustice served upon my clan is at an end. And that includes the prosecution and persecution of Maradhor and Atinna."

Most of the lords sat, mouths agape. Krendhal's one brow raised in subtle triumph; aye, he always believed Ch'shalna would one day reclaim the throne.

~*~

Tam stood when her uncle entered, as did all the chiefs and family present in the Thane's suite. Her hands wrung together.

His black eyes and the set to this jaw bespoke the decision had indeed been made.

"Stars, Alcandhor," Sarinna whispered. "What have you done?"

"What was necessary," he murmured.

What new rules of etiquette needed to be followed now? Everyone bowed, so Tam followed suit.

The Thane, nay, their king, inhaled sharply and met Tam's eyes. "Have the drums send a message to Maradhor that he and Atinna are safe, and they are to return to Laird Hall. Have it sent in the newest code, created for when we tracked the Rogues."

"Aye, Uncle. I mean... Sire? I know not what to call you now."

"In public, I fear we must follow all protocol in every detail to assure they comprehend this is no game or whim, but for our clan, in private, I wish no change in address or formality."

"Or lack thereof?" Marcalan blinked, brows raised.

Her uncle shot her husband a glare, but said, "Publicly, I am 'Sire' or 'Your Majesty.'" He stopped, grimacing as if he ate something that tasted terrible. His gaze fixed on Tam. "Not only that, but as heir, you are now 'Your Royal Highness' and in direct address, 'Princess Tamissa' or 'Lady Tamissa.'"

"Princess?" Words fled Tam's mind, and she finally managed to whisper, "I wondered how this would affect heirship. But need I be called princess or lady? I am but a Ranger."

"Ask Lamadhel or Andhrel or"—he waved a hand toward her dark-skinned uncle—"Mattan for details on proper address. I am more worried about Maradhor and Atinna. Go. Send that drum message."

"You should also drum out that Claim was made, and that we now have a king," Mattan added.

"Aye." Lamadhel stroked his chin beard. "The scribes will be busy copying the proclamation, but news of it should spread quickly. Knowing the Than—the king's intention, we have prepared a copy for the drums." He handed a scroll to Tam. "Go, child."

Tam nodded. Should she bow to her...her *king* before leaving? She compromised with a bob of her head. One hand on the door, she turned. "I forgot to say—they are missing. It is said they are probably on their way to North Port to find a ship."

Alcandhor frowned. "We will find them, or they shall hear the drums and return of themselves. But in any case, send word out to watch for them in North Port."

After a proper bow this time, Tam left, her thoughts whirling, not noticing her surroundings as she descended stairs and crossed the Great Hall. Shivering, she hurried across and the bailey; she had been so stupefied she had not even grabbed her cloak!

The long ascent up the winding stairs of the drum tower seemed to help further twine her thoughts into a muddled mess.

She stepped out into the large, circular chamber and stared at the two Rangers, one leaning against an embrasure, a steaming cup in his hands, and the other squatting to poke at smoldering wood in the open hearth. Both noticed her and straightened.

"Tam, is it?" one asked. "Have you word for us?"

Nodding, she swallowed, unable to force herself to correct them. "Two messages are to go out. One is that Maradhor and Atinna are safe and are to return to Laird Hall, and it is to be sent in the new code used in the search for the Rogues." She held out the scroll, her hand trembling but not just from the cold. "This is the other."

The one Ranger set his cup down and took it. She held her breath as he unrolled and read it.

"By the Bells and both moons! Is it true?"

"What?" The second Ranger took the scroll. His eyes scanned the proclamation, then he gazed at Tam. "Truly?"

"Truly." Tam lifted her chin, afraid of how this would affect her future—Thaneship was frightening enough, but heir to a *throne*? She had best follow the order her uncle, her *king* had given her. "I am informed that correct address to me is now—" She could not make herself use that one term but managed to choke the words out. "'Lady Tamissa.' The king has decreed we should follow protocol to be certain no one takes his Claim lightly."

Both Rangers bowed, murmuring, "Lady Tamissa."

~*~

Lamadhel answered the knock at the door. The Laird entered, face pale.

Alcandhor stood, his eyes not leaving his former pupil's. "Leave us," he ordered his kin.

They bowed and obeyed. Mattan lingered, hand on the door, then closed it.

The Laird threw his arms out. "What do I call you now? Your Majesty, I suppose?"

"Or Sire, or—" He forced the words out: "King Alcandhor."

"I thought we were friends."

"Why are we not? How has this changed anything?"

Tears filled Randhal's blue eyes. "You always said this could never happen. Impossible, you said. Was that all a lie?"

"Nay, you know 'twas not. But what choice did I have?"

"For a mere two people, you would do something so drastic? 'Tis said it was but an excuse."

Likely by Krendhal, at least, if not others. "Not just for two people. And not for seeing my people tethered, rules laid upon us that no other clan endured. Nay. Give thought, my Laird! The lords declared they would train their own forces to replace my clan if I withdrew my men as peacekeepers. That of itself is against the Laws of the Enaisi. But beyond that, did they once mention training men to roam bounds as *Rangers*?"

"What do you mean?"

"Why do you think my clan was given the appellation 'Ranger clan'? Our people were ceded this planet by the Enaisi with specific conditions. Laws were instituted that my clan roam or 'range' bounds to ensure nature was not despoiled. Their decision would disclaim and abandon the Laws of the Enaisi if they did what they proposed. You know our history, or if you do not, you can ask Mattan. He was there when my clan became more than just peacekeepers but also *Rangers*. So then, what would you do in my place? Tell me, my Laird."

Randhal shook his head, hunching his shoulders. "Am I still Laird? And what of Lord Krendhal? He acts as provincial lord so that the Laird can deal with matters concerning all the provinces."

"Viltara was always the right hand and main advisor to the king in

375

ancient times. Think you I will sweep away all lords and nobility? Much remains the same. Now, instead of decisions affecting our world coming directly from the lords' conclaves, the lords will advise me, and I make the final decision. How you and Lord Krendhal decide policy within your province is between the both of you, but you are still my main advisor, and the one to whom I turn for help in administration. Little changes, my Laird."

"And what wisdom have I to give you? I am young, and no experience."

"You are clever, and look at hearts as much as at law. This I know of you. You can help keep my feet on the track."

"But you can decide what you will."

"Think you I will not need, or indeed heed, advice and counsel? And the lords can convene if they disagree with my decisions and plead a case to my chiefs."

"That does not sound reassuring."

"What I have done does not give greater privilege, but greater responsibility. Are you so afraid of me, of what decisions I might make? That I will abuse power?"

The lad's eyes met his. "Nay. I...I do not fear you. But..." He took a breath. "Is it permanent? I remember what you used to say. If such a thing did ever take place it would only be a temporary stratocracy. Do you hold to that?"

"I did not desire to make this decision in the first place. I do not wish to clutch it in my hands for the rest of my life, nor pass it on to Tam. But while I do hold it, I must first determine what I may accomplish that has been hindered."

"Hindered?"

"You certainly know the concerns your father had about some of the provinces and those who ruled them."

"But those traitors are gone."

"Can you say for certain that Lord Lorwith can be trusted? What of the new lords? Be you sure they are also not traitors, either in following the examples of their predecessors or setting their own schemes in place, for greed, power, or both? Shall I not take this opportunity in both hands, my Laird? Will you back me?"

Randhal licked his lips, his eyes darting about the chamber. "I...think that could be a positive move, but I doubt if mentioning it to the lords themselves is wise."

Alcandhor barked a laugh. "Aye, my Laird. In that we do agree."

The lad's tentative smile grew wider.

"Still friends, then?"

"Aye."

He clasped a hand on the young man's shoulder, and the Laird returned it.

"Good." Alcandhor turned to the sideboard, still laden from luncheon. At least it seemed his relationship with Randhal had not been entirely riven. "Shall we have tea and discuss matters facing us, my Laird?"

~*~*~

Thank you for reading *Laws and Prophecies*. If you enjoyed it, I'd love for you to leave a review at your favorite retailer.

~L.S. King

ABOUT THE AUTHOR

L.S. King has novels published in two series: Deuces Wild and the Sword's Edge Chronicles.

Besides having short stories published in *Deep Magic*, *The Sword Review*, *Dragons, Knights & Angels*, *Digital Dragon Magazine*, and *Residential Aliens* (the fact that several of the publications which have released her stories are now defunct has nothing to do with her, honest), she also authored a column for writers, has worked as a submissions editor and a copy editor on several magazines, and was a founding editor of the semi-pro online magazine *Ray Gun Revival*, currently on hiatus.

~:~

Check out my website: http://loriendil.com
Follow me on Twitter: @Loriendil
Facebook author page: @AuthorLSKing
Facebook fan group: Loriendil's Lair
Subscribe to my blog: http://loriendil.wordpress.com/

www.ingramcontent.com/pod-product-compliance
Lightning Source LLC
Chambersburg PA
CBHW060148260626
47160CB00001B/176